The Hidden

Also by Tobias Hill

Fiction

Skin

Underground

The Love of Stones

The Cryptographer

Poetry

Year of the Dog

Midnight in the City of Clocks

Zoo

Nocturne in Chrome and Sunset Yellow

The Hidden

A Novel

Tobias Hill

HARPER PERENNIAL

NEW YORK • LONDON • TORONTO • SYDNEY • NEW DELHI • AUCKLAND

HARPER PERENNIAL

First published in Great Britain in 2009 by Faber and Faber Limited.

HarperCollins books may be purchased for educational, business, or sales promotional use. For information please write: Special Markets Department, HarperCollins Publishers, 10 East 53rd Street, New York, NY 10022.

FIRST U.S. EDITION

Library of Congress Cataloging-in-Publication Data is available upon request.

ISBN 978-0-06-176825-5

09 10 11 12 13 RRD 10 9 8 7 6 5 4 3 2 1

I have hidden something in the inner chamber
And sealed the lid of the sarcophagus
And levered a granite boulder against the door
And the debris has covered it so perfectly
That though you walk over it daily you never suspect.

ANTHONY THWAITE

The power of hiding ourselves from one another is mercifully given, for men are wild beasts, and would devour one another but for this protection.

HENRY WARD BEECHER

Every thing secret degenerates.

JOHN DALBERG-ACTON

I

Notes Towards a Thesis

It has been said that history is written by the victors. The truism is false in one case. The Spartans were once masters of all they surveyed, prevailing over Greece through fear and war, yet did not trust their prevalence to writing.

The written word is unselfish. It gives up its secrets readily: it speaks to friend and foe alike. For this reason the Spartans entrusted few things to its care. They were a secretive people. They wrote little plainly, and little even of that little has survived. The Spartan writings that have come down to us – Alcman's joyful Maiden Songs, Lysander's vainglorious inscriptions – are not the missing pieces of the puzzle so much as the only pieces left of a puzzle which is itself missing, so that the nature of the puzzle – the nature of Sparta – has itself become a riddle.

It is hazardous to assume almost anything of such a reticent people. It might be assumed (for example) that our uncertainty would satisfy the Spartans, but there is no certainty even in this. That they have left no explanations for the world would not concern them unduly, since they had scant concern for the opinions of the world. That they would be judged not by their words but by their actions might have seemed to them fitting, since they were a people who did much but said little. And that their own history should be based on little more than guesswork, such as these guesses of my own – that their secrets should still hold, two and a half thousand years on – that might also have pleased them.

Would it please them to be remembered at all? Those who dealt with them describe a proud people. No one likes to be forgotten. But the curiosity of history is a relentless thing, and the importance of Sparta is such that the good historian cannot pass it by. What remains is endlessly scoured for the gold of the truth. The motives of the generals and kings are examined and re-examined, doubted and picked apart. The rare achievements of archaeology are magnified in importance, sometimes beyond their due. And the known actions of the Spartans assume the prominence of legends, so that the mythology of the city has come to have more influence than its archaeology may ever possess.

For example, there is the legend of the Battle of Thermopylae. It goes like this.

Four hundred and eighty years before Christ, the Persians set out to conquer Greece. Their army was as vast as their empire itself, which stretched from the Nile to the Indus. So inevitable was their victory that the Great King Xerxes travelled with his people to see his conquests with his own eyes. So overwhelming was his power that much of Hellas made peace before the Great King reached Greek lands, offering him earth and water, the Persian tokens of submission.

Those who resisted were led by the Spartans. Few, though, were willing to speak of war against the empire, and fewer to back up words with men. The Persians had reached as far south as the pass of Thermopylae, two hundred miles from Sparta, before any Hellene stood against them.

Thermopylae: *The Hot Gates*. The pass was named after its springs – which were volcanic and sulphurous – and after its three narrows; its gates. It was a low road, overhung with cliffs to the south and overlooking the sea to the north. Inland there were only interminable mountains, high forest and crags, land good for goats and not much else. At its gates the pass was no more than fifty feet across. The Persians could have found other ways south if they had wished to seek them. But they did not wish. They did not need to wish. They chose to go through Thermopylae, where their enemies had gathered.

Xerxes' enemies were commanded by Leonidas, King of the Spartans. He led five thousand two hundred Greeks. Among them were three hundred Equals, the men of Sparta, who spent their lives in nothing but the practice and execution of war.

They faced three hundred thousand Persians. Across the Hellespont, and westwards, the Great King had brought an even greater force: in his vanguard's wake came an army of eight hundred thousand. Xerxes felt no need to bring his full million to bear against the few at Thermopylae. With him were his Immortals, after all, the finest ten thousand soldiers of the empire.

Xerxes was merciful. For three days the Great King waited for the Greeks to give up the pass. But they did not do so. His scouts informed him that the foreigners were rebuilding an old wall that spanned one gate. Against such odds, the Hellenes meant to make a stand at Thermopylae. And there was something else, even more bewildering. Among the Greeks were men in red cloaks. These men were not even readying themselves for battle, as the others were. They were performing exercises. They were seen to be combing their hair. The informers of the Great King told him that these were the Spartans. By making their heads beautiful, the informers said, the Spartans were preparing themselves to die.

When he heard this, the Great King ordered his army on. His pavilion was pitched on the highlands above Thermopylae. There he sat to witness the demise of his enemies.

The Battle of Thermopylae lasted three days. On the first morning the Great King sent out his Medes and Cissians. His orders were that the Greeks be taken alive: but the Greeks drove back the Persians. In the afternoon the Great King withdrew his common troops and sent forward his Immortals. They too were repulsed. Three times the Great King was seen to leap from his chair as he watched. As night fell the Greeks still held their wall.

The second day began as the first had ended. The Great King sat and watched his men die. The Hot Gates were a killing ground. In their narrows the Persians could not bring their numbers to bear. Their archers carried bows as long as they themselves were tall, but when they came up the Greeks lay low behind their makeshift wall. The Persian infantry were deft, but their spears were overreached by those of the Hellenes. Sometimes the men in red cloaks would take their turn in the fighting. Sometimes their lines would seem to break, their men scattering away in the terror of battle only to suddenly reform, their shields coming together with a sound like a rolling of drums, the onrushing Persians impaled on their spears.

It was the season of summer storms. The days were hot, unbearably close. At night the moon shone near full through the rain. The

Persians were far from home. The mud matted their skin and hair. Their eyes stared white from their darkened faces. The air smelled of urine and brimstone and ozone.

On the afternoon of the second day a local man was brought before the Great King. He knew, he said, of a path through the mountains. If the Great King so wished, he could send men along the path to the far end of Thermopylae. The Greeks would be trapped like quail in a net.

At nightfall on the second day, at the hour when the lamps are lit, the Great King ordered his Immortals to take the mountain path. Leonidas had known of the path and, fearing its discovery, had put a thousand men to guard it. They could not stand against ten times their number. They fell back through the forests, sending word to the allies that Thermopylae was lost.

Leonidas dismissed all those who wished to go home. Most wanted no more than that, and left under cover of darkness before the enemy could surround them. But the Spartans did not abandon the pass. Nor did they remain alone. Fourteen hundred Greeks stayed to fight under the Spartan king.

As dawn broke on the third day the Persians came down again from the west. The Greeks had been fighting for some time when the Immortals were sighted to the east. With nowhere left to shelter, the Greeks drew back to a small rise. Most of their spears were already broken. They fought until their swords were clubbed out of their hands. King Leonidas fell dying. They dragged his body back three times. They fought with their daggers, hands, and teeth. The barbarians buried them in missiles. They were massacred to the last man.

When the battle was over Xerxes ordered a search of the carnage. He wanted the body of the Spartan king. When it was recovered he had it mutilated. The head of Leonidas was cut off and put up on a pole. Unburied in such a way, his soul would never pass on to the world of the dead. Then the Great King went on with his armies, his eighty thousand horsemen, his twenty thousand charioteers, into the heartlands of Greece.

The battle for which Sparta is best remembered is not a grand victory, but a splendid defeat. It is one of the earliest illustrations of the potency of martyrdom. As the story of the sacrifice at Thermopylae spread, the Greeks took heart. Few sent new envoys to Xerxes with earth and water. Instead the Hellenes drew together. The invasion went on, and was terrible – Athens was razed to the ground – but in the same year that Thermopylae fell the Persian navy was destroyed, and one year after the death of Leonidas the Greek armies that remained met under the leadership of the Spartans. At the Battle of Plataea they faced the Persians together, and obliterated them.

Thermopylae. It is a good story. But it is only a story. Did five thousand men stand for three days against three hundred thousand? Did the Great King start three times from his seat? Did the Spartans drive back the Persians three times from the body of their fallen king? There is truth in all this somewhere, but it is remote. The chronicler of Thermopylae, Herodotus of Halicarnassus, was as much a storyteller as a historian. His account bears all the hallmarks of fable. It does not give us the answers that history demands. Why did the Spartans choose to die so far from the home they cherished? Why would their own king give his life? What is the meaning, the political meaning, the human sense, of the inscription they left behind?

> *Go tell the Spartans, stranger passing by,*
> *That here, obedient to their words, we lie.*

The Sparta of Thermopylae comes down to us through a story, not a history. The good historian is a sceptic. He cannot be content with stories. As the audience to a story he must suspend his disbelief; but as the student of history it is belief he must suspend. In the story of Thermopylae, King Leonidas dies for the freedom of Greece. In history, no one comes off so clean. *The pure and simple truth*, it has been said, *is rarely pure and never simple.*

Would the Spartans be pleased to have become fictions? The Spartans of Herodotus are so fierce and inscrutable that they lose all human proportion; they become a single monolithic entity, fearless and hopeless: Sparta.

Herodotus leaves so many questions unanswered. But then the Spartans did not like to answer for their actions. They answered to no one. They knew the value of fiction. They would be content.

Transcript, public lecture,
Cherwell Historical Society,
Ben Mercer, Oxford, 2003

II

Metamorphosis

He left at night and arrived before morning.

It was February, and Athens was wet as any northern city. Those first days he revelled in the rain. He found a boarding house by the Hill of Wolves and walked up to the summit each day, his heart hammering at the gradient, the groves of wet cypress and pine soaking him when the wind caught them head on, the air under them awash with the smell of retsina.

And then, all at once, the weather began to weigh on him. It reminded him of Oxford and all that Oxford entailed. It became a burden of water he carried from place to place with his head bent, as if the rain chastened him.

ꝏ

He had told those he had left that there was work waiting for him. Three months of private college teaching. A lie to put their minds at rest, or to quell unwanted questions; it depended who he had been telling. Only Emine had not believed him.

As often as he could he lost himself in walking. The city did not embrace him. In Athens, in winter, there were too few tourists and not enough work for anyone. The papers were full of bad and worsening news. In Istanbul, the Great Eastern Raiders' Front insisted on the privilege of having killed the British Consul General. Contractors for the Athens Olympics were running eight months behind schedule and four times over budget, and who would pay in the end but the man in the street? Three boys had died on Symi celebrating a wedding with dynamite, the charges stolen from a road crew's hut, the explosion leaving nothing behind, the bodies vaporised. A retired general had been kidnapped from his yacht at Laurium, the vessel found drifting like a ghost ship in a seaman's tale. Anarchists had firebombed a ferry company in Piraeus, and the Association of Kiosk Vendors were threatening to strike over the licensing of Albanians, the concessions having always gone to disabled war veterans; and their popular cause, more than anything, soured the general mood. The city was neither welcoming nor unwelcoming, but unnoticing, with a gleaming, hurrying coldness that reminded him of the worst of England. He sat alone under the rafterless eaves of the temple of Athena Parthenos, rain dripping onto the steps, and remembered what he had left behind.

He needed work. He needed to be with others, working, and there was nothing. Already his money was short, but it was not the living he needed so much as the life. There was always that hurry in him. To be with someone; to be a part of something. He was not a man who was happy alone.

The boarding house manageress saved him the local jobs pages. He found two positions he might have filled, both menial by his standards, one in the harbour subcity of Piraeus and the other miles out in the industrial conurbations of Mégara; but both were taken when he telephoned, with no expectation of further vacancies.

The days were insubstantial, fast-changing, always threatened by rain, but with bursts of sunshine that lit up the avenues and squares with spells of sudden clarity, so that he would stop dead in a street of lock-up shops, or under the dusty orange trees, trying to understand how the place could have become glorious, even as the clouds moved on and the moment passed.

He dreamed of the women in his life. They were on the plane with him. Somehow – he did not know how or why – they had come away with him.

Emine was in the window seat, looking at the stars outside. Her eyes were not hers, were not human at all. They were wide and ferocious as those of a bird. Vanessa slept in her arms. He wanted it to be true, at first, despite that inhuman gaze, despite knowing in some fold of his brain that it was not. Then a wave of claustrophobia washed over him.

– You're not here, he said to them. – You shouldn't be with me. Go home. Go home!

But Emine only smiled and shook her head, and Nessie woke and began crying. Her lips were sewn together. The loose ends of the thread were crusted with old blood.

ꙮ

On Monday, as he tried to buy roast chestnuts in his antiquated Greek, two students from Corinth came to his aid. Over coffee and cigarettes they asked him about England, showed him pictures of London as they knew it – a college bar, a kebab shop hoarding dimmed by rain – and were eager to help when he mentioned employment.

On one of the girls' jewel-like mobiles they called their uncle, the owner of a meat grill in the suburb of Metamorphosis. He agreed terms without a second thought: yes, he would wait tables and wash up (could he wash up? Yes, he thought he could) in exchange for tips and something on top, plus meals and a room. Could he cook a steak? All the better. It was Ben, was it? A good bible name. The clients were a little rough that winter, construction workers down from the North, he shouldn't expect them to be a gold mine. At least they would find his Greek amusing, the uncle said, and with that settled he told Ben to put his pretty nieces on again.

The boarding house manageress was disappointed in him.

– Such hard work for soft hands, she said, leaning close across the counter, raising her pencilled brows, and he told her that it was good work, that it was nothing to be ashamed of.

By way of a parting gift she drew him a map on the back of an election flyer. An X marked the meat grill like buried treasure. He walked to Constitution Square and took the bus to Metamorphosis.

He had been to Athens before, twice to speak and once to dig, but had never ventured out to the suburbs. They seemed to be built entirely of postwar concrete and plate glass, as if the city were nothing but an invention of the twentieth century. The bus soon threatened to overheat, the driver getting out to hammer the hot bonnet open with his shoe while the passengers shifted and muttered. The windows were gummed shut with eluvium, and when they got going again the heat built up, pleasant at first, then uncomfortable and finally alarming, the metal frames of the seats too hot to touch. No one got out unless they had reached their destination. In Metamorphosis, it seemed, even a bus half on fire was better than no bus at all.

He disembarked when he recognised a street name from the map. There were few signs and he took his direction from the light. The shopfronts on each side were cavernous and contained nothing but pet stores and tractor showrooms. They were large enough to accommodate the orange and green chassis of the tractors, so large that the sounds of canaries and cockatiels echoed and multiplied, as if there were flocks of birds gone wild in the recesses of the buildings.

He crossed a public park, deserted in the rain but for a single black woman with Ghana braids who sat on a bench by a clock tower with her head in her hands. By the time he reached the restaurant he was an hour late and the owner, Mr Adamidis, scowled and bundled him out of sight before the customers could judge him.

The room upstairs smelled of men and cockroaches. On the wall by the door were a washbasin, a mirror and an Agricultural Bank of Greece calendar. A defunct deep-fat fryer stood in one corner. Four mattresses were laid out on the floor as far from one another as possible, their sheets in various stages of disorder, a suitcase beside one, a sports bag by another. On the mattress nearest the window a long-faced man lay smoking. He turned his head as Ben came in, then turned away without interest.

– Sleep where you like, Mr Adamidis said, his accent heavy, gesturing at both the man and the mattresses. – Any valuables, you can leave with me. Come down when you're cleaned up. He looked Ben up and down. – You have anything valuable? Fine. You want a drink? Some water?

– No, I'm okay.

– Okay, well, that's okay. I was only offering. I'll see you downstairs in half an hour, right?

He ran his eye over Ben again, his hand on the door. He looked as though he regretted having listened to his nieces. The smell of meat and the sound of laughter drifted up in the moment before he closed the door behind him.

Only one mattress had no accompanying territory of belongings. He shucked off his rucksack, laid it down. The bedsheets looked clean, but the smells of sweat and insecticide contaminated everything.

How did I get here?

He had left England with almost no ambition beyond leaving. It had hardly mattered where he went, only that he put some space and time between himself and the life he had damaged beyond repair. Three months had been the most he could take off from his obligations, and Athens was somewhere he knew, a destination that would not seem untoward to his colleagues and friends.

And so now here he was, in Athens. The sweat was cooling on his back. He was shivering with the cold. The discomfort of the room was nothing to him, but now that he had come to a stop he found himself uneasy. It was unsettling that he should have stepped out of his old life and ended up so quickly here. In a room above a meat grill, in the backwoods of a foreign city.

It was as if he had gone wrong somewhere. As if, at some point, he had turned down the wrong road without ever realising it, so that now he headed on towards some dark and unexpected place.

– Is not so bad.

When he turned the man was watching him. He had spoken in English. He transferred his cigarette into his left hand and held the right outstretched.

– Kostandin.

– Ben.

– English, right?

– How do you know?

– You look English, Kostandin smiled. It was a good smile, crooked and wry. – And maybe the boss said.

– What's he like?

– Like a boss. Sit, sit!

He motioned to Ben, drawing his legs out of the way, nudging his cigarettes across the sheets. His eyes were deepset, the skin darkly pigmented within the sockets.

– Most of the time is on vacation. When is here, he never trust no one. He nodded his chin towards Ben's rucksack. – Not me, not you, not his wife. Only his son. Watch out for the son. Where I come from we say, *Shake hands with a Greek, then count your fingers.* With the boss you count them, with the boy you look for blood.

He nodded, awkwardly, searching for the right thing to say.

– How long have you been here?

– Too long. Two years. The pay is shit, the food is good, the room . . . as you see. Long hours. Is better when we are busy, then the time goes faster. But the boss is okay. The room is free.

He was still cold. His clothes were wet. The man's tobacco lent him warmth.

– Where are you from?

– Albania.

– Apollonia is in Albania.

He was gratified when the man's face softened, becoming unexpectedly tender, his features losing their mournfulness.

– Our beautiful city of the Romans. You been there?

– I read about it.

– Why?

– It's what I do. Archaeology.

– *Arkeologji*, Kostandin repeated, and nodded. – Ruins, sure. We have plenty of ruins in Albania.

When his cigarette was finished Ben got up, fetched a towel from his pack and went to the washbasin. A sliver of green soap lay congealed between the taps. The water began to warm. He took off his shirt, scrubbed his face, hands and armpits, dried his hair, clothes and skin.

– Now you don't do it. This archaeology.

– Not right now.

– So why you come here?

– I needed a place.

– But how come Greece?

– It's my area. It's the place I know best.

– Sure, in archaeology. But England is old country. Buckingham Palace, Windsor Palace. You do archaeology in England. Is better.

He rescued the soap from the plug, replaced it between the taps, rinsed its grease from his hands. The agricultural calendar was open to February. Under the picture, *Auster Slaughterhouse Ltd, Kalamata* was captioned in English and Greek. In the photo, an interminably bored young woman was severing a pig from snout to anus.

– Why not stay in England? the man insisted, and Ben shrugged, to delay, perhaps to postpone the need to answer, his hackles rising. – You going to do some archaeology here?

– No. Look, I told you, I just need somewhere to stay.

– What are you, then, a teacher? A student?

– Both.

– You look like a student. But students have their own places. Maybe you are kind of something else.

There was a cataclysm of pans from downstairs, the sound of voices briefly raised. Ben pulled on his shirt. – Maybe I'm something else like you.

– No. Kostandin's own cigarette was finished. His arms lay across his upraised knees, his eyes motionless on Ben, his lean body folded away against the wall. – Not like me. Nothing like me. You are another kind of something else.

Archaeology. From the Greek *arkhaiologia*, meaning *discourse on ancient things*.

He didn't think of it that way himself. *The study of secrets*: that was what it was to him. The way the past could be put back together, piece by piece, by force of ingenuity and rational intelligence. The way history could be bared.

The body in the gravepit and the notch in the skull; the meaning of its jewels and the method of its sacrifice; the pollen in the poison in the wineskin at its feet . . . it could all be discovered. Could be rediscovered. All things would answer, in the end, if you knew how to question them. If you were patient, if you listened, the earth itself would speak.

He remembered Nessie's voice, the day that he had left her.

The dawn fog had begun to lift. The sky beyond had been a flawless grey, as if Oxford lay under a northern sea. He had stopped the car on Foyt's square and turned off the engine, cautious as a stalker. The house had been visible through the pines. There had been lights on downstairs. Foyt's car had still been in the drive.

He had meant to see her, one more time, but when it came to it he couldn't face Foyt again. Instead he'd sat there like a coward and called up the number on his mobile. The streetlights had still been on, their circuits set to winter time, their heads ringed with lit fog. He had stared through the trees at the house while he waited.

The au pair had answered, a nondescript girl with a name he always forgot. Foyt had hired her himself through one of Oxford's many language colleges.

– It's Ben.

– Ben?

– Vanessa's dad. Can I speak to her?

A voice in the background, the girl covering the mouthpiece. He had caught the sound of his own name and Foyt's voice. *Tell him . . .*

Then the au pair had been talking again, Foyt leaving her to it. Delegating him.

– You can ring later? She has her breakfast now, and then we go to the nursery . . .

– Just for a minute. Or look, I'm just round the corner, I can come by–

– Now? No, now is not good.

Sunniva; that was the name. She had always looked sullen when he came for Ness, and she'd sounded sulky then, as if she had been waiting for a boyfriend to ring and picked up on a telemarketer.

– You can ring us at the nursery?

– What? No. Look, Sunniva–

– *Su*nniva.

– That's what I said–

– You're going away, yes? A holiday. Greece. Emine said so.

– It's not a holiday.

– It will be nice for you.

He had closed his eyes. The anger had welled up in him, then, useless and hopeless. It did that so often now. It was as if his reserves of it had grown during the months of separation. It was as if there were a sea of it inside him, cold and tidal and unkind. It terrified him. He would grow angry so quickly, sometimes with total strangers, like Kostandin the Albanian, but more often with those he loved, with Emine most of all, so that however much he wanted to see her he no longer trusted himself with her. He would dream of such terrible things. Breaking open her skull, prising the fragments apart, to find out what there was left in there for him.

Only thoughts. He would never have touched her. But then he had already done so once, in his own needful way. Once had been more than enough for both of them.

– Hello?

The girl's voice had changed. It had become prim and brisk, the tone she would use with a recalcitrant child.

– I'd like to speak to my daughter.

– We are late for the nursery, and she is not dressed yet.

– I don't need her dressed, I just need–

– If you want you can speak to the professor.

– Oh, for Christ's sake–

From somewhere in the distance, garbled by transmission, another voice had reached him; a falsetto bellowing. There had been a sigh, then the clunk of the phone; an altercation, coming closer; then, finally, heavy breathing.

– Daddy.

– Shrimp.

– My name's not Shrimp.

– No? I've got the wrong number, then. Who is this?

– It's me but my name's not Shrimp.

A shadow at the kitchen window. He had watched the blind darken, his enemies looming up and away.

– What is it, then?

– You should know because you named me.

– Is it Nessie?

– Yes.

– Hello, Nessie.

All the anger had drained out of him in the time it took to say her name.

– Daddy, how old are you?

– How old? Oh, ancient. Why?

– Mark's dad is fifty.

– Mark who?

– It was his birthday party we went to, silly!

– Right. Head like a sieve. Did you sleep well?

– Hm. We're eating breakfast now. Me and Sinny. That's what I call Sunniva now, Sinny, it's a nickname, like Shrimp is a nickname, but better.

– You don't sound like you're eating.

– Not *now*. After and before. What's so funny?

– Nothing. Mum said you wanted to talk. She said you wanted to ask me something?

– . . . I did, but I forgot.

– Oh well. Listen, I had a good time yesterday. How about you?

No answer. He had still heard her breathing, but her attention had gone elsewhere, drawing away. Already he had been losing her.

– Hello? Hello, Nessie. I want to speak to you. Hello? I want to speak to you. Nessie, he had said, trying to be calm; and suddenly she had been back again, louder and much closer than before, like a radio signal emerging through interference.

– Daddy, are you going away?

He had told her about it many times, ever since he had been certain of the necessity. She had never seemed to understand. He had almost regretted it, then, that she had grasped it at last. He had wondered who had explained it to her, or if the information had been there all along, dormant, waiting for acceptance.

– Are you?

– Yes. Yes. We said goodbye yesterday. Did you forget?

– We always say goodbye.

– Yesterday was different.

– I didn't know.

– It's just for a while. Is that alright?

– I don't want you to.

– I have to.

– Why?

– For work.

Such a lie. Had it ever been a white lie? It had been so easy to lie to his child.

– Where are you going?

– A place called Athens.

– *Athens* is a stupid name.

– It's just for a bit, love.

– When will you be back?

– In the summer.

– When's the summer?

– You know that. After the spring.

– Is it spring now?

– Almost, he had said. – Almost spring.

No sound. A car had gone past through the grey, and then the square had been silent again.

– Nessie?

– Okay. You can go.

– I'll be back before you know it.

– No you won't. I'm going now.

– Wait–

– I've got to go. We're very busy here.

– Nessie?

But his child had gone, and it had been only the girl he would soon forget who had came back to the phone to say goodbye.

There were nine of them at the grill. Lowest in rank were Modest and Florent, Albanian brothers arrived that winter from just over the border. Less junior by virtue of culinary skill and age were Kostandin and Ben. Some weekends Mrs Adamidis's nieces would help out with the waiting for pocket money. Adamidis and his wife oversaw them all, and had worked the restaurant together for thirty-eight years. But the pinnacle, the top of the grilled meat food chain, was their son, Nikos.

Kostandin had earned more trust from Adamidis than he liked to admit: to do so would flatter the Greek too much. Often the owners would be away, on business or pleasure, and then Kostandin would be entrusted with the role of front-of-house man, not only cooking but hurrying out to greet and entertain, sometimes distributing largesse, the sparse courtesy of a glass of three-star brandy where it would bear fruit later. In any case, whether Adamidis was there or not, the kitchen work and much of the waiting were left to Ben and the Albanians.

Every day it opened the restaurant was busy. It filled up for the lunchtime main meal and filled again late in the evening, when the midday crowd of construction workers would be interspersed with couples in search of corner tables, hangdog travelling businessmen who smoked as they ate alone, students from the local college, and the occasional family, complete with children for Adamidis to dote on and spoil with spoon sweets and Pepsis. Few foreigners came to Metamorphosis, but the meat grill had no need of them.

The work was relentless. He had taken the job as a temporary thing, a stopgap, but it did not feel that way. By the end of the first night scars and burns had already begun to mark his hands and forearms. The burns crawled with pain, as if there were something lodged and living under the welted skin. In the days that followed the wounds healed slowly and imperfectly. There was a permanence to them that was disturbing.

There was the smell, too. From almost the first moment he set foot in the place its odours crept into the fabrics of his clothes and self – ammonia, cooked meat, raw meat – so that even on his mornings off, when he read or walked in the park, the impression of hunger clung to the edges of his consciousness.

He was not always unhappy. It was hard work for soft hands, but he knew he could survive it. He knew enough about shame not to be ashamed of it. When he contemplated the endless appetite of the customers, the food that came back to the kitchen as waste, the place disgusted him, and away from it, too, he loathed the mindlessness of the work. But it was sometimes different when he was there. The shifts were backbreaking, yet there was a rhythm to them which he found himself caught up in when he considered it least, a pattern of tasks which gathered up all his attention, a dancer's understanding of those around him, a pack mentality, so that he would look up from turning meat, giving orders, taking orders, to find to his astonishment that hours had passed, and the sun gone down into dusk outside.

To be with someone. To be a part of something.

It was something that happened most completely when the place was at its most hectic, when the temperature and grinding nervousness in the kitchen were almost unbearable, so that he would step from its oven-heat into the cool and civil noise of the dining room with no time to feel relief. Kostandin had been right: the work ate time. It devoured not only hours but days – years, perhaps, given the chance – so that he woke one morning into nine o'clock quiet and lay still, counting the days to find that he had been in Athens a fortnight. Two days before his birthday had passed uncelebrated. He had turned twenty-five without knowing it.

He dreamed of his wife and child again. They were just the same, paused, as if they had been waiting for him on freeze-frame. The stars shone through the porthole behind them. They flew together through the darkness in darkness.

How wrong he had been to leave them. In his dreams his leaving was revealed as the mistake it was. He should never have left Oxford. He had given up too easily, however far he and Emine had gone wrong, whatever wrong he had done them. The moment he had left he had gone wrong again.

The tears were wet on Nessie's face. The thread in her lips was coming loose. Her mouth moved against its ligatures.

He shook his dream-head at her. His daughter was trying to tell him something. She lay as she always did in sleep, one hand curled in her hair. Her mother's arms held her away from him. He leaned down to make out her words. The crude threads brushed against his ear. Her hand crept into his like a thing seeking shelter.

You haven't gone wrong, Ben. You haven't left us. One day you will, she said, and her voice was not her own. *But not yet.*

❧

He began to count the time in shifts. His world narrowed to that of the kitchen and the front of house. The raised forestage and the treacherous step. The flare of incendiary fat. The thutter and blurt of meat. The steel pans gilded with oil. The fish as green as celadon, as dull-bright as lead, as pink as grazed flesh. The rare laughter of the Albanians. A gallon jar of cucumbers, broken in the kitchen yard, the pickles shrivelled in the sun like the cadavers of lizards. The neat sheaves of scallions. White tiles grooved with chicken blood. The gutters full of guts. The drunks crowing in the street beyond, the whole dark night their oyster.

❧

When he had arrived at the grill Nikos had been skiing with friends in the mountains. It was a while before Ben met him. His father was a heavy man, lazily pugnacious in the old photos above the bar, mellowed and gone to fat after decades in the business. Nikos was different. He was clever, the first of the family to go to a top-notch university. He had a busy look, his eyes never settling long. He was lean as tenderloin. He did not drink. He enjoyed hash, Ben observed, and sex, if he was to be believed. Occasionally he would come back to the grill with a girl in tow, but he was unkind to them, with a coldness Ben hated, and perfunctory with his cousins, Demi and Chara. He exercised at an international hotel gym near Constitution Square where he could meet foreign women. He carried no apparent trace of muscle. Kostandin said he was stronger than he looked, and said it as if he knew it.

Once, while Kostandin was teaching him how to gut squid – drawing the calyx from each soft body like a glass pen from a well of ink – the Albanian told him a story of Nikos. When he was seventeen, the boy had gone to watch a football match with friends, and afterwards had been caught up in a fight with three Englishmen. He had not been hurt, but a friend had taken a cut to the hand, which required stitches.

Somehow, by the evening, Nikos had discovered where the men

were staying. He had gone to the hotel alone. The men had been in the restaurant. It went without saying (Kostandin said) that they were drunk as rags. Nikos had walked up to their table and had congratulated them on the victory of their team. He had taken a pair of bikers' gauntlets out of the bag he carried, and still smiling, had put them on: then he had reached into the bag again and had taken out a motorcycle chain. He had flogged the nearest man with the chain. In trying to defend himself the man's hand had been partially severed. He had almost died from the loss of blood.

It had taken a number of people to drag Nikos off. The man had taken out a civil suit which the Adamidis family had settled privately. Nikos himself had been released from prison a week before his eighteenth birthday, a model first offender with time reduced for good behaviour.

In summer, by his own account, he would cruise the city for female tourists, who were always eager to ride first his Honda and then Nikos himself. In winter, though, the fishing seemed poor. More often than not he would come back to Metamorphosis before midnight, pallid and sullen, to eat what little he wished for, to stare at his father's foreign workers, sometimes to talk with them.

– So you're an Englishman?

– Yes.

– I like Englishmen.

– Really.

– Really. You know what your grandfathers did for my grandmothers?

Saturday night, ten to nine. The evening rush about to begin. Nikos prowling by the yardside door. He was smoking – hash, always hash, never leaf – the joint held out into the clean night air. It was something he would do on the premises only if his parents were away. Occasionally he would punctuate his talk by pointing the joint into the kitchen, sometimes at the workers, sometimes at the intangible force of his own words, and the acrid spice would linger, mixing with the other smells of the place.

– You don't know? You English are so funny. Always forgetting your own past. You freed us from the Nazis! You and the Americans too. Isn't that great? Don't you think I'm grateful?

– Sure you are.

Better not to talk too much, with a boy like Nikos. Better not to listen much, and to talk less.

– I'll tell you, I'm not grateful. My grandmother is grateful – there you have your gratitude. But my grandmother is a peasant. Me, I study my history. I know what the English did *firstly*, for my country and *secondly*, to my country. You helped us and then you tried to control us. I don't want to be rude, but we are all men here, right? So let me be plain. You told us to bend over and take it like ladyboys. You became capitalist interferers, then arselicking war criminals, no better than the Americans themselves. Oh, you earned our gratitude, but then you spent it as though it would last forever. Like the Guns and Roses song – nothing lasts forever. Right? You still walk around like we are all friends, but you only remember the good times. You forget that you gave us the Colonels. You gave us those monsters, but you don't remember that. Do you even know what I'm talking about? You still come to see us, but you are like old idiot guests who forget the names of their hosts. And so many of you! You go sniffing around our country like dogs running after dogs. What is wrong with you all? Is England so nasty that you all come here to escape? Well, I understand, my country is beautiful, no doubt about it. All the foreigners love Greece. They all want a piece of us. They buy their little places on the islands with the pools they never use. But you English . . . well, I hope you don't come expecting favours. My grandmothers already gave thanks to your grandfathers. You won't get any victory parade out of me.

Other nights it would be the Albanians he would bait. For a long time he didn't speak to Florent, but he would talk to Kostandin and Modest. Sometimes he would be amiable, chatting with them, picking over the last night's sports, but he could turn on them suddenly. Kostandin held little interest for him. Modest was his favourite, Modest with the kicked-dog eyes. With him, most of all, the talk could take on a dangerous edge.

Burnt Thursday was the day of meat, the Carnival, a last excess before the seven weeks of Lent. The meat grill opened early and went on serving until first light. Mrs Adamidis worked the front of house with the girls while her husband threw himself back into the old routines of his kitchen, stripped down to an AGED TO PERFECTION T-shirt, driving the rest of them on with promises of extra cash, then when the promises were no longer believable, with cold beer and brandies and cigarettes. The next morning Ben slept until eleven, the Albanians leaving him to it. It was Chara and Demi who finally came up for him, stopping at the threshold of the men's room to tease him down.

They were eating, the four of them, in the lull after lunch, the kitchen scrubbed and ready for the evening. There was rice, a bowl of greens, and more goat rib-chops than they could stomach. Nikos had come in early, bringing a chair and a newspaper to sit in the warm. The ovens had retained their heat all day. They had all been talking, the five of them almost at ease. When the meal was finished they cleared and made coffee. It was a quiet day, and in the afternoon there was never enough work to make the time pass.

– So, Englishman. How are you today?

Nikos was stretching his legs out by the ovens, still dressed in his bike leathers. – Not working too hard, I see. Me, I was hard at it all night. You don't believe me? Two German girls. Both of them wanted to sleep with me, so I did my best for them.

– How did you know?

– How? Because they said so.

– They spoke Greek?

– German. German comes from the Greek, it's no problem for me. I know what they were talking about. Some things don't need language. Are you making fun of me?

– No.

– That's good. So tell me, are you married?

Already the conversation had gone on too long. He was not wearing his ring. He held up his bare hand in reply. Nikos gave a grunt of acknowledgement.

– So you are a bachelor like me. A free man, searching the world for adventure. *When you set out from Ithaca, pray that the way is long, full of knowledge and adventure.* You know this? Greek poetry.

– I don't really like poetry.

– You don't like our Greek poetry? Why do you come here, then,

I wonder? No, I can guess. Your English girls, they are just like the Germans. That blonde hair is so pretty at a distance, but get up close, ouch! You find they don't take no care of themselves. So you come to the only country where you can find real beauty. What about you? Albanian boy.

They both looked up, Modest at the washing-up sink, Florent leaning with a cigarette in the doorway to the kitchen yard. Only Kostandin went on working, his head down as he boned a rabbit. Already he was almost done with it, the last of the meat coming away in nuggets and knots.

– Yes, you. What's your name again?

– Modest, Modest said. He was the youngest of them. Nineteen was the age he had offered Ben when they had met, but he seemed much younger.

– You're married, I bet. You've got the look. To an Albanian girl?

– Yes. Modest turned back to the sink, his hands weighing dishes in the grey water. From where he stood, Ben could see him smile.

The quiet returned and held. Already it was getting dark outside. It was turning out to be a nice evening, peaceful, when Nikos wasn't talking. A blackbird started up. If he didn't listen too hard – if he half-closed his ears – it was almost intelligible, expectant, the syllables falling into words.

You're late you're late you're late

hurryup! hurryup! hurryup!

– Her name is Flutura, Modest said into the birdsong, and Ben's heart fell.

– Is what?

– Flutura.

Nikos laughed. – My God, what the hell kind of name is that?

– It means butterfly. Kostandin spoke without looking up from his work. His voice spread the smile across Modest's face. In the doorway, Florent laughed.

– Because she dance like a butterfly, he said, and his brother began to giggle. Florent was bigger and older than his brother. His frame blocked out the illumination from the streetlight beyond the yard.

– Well, I'm happy for you. You're a lucky man, eh?

– Lucky. Modest nodded and shrugged. – I miss my wife.

– But it's lucky for you that you found an Albanian girl. Lucky for her too, yes?

– Yes?

– You know why?

– No?

Even in the last daylight, Ben could see the blush creeping across Modest's face. As if he had already been slapped down. Kostandin's features were unreadable in the diffused shadow of the extraction fan.

– Because no woman except an Albanian would let you nuzzle between her legs. And no man except an Albanian would want to do her the service. Don't you think so?

No one answered. After a moment Nikos began to talk about something else, the basketball, the lottery, meaningless things. In the doorway Florent stirred. Kostandin and Modest both turned to watch him. Only when he dropped his cigarette into the yard, stepping down to put it out with his foot, turning his back to the men in the kitchen, did the other Albanians look away.

– Trouble, Kostandin said. They were alone, the night's work finished, the grill cleaned for the thousandth time, ready for the next day's custom. They sat in the park drinking beers still cold from the chill cabinet. It had become their habit, the empty park a cure for insomnia, the small theft of beer an equalising freedom. The brothers were always asleep on their feet by the time the kitchen was scoured down, but Ben slept less readily himself, even tired to the bone. The adrenaline took time to ebb out of him. Kostandin was the same. Often they were too exhausted to talk and would do nothing but drink, side by side on the bench by the park clock tower. Some nights Ben would teach the older man English, other times Kostandin would correct his Greek.

– What did you say?

– I said, there is going to be trouble.

– Because of Nikos?

– Because of Florent! I don't say it is easy for anyone, Kostandin said, But for him it is hard.

– Being here?

– Being here. Having to listen to foolish talk.

He dangled a Mythos in both hands. His head drooped over it. His voice was so tired that Ben was sure they must both fall asleep, one from talking, the other from listening.

– A brave man would turn the other cheek.

– Isn't he?

He tried to picture Florent. He could imagine nothing of him but his silhouette in the kitchen door. – He seems brave.

– How would you know? No, he isn't brave, he's too young to be brave. He's as bad as the crazy Greek boy.

– How do you mean?

– He got into problems at home. Modest told me. Something in their village. I don't know what so don't ask me. Some things are unforgivable, whatever the priests say. Whatever this thing is, it is bad enough he has to leave the village. He is the head of the family, so the family comes with him. Anyway, the old folks are dead, it is only him and two little sisters and Modest and Flutura left, it is not so hard to leave. Florent finds somewhere for them a long way from home, down near the Greek border. A new town they are building, so there is plenty of work. Then the town is finished and suddenly there is no work. So the boys come here.

He tipped the bottle back, trying to listen. His thoughts moving with narcotic slowness, the beer sweet and cool as rain.

– And what do they find here? Shit work, shit money, and a boy with no heart who wants to spill blood.

– It's just talk. He's just having fun, he won't do anything.

– Just talk! If you think that then you shouldn't talk about talk. You don't know what you're talking about.

– I know what I'm talking about. I have to listen to enough of it from Nikos.

Beside him Kostandin laughed and sighed in the dark.

– Listen, you don't know. I'm not talking about Nikos. These boys are new in Athens. Where they come from *no one* would talk that way about a man's wife to his face. They grew up in a village in the mountains. They are Ghegs. The Ghegs are very proud people. Up there people take care what they say about their neighbours. They don't even talk to strangers. They know that talk is dangerous. Florent is an old-fashioned young man. He loves his family. He has looked after them, maybe not so well, it's true. Maybe he wants to do better now. He is the eldest son. You have little brothers, sisters?

– I'm the youngest.

– That's nice, everyone loves the youngest. So in Albania it's a big deal to be the oldest. When the old man dies you look after the family. Kostandin tapped his chest. – I was the oldest, too, but in the cities it's not so serious. For Florent it's serious.

– What's going to happen?

– I told you. Trouble.

– Does Adamidis know?

– No.

– You could tell him.

– So could you.

He looked sideways at Kostandin. Outlined in the dark, the man's head was no longer quite human. It became that of a mule, the shape of it was so long, the bones of his cheeks and sockets so habitually mournful.

– Better to leave it. What happens happens. And afterwards they round us up and we all go home.

– Come on, it's not that bad. Nothing's happened yet, he said, but Kostandin shook his head, and for a while they sat in silence.

The nights were getting warmer. Through the clouds and the haze he could make out the moon and a scattering of stars. A plane crawled between them. He tried to imagine himself back into that distance, but it seemed as remote as England itself. Beside him Kostandin hawked and spat.

– What time does it say up there?

He looked from the sky to the stack of the clocktower. – Past three.

– Late.

– You want to go back?

– Not really.

– Maybe we could find somewhere else to drink.

– Maybe. We have no money.

– That's true.

Silence again.

– Maybe I'll go home anyway. You should come. There's a bus to Vlora tomorrow. The beer is cheaper. You can go dig holes in Apollonia. Find some treasure. What keeps you here?

Nothing, he thought numbly, and said finally, – Nothing.

– Nothing. Maybe the Greek boy will learn when to stop talking, Kostandin said, and stood up to go.

❦

He thought of the times Emine had cooked for him, as he now cooked for strangers. She had not done so often. She had a generous spirit, but in that she had always held back a part of herself; a talent. It was something she had chosen to distrust before they had ever met: she had made up her mind that cooking for a man would be offensive to her. Her mother had cooked for her father for years, she had told him once, and look, they had hated one another anyway, so what was the point?

Better to learn something useful, she had said. *Like how to earn our daily bread in the first place.* And kissed him, to draw out the sting.

She had kept her ability to herself, as if it were a weakness. Only once had she let it show before they moved in together. He had been staying at her place, and his brother had come to visit. She had never met his family and had been anxious to impress. She had made coq au vin, the real thing, hunting down a cockerel through an enamoured butcher at the Covered Market, working on it all through one afternoon.

He had helped her peel away the wrappings of bloodied newspaper. The cockerel had been an ugly thing, red-crested, with a great pale bloom of chest and massive scarred claws, black-scaled, reptilian, made for fighting as much as digging. Its blood, heart and liver had been set aside for Emine in a canopic polystyrene cup. He had not liked the look of the claws, but the final meal had been so good he had been speechless, and Ted had laughed at them both.

What are you so gobsmacked about? You look like you never sat across a table before.

It had been an oddity for them back then, that momentary bewilderment. It had only been towards the end that such awkwardness had expanded to fill their lives. Then, their conversation would often descend into small talk and puzzling silences. They had come to move around one another like magnets laid North to North, all their old attraction turned to bafflement and repulsion.

In the end they had met twice at the offices of a solicitors in Cowley – not Emine's partnership but another, cheaper and neutral outfit – the room where they convened windowless and still somehow full of a wintery grey light that seemed to subdue Emine and the lawyers just as it did Ben himself. Neither meeting had gone well, and the second time he had left in a rage, shaking like an old man, palsied with anger. He had agreed to everything demanded of him all the same. Emine hadn't asked for much. She had always avoided dealing with divorce law, and had seemed almost as innocent of the practicalities as he had himself. But she had never needed his money and whatever else it was she had once desired of him, she no longer wished to bind him to it. She had agreed to joint custody. There would be no annulment from the church, but the civil divorce would be done by the summer at the latest.

He knew it was the opinion of the lawyers that he had come off well. *Got off lightly*, was how his own solicitor had put it. *Relatively, you know. Could have been messy, with her like that. I mean religious. And in the business. A nice clean break, apart from the girl.*

Sometimes he would run into Emine at the Institute of Archaeology or at their college, with Foyt in tow or without. Somehow both places had become theirs. Somehow he had been dispossessed. And even after Emine had left, she would still be with him in the eyes of others, the ghost of a wife. There would be the sidelong glances, the conversations stopping as he entered a lecture hall or the common room. The unbearable English lulls and silences.

He had considered giving up on Oxford, leaving it to Emine and Foyt and going home to whatever he could find in London. He had begun to drink, not for the enjoyment of it but with a savage, bottomless desire he had never felt before and which he recognised. His father had drunk in the same way. He had feared and hated it as a boy and loathed it all the more in himself. He had become aware of how fragile his normality had become. There was a delicacy to his sanity he had never acknowledged before. It was as frail as water tension.

He couldn't leave for good. He was not about to give up on so much. His life was too deeply rooted to break as cleanly as that. But he had left all the same. He had run away, like the coward he was.

And who had he had run from, if not himself? As if that were possible. As if he could ever escape himself.

Even when Nikos wasn't there the meat grill could be dangerous. It wasn't the trappings in themselves – the knives, the meat sat in its blood, the means and proof of harm – so much as having all that at hand in a place of tension. Tempers could flare up over the most insignificant things. An order misread could be a catalyst one day and a joke the next. A borrowed spoon might do it, or a pot of beans left unattended. Whenever it came, whatever it was, the wrong thing would be like a pinch of salt dropped into scalding water.

The atmosphere was worse at lunchtimes when the construction workers crowded in, roughnecks from Vólos and Lárissa. Half of them worked graveyard shifts and would be tired and intemperate by two. Their orders would come all at once and if anything went wrong the kitchen could be overtaken by mayhem. When it happened Modest would talk too much and Florent too little, and Kostandin would mutter oaths under his breath, unspeakable storms of consonants that sometimes made the Albanians giggle like boys, but could also propel them all into anger, Modest standing over the charcoal with his teeth bared in a snarl, Ben screwing up botched orders, Florent turning from some task with an expression of such blind savagery on his face that they would all be reduced to silence.

Nikos had lost interest in him, and Florent was not his problem. They were not his enemies but one another's. The atmosphere between them was one into which he could walk without realising it until too late. It was there in the way the others would go quiet when they were in the same room. It was as if they were all counting the seconds after lightning.

൭൭

He considered bravery. He was not brave himself. There was one year, as a boy, when he had been sick, seriously ill, with double pneumonia. They had kept him in hospital for a fortnight. In the beds nearest him had been two boys and a girl. All three had been more obviously unwell than him. All had seemed to him brave.

He had envied it in them. He remembered lying in the back of the van, on the way to hospital – the road veering under him, his mother's face pallid above him – and the creeping realisation that he was, perhaps, in danger. He'd had no dignity after that.

His mother had told him once that before the pneumonia he had been the kind of child you couldn't take your eye off, an explorer, a talker to strangers. He had changed after the sickness, she had said. He had not disagreed with her, but he had wondered. Had he really changed? What had he had to be scared of, before that time?

Maybe the sickness had only been his first taste of fear. Maybe, until then, he hadn't had the imagination to understand that he was not the centre of the world. That he was not the motive force at the heart of things, the hero, beyond all harm. That anything might happen to anyone.

Once he woke in the middle of the night with a feeling of claustrophobia so strong that it was like a fire alarm going off in his head. For minutes he sat there, the sheet clinging to his sweat, before he remembered where he was. The room, the basin, the calendar. The fryer leaning in its corner, the other men sleeping around him. He sank back down without relief.

What keeps you here? Kostandin had said, and he had said *Nothing*. And that was true, surely, because how could it be otherwise? It was only the slightest of connections that had brought him to Metamorphosis. There was nothing there for him that was worth the violence Kostandin saw coming. He could go to Albania if he wished. He could go anywhere.

Then Eberhard came to Metamorphosis, and Eberhard changed everything.

III

Notes Towards a Thesis

Transcript, Doxiades lecture,
'Spartan Gods: Spartan Monsters',
Eberhard Sauer, Oxford, 2003

The fall of Sparta is one of the great mysteries of the ancient world. In the absence of Spartan writings there are as many theories for the city's decline as for the extinction of the dinosaurs. At the time of Lycurgus there were said to be nine thousand Spartan men, and, two centuries later, the Great King of Persia was informed that there were eight thousand, just like those hundreds he had seen die at the Hot Gates. Yet only eighty years after Thermopylae, Sparta could muster no more than three thousand spears, and three decades later, when Sparta was defeated by Thebes at the Battle of Leuctra, there were only fifteen hundred remaining. One year after that loss, and for the first time since antiquity, Sparta's enemies came within sight of the unwalled city itself.

By contrast, the rise of Sparta is not mysterious at all. It was built on the backs of hoplites and helots.

The hoplite was the archetypal Hellenic soldier. The name derived from the hoplon, the great round shield that he carried. He was armed with a spear of cornel wood and iron – ten foot long from spike to blade – and a short sword for nice work. His left side was shielded by his hoplon. His right was guarded by the man beside him. This was a spur to steadfastness: a hoplite who broke and ran could no longer defend himself, and condemned the man who fought beside him.

A hoplite army fought as a phalanx, a massed force of spears, eight men deep and many men wide. A phalanx of five thousand would stretch for half a mile. As the fight approached the phalanx would utter a paean, or war-song. Only the Spartans came on without a battle cry.

Every Spartan boy was raised to fight, and only to fight in this one way. At seven he left home and began instruction. At eighteen the instruction was complete. At twenty he would become a hoplite. He would remain as such until he was sixty. All other ways of life were forbidden to him. He could not trade. He could not use money. He was born and bred only for war.

The Spartan who fought with passion alone was not admired. Excellence was sought through unity. The hoplite who fought alone could not even defend himself: his strength lay in solidarity. Sparta's victories were won through the discipline of the phalanx. The Spartan lines would charge and wheel, mock-retreating, regrouping.

The word helot means *captive*. The first helots were peoples conquered by Sparta in what came to be their kingdom of Lacedaemonia, which today is called Laconia: to those would later be added all the people of Messenia, to the west. Their captivity would last beyond death. To be called *helot* by the Spartans was to be changed not only in life but after life. The descendants of the first helots were born into helotage. The lineages of the conquered were bound in perpetuity. *Helot* became a name that ran in the blood.

The helot was not a slave. As a rule, the slaves of Greece were barbarians – aliens from the horse-tribes of the North or the deserts of Libya and Asia. The Spartans made helots of Hellenes. Nor was a helot a chattel, as a slave was. He could not be bought and sold. He was not an object, as a slave was. He was not considered inhuman. To kill a slave was not murder, any more than would be the breaking of a jar, or an overburdened axletree.

(*Tools*, Aristotle wrote of slaves, *may be animate as well as inanimate*.)

Thus, as the Spartan hoplite was more than a soldier, so the helot was more than a slave. He was an enemy defeated in war. He would forever be a captive foe. Each year Sparta would declare war again on its own helots, and in that way the laws allowed a helot to be killed, not as if he were a slave, but as if he were an enemy.

They were the captives not of Spartans but of Sparta itself. They did as the state commanded. They were bound to the land they kept as firmly as the hoplite was bound to his shield and spear. They did everything that the hoplite did not, which is to say they did everything there was to do but fight. Without the helot to serve him, the Spartan hoplite could never have existed. Without the hoplite, the helot could never have been conquered.

It is one of the longest wars in recorded history, that waged between Sparta and its own subjects. Nor is it only the duration of the status quo that is notable. More remarkable still is that Sparta should ever have been able to hold such power at all.

At the height of Sparta's strength there were nine thousand Spartan hoplites. With half that force and less, the city held dominion over Lacedaemonia and Messenia. With fewer than ten thousand men, Sparta held one hundred and eighty thousand helots captive for over three hundred years.

It was a rulership that could never have been contrived by force of arms alone. For so many to be bound by so few, for so long, the helots had to believe in Sparta. To have so little faith in themselves, to have such scant hope of liberation, they had to think their rulers invincible. Sparta required their hopelessness. Its power relied on more than strength. Its system needed terror.

The title of this evening's talk makes mention of gods and monsters. I haven't spoken yet of either, but I would like to do so now, since terror leads us neatly to them.

It is said that to understand a people one must only comprehend its gods. To that I would append *and monsters*. The knowledge that the United States is predominantly a Christian nation goes only part-way to explain its history in this, our Age of Terror. An awareness of that country's popular mythologies – of America's monsters, from the Red Scare to the Enemy Within – brings us significantly closer to understanding its secular workings.

When it comes to monsters, many of us take our native term from the Latin *monstrum*, meaning a warning. The Ancient Greek *teras* has this implication also, denoting not only a deviation from nature, but more generally a supernatural portent. We apply our modern usage to a familiar bestiary of terrors, even as we dispense with the subtleties of the ancient applications.

In Hellenic archaeology monsters are found adorning everything from the potsherd to the death mask. How are we to interpret their prolific representation? How can we understand their terrorisation of those upon whom they are visited? East of the Hellenic world, the Abrahamic God would soon be sending angels as his messengers, yet the deities of the Greeks had no such benign intermediaries. Instead they appeared themselves, and when they did not, it was monsters that came in their place.

Inarticulate and bestial, the monster seems a poor messenger, until one understands this: that the monster is the message. The will of the gods is embodied in the creature itself. The Gorgons who turn to stone those who look on them, the Sirens who destroy all who listen to them, the Minotaur born of excessive female sexual hunger; these entities are vehicles of punishment and thereby of warning. Their role is uniform: the monster chastises the one who wanders too far or wonders too much.

Invention – exploration – these things are not rewarded. On the contrary, what is good for the gods proves fatal to mortals. It is when the hero ceases to abide by natural laws, when he emulates the ambitions of his divinities, that monsters are visited upon him.

The message of the monster is that the behaviour of the gods is not to be aspired to. The *monstrum*, the warning-in-flesh of ancient text and oral mythology, is a jealous *demonstration* of fate or divine power. Monsters are the terrible punishments exacted on the errant inhabitants of the earth.

What, then, can we learn of Sparta, from its mythologies?

The Spartans worshipped monstrous gods. Their deities were terrors personified. All gods have their share of terror – I would suggest that no one would get down on their knees for less – yet the Spartans had a high threshold for awfulness. An unusual tolerance for dread. Their gods are more frightening than most. That is their common theme, that dense preponderance of fear.

Are those who worship frightening gods frightening people? The opposite may also be true: that those who worship frightening gods pray to allay their fears. Were the Spartans fearful? One might ask what they – of all people – ever had to be frightened of.

They were devout, and unusually so. Because of their gods the Spartans refused to fight battles they could only have won, or fought those they could only lose. Their generals would sacrifice and read the entrails of animals again and again – at each river crossing, at each battlefield, at each charge.

The other Greeks did not understand them. The Athenians feared them and were shocked by them. The Spartans were Greeks, believed themselves Greeks, fought for the ideal of Greece . . . yet they made captives of Greeks, too. They were obsessed with their own privacy. They were alien to both those they defeated and those they led to war. They were set apart by gods and laws and mountains.

Why even say they were Greek? What does it mean to be Greek if it can be so alien? Many of their gods, it is true, were worshipped throughout Hellas. Apollo was adored and feared. He was an ambiguous deity – Carneius and Lyceius and Smintheus; *Apollo the Ram-Like*, *The Wolf-Like*, *The Mouse-Catcher* – and the harsh god of plague and prophecy, predictable only in his vindictiveness, killing and cursing and flaying alive all those who challenged him.

The Spartans loved Artemis, too, Apollo's twin and female mirror. Keepers of the sun and moon, offspring of the goddess of night, they were ruthless siblings. The choice is significant. The Spartans could have prayed to kinder deities.

What does it mean to say that Artemis was a god of the Greeks? How many goddesses were called Artemis for the sake of authorial convenience? There was the Artemis of Ephesus – an inhuman cascade of breasts, an Asian idol, fertile and benign – and the terrible Artemis of the Tauric Chersonese, to whom all shipwrecked strangers were sacrificed. There was the Artemis of Athens, who was *The Best* and *The Good Advisor* – and of Sparta, who was Cnagia – *The Burning One* – and Ambulia – *Death-Delayer*, and Derrhiatis and Aeginaea – *Leather-Armoured* and *Armed with Javelins*.

She was the untamed, the destroyer, the matchless huntress, fierce as a bear. She was the virgin watcher over childbirth. She was a bloody goddess, a woman's goddess, the power of women made flesh. There was more than one kind of Artemis, which is to say – isn't it? – that there was more than one kind of Greece. Or that there was barely such a thing at all.

Then there were the ancestral gods. On a narrow plateau in the hills above Sparta stand some curious pyramidal ruins. Under and all around those stones are older structures, ruins buried under ruins, ruins already ancient when the Classical Sparta of the hoplites and helots was in its prime. There are palaces there that are Mycenaean, and graves and weapons that are older still, stone blades from the ages before the forge. In the travelling journals of Pausanias the place is called Therapne, and it is the citadel of Menelaus, the red-haired king who waged war on distant Troy for the return of his stolen wife. The pyramid marks the remains of three great limestone terraces. Atop them there once stood a shrine to the Mycenaean king and queen, a Classical monument, built three centuries after the last of their palaces were burned. It is still called the Menelaion, the Shrine of Menelaus, but others were worshipped there too, both Helen herself and her half-god brothers.

Leda, Queen of Sparta, was raped by Zeus in the form of a swan. She gave birth to two eggs, one mortal, one divine. From the divine egg hatched Helen and Polydeuces, her immortal brother. From the mortal egg were born Castor and the murderous Clytemnestra.

What did the Spartans worship in Helen? She was a goddess of vegetation, once, but her essence came to be her physical perfection. She was inhumanly beautiful. In Sparta, offspring born imperfect were taken by the state and left in the mountains to die. Imperfection equalled monstrosity. It was not vanity to pray for a perfect child.

Castor and Polydeuces were soldiers' gods, brothers in arms. When Castor was killed, Polydeuces, undying, wept for not being able to follow him. Their father, the All-Father, was touched with pity. Taking half the immortality from Polydeuces, he bestowed it on Castor. Thereafter the brothers lived and died on alternate days. In time Zeus set them in the heavens, in the constellation of Gemini.

Ares was a distrusted god. Few peoples chose to cherish the deity of savagery. Athena was a kinder force: the war-prayers offered up to her were for victory. To pray to Ares was not only to hope for fortune, but for war itself. Among the Spartans he was held in high regard. His epithet among them was Thereitas, meaning *The Beastly One*. His sanctuary stood on the ancient road from Sparta to Therapne. Black dogs were sacrificed to him, and men, too, before the fight. His companions were Alala, daemon of the battle cry; Kydoimos of the battle din; Enyo, the daemon of horror; and his sons Deimos and Phobos, *Terror* and *Fear.*

Finally there is Orthia. Artemis-Orthia, she is called now – she is yet another Artemis – but only in Roman times were the goddesses worshipped together. Artemis was many-faced and ambiguous. Orthia was a simpler thing. Her story goes like this.

Once upon a time, in the deep forests, two brothers found a pillar of wood. It was broken or grown or carved in such a way that a face or a form could be made out in it. It stood upright among a thicket of willow trees. It was as if the trees themselves had grown to hold it upright. It was as if it had been waiting there for those who discovered it.

The brothers knew power when they saw it. They brought the pillar out of the forest. The Lacedaemonians worshipped it, naming it Orthia and Lygodesma, meaning *Upright* and *Bound by Willows.* No good came of their devotion. In the pillar's wake came awful curses. The brothers who found Orthia went insane. Disease and madness inflicted Sparta. To appease Orthia a temple was built by the river. Sacrifices were made there. Offerings were left. The Spartans discovered that nothing satisfied the goddess but blood. The priestess would hold Bound by Willows aloft to weigh her satisfaction. If the blood spilled was sufficient, the pillar would become lighter. If not, its burden would increase.

They are uneasy gods, those of the Spartans. They are half-gods, fragile, capable of death. Or they are cruel immortals, double-edged, hungry for destruction. They have nothing much in common except terror and blood. They are all both gods and monsters . . .

IV

Monsters

It was true about poetry: he had never liked it. It was too refined for him, too clear. It demanded too much, and demanded it as if it had the right to demand anything. It was like having the truth stuffed down your throat.

Foyt liked poetry. Sometimes, in their morning lessons, he had given them verses to translate, back and forth, from Classical Greek to English, from modern to Koine.

> *When you set out from Ithaca,*
> *pray that the way is long,*
> *full of knowledge and adventure.*
> *The giant eaters of men, and the Cyclopes,*
> *the ragings of Poseidon – do not fear them.*
> *You will never meet them*
> *as long as your thoughts are dignified,*
> *as long as dignity*
> *steers your spirit and your body . . .*

On his desk Foyt kept a statuette of Calliope, muse of epics, cast in silver-bronze in Ephesus three hundred years before Christ. It was small, quite rare, and valuable. A rumour among Foyt's students was that a curator from the British Museum had offered Foyt two thousand pounds for it. Ben was prepared to believe it, though he had always shied away from the thing.

The statue was of a young woman, conventionally beautiful, smooth limbed, unmuscled. The muse and her sisters had been born from nine nights of godly lovemaking, but the Ephesian sculptor had made his Calliope too pristine to be erotic herself. Her pose was unusual, and that was what had attracted the man from the British Museum. The goddess had been presented standing, more in the stance of an orator than a singer, her head raised, her mouth ajar, one hand raised in a decisive gesture of emphasis.

What Ben disliked about her was her look. Foyt's Calliope stared. It had the kind of gaze a living creature wouldn't turn for long on anything but kin or prey. It was wide-eyed and unerring. It had eyes like a hawk, unnerved and unnerving. Wherever you sat in Foyt's dark study, the Calliope would be staring at you.

Eberhard Sauer had something of that look. Ben had met him for the first time in Foyt's lessons. Before that, their paths had crossed without ever colliding. He had seen Sauer in lectures and at formal halls, had known him by reputation. He had envied him from a safe distance. Sauer had been one of those who was at home at Oxford, born to it. He had a gaunt assurance, and more than that a gauging look, as if he were assessing the standards of those around him; a measuring way of looking at the world, where Ben only ever measured himself against it.

He remembered the day they had met, if it could be called a meeting. It had been in his first lesson with Foyt. Emine and he had still been studying together, then, before she gave up on the past for more profitable work in law. They had arrived late to find Eberhard and the others already there. Emine had sat near Eberhard in an armchair by the bay window, the room's only sunlight stretched in her lap like a cat. Ben and the others had been left with seats in front of the desk.

He had been closer to Foyt than the others, with the Calliope staring a hole in his head. He'd had a sense that Eberhard had been watching him, too, had felt the hairs tightening on the back of his neck, but when he had glanced round he had met only Emine's distracted look. Sauer had been gazing out of the window, as if his thoughts were well occupied elsewhere. He had been very still, only his hand moving, stroking the furred leaves of the African violets Foyt kept in rows along his dim stone windowsill.

⁂

Lent had begun.

– In the old days, Mr Adamidis said, We would close the place, but religion isn't what it used to be.

The roughnecks bulked out the lunchtime crowd. In the evenings, though, the grill was quieter, and the hours dragged. Only the younger customers and the old regulars still came in numbers, lingering over light suppers and small beer. Adamidis would sit with them, doing the books and grimacing, as if his presence front of house could dissipate the smell of meat.

It was still early. Ben and Kostandin were sharpening the knives, one ear each cocked for customers. Florent was cooking the salt out of vine leaves. Modest was washing potatoes while he told an interminable joke about a one-legged beggar and a three-legged dog, incomprehensible to Ben even with Kostandin's translations.

When the knives were done he went front of house. It was Friday. There were a few people in. The television was on, an old priest chanting into a microphone. Mr Adamidis sat by the bar, under the framed pictures of his younger self, filling in a sudoku. As Ben came out he folded the paper and waved him over.

– Come keep me company. How are you finding things? Take a seat.

He took it. The priest droned over their heads. *Wash yourselves, and ye shall be clean.*

– You know, my nieces did me a favour finding you. You turned out to be a safe pair of hands. A head on your shoulders too. You like the place?

– I like the work. It's better for us when it's not so quiet.

Though your sins be scarlet, I will make them white as snow; and though they be red like crimson, I will make them white as wool . . .

– Better for you, better for me. Carnival is like all my name-days come at once, only afterwards I get to pay for it.

There was a tulip-glass of tea on the table. Adamidis dropped in a cube of sugar, stirred it through, the spoon chiming. – My boy's been spending a lot of time out there with you. He's behaving himself?

But if you desire not, nor will obey me, the sword shall devour you, for the mouth of the Lord has spoken it.

– I don't really notice him. Too busy.

– He's a good boy. Adamidis's eyes hung onto Ben's. – He has a temper. He gets that from my side. But he's a smart boy.

– He seems clever.

– See, I like it when he hangs around here. He says he doesn't want to run a place like this. It's not for him, he says. Politics, that's his thing. Does he talk about this with you?

– No, never.

– No, well. He won't talk to me any more. Fathers and sons shouldn't talk politics together. That's what he says. You seen this?

He jabbed the newspaper at the television. The priest had gone. A split-screen image showed two men engaged in furious argument. It was ten days until the general election. In the last week the campaigning had shifted gear from the Byzantine to the hysterical, with televised mass rallies and marathon pop-eyed debates.

– This is politics. Three months of men in bad suits trying not to look like carpet salesmen, Mr Adamidis was saying. – God save us all from politicians. But Ben was no longer listening. Beyond the television, sitting alone in the corner, was Eberhard Sauer.

His back was to the empty room. Even so, Ben knew him at once. He was tall, so tall and thin that, sitting, he always looked a little uncomfortable. His fair hair, already thinning when Ben had first met him, was combed back against his skull. He was in shirtsleeves, his jacket hung carefully over the back of his chair. He had a book spread on the table before him. His head was tilted as he read, like someone listening for an echo.

– I should get back to work, Ben said. As Mr Adamidis began to agree (– Sure, don't let me stop you. And make up something, just some little somethings, for me to give out later –) he stood up, moving back to the kitchen door, watching Sauer as if he might disappear.

There was a burst of laughter from the kitchen. He half-stepped back through the swing doors, but Eberhard didn't look up from his book, didn't move at all. There was a menu beside him still folded around the cruet, a carafe of water with a glass capping its neck, a pannier of bread, all untouched. If he had come into the grill to dine he had forgotten it already. He might have been in a library; the Sackler, where Ben remembered coming upon him once, a great gloomy figure, or the Centre for the Study of Ancient Documents; or Foyt's study, with the bronzes and violets.

Without thinking he turned and went back to the kitchen. Modest was finishing his story, giggling, helpless, the others laughing regardless of the outcome of the joke. He felt a hand on his shoulder and, looking up, found Kostandin there.

– Listen to this, listen! So there is this beggar with one leg and this dog with three legs. The beggar goes from house to house asking for a bit to eat, but every time–

– Not right now. Tell me later.

– Sure. You okay?

– I'm fine.

– You don't look so fine.

– There's someone I know out there.

– From home? A friend?

– Not really a friend.

– You don't want her to see you?

– Him.

He went past Kostandin to the spits and scored the meat, testing it. He should not want to see Eberhard. They had not met in a long time, certainly not since Emine had left him; but Eberhard knew Foyt, of course. From Foyt he would know how things stood.

A runnel of hot blood slid over the hilt of the knife and he swore, turned past Kostandin and ran water over the new burn. His hands were raw, marked in a dozen places. No, he shouldn't want to meet Eberhard. And yet, seeing him, his first impulse had not been to avoid him, out of shame or anything else. He had thought that he might talk to him.

– Why is he in Metamorphosis?

– How the fuck should I know?

Kostandin came over and began washing his hands. – Hey, shh, it's no problem. Modest tells you his joke, I take front of house. I serve your *friend*, you get your smile back. Okay?

He rinsed the little knife and hung it on a rack of skewers, the lengths of metal jangling. Florent said something behind him in his own language. Modest laughed, less comfortably than he had at his own humour.

– Okay?

– No, look, I'm fine with it. Thanks.

– Why? You're sure, Kostandin said, as if it were not a question at all but a response to something too bizarre to agree with. – But you don't want to see him, right?

– I didn't say that. Or maybe I did. If I did, I changed my mind, he said, smiling to show them it was alright, that he had no issue with them, at least; and taking off the apron, wiping his hands, bracing himself, he went back through to the front of house.

A few more regulars had arrived, men he knew without knowing their names, bachelors with no one to cook for them, widowers with no one at home for them. Two of the old men were getting worked up over the TV debate, slamming their palms on their adjacent tables. Ben took their orders and called them through to the kitchen, then worked his way back to the corner table.

As far as he could tell Eberhard didn't see him until he stopped beside him. He was still reading, and as Ben began to speak he went on doing so, slowly turning another page. The book was no more than a pamphlet, white-bound but yellowed, printed in Italian, with dense strata of footnotes.

– What will it be?

– Ah. I'm not especially hungry, but I ought to eat. Something sustaining. What would you recommend?

His Greek was modern, nondescript, unaccented. In itself that was a surprise. At Oxford Eberhard's ancient languages had been admired. Like some of their teachers, though, he had always seemed to have a limited sympathy for the everyday world, a disinterest in modernity that bordered on antipathy.

When there was no quick answer he glanced up, the light striking off his spectacles like a flashbulb. He cocked his head and the spectacles went clear. His face reminded Ben of Lorne, the Professor of Egyptology, a man who had looked at all others with benevolent, spoiled incomprehension, like a child in a car watching walkers hurrying through snow. Then Eberhard's expression altered, the smile physically indifferent but no longer meaningless, the Calliope stare coming into his eyes.

– The meat is always good.

He was still speaking in the demotic, and was glad when Eberhard hesitated. He would have preferred not to have recognised Ben and was wondering whether he could avoid their meeting; was wondering, therefore, if he had been recognised himself. Then something must have shown on Ben's face, and Eberhard closed his pamphlet and took off his reading glasses, folding them away into a dented metal case.

– It's you. What are you doing here?

– I'm waiting on your table.

– Evidently, Eberhard said. Really?

– Really.

Sauer was quiet, his eyes resting on Ben; then, pocketing his pamphlet, he looked past him, taking in the front of house – the nicotine-stained ceiling fans, the old men growling over politics, Adamidis slouched by the bar – all at once.

– That seems a waste. Are you allowed to sit down?

He shook his head, sat anyway, shook his head again and discovered himself beginning to laugh. – It's so strange, seeing you! I never thought I'd meet anyone, here.

– I imagine you meet lots of people. Rather too many, if anything.

– You know what I mean.

– Yes, this is a surprise. Eberhard was smiling faintly, as if the situation were amusing or ludicrous or perhaps distasteful. – But it is a small world, ours, and getting smaller. There is no escape these days. A shame we don't meet in better circumstances.

– It's not so terrible.

– How is it you come to be here?

– Luck.

– You call it *luck*?

– Bad luck, then.

– Oh, I'm sure there are worse places to be. Still, an ordinary suburb shouldn't have such an extraordinary name. *Metamorphosis* only invites disappointment, don't you think? I was expecting streets of gold.

Now he was pouring himself some water. – There's only one glass, I hope you don't mind, he said, and after a moment glanced up, waiting again for Ben's answer.

– I'm not that thirsty.

– You look tired.

– The shifts are long.

He didn't know what else to say. Already he wished they hadn't met: they had nothing in common but shared history. He checked the room. Adamidis was hunkered over his puzzle; the old men were winding down their argument. A bevy of office girls was settling the window tables. Soon he would need to fetch their orders, and find something for Adamidis to give the old men on the house.

– I heard about Emine, Eberhard said, and just like that, as if a switch had been pulled, a light turned on, he became aware of the source and direction of his anger.

– I knew you would have. Good news has a way of travelling, doesn't it? Thought I might get away from it here, but you're right, it is a bloody small world . . .

He stopped himself. His hands were sweating. His accent had revealed itself, stripped raw. Eberhard was looking at the table.

– I am sorry, Benjamin.

– Yeah.

– I heard you were planning to leave, there was a rumour to that effect, but I had no idea you were coming to Greece. You couldn't find anything better than this?

– I never got around to looking.

– You should make the time to do so. You could find some real work, surely.

– I might. I'm alright here, for now. It's not like I came here for the work.

– I see. For the air, then. Fresh air, fresh pastures. That's understandable.

– Is it?

– Yes. I suppose you must feel–

– You don't know how I feel.

– No. Well, at least your Greek has improved.

– Not much.

– Oh, quite a lot. If you weren't so well mannered you'd sound like an Athenian taxi driver.

– Is that good?

– Why wouldn't it be?

– I don't think of you admiring modern Greece.

– I wasn't aware that you had noticed. Still, any classicist should envy these people their Greek fluency. Physicists and mathematicians never have to experience that kind of jealousy, there being no citizens of the Nation of Physics or the Republic of Numbers. It would do their egos good if there were.

A yell from the kitchen; the curt exclamation of his name. He stood with a sense of release, an eagerness to be gone.

– Did you want something to eat, in the end?

– Certainly.

Eberhard picked up the menu, glanced at it, then put it down, as if he were unsure what to do with it. – Perhaps if you could bring me whatever it was you recommended. The . . . meat, wasn't it?

– The meat, he said, and Eberhard sighed.

– To tell you the truth, I only came in looking for some quiet. I don't like to drive when tired. I imagined a meat grill during Lent would be a peaceful retreat.

– But instead of peace and quiet you found me.

– That's not quite how I'd put it. Eberhard pushed back his own chair and offered up his hand. – May I make a suggestion?

– If you like.

– Granted the university is full of students learning to take orders in Starbucks, but seven years at Oxford might qualify you for better than this.

– I'll bear that in mind.

– Do that. Don't be cross, it's only advice, well meant. I'll say goodbye again before I go. How long will the meat take?

– Not long, if you're in a hurry.

– Thus the early supper.

– Where are you headed?

– Corinth tonight, Eberhard said, and then, softly, Further, if the roads are clear, but Laconia will still be there tomorrow.

He reached for the menu again, opened his spectacles case, unfolded the glasses and put them on, not seeming to notice Ben standing beside him. When he looked up his eyes were magnified, owlish at finding Ben still there.

– Laconia?

– Yes.

– You mean Lacedaemonia?

– Yes. Look, Eberhard said, and held up the menu. – It says you have milk-lamb–

– Not until Easter. What's it like?

– I've never had the pleasure–

– Not that. Lacedaemonia.

– It's . . . striking. I don't suppose it's for everyone.

He sat down again, Eberhard shifting his chair back. As if to make room for them both, though there was no lack of it.

– I've never been.

– Well, Oxford is theoretical to a fault, but in this case they have a point. There isn't much to make the trip worthwhile. I'm afraid it doesn't merit your laudable curiosity.

– I was writing about it, that's all. Laconia. Sparta. Some lectures, a bunch of articles. I was thinking, last year, anyway, that I might try and work it all together, get a thesis out of it–

– Better not, Eberhard said. – If I were you. There's so little to write about, in terms of archaeology. So little has survived.

– I know, of course. I always loved it, though. Or the idea of it. Athens and Rome didn't really interest me, but there was something about Sparta . . . I mean I used to read about it all the time, when I was growing up. *Hollow Lacedaemonia.*

No answer. Eberhard closing the menu, looking down at its closure, as if the mention of love offended him.

– I suppose it'll be beautiful, in spring.

– Oh, it's beautiful already. And at any time. Though I'm afraid no one calls it Lacedaemonia any more. Not even us.

– Us?

Sauer folded his hands on the table, the fingers interleaved, sheltering. – Those of us who are working there.

– Working on what?

– It's a small project. Hardly newsworthy.

– A project? You mean an excavation?

– That's rather a grand name for it. We're just fossicking over old ground. A bit of digging also, now. The earth is still cold, but it will get better.

– At *Sparta*?

– No, no. But close.

– I don't suppose there's any–

– No.

– Right.

– I'm sorry.

– No. You were right, though.

– Was I?

– I wouldn't mind the work. I mean, if something else came up, something like you've found . . . and then you turn up here. That would have been good luck, that's all.

– Yes, wouldn't it? Eberhard said, smiling in bland sympathy; and then one of the office girls was waving for service, and Florent was whistling from the kitchen, the old men's plates balanced precariously on the swing doors, and he had to go.

He had not said goodbye, after all. When Ben had brought his food Sauer had been there waiting, and later, going to and fro, Ben had seen him reading as he ate, methodically, his hands set square on the table top, the pamphlet weighed open again with oil and vinegar. Then Modest had broken a bowl of offal, and by the time the two of them had cleared up the verminous mess the corner table had been empty. It turned out that Adamidis had dealt with the bill. The customer had been in a hurry, and not too chatty, though that happened sometimes with the English, it was a genetic thing, and what did it matter when he had tipped so well?

Sparta . . . There was little to see there, he knew, and he had never had the money or the time to go, nor had his research ever demanded it. What would there be there, that Eberhard might be digging for? Sparta was not Athens. The Spartans had left nothing behind that reflected their greatness. They had become no more than rumours of rumours in the histories of others, Romans and Ionians, Macedonians and Athenians, each outsider contradicting the next, a chain of Mediterranean whispers.

He wondered how it would be, not to be running from, but towards. To have something or someone to go to: to have a destination.

He had perceived, at Oxford, that even the cleverest of people could make fools of themselves. He was sure that Eberhard had lied to him, and lied ineptly. There was work to be had in Laconia, and he had not wanted Ben to know it. Caught off guard by their meeting, he had improvised clumsily; or he was an unnatural liar to begin with, heavy-handed with mistruth.

Either way, Ben didn't hold it against him. He had never known Eberhard well. Sauer had always looked unapproachable, and the looks had not been deceptive. He had not been much interested in the social life of the university, though Ben knew he'd never been short of invitations from those seeking a challenge. His reputation had made him a desirable commodity, but he had also seemed too clever to know, even at Oxford, his intelligence like an armour. Or more than that, like a panoply: both armour and weapon.

They had been colleagues at best, never mistaking one another for friends. They had nothing in common – he had thought so himself. Why should Sauer share his good fortune with him?

It was just that it was curious. That their paths should cross like that at all, however small the world. That Eberhard should lie, and lie so poorly, when there seemed nothing much worth hiding. Only the chance of work, at best, and badly paid, no doubt, as their work often was. The truth might have made them colleagues again, of course. He wondered if that was what Sauer had meant to avoid.

For the first time since leaving England, he felt a lightening, a faint stirring of the spirit. His curiosity was a spur, goading him into – not action, yet, but a consciousness of inaction. A fragile, fledgling eagerness.

൭൭

At night his thoughts were always darker. His mind lingered on the first time he had met Eberhard. It was the same day that Emine had met Foyt. She had thought the professor ridiculous, then. She had been angry with him on the way home from that first class. And Foyt had seemed easy to deride, then, with his mannered shyness, his dry lechery and polite pride. The vanity of a handsome man, one famous only within the confines of his world.

They had been together only a few months. Emine had moved out that term into a flat in Risinghurst with girlfriends, a sprawling place well beyond his own means, so that he had stayed on in his college rooms and spent more nights than not at hers. They had got in early for the seminar, had bought coffee and marble cake to share and had gone to sit by the sunken garden. Emine had been restless with the wait, nervous about the new term and tutor. Foyt's study had overlooked the Cherwell, and Emine had kept glancing in that direction. She had been talking about her school days – a nun she had fallen in love with, a summer in Limoges, a trip to the Ile de Ré – when she had abruptly changed tack.

– Which is his room?

He had leaned past her to point it out; aware, in the cold, of the heat of her against his arm. – By the Fellows' Garden.

– I'm going to look.

– Why?

– Because I'm bored. And because he's famous.

– *Famous!* he had laughed. Emine, come on . . .

It had stung him into using her name, the fear that he might bore her.

– You come on. It'll be fun. I want to.

And because she had wanted to they had crept down together, of course, slipping on the morning green, Emine shushing his mutterings. He had not expected anything, but in fact Professor Foyt had been there, unaware as a fish in a bowl. Not dressing or in disarray, but absurd nonetheless. A dapper man, no taller than Emine, he had been stood at a long mirror in the gloom of his study, regarding himself with an expression of rapt concentration. As they watched he had raised one hand, cupping the palm in front of his mouth and nose, the gesture both strange and familiar. Checking for bad breath.

In the event the seminar had been remarkable only for the presence of Eberhard, Foyt as uninterested as most professors in his students, going on too long about the Primary Laws of Archaeology, the modern subtleties of the Law of Superposition, the dangers of excavation, his gaze only now and then drifting to Emine where she sat, her legs crossed at the ankles in the sunlight. Most men would have done the same.

– Excavation must be our last resort. In our exploration of the past it is our most powerful tool, but it is also the most destructive. It is inevitable that the act of excavation will lead to destruction. If the archaeologist does not recover all that can be recovered, the answers he seeks may be lost forever. The moment we begin to dig, we begin to lose that which we seek to find. There is no recourse in the process of excavation; there is no going back . . .

At one point Emine had raised her hand to her mouth, the gesture like a yawn but not, her eyes as they slid to his brimming with mirth: but afterwards, on the bus back to Risinghurst, she had been ill at ease.

– I don't like him. Foyt. I can't stand him.

– Why?

– Because he is . . . Her accent had grown stronger, as it did when she was irritated; as did his also. – He is a dirty vain old cockerel.

The turn of phrase had struck him as funny. It had reminded him of the meal she had cooked his brother, and he had laughed, even knowing it was a mistake.

– You think I'm joking?

– No, of course not. Why would you?

– You're such an idiot. You didn't even notice.

– Notice what? Was he going at it like a piston under the desk?

– Don't be vile.

– Vile and Vain. Evil twins, separated at birth.

– It's not funny.

Belatedly he had noticed the red starting in her cheeks, the sign of real anger. – Hey. Okay, he's a vain old cockerel. Did he touch you?

– . . . It wasn't like that.

– Well then, what?

But Emine had just looked at him, then, her eyes giving away nothing. He had felt as if he had done something wrong himself, and when she spoke again it was to change the subject. And after that they hadn't really spoken of Foyt for years, nothing that mattered, right up until the night she had told him that he was a danger to her, body and soul. That she was leaving him, and who she was leaving him for.

. . . *It wasn't like that.* Had she paused, then, before answering? Or was he imagining things as he recalled them? How easy it would be to falsify those memories with hindsight. It was years ago, now, and he couldn't be sure.

ᘓᘐ

He dreamed of Sparta and remembered nothing of that, and dreamed of Emine and recalled everything. It was a better dream than those which had come before it.

Her hair lay on the pillow beside him, the strands of it like light and dark honey together, summer-bleached; and turning, following it (both pillow and hair far too long), he discovered her also there, waiting for him. He kissed her, felt her reaching for him, felt her drawing the sheet away from them both. Her pupils were dilated with desire. It was as if nothing had ever gone wrong between them. When she came her fingers covered her mouth, as if her pleasure were something long-forgotten.

He woke knowing where he was going.

ᘓᘐ

He telephoned the British School. It was an old archaeological institution, not far from the boarding house where he had spent his first days in Athens. Two days later he received a call at the grill. The School had made enquiries, as he had asked, about excavation work in Laconia. A Dr Fischer would see him now.

Already the day was warm. Spring was approaching. He walked to the British School. Beyond its green enclosure, flat rooftops and striped awnings climbed towards the Hill of Wolves. A sallow faced assistant led him to Dr Fischer's office and closed the door behind him.

The room was empty. Two walls of books bordered one of pictures. Archaic photographs. A woman in rusted monochrome, standing astride a cyclopic ruin as if it were the body of an elephant. A shot of Delphi at dawn, horse riders among the columns. The grand moguls of archaeology, claiming hoards of gold in the names of empires: Schliemann seated before a crowd of engineers; Layard posing with a battalion of tunnellers; Carter signing autographs, fresh from the plunder of Tutankhamun, the darkness around him stellar with flash-powders . . .

Behind the desk a pair of sash windows were crowded with aloes, their fronds pressed against the glass, rendering the room jungle-green. The desk was heaped with stuff. Facsimiled inscriptions in Etruscan, Phoenician and cursive Elephantine. A blue box of Glacier Mints. An article in French about the synagogue bombings in Istanbul. An old pamphlet – *Summary of the Doctrines of Zoroaster & Plato* – splayed under a glass-flower paperweight.

These are the principal doctrines that ought to be acknowledged by one who will be wise. The first of these is one about the gods: that they are. One of the gods is Zeus, the sovereign. Poseidon himself then begot from Hera, other gods within the heavens, both the celestial offspring of the stars and then the chthonian offspring of the spirits who are close by us . . .

– Gemistus Plethon of Mystras, a cracked voice said, and he jumped, knocking the paperweight sideways, catching its flower-bubble before it hit the floor. The doctor stood behind him, a small old woman in dogtooth tweed and sunglasses that were too large for her.

– You've read him?

– I– no, no . . .

– Not your period, perhaps. Fourteenth century, though you might not guess it. The last of the great Hellenic philosophers. Some people would say the last lost hope of Byzantium. Constantinople fell to the Turks only a year after his death. His *Laws* were supposed to be extraordinary. So extraordinary, alas, that the only copy in existence was burned by the Patriarch of Byzantium. This is only his *Summary*, preserved by a faithful pupil. As you can see, Plethon advocated an acceptance of Hellenic paganism . . . thus the burning. Please sit. Have you been in the country long?

Fischer was lowering herself into her seat, rearranging her papers and candies. A month, he said, and she tsked.

– You sound as if you have a cold. If you are going to Laconia you will have to dress sensibly. The Greek winter can be surprising to those who know only her summers.

– There is a dig at Sparta, then?

– Indeed there is. Ah! Here is the tea. Thank you, Nyssa.

The sallow-faced assistant came and went. Fischer took off her sunglasses and poured. Underneath her eyes were a fragile blue, seamed with a multitude of smile-lines.

– Well! To business. You are Oxford, yes?

– Yes.

– And you have much experience of fieldwork?

– Well, no. I wouldn't describe myself as a practical archaeologist–

– No doubt that will make it all the more thrilling for you. Personally I hope never to heft a shovel again, but for you it will be a privilege. The completion of your education, yes? So, now: just as you have heard, there is a dig. We were asked to fund it ourselves, in fact: at that point the project was intended to mark the centenary of the School's first work in Laconia, with subsequent exhibitions to be held here and in Sparta. We are sent so many proposals, however, and the director in this case was young and inexperienced and . . . well, there have been so many digs at Sparta, and there is so little to show for them. Nevertheless she has persevered, and, to her credit, it seems the dig is now under way. Even so, as things stand there is backing for only a single season. So they will be hard at it down there. Long days. No picnics. And they are searching for findspots on the fringes of the main Spartan sites. They will be excavating pigsties, not palaces . . . a pigsty would be a considerable find, in fact. Do pigsties hold some appeal for you, Mr Mercer?

– I'm sure I can

– Well and good. In that case I have more news for you. Firstly, the digging began a month ago. The sites will be reburied in the autumn. The director is putting into practice some new ideas on working out of season to minimise tourist interference; they seem a little New School to me, but they offer a rare chance for you, so early in the year. Secondly, though there is only funding in place for a single campaign, that financing comes courtesy of the Cyriac Foundation. You've heard of them?

– I'm afraid not.

Fischer drank off her tea, then leaned forward over the desk.

– Cyriac like to keep a low profile. In America they are a designated Cultural Resource Management firm; here we simply call such bodies rich. The Greek government has precious little to invest in ploughing up its past, and in this day and age the universities are not much better. Besides, none of them are much interested in digging over such well-trodden ground as that of Sparta. By contrast the Cyriac Foundation are rich as the proverbial Lydian king. I understand their workers are all paid something, and their per diems are the envy of fieldworkers everywhere. Would you like the rest of my good news? Fischer said, and in her enthusiasm rushed on, the empty tea cup gripped in one thin hand. – I have already 'touched base' with the project director. Her name is Dr Missy Stanton. I am afraid she is American, but there is no getting away from them these days. I have expressed a warm interest on your behalf, and Oxford speaks for itself. Dr Stanton will be overjoyed to have you. She would like you there within the week. Now then, you must tell me, how is England, these days?

~

– A little bird tells me you're leaving.

Evening, the kitchen laid back after the day's sunshine. Later they would regret the warmth, unaccustomed to it; but at sunset everything was slow and sweet, as if the oil in its plastic casks had risen up and submerged them all.

– Laconia, the bird says. Is that right, Englishman?

– That's right.

– Such a shame. Like the singer says, I hate to see you go, but I love to watch you leave.

He had been trying to gather up what he knew of Sparta. He worked at the knowledge as he worked at the mixing bowl in his grip. Each fact was like a tooth loose against the tongue; each one would hang close but would not quite come free.

Tomorrow he would go to the British School library. He would have the morning to read and the coach ride in which to write. With time in Sparta, it might be enough to begin work again on his thesis.

Letters had come, too. One from Emine, and a card signed by

Ness, delivered, as arranged, to the post office on Constitution Square. He would read those too, when he was ready.

– A great city, Nikos said, A noble city, Sparta.

– You'll send us a postcard? Modest asked, and Ben had to smile.

– They used to say Spartan women were beautiful.

– Then send us a hundred postcards!

– If they used to say it they might all be grandmothers by now.

– That's true. I don't need a hundred postcards of grandmothers.

Small talk. The comfort of silence. He was making egg and lemon sauce, whisking the water and whites to a foam, beating in juice and yolks and bloodwarm stock. He worked carefully, easing the elements together. Bats were hunting in the yard, black rags flitting through the light.

– When I was a kid, Kostandin said, I could still hear them. Now I can hardly see them.

– When I was a kid, Florent said, My mother tell us they are the angels of mice.

Laughter without malice. This is how it should end, he thought. I should leave now, tonight, when I feel as if I could stay forever. And then Nikos was rising from his spot by the door, coming to stand at his shoulder.

– Sparta. A great history, that place has. But you know that. My father says you know all about the history of my country. He says you are a clever fellow. Is it true?

The mixture was turning an alchemical yellow, brighter than either the yolks or the lemons. Almost there. A little more broth. One more yolk. He reached through Nikos's long shadow.

– Is that true, Englishman? You never said.

– Your father is wrong.

He cracked the last egg into a tea cup, lifted the yolk out whole, rolled it free of the white, slid it down his fingers into the mix. He began to beat harder, leaning into the motion.

– My father is never wrong. You and me, we have something in common. We have brains in our heads. Not like these others. Modest, here, he has nothing in his head but dirty pictures. There is nothing but cock between his ears. What can we do for him? I know. Let's tell him a few things, you and me. Let's teach him about the glory of Sparta. Okay? I'll start. Once upon a time, Sparta and Athens were mortal enemies. The Spartans could not be beaten on land, and we were masters of the sea. Then we got too greedy. We tried to conquer a rich city far away, but we were defeated. The clever Spartans built their own ships, and our scattered fleets were hunted down. Am I doing well?

– I'm busy, Nikos.

– No, no! Now it's your turn. When the Spartans caught our sailors, what is it they did to them?

He stopped beating. His heart was going faster than he would have liked. His fingers were glued-up with egg whites. And there was something wrong with the mix, a resistance to his work, the whisk clogging up with something. A snag of solidity, as if the stock had been too warm or trickled in too impatiently, so that the eggs had cooked too soon.

– Did they kill them?

– That's not right.

He drew out the whisk. Bits of matter clung to the wires, grey-pink. He laid the whisk to one side and bent closer, trying to work it out. The colour of the mixture had changed, too. It was no longer shining but dull, the plastic yellow tinged with brown.

– Come on. What did they do to them, Englishman?

– Leave him, Nikos.

– What's up with you? We're just telling Modest a story.

– It's Ben's last night.

– Are you telling me what to do?

– No.

– Are you ordering me?

– Come on.

– ARE YOU TELLING ME–

– Their hands, he said. They cut off their hands.

He stood looking down into the bowl. A flaw of blood rose to the surface. At first it was only a crack in the yellow, gaudy as a lava lamp. Then it became a bubble, breaking and spreading. More blood than he would have imagined possible.

He heard Nikos exclaim and step back. In the blood's wake the foetus itself was rising up. It was big, almost ready to be born, its skin already a stubble of wet feathers. Its form had been beaten to a bulging rag of flesh, the symmetry flayed out of it. It was bodiless, headless, natureless, protoplasmic. It was a thing transfigured.

Dear Ben,
I hope you are well. I am writing and hoping this reaches you soon. We are all fine here. Nessie has a cough but it's nothing, all her friends have it too like a fashion. She misses you. Papa came to stay for a few days. He sends his regards. He also wishes you well.

It is still cold but some of the trees are coming into their leaves. By summer they will all be the same green, but now they are young and every new green is different.

Ben, the papers have come through. Actually they came through the week after you left. Our situation was not difficult so it did not take so long. So it is done now. I wanted to tell you on the phone but you need to know and you haven't rung, and maybe this is better.

I wanted to say I am sorry. I am not apologising for anything. I mean I am sorry for us. It is hard to write these things, but easier to write them than to say them to your face.

Here is something else I would not say. I know you still love me. If I could still love you I would. It would be better for all of us.

Ring me. It is terrible that we did not say goodbye. It is not the way we should be. I feel like I have lost touch with you. It feels as if you are so far away from us. When you said you were going away I didn't know it would be like this. Ring me or write. Will you still come home this summer?

Emine.

Dear Nessie,
Here is a picture of a dolphin. As you can see I drew it myself (as you know, your dad is a terrible liar).

In Greece the dolphins are famous and everyone loves them. They are friendly as dogs and swim along with the ships. Maybe they think the ships will race with them? Maybe they think the sailors will throw them some dolphin-friendly tuna? You will have to write and explain it to me.

I am not on a ship, but I am on a bus. The bus is so big it has its own TV and toilet. You would like the TV, it shows nothing but old films. The bus has a sign of three magpies on the side. Magpies are the birds for which you say, One for Sorrow, Two for Joy . . . Three means a girl, which makes me think of you.

Now the driver has turned off the TV. I don't think he likes old films as much as you do. Outside I can see mountains on one side and sea on the other. The sea here is blue as a picture. I have been looking but I haven't seen any dolphins and now I'm running out of room, so I must write like this. I'll be back in the summer – don't forget. Today I am going from the place called Athens (silly name!) to a place called Sparta. If you ask Mummy or Sinny for a map you will be able to see exactly where I am. When I have an address in Sparta I'll send it to you and they can help you write back to me.

Love xxx

Feb 29th 2004

Dear Emine,

From Nessie's card you know where I am. All that matters is what I've told her. Don't worry about me. I've got work in Sparta, an excavation there. By the time you get this I'll be up to my neck in ancient pigsties.

We're divorced, then. That's good. I don't want it not to be. I hope you're happy. I know what that sounds like & I don't mean it like that. ~~*I wish you*~~

When we talk we say nothing these days but it is much harder to write nothing. What else can I say? We've just stopped at the Corinth Canal. The men are all smoking while the women head off for a group piss. The bar is full of fat bikers and old-timers. The old-timers wear Kangol caps and one has only one sock on. The bikers watch football and eat doughnuts. I'm writing these postcards and some fresh notes on Sparta. I hope they might help with my thesis. I miss you.

Things to make you laugh:

A boy who believed bats were mouse-angels.

A girl called Butterfly.

A T-shirt: AGED TO PERFECTION.

Now I can imagine you are smiling, so I'll stop. Take care. Don't worry about me. I'll see you soon,

Ben.

❦

Athens. The mountains and the sea. The blue battlefields of Salamis. Plains wasted with factories. Sunlight catching him like a speed camera.

Olive trees silver in the last sun. Olive trunks full of lumps and rumps, love handles, sumo thighs, double chins, breasts and warts and genitals, whittled slits, murder holes, clefts and crevices, wing-bones and filigrees. Olive groves full of secret things: car wrecks, gypsies and horses, shoulders of ruin.

A dog in a ditch, dead and swollen as a fruit. The Corinth Canal, deep and sleek as a gun. The smell of grilled meat at the truck-stop at sunset.

⌖ ETNIKISMOS ⌖
KKE
ALBANIAN ETNIKE LEGIONE

Derelicts sat in the doorways of derelicts. A green tanker in a petrol station. Cats outside a kafeneion, every old man their sugar-daddy. A street full of motorbikes. A street full of statuary. A square full of lights and dancing children.

Dusk. An owl quartering the fields. The far-silent fields of the night. The empty habitations and hollow realms.

Mountains. Cold translating the glass. Snow holding its position. Deadfall under hemlocks. Dead trunks and stumps of pine. The obduracy of winter. Reproach and uninhabitation.

The road down. A whiff of woodsmoke. Hunting shops still open. Light spilled across ruts. Hardware shops still open.

Windows full of knives, handsaws, sickles, machetes, gutters, throat-cutters.

A last treacherous turn, the old woman in the next seat white-eyed and praying. And then the plain opening out. The land opening itself like hands. The soft darkness of trees. The city picked out in small lights. The mountains beyond and behind blocking out half the stars.

Hollow Lacedaemonia.

V

Notes Towards a Thesis

Storytellers have many motivations. The truth is not always one of them. Archaeology offers the historian a firmer ground: but Sparta has always resisted the archaeologist. It is not an Athens, with its Parthenon and its Tower of the Winds, its philosophies and histories. It is not a Mycenae, with its human face of sheet gold. In Laconia the rewards of excavation are rare and cryptic. Precious little has been brought to light through the centuries, though there has been no shortage of those who meant to do the glorious up-bringing.

Half a millennium after its decline and fall the Romans came in search of Sparta. They would sail to Gythion, buy their souvenirs of purple murex and porphyry, and ride the twenty miles north to the city of King Leonidas. They found something there, if not quite what they were looking for. Sparta still stood, but the heart had gone out of it. It had been stripped of its strength ages before. Without strength its people had no dignity.

At one sanctuary the Spartans built a theatre for their imperial masters. By way of entertainment, young boys were flogged to death at the altar of Artemis-Orthia. Afterwards, the visitors might go to see the swan's egg from which Helen of Troy was born. The only Sparta the Romans discovered was an amusement, an assemblage of sideshows, of the cruel and ludicrous, a mythical beast stitched up from old carcasses: a parody for tourists who cared no less or knew no better.

Cyriac of Ancona visited Sparta in the fifteenth century. Merchant, diplomat and scholar, he came to mourn the people who had driven back the Persian Empire. What he found were fields and fields of ruins – the whole valley full of them – and fallen and failing powers. Greece then was a fading moon in the dying system of Constantinople, Sparta a force long since spent, sacked by King Alaric of the Western Goths a thousand years before. The Ottomans were massing in the footsteps of the Persians. Cyriac's Sparta was a forgotten town lost in the Far East of Christendom, barely Christian itself, braced against Islam, ruled by the Despot of Morea from the walled heights of Mystras.

Cyriac looked for what was lost. It was another four hundred years before anyone dug for it. Mercifully little was discovered. At that time there was little distinction between the archaeologist and his more avaricious counterparts: the antiquarian, the treasure hunter, the grave robber, the tomb raider. There were excavations at Therapne in 1833 and 1841, and again at the turn of the century. Schliemann of Troy and Tsountas of Mycenae came and went, sniffing for Homeric gold and finding nothing to their satisfaction. The Americans tried their luck but returned to Athens with no glory for their troubles.

In 1904 the British School struck out across Laconia. In photographs they sit in trilbys and riding boots, arms folded or akimbo, pipes stuck in their gobs, their coolies sinking trenches with the hunger of oil prospectors. They reached Sparta in 1906, excavating the Sanctuary of Athena of the Bronze House that year.

According to the legends Odysseus built the Bronze House to celebrate the winning of Penelope, his Spartan bride. Herodotus, too, tells a good story of the House. A Spartan regent, accused of treachery, sought shelter from reprisal there. By custom he could not be forced from a sacred building. But the Spartans were a patient people. The elders ruled that the regent be immured. His body was brought out on the brink of death, that the goddess be spared his corruption.

The stories proved richer than the archaeology. Little bronze was gleaned from the Bronze House. An excavation like that would be big news now. Now, even a single shard of pottery can be dated by thermoluminescence, the residues of wine traced to their place of origin, the fats on its innards studied, the ecofacts of pollens analysed, the style interpreted, the technology of the firing gauged, the sediments that buried it – century after century – dated like the rings of trees; the trees that grow in those sediments – conifer and angiosperm – opened and read like secret messages. A century ago, a potsherd was a fillip, an X marking the spot where true treasures might be buried. Now there are as many secrets in one shard as Schliemann found in all his Trojan gold.

In 1906 the British abandoned the Bronze House. They moved down from the acropolis to the banks of the Eurotas river and began new excavations there. They had a stab at the Sanctuary of Artemis-Orthia, where the Romans had once watched spectacles of blood. Their renewed hope is plain in the five years they spent there, their increasing frustration in the brutality of their work.

These two last [altars] had to be destroyed to get down to the lower levels, and it was, in fact, only when the Archaic altar was found that the broken remains of the Roman altar were recognised for what they were . . .

More often, in the wake of the Second World War, it was the Greeks themselves who explored the ruins of Laconia. Most of the foreigners had come and gone, moving on to richer hunting grounds. The French came to root in the rubble. The Dutch sieved the rivers and ransacked old middens, and the British – always the British – did all of that and came again to dig at the Basilica of Nikon the Repenter. An Orthodox missionary, the Repenter had come to convert the Lacedaemonians, many of whom still worshipped the old gods a thousand years after the death of Christ. As proof of the power of his beliefs, Nikon offered to cure a plague if the Lacedaemonians drove out the Jews who had lived among them for many centuries. Which they did. *The people heeded me*, the Repenter wrote, *and loved me as incense . . .*

One hundred and eighty years of archaeology, and what has been found of Sparta?

Nothing that proves the presence of a great city. Nothing but wooden masks, bone flutes, stirrup jars. Bars of lead. The head of a god. Only the golden cups unearthed near Amyclai possess any sense of grandeur. The gold of those vessels is so pure and thin it seems as if the light shines through it. But the cups were discovered in a beehive tomb, a burial place of the Mycenaeans. They are as old as the legends of Helen and Menelaus. They were made half a millennium before the great ascendancy of Sparta.

There is no hint of magnificence. There is no proof of the city the world sat up and noticed, the seat of power to which King Croesus and the High Priest of Jerusalem appealed for help from far-off Lydia and Judaea. It is as if the Spartans crawled away and died, taking with them all trace of themselves. As if they were never there at all.

It is a mystery archaeology has failed to solve. No one has found anything better than the fictions of fable and story. Sparta is all secrets and no answers, all actions without substance. All rumours and chatterings and whispers.

Oh most detested of mortals among all humanity,
Inhabitants of Sparta, council-house of trickery,
Masters of lies, weavers of webs of evil,
Thinking crooked things, nothing healthy, but always
Devious . . . are you not found out always saying
One thing with the tongue, while thinking another? . . .

No longer – maiden voices sweet-calling, sounds of allurement –
Can my limbs bear me up. Oh I wish, I wish I could be a sea-bird,
Who with sea kingfishers skims the blossom of the sea
With a heart free of care. Sea-coloured, sacred bird of the waters . . .

Their city is not built continuously, and has no great temples or other works. Instead it looks like a group of villages, like the ancient towns of Hellas . . .

The Spartan – that cicada! Always ready to sing . . .

Long hair makes a handsome man more beautiful, and an ugly man more frightening . . .

If Lacedaemonia were ever laid waste, and there remained only the ruins of the temples and public buildings, those born into the world of the far future would find it hard to believe that the power of Sparta had ever been equal to its reputation . . .

VI

Lacedaemonia

He woke up to Madonna. Somewhere outside a radio was playing, and as he lay listening a car started and moved off, 'Material Girl' carried away with it.

Churchbells in her wake. A cockerel crowing. A carillon of bells and cockerels.

He closed his eyes in happiness. He had slept well, had rested wonderfully, but felt no regret as he woke. Had he been dreaming? Certainly he knew where he was as if he had been dreaming of it all night. There was no disjunction between sleeping and waking. He was in Sparta; he had made it to Sparta, the city without walls. That was the source of his elation.

He sat up. The bed was hard and the room, too, was spare, though the stairs and halls he dimly remembered had not been Spartan at all, had been all plush carpets and deluxe velvets. Emine's letter lay on the floor. He had been reading the thing again before bed. He got up and pocketed it, her writing snagging at his thoughts.

Ring me.

He went to the window, pulling off the sweatshirt he had slept in. The view was of nothing – the hotel pool, balconies, a wedge of street – but beyond he could make out mountains. Shades and shades of blue. The air was colder than Athens. Everything was washed in sunlight.

He went through to the bathroom. The fittings were black and white, marble and steel, the towels in matching livery. The little soaps and bottles were lined up, straight as ammunition. It was like walking into an old photograph. After Metamorphosis the austere luxury of it was overwhelming. He stripped, turned on the shower, sank his head into the deafening heat.

Dr Stanton had got him the room. *Missy*, she had said. *Please call me Missy. I tell them all the same but no one ever does.* Her voice had been warm and pleading and distant. He had been standing in the meat grill, Mrs Adamidis hoovering round him, the voice on the line hard to extricate from the din of suction. There was a problem with his sharing lodgings, he had understood, so he would be in a hotel for now. Of course the Cyriac Foundation would pay for it. The where? The *where*? The Menelaion, on Palaeológou. And about the dig, there would be instructions for him at reception. Someone could leave him instructions. Or maybe someone would come for him in the morning. Was that alright? Did that make sense? They all hoped he didn't mind . . .

He got out of the shower, wiped off the mirror and shaved, watching his face emerge. His eyes glared back at him. Even his smile was ferocious. He had not shaved in a fortnight. He grazed the skin along one cheekbone, dabbed at the blood and kept going.

There was no one at reception. A cat scrutinised its claws in the sunlit entrance. A pedestal cage stood out of place on the steps like a sofa moved for spring cleaning: its cockatoo denizen peered back into the lobby with aldermanic affront. A stick-thin boy with slicked-back hair polished brasses between animals. He stood when Ben called good morning, ferreting a headphone out of one ear, shoving it in his pocket, death metal coming faintly through his trousers.

– Sir?

– Good morning! he said again, but the boy only smiled and frowned, as if a foreigner's enthusiasm might be a trick and he meant to cover all contingencies.

– There's a message for me. Room 39?

There were no messages. The boy took Ben's key and peered into drawers and pigeonholes. In the hotel bar someone began to play the piano not particularly well. A flock of women were entering and settling there, all dressed in their best, a waiter bringing them cakes on a trolley – *Oh my goodness! No, that we must save for Glykeria* – a priest in orthodox habit watching over them like a shepherd.

– There is nothing, the boy said finally, and crossed his arms over his ribs with nervous satisfaction.

He breakfasted alone, the women and the priest ignoring him, the pianist giving him a wink, the waiter taking his order sternly, as if breakfast were not a meal to be trifled with. When he finished there was still no message and no one had come for him.

His impatience grew. Outside the morning was going to waste. He could be sightseeing or looking for the others himself. Stupid to sit and do nothing, with the sun out and Sparta on the doorstep. He left a note at the desk on his way out, stepping over the boy's gleaming MENEΛAION on his way down to the street.

And there was Sparta, the source of his waking joy. A broad road – a boulevard – lined with orange trees, crowded with people late for work, with booths selling Chiclets, chocolates, matches, watches, paperbacks. An avenue of bulbous palms, ivy growing up their flanks like military winter coats. A square bordered by colonnades. A pack of schoolgirls eating chips. A custom pickup cruising past with speakers pumped up to the max. A flatbed full of yelping dogs. A pair of jeeps packed with cadets. A rigid geometry of streets. Umbrellas hung from barred windows. The sun going in, the sky ironclad. A shop selling onions and eggs, comics, chestnuts, shotgun shells, and fourteen brands of cigarettes. A plane tree, spreading down, its tentacular arms harbouring four tables, three old men, two children, one backgammon board.

It began to rain, at first only damping the dust but then with increasing resolution. He stopped to wait it out under a row of carobs. Others were there before him. An old woman nodded at him and looked away, as if they had met there so many times there was no longer any need for small talk. A man in shirtsleeves came out of a house and began washing down a car with a broom. The old woman took a mobile from her purse and frowned at the upsidedown time.

Ring me. Here is something else I would not say.

One by one the other loiterers abandoned the trees. There was no one left but him when the rain began to penetrate the foliage. He turned round, looking for better shelter. Behind the carobs a public garden ran along for a block, its footpaths meandering between rain-dark statues. To one side stood a doorway flanked by caryatids, words inscribed on the entablature above them:

MUSEUM OF ANCIENT SPARTA

He upended his jacket and ran for it. The doors were closed and for some time he knocked, run-off seeping down his neck, before he tried them and discovered them unlocked. He pushed them open, wiping his face and hands.

Dry church air: the taste and smell of limestone. The atrium was empty and unlit, cornered with columns, hollowed out with galleries. Less museum than mausoleum. He took another step and a light came on in the chamber ahead. He caught a glimpse of a room – one wooden chair, a one-bar heater – and then the curator was shuffling out, sighing, waving his coins away as if they were a crude offence, as if his presence were a personal affront to her.

Dim lights flickered on in the side halls. The curator was grumbling over a dead bulb. He wandered away from her through a room full of weapons. He could still hear her behind him. She was dogging his footsteps, her face hovering between a display of spearheads and sword blades, her expression one of unabashed suspicion. He turned back to the exhibits, pretending to ignore her, biting back both irritation and laughter. Finally he lost himself in study, so that he did not hear her leave, only noticing that she had given up on him when he glanced up to find her gone.

So many snakes. That was surprising, and he was no longer in the mood to be surprised. What had snakes to do with Sparta? Here was a man striking a serpent down, here a man stretching out a hand to one, as if . . . feeding it, maybe, or offering it himself. Here was Apollo, who once killed the great serpent Python. Here were Castor and Polydeuces, the god-born brothers, rendered in the forms of snakes. Here, in a clutter of tiny bronzes, was the Amphisbaena, the monster born of the blood that fell from Medusa's severed head; and beyond it, rendered in Roman mosaic, the face of Medusa herself.

He went on. A line of bas reliefs, labelled only *Chthonic Deities*. The same scene repeated over and over like an occurrence in a nightmare: a man and a woman seated side by side on lion-footed thrones. The man's hair was dreadlocked like that of a Spartan warrior. His gaze met that of the onlooker and was not unkind. In his hands he raised a two-handled bowl. In one relief a snake coiled upwards, its head over the lip of the bowl. In another a dog cavorted under the thrones. In a third, two kneeling worshippers rendered the seated gods gigantic.

He stopped to put his jacket on. The museum was as cold as the streets outside. When he had seen the sign above the door he had been relieved, as if it were a familiar address, but the place was not what he had expected. The labels were cryptic, as if whoever had written them had wanted to be as secretive as the Spartans themselves. And he shouldn't need labels after all. He should know Sparta.

He came to a wall of gravestones. Some of them bore names, some only reliefs of men fighting beasts and monsters. Those he understood. Sparta had been no place for monuments. Only those who died as heroes would be honoured with names on their graves.

But then beyond the stones . . . what was that? A basin, a massive pale urn, carved with women – three of them – each standing on the back of a lion. Who were they? What did they mean? And beyond that, laid side by side, were clay masks from the Sanctuary of Artemis-Orthia. A row of devilish old men, pucker-mouthed, sphincter-lipped, a clutch of scalped faces grimacing at the ceiling. He stood looking down at them, glad of the intervening glass. What did old devils have to do with Artemis, god of women?

A lightstrip fizzed and pocked above him. He turned back towards the atrium. Unease caught at him, as if he had swum out too far. In a corner stood a Roman bust, another relic of the centuries after Sparta had given way to younger empires. The head was tranquil in profile, but as Ben passed its expression seemed to change. Face-on, the look it bore was one of pure viciousness.

He called out thanks to the curator, not waiting for a reply. Outside the rain had eased. He hurried back through the garden of statues, finding to his relief that the far end came out by the main road and only a block from the hotel. The city was smaller than he had imagined – no more, really, than a country town – but a clock on the corner said he was later than he had meant to be.

No one waited for him. The slicked-back boy was gone. The birdcage had been moved inside. Two women sat at reception. One was doing a crossword, the other a sudoku. They looked alike as family, almond-eyed, henna-haired. They worked at their puzzles as if they were in competition. Only when he rang the bell did one put down her pen.

– Are you lost?

– No, I'm staying here, he said, and the second woman nodded, as if the fact were unpleasant but unsurprising. One of them fetched his key while the other looked him up and down.

– Caught by the rain, I see.

– It's not so bad. There's a message for me . . .?

– No messages.

– You're sure?

– No messages. No one came, not for you. You know, you could do with an umbrella, Crossword said, as if suggesting a haircut to a delinquent.

– Does it rain much here, in winter?

– Did you hear that, Marina? What do you say to the boy? Does it rain much in the winter?

Low laughter, a mannish chuckle. – It rains all the time, Sudoku said, In winter.

He went upstairs to wait. His clothes were wet and he hung them up and crawled back into bed for warmth, going on with the thesis notes. A rock drill was gearing up outside and he turned on the TV to drown it out, an old film interspersed with local business ads. Mystras roofing, the Aspis bed emporium, the Spartina lemonade cannery. The Predator crouching over Arnie, dreadful, dreadlocked, monstrous.

At some point he must have dozed off: he woke to find noon come and gone. He got up in a muddle, drooling and lost, cranky with himself and with the waste of the morning. The clothes were not yet dry but nothing else was remotely clean, and he shrugged them back on and went down again to the street.

The sky was an unbroken grey. He bought an umbrella from a street vendor under the pineapple palms, asking for directions with his change. Fischer had said the Cyriac dig would be near the major sites, and there were not many of those in Sparta. Already he could see the old acropolis, its heights nothing much after Athens.

The vendor came out of his booth. Down by the river, if he so pleased, he would come to the Sanctuary of Artemis-Orthia. Across the river and up in the hills – up the first good road after Afisou – he would find the Menelaion . . . but that was far, the vendor said, and besides, there was nothing there but stones, old stones.

– Better you come back in the summer, he said, and handed Ben a red umbrella.

He went north. The streets gave way to a football field, the field to olive groves, witchgrass and meadowflowers, chickens ducking between the trees. It would not be so bad, he decided, to find the excavation this way; to show himself capable, to show willing. He passed a ruin rutted with biker tracks, then two tourists toiling upwards, bedraggled and bickering, French girls, or Belgians, in floppy hats and gingham shorts.

At the summit he stopped to catch his breath. The air smelled of pines and woodsmoke. There was no sign of the archaeologists, but already they seemed remote, while Sparta was immediate and unexpected, exhilarating and familiar from the thousands of pages he had read. He was a fool not to have come here before.

He would try and find them anyway. Just to show them; just to show them. There were not so many other places to check. He would make for the Menelaion while the weather still held and go by the Sanctuary of Artemis-Orthia on his way home. And if he hadn't found them by then, well, they couldn't say he hadn't tried.

The girls had reached the theatre below. One of them began to dance while the other filmed her with a mobile. The ruins carried their laughter upwards, as they had been made to do. They sat on the broken stage, talking together in soft voices. When they began to kiss he looked away.

A horse whinnied in the olive groves. Beyond them, Sparta was laid out bare. Simple buildings, white as salt.

He began down towards the river. He heard the highway before he reached it. The buildings around were gutted and abandoned, the town fraying at its edges. Irises grew in the ruins. Someone called to him from a doorway. An old woman was leaning there, on a forked staff taller than herself. White teeth and dark skin; white-and-dark eyes. A gypsy, he realised, and wondered how it was he knew to realise it. She was waving something at him – as he passed he caught a flash of some trinket – and he shook his head and went on.

He came to the bridge out of town. The river was swollen with rain, full of log-jams of oranges. He crossed and went on along the highway, stepping around the deepest ruts, tankers thundering past him.

He was used to walking, used to the directions walkers were given, the distances never as great as kind strangers would have one believe; but he had gone a way already, two miles or so from the hotel. He skirted a village and doubled back, following the river again. The banks were overhung with oleander and giant grasses, the stems and blades as tall as trees and thick as the trunks of saplings. The hills were closing in. The air felt colder. There was a stillness to the landscape, as if it were waiting for something. He caught a whiff of oranges, the odour mixing with his sweat and seeming for a moment salt, as if the smell of the sea had been blown twenty miles from the coast.

A peal of thunder rolled between the mountains, echoing down the ranges. He began to walk faster. The road was single-lane and empty most of the time. A tractor passed, heading back to the highway. He stuck his hands in his pockets and kept walking.

He tried to think how far he had gone. Four miles or so from the hotel, and surely it couldn't be much further. The umbrella vendor had said to take the first good road up to the hills. A truck came down a muddy track ahead, and he stopped beside it, looking up in indecision before going on as before.

The rain began, so softly at first that he was hardly aware of it until he saw the blacktop shining. He stopped to open the umbrella. He had not noticed when he bought it, but now he realised it was printed with the face of a familiar right-wing politician. Under the beaming face, a slogan: *Shelter In Any Weather.* Something hissed past, going his way, and he looked up from the politician's leer too late to wave it down.

The cold was leaching through his clothes. Stupid to have worn them damp. He started walking again. Up ahead was a stand of pines, whip-thin things with no shelter. He reached them and kept going. The rain was soaking through his shoes. He passed a roadside shrine, the offerings in its tin-and-glass box – a packet of Kleenex, a bottle of Claymore – as faded and dry as bones.

Lightning, and then thunder again, gigantic between the valley walls. It was becoming hard to go forward. The blacktop was plunged in downpour. He saw headlights coming up behind, stuck out one hand, shouted a filthy curse at the car and himself as it ploughed on through the rain.

He came to the one good turning. The umbrella-man's road was sunk in mire. He climbed through the undergrowth until he reached higher ground, pulling the umbrella behind him.

He advanced with his eyes on his feet. He seemed now to be walking on water. His steps slid and skated and bit. Something – an animal? A rock? – went crashing away through the scrub. When he looked up again the road was ending. The concrete ran out where it turned. There was nothing beyond but a dirt track churned to milk.

He stopped at the edge of the concrete. The rain pelted his scalp. He recalled Emine again, the memory forcing itself up. The sense of her was so strong it was like a presence. Emine would not be doing this. She had always been the sensible one.

He shook his head, spraying rain. There was no going on. He would have to go back the way he had come. He looked down the hill, baring his teeth, and saw a building set back in the trees.

The door was unlocked. He went in blindly, not caring to mind himself in the dark. The place stank of incense. After a while he could make out an altarpiece. A row of unlit lamps, the olive oil to fuel them congealed in plastic bottles. Matches. His hands were shaking as he opened the box. He broke three sticks before he got a lamp to take. The chapel flickered around him. On the wall, a superman rode forth in his chariot of fire. Below him, men fell to their knees in the untilled fields.

He pulled out a wooden chair and sat. There was a clattering somewhere, and he wondered if it were rats before he realised it was his own teeth. His thoughts moved sluggishly. He wondered if he should thank God. He wondered if he should have gone back. It seemed too late now, and beyond him. He wouldn't have gone back now if he could.

It was some time – he didn't know how long – before the downpour slowed. When the sound of it on the tiles had almost ceased he went outside and stood under the eaves.

The rain was moving off westwards. Out of nothing the sun had appeared. He stepped out of the shelter, shivering. There were rainbows across the valley, bent low between mountains and clouds.

He began to follow the track upwards again. The mud treacherous underfoot. The mud full of olives and shotgun shells. A labyrinth of puddles and tractor ruts. The river shining miles below. Goat bells ringing in the high pastures. The shirt drying on his back. The sun on his head a blessing.

And then voices ahead. A question like birdsong, asked and asked again in answer. A green plateau between green hills. A guerrilla encampment among the trees. People rising up from the ground, sudden and strange as centaurs. Eberhard there among them, his face cold as he turned away. A blonde girl in blue jeans and Terminator shades. A thing like a pyramid at the edge of the heights, a ruin like something flown up from Mexico. A woman waving a hat, a ridiculous floppy sunhat, calling out across the grass and wild tulips and cyclamen.

– Is that you? Is that Ben Mercer? Oh, *Ben*, you made it! We're so glad you made it! We've been waiting for you so long!

VII

Shovelmonkey Number Five

– Ben! the woman in the floppy hat said again, as if it were the most adorable name in the world. – It's Missy! Missy Stanton. It's *so* good to see you. Where *have* you been?

– Waiting? he said (how stupid he sounded; his lips were numb).

– Waiting? she said, and she laughed, hugging him, holding him back, as if they were relatives who hadn't met in years, as if she meant to kiss him or shake some sense into him; as if it was not *Where have you been?* she meant to say but *Where have you been all my life?*

– Waiting for what? Couldn't they find a cab? Did you *walk* all the way up here? Why? Look at you, you are so trashed.

– Trashed, he said, and laughed with her, his voice queer as an echo. – Yes, I'm afraid I am.

– Oh, we better get you dry. You better get out of the wind. Are you okay?

– Really, don't worry, I'm just–

– Your clothes! The guys can lend you something, I guess. You're about Jason's size . . . are you sure you're alright?

She was wringing her hands. It was not something he remembered actually seeing anyone do. The quaintness of it embarrassed him for her. *No, look, I'm really fine*, he began to say, but as he spoke the wind picked up, glossing the grass flat and bright, pressing his clothes against his skin, his teeth chattering and locking on *No*, the cold going right through him, as if his flesh had become porous, and the last pleasure faded from Missy's face.

– No you're not, are you? Oh dear, oh no . . . we'll get you under cover. You'll be better in no time, I promise. Guys? Guys!

She had turned away from him to call across the uplands. There were excavations at each end of the plateau, and people all along it. Already they had started down in twos and threes. For a moment he felt the indignity of it – his arrival a joke, the opposite of everything he had hoped for – and then there was only the release and surrender of relief.

He caught sight of Eberhard again, the girl in the Terminator shades walking beside him, their heads bent together in rapid conversation. A second girl was tagging along behind them, a more disconsolate figure, pale and wan in a Hello Kitty T-shirt. Then they were all around him, almost a dozen of them, all except Missy holding back, as if he were an exotic animal, a creature that might prove curious or distasteful or even, somehow, dangerous.

– It was further than I thought, he said, a tame apology to no one in particular, and Missy took his arm.

– Guys, this is Ben Mercer, the one I was telling you about. He ran into some hitches getting up here. Jason, can you lend him something dry? Oh, tea! Do we have–

– We drank it all this morning, the blonde girl said, and Missy turned on her.

– Oh gosh, you can make some more, Eleschen, can't you?

– Well, sure.

Her gaze – Eleschen's – stayed on him as she shrugged. Her look was politely curious; no more and no warmer than that. Her accent was some kind of American: there was a burr to it he didn't recognise. She was striking: so thin, and her eyes such a glorious blue, that the rest of her seemed faint by contrast. The light seemed to shine through her, like the gold of the cups from the tombs at Amyclai.

– What happened to him? an English voice asked behind him, and then they were speaking all over one another, arguing over him, as if he were an artefact of doubtful provenance, their voices coming and going so quickly that he gave up listening. There was a sign beside him – CAUTION! DEEP EXCAVATION! – and he leaned against it, losing track of everything except his own fatigue, his body so weighed down with rain it was as if it had saturated him, not only his clothes and hair but his bones and blood, his organs hanging heavy in their allotted places.

– He just got a bit lost, is all. I don't know why he tried to walk, I said to get a cab–

– Is he sick? He looks sick.

– He doesn't look sick, don't be silly.

– What kind of sick?

– Looks fine to me.

– *Talis iste meus stupor nil uidet, nihil audit . . .*

Laughter – a girl's – as cool as a wind chime. A shudder went through him. When it passed he found that their excitement had begun to annoy him. He shook his head, as if to extricate himself from them all, and realised that someone was cupping his chin, Missy staring into his eyes.

– . . . Ben?

– I'm alright, he said, pettishly, though his teeth were threatening to chatter again. – Let go of me.

– Alright, okay, let's get him into the Findhut–

Another voice, measured and familiar. – No. Any of the cars will be warmer.

– Yes, that's . . . thank you, Eberhard. Jason, will you . . . no, the other arm. Thank you, Max. *Jason.*

– Alright, keep your bloody knickers on.

– And can someone open . . . and *there* we are!

The *thunk-thunk* of car doors closing. Blissful silence. The smell of leatherette. He closed his eyes and let the warmth leach into him. The car was a suntrap. Now and then he could hear the buffeting of the wind. The vehicle rocking gently, as if he were drifting out to sea.

When his eyes opened again he was unsure whether he had slept. The daylight did not seem to have altered, but he felt alarmed, as if he had dozed off in a lecture. He could see Missy outside, bent over a mobile, and two of the others beyond her, the blonde girl – Eleschen – and a skinheaded man with an acne-scarred face and the squat build of a wrestler, the two of them looking off towards the eastern mountains.

He had found them, at least. At least he had that to his credit. He had found Therapne, the Sparta of the Ancients. Then the humiliation of it all began to come back to him, and he groaned out loud at the recollection.

He was propped up in the back seat of a hatchback, leaning against a heap of stuff. Ziplock bags, Tupperware, a tripod sieve folded in on itself. A pile of clothes, less esoteric and faintly erotic; a pair of jeans, a white bra, a sky-blue T-shirt with a Disney bunny and a message. *All This And My Daddy's Rich*.

– Don't get ideas.

A boy was sitting in the driver's seat. He was so still it was as if he had suddenly appeared, prodigious as a rabbit snatched from a hat. His face was rabbity, too, almost hare-lipped, though he had done his best to hide the fact. He wore a lived-in Hawaiian shirt, a frayed T-shirt poking from under it, a diver's watch and a goatee, although the beard was new and coming in unevenly, a surf-dude's mange. He was tanned and dusty, so dusty it was hard to tell where the tan ended and the dust began. His smile was wolfish and not entirely pleasant, as if he were in on a joke he wasn't yet willing to share.

– Ideas? he said, and the boy nodded at the clothes.

– Natsuko's. Don't get your hopes up though. First time I saw her I thought the same thing.

– What was that? he said, and the boy snorted.

– If you don't know I ain't going to tell you.

His accent was that of London or one of its countless suburban satellites. There was something about him which reminded Ben of the street markets where his father and uncles worked. A wide-boy slyness: an impishness. The boy turned away, hunching over himself: there was the scritch of a lighter, and then he was holding out his free hand between the seats, breathing out smoke with the syllables of his name.

– Jason.

– Ben.

– I know, Stanton told us about you, he said, and drew on his cigarette, eyes running narrowly over Ben, like those of a tailor or a boxer.

– I hope she was nice.

– She's always *nice*.

– What did she say?

– That we'd be getting a new shovelmonkey. Which made all us mooks happy, of course, more monkeys meaning less shovelling. That was quite an entrance, by the way.

– Was it?

He heard the catch in his own voice and hated it. He saw Jason's grin widen.

– Don't worry about it. Listen, there should be a towel back there. She goes for a swim most mornings. There it is, look. Go on, she won't mind.

There was still a smell to the towel, complicated and not unpleasant: perfume, chlorine, a female tang. As he scrubbed at his hair Jason passed back a sports bag and a gigantic thermos flask emblazoned all over with the green clovers of the Panathinaikos football team.

– Tea. Made it myself. Hope you take sugar. There's wellies in the van if you feel up to working.

He opened the bag. A tie-dyed T-shirt with a silhouette of Indiana Jones and another slogan, *LORD OF THE TROWELS*; a garish tangerine Fred Perry sweatshirt; army surplus trousers; two pairs of socks; a paisley handkerchief. Jason's shed skin.

– Couldn't find you a hat but the hankie'll do. Wise Shovelmonkey Number Five say, never go digging without a hankie on your head. It's all clean, he added, as if he were a salesman and cleanliness a not-to-be-expected bonus.

– Thanks.

– Couldn't find you any waterproofs either. You have got your own waterproofs? No, you haven't. Bloody hell. Haven't done this much, have you?

– Not much.

– First time?

– Not quite, he said, defensively, and began to change. His body felt damp and unkempt as his clothes. He could feel Jason still watching him, as if he had been laid on for his amusement.

– So, you know Eb.

– Eberhard? A bit.

– Small world. Friends?

– Pretty much.

– Yeah, right.

– Why ask if you know different?

– More fun that way, isn't it?

Their eyes met again across the seats. There was no real aggression in Jason, only a fierce mocking antagonism. *Go on*, his eyes said. *Lose it with me. What a laugh that'll be! What a riot!*

– You should've seen his face when Stanton told us you were coming.

He worked at the clothes in silence, gingerly sullen, waiting for the inevitable; for Jason to start in again.

– What's the story, then?

– There is no story.

– Course there is. You don't know us, you don't have mates here, and you don't know how to dig. What made this shithole seem like a good idea?

– It doesn't look that bad.

– No? You wait, Jason muttered, examining his cigarette as if it were defective. – It's like the Foreign Legion here, no one joins up unless they have to. How'd you get wind of us?

– I don't remember.

– Come on, don't get sulky.

– Don't get sarky then, he said, rising to the bait despite himself, and Jason cackled and put up his hands.

– No more sark, then. On my life.

– Eberhard said there was something going on down here, and I wasn't–

– Eb told you about us?

There it was again, that *Us*. He had heard that before. There was something Eberhard had said, that night in Metamorphosis, his *Us* carrying this same light weight.

– He just said there was a dig.

– And so here you are.

Jason was still smiling, the expression barely faltering. His cigarette had gone out unnoticed. His eyes were very white in his dust-tanned face.

– What's wrong with that?

Jason cocked an eyebrow and glanced at his watch. – Not like Eb to be so chatty, that's all. Well, you're all kitted out now. Stanton said to tell you to take it easy. Have a sit down and a nice cup of tea. Come and have a dig later if you think you're hard enough. Not that I would if I were you. Enjoy it while it lasts, mate. Lie back and think of England. I'll see you later, alright? No rest for the wicked shovelmonkey.

He winked and held out his hand again, waiting an age for Ben to take it, then mockingly formal, a customs officer returning a passport.

– Welcome to Sparta, Mr Mercer. We do hope you enjoy your stay.

He lay back and thought of England. He had been gone for a month. It felt like no time and like forever. A part of him still waited there and yet it was impossible to imagine himself back into that distance.

He remembered Oxford that last morning. The fog going out through the streets to the rivers, the Thames and the Cherwell, the Evenlode and the Ock. And the city always secretive and all the more so at that hour, as it slept, its acres full of unseen courts and cloisters, its lodgings and stairs full of lives held in waiting, pending morning.

He thought of Emine and her letter and then – sharper, sharper – of Nessie, a month older without him to see it. He wondered how long it would be before she began to forget his face, as he had half-forgotten his own father's. He tried to remember hers. It was clear until the moment he sought it. The harder he tried the fainter it became. She faded away from him like the fog.

He drank sweet tea and watched the dig. He had studied Therapne at Oxford and had refreshed his reading in Athens, but the reality drew him out of himself. He recognised the lay of the land, the hills and saddle that ran between them. He knew the history of the ruins on each, the palaces and shrines and graves built one atop the other, like corals, the living on the dead. But the green of the slopes in the sunlight, and the flash of spring flowers; and beyond the ziggurat-steps of the Menelaion, the clear air across the valley, and the city below, and the mountains beyond the city, white-capped, momentous . . . it was spectacular. Nothing he had ever read had thought to mention that.

The archaeological encampment was startling only in its ugliness.

Mud everywhere. Muck and dust. A Transit van and assorted cars sat gathered under a stand of cypress. A Containex toilet cabin stood askew. Four men worked at two pits nearby with all the subtlety of road-diggers. A third pit lay empty, its clean-swept terraced depths as meticulous as any excavation he had seen during his stints of Oxford fieldwork. Halfway along the saddle stood two wooden huts, high-eaved, double-doored, expensive things with styrene windows. Incongruous striped awnings had been added to their lee-sides. Folding tables and chairs stood under them. At the top of the second knoll, by the Menelaion, Jason stood over the tripod of a surveyor's laser plummet, almost motionless, his head bent to the readout. On the furthest rise stood a chapel, much smaller than the one in which he had sheltered, a tiny thing with a wide sheltering roof and a bell hung under the sweep of the eaves.

There were only three women: the girl he supposed must be Natsuko, the one called Eleschen and Missy herself. Their work often seemed to draw them to the huts, although Missy was everywhere, boundlessly energetic, digging and sifting, washing and hauling. The seven men came and went, all of them out of sight at times in the pits. He saw Eberhard stalking between ruins, and the wrestler below the shrine, lying flat out, his head and arms underground. The others looked to him like Greeks, their clothes more formal and less youthful than those of the foreigners, their faces clean-shaven and sun-leathered and worn.

No one seemed to be telling anyone what to do. That too was unexpected. The excavations he had taken part in at Oxford had been controlled in the extreme, their hierarchies military in their severity. He saw Missy give an order only once, one of the Greeks going to fetch wheelbarrows from the nearest hut. Otherwise they all went about their business as if according to some unspoken agreement, without a word to their overseer. Eberhard and Natsuko worked alone, Sauer in splendid isolation, the girl hunched miserably over the worktables under the awnings. Then it rained again and for a few minutes they did work together, pulling sheeting across one distant trench, abruptly as organised as sailors, the sky above and beyond them marbled with clouds.

He found a site plan in the back of the car, the dig hand-drawn in pencil with more skill than he could ever have achieved himself. There were the saddle and the three miniature peaks, *North Hill*, *Aëtós Hill*, *Elijah's Knoll*. The surrounding acres were crowded with the arcane names of ruins and a hundred years of excavations, the ground dug and reburied decade after decade, the new pits with faint working titles of their own like the names of old villages – *Long Hearth*, *Bronze Trench*, *East Midden* – and all around and over them contour lines and context numbers and stratigraphical notations, the design in its entirety so busy and crosswritten it was as if it had been encrypted.

At the bottom was a name, precise as a cemetery engraving, and so small on the translucent paper it made his eyes ache to read it.

Matsumoto Natsuko
Sparta,
February 2004.

He was still bent over the plan when the door beside him opened, almost spilling him out, the wind tugging at the Permatrace, Missy leaning in.

– Boy, you look sketchy. You just had to go and be Jason's size.

Her mouth was set hard in distaste. He got a hold on the wayward map and began to apologise even as she overrode him.

– No, it's okay, you'll fit right in. Don't mind me. How are you feeling?

– A lot better, thanks.

– Good for you. Can I squeeze in there?

She was trying before he could reply. Up close everything about her seemed excessive; her voice, her Yankee health, the wide bones of her face in the freckled shade of the straw hat.

– Ben, I just found out about the message. I am so *so* sorry. What you must think of us I don't know. What happened was that Natsuko was supposed to leave it for you at the desk because she goes for a swim at your hotel every morning, but she felt sick and didn't go today and . . . well, she just forgot. It's not like her at all. She's really so apologetic and actually ashamed. I think she's so sorry she can't even tell you sorry yet, you know?

There was a faint smear of suntan lotion on her nose, a line she had missed. She was so close he could smell it: salt coconut. He resisted the urge to rub it in.

– Anyway, how's the hotel? Settling in? Cyriac knows how to look after its hardware. Speaking of which, I can't believe you tried to walk. That wasn't real smart. How did you even know we were up here? Listen, okay, in future, you really don't want to mess with the weather here. You want to show it some respect. This is the country that invented the thunderbolt, okay? It must have been a heck of a walk! When it gets like that we just dive for cover, we're out of here like prairie dogs; oh, we just hole up in the huts or the chapel, and we, you know, we just play strip poker, drive each other crazy up here. I mean we do that anyway. Not the poker, actually, I'm kidding . . . wait, you're not religious too, are you? Oh thank God. Me, you dump me on a bare hilltop in March and I'll trade my soul for a dry butt any day . . . I'm talking too much, aren't I? I know I talk too much.

He was laughing, and she blushed before laughing back at him.

– Well I'm glad you find me amusing. Okay, how about introductions? No, you stay put, I can pick out the wildlife from here . . . So there's Jason, who you've met, and Eberhard you know, right? Jason is annoying as hell but he really knows what he's doing, he's been shovelling a long time, the day he was born he turned round and dug right on back in, you know what I'm saying? And Eberhard is kind of hard work too, but I guess you know that. Then that fine figure of a man with his head in the ground, that's Max, that's just a nickname but he likes it, we all kind of do whatever Max says . . . he's bossy that way. Max is our magician. He sees colours like nobody I've ever worked with. You show him dirt, he'll show you pay-dirt, I swear it's like he's got X-ray vision, we'd never have found the Skull Room without him . . . and there's Natsuko, she's our illustrator, she's nice but she's a – what do you English say? *A funny old bird*? And Miss World there, that's Eleschen. Our finds specialist. Then we have our dear locals, Chrystos and Giorgios, whose family actually owned this land way back, and that's Themeus, and his cousin Elias will be underground . . . and that's it. Except for me. Dr Missy Stanton, but like I said just call me Missy. And here you are and none the worse for wear. So welcome to my palace!

– Your what?

His voice sounded weak in his own ears. Her exuberance was boxing him into a role, a sympathetic uncertainty. He felt frail again beside her, insipidly English. She spread her arms, filling the car; palms up, like an oil tycoon or a televangelist. *Praise be!*

– Therapne! Actually it's supposed to be the palace of Helen and Menelaus, but they're ancient history and I'm project director, so I reckon that makes me the Daddy. *Bow down before Queen Missy of Sparta!* Listen, Ben, I'm so glad you're here. We really needed a new face, things were kind of weirding out recently. And you're going to love it. I mean will you look at it? And it's even more beautiful underground. I promise you could spend your whole life digging here and never get tired of it, and what is that if it isn't love?

She was unpacking a bag now, heaping things in his lap, still chattering on.

– Did you have lunch? I stole you a little smorgasbord. Here we have coffee in case Jason's tea is too nasty, which it probably is, and this is *bread* and this is *cheese* . . . and this is bug dope, don't eat that; and *these* are the famous Greek Bread Rusks, have you had these? Oh. My. God. You know they dug some of them up, seventeenth-century site, and they could still eat them? I mean I don't know if they did, well I guess they must have, otherwise how would they know? Anyway, that's what these things taste like, four-hundred-year-old bread. Edible is relative. Don't say I didn't warn you. Eberhard likes them. Personally I'd rather eat bug dope.

He picked a Jack Daniel's bottle out of the pile and held it to the window light.

– Moonshine. Reckoned you could use a shot. Chrystos makes it himself. Go easy or we'll be digging your brain out of the upholstery.

He unscrewed the bottle and sipped carefully. Immediately the reek of aniseed filled his mouth, the fumes searing his sinuses. His throat clenched and he doubled up, coughing, felt the bottle pulled from his hands, heard a snort of disdain and the sound of the bottle being swigged, and looked up in time to see Missy wiping her mouth.

– You'll get used to it. Let's get some food down you at least. You eat, I'll talk, it's what I do best. Did that Fischer woman tell you what we're doing here?

– Not really–

– Not that she understands, or she would've funded us. Ben, what we're doing here is really important. See, no one understands any of this. Is the North Hill Mansion really the palace of Menelaus? If we dig under the shrine are we going to find Helen of Troy? The skull that launched a thousand ships? Let alone *Classical* Sparta, no one understands *that* at all. Digging for Sparta is like trying to squeeze blood out of a stone . . . Fischer would say so anyway, those old-school guys are all doom and gloom, but they don't know how hard we're going to squeeze, they don't know we're going to *juice* these stones. So right now we're looking for secondary findspots at the peripheries of the main sites. That means here and the Sanctuary of Artemis-Orthia this season, and the acropolis and Amyclai when I find someone to grease my palm again. We're working a long season to do that much this year, nine months through October. Long hours, six days a week, but every find makes it worth it. So, ready to get juicing?

– Now?

– Of course now, now you're feeling better. Look, I called the doc and she said get you warm and rested and you'd probably be fine, so we have and you are. Probably. And there's nothing like work for keeping warm, is there? What are you good for? You're Oxford, right? Arch-Anth?

– Class-Arch, he said, his eyes still watering from the moonshine, and Missy wrinkled her striped nose, as if his education were something to be ashamed of. – I have dug before. I can also catalogue–

– Yeah, well, it's a funny thing, but everyone wants to catalogue. That's the icing on the cake, my friend, the extreme cream. What else?

– I can draw.

– Can you dig?

– Of course I can dig.

– My hero, Missy said, and leaned in to kiss him on the cheek, the taste of aniseed still on her breath. – Like I said, you're going to fit right in. So, are you ready to go make holes?

She held open the door for him like a gentleman. He stepped back into the wind, glad for Jason's two layers. Somewhere a radio was tuned to a Greek station, but turned down low: over it he could hear skylarks dwindling in the clear air.

– Boots, Missy said decisively, and took his arm, steering him towards the Transit van. He sat on the mudguard to fit them, watching the others as Missy rambled on. The group had spread out now, only the Greeks working together in pairs, and only the wrestler – Max? – seeming to notice him, looking up from the lip of the hole at which he sat, his expression neither friendly nor inimical. He saw a muscle flex in the man's flat cheek, like something parasitical.

– . . . Just light housework today, Missy was saying, one hand holding her hair out of her face. No point beating a dead dog. So I'll give you the grand tour tomorrow, but what you see is what you get. We've struck gold twice around North Hill and the same below the Shrine. Skull Room's the really interesting context, but I think maybe we'll leave that to Max, he gets prickly about me interfering . . . let's put you on Long Hearth. Aren't you done yet? What's the problem, you got two left feet? Come *on*.

As it turned out the tour would not wait. Once she had started showing off the site Missy wouldn't stop. He trudged behind her, nodding to those whose work they disturbed, nodding again at Missy's explanations, one thing leading remorselessly to the next, the beauty of the site lost in its details.

Eberhard's lie had been thorough: there were excavations everywhere. Circling each rise were minefields of test holes no wider than a hand's breadth, burrows where the magnetometer had picked up a signal only for the spade to turn up a petrol can or a bale of rusted wire. Work was continuing on six pits, two that were still no more than clean pegged-out earth, four that already went deeper. He stood at Missy's shoulder, hunched against the wind, as she went through the potsherds laid out by the Findhut, a broken kantharos inside as massive and pale as a horse's skull.

– And here's two Spartans we discovered with the hearts still beating! Hey, guys. Chrystos, this is Ben, he's yours for the afternoon. Go easy on him, he's still fragile, okay?

For the last few hours of that first afternoon it was Long Hearth he worked on, with the Maxis brothers. The Greeks dug at the pit floor, Chrystos with a trench shovel to the south, Giorgios to the north with brush and trowel. Each bucket of earth that was cleared was passed up to be sifted through quarter-inch hardware cloth. At first the loads weighed nothing at all. Only slowly did the ache in the muscles set in.

Chrystos put him to sifting. He did not know enough to be grateful for that. He sat on the goat-cropped grass, unduly annoyed by the damp, the chill of the walk still in his bones, peering at the men below. Max's Skull Room was the widest hole, and even the shallowest terrace of East Midden was deeper, but Long Hearth was the biggest, lean and dark, widening to the north like a cyclopean keyhole. Four feet down at that end the sandy topsoil and underlying clay had given way to a gigantic circle of hearthstones, but to the south there was nothing at that depth, and below it only layers and layers of ancient ash, a black record of repeated cataclysm at two feet, four feet, five.

The brothers spoke little between themselves and less to him. He sat listening to their coughs and sudden sighing breaths as they worked. The panting in the dusty air. Once Giorgios waved him down to hold a torch while he brushed at an imploded nest of broken pottery. The heat took him by surprise. The rain had been cold, and the ground of the hillside was still hard from winter, but the pit itself was humid enough to make them sweat. The last sun angling across the muddy lip, their work warming the trapped March air.

They kept on until the light began to go, breaking camp at six. It wasn't until then that either of the Greeks did more than mutter an order to him. Chrystos was the first to offer his hand. His grip was hard and cool as bone, his face caked with dust, ingrained with it, as if Missy had not been joking; as if he had just been dug from the ground himself.

– Welcome, he said, solemn and grim, and somewhere in the dusk the bells of the goats set off ringing.

The brothers drove him to town, the van leading the other cars back down the umbrella-seller's road. As far as he could tell they had found nothing for all their work on Long Hearth but the nest of pottery and another stratum of ash, but neither of the Greeks seemed dispirited. Aside from an offer to pick him up in the morning, what talk there was passed between them as if he was not there. Even so, invisible among half-strangers, he felt content.

More than that. As they turned down under the streetlamps of Palaeológou Street he felt gripped by an inexplicable excitement. Only days later did he understand it as a feeling of arrival. Of knowing that he had not gone wrong after all. That his weeks in Athens had not been for nothing. That he had finally arrived somewhere he might belong.

It was a clear night, the clouds rained out to nothing. After Chrystos dropped him he loitered on the hotel steps, reluctant despite everything to call an end to the day, his wet clothes a malodorous bundle under one arm, the lobby spilling light above him.

There were constellations rising over the black of the mountains, abstract and familiar configurations, superstrings of stars. He was still trying to remember their names when a car horn sounded behind him, and turning, his heart sinking, he saw Missy there, waving, working at the window.

– Hey!

– Hey.

– Want to go for a bite? I guess you're too tired, but here I am asking anyway . . .

– I am pretty tired, he said, and regretted it even as her grin faded.

– Just an idea. She shrugged. Then; I could do with the company.

– What about the others?

– The others. Are you kidding?

She looked younger now: she was not much older than he was himself. It was as if the excavation endowed her with some seniority that she had left behind, up among the pits and ruins. Her eyes were dark in the gloom of the car. Stripped of ebullience, her voice was soft and serious.

– I don't really hang out with the others.

– Oh. Well, if you don't mind waiting, I'll just–

– Listen, forget it, bad idea. I don't know what I was thinking, you must be bone-tired–

– No, I'll come.

Her smile broke through again. – Sure?

– I'd like to.

– Great! Get in, cowboy.

He jogged round to the passenger door. The car was already moving as he ducked inside, the door swinging shut as Missy accelerated into the evening traffic. She drove fast and not well, the SUV deceptive in its solidity, an armour of steel and glass between them and the lights they hedged, the trucks they overtook, Missy's hand raised to each in lazy apology.

– Where are we going?

– Wherever the eating looks good. Got to keep your strength up.

– I'll have to get it back first.

– Poor Ben. It'll get easier. If you take care of yourself it will. Turning up in the rain like that, that's no one's fault but yours. I swear I've got dogs back home with more sense . . . wait, maybe here! Let's see! I promise it'll beat room service.

They tried four places before Missy was satisfied. It was early to eat, the tavernas were still closed for Lent or until the summer, and the hotels were too rich for their pockets. There were cheaper places around the town square, grills more ramshackle than the one in Metamorphosis, a few cafés and ouzeries. In some the talk would stop as they entered and the food would be brought out with reluctance for inspection. In the one Missy settled on she was met with welcomes from the old men, and Ben with questions in Greek and German – *Where are you from? What is your name?* – then with drinks sent over, the farmers and factory workers slapping the tables and whistling for fresh wine, the stereo bellowing music, the TV broadcasting bombings and election rallies.

By the time the food came he was ravenous. He let Missy's conversation wash over him, the food and the talk rough and strange and his mind on other things half the time. The ancient city he had fallen in love with as a child. The streets below the streets below his feet, buried like old writing on a palimpsest.

On the television people ran towards what might have been bodies or bundles of clothes. Three men in a row stood facing a burned-out car, as if it too were a body: but beside him Missy was still talking, ruddy, laughing, telling tall stories. The dry desert light of Abu Simbel, the marbled rock tombs of Petra. The grandeur of Ephesus, the shafts of Troy, the whispering galleries of Ebla and Ur. And the wine as pink as cochineal, the lamb baked with laurel, the pork roasted with juniper.

He slept well that night. He did not recall dreaming. Only just before morning, as he woke, did he find himself lying in the dark, thinking of Metamorphosis. The cacophony of the meat grill, the alarums of metal and the hotchpotch of languages. Then Eberhard's voice, cool and sure, echoing afterwards as he washed and dressed and went down to the dark street.

– *I'm afraid no one calls it Lacedaemonia any more. Not even us.*

– *Us?*

– *Those of us who are working there.*

His hands on the table, the fingers interleaved, sheltering.

∾

In the mornings he would wash quickly, then boil up the kettle and take the one chair to sit by the window. He would be there before six, but already then Sparta would be awake, the fields and factories waiting for no one.

He would drink his tea and watch the town come to life. The sunrise would be somewhere behind him. It would creep down the Taygetos mountains. Sometimes the first light was clear of all colours except those of the snow and stone of the mountains. Other mornings it was red as blood.

Just after six the slicked-back boy would steal out into the yard, roll back the cover on the pool, then loiter, smoking a fretful cigarette behind the stacked-up sun loungers until Natsuko appeared.

Seeing her before Ben could, the boy would flinch galvanically, then get to work, wiping down chairs, sweeping the tiles as she swam. From Ben's window she looked foreshortened when she first came out – small as a child in the yard's dim light – and then elongated as she dived, splash and ripple transforming her, her fierce, neat strokes eating up the pool, echoing up the courtyard's well. And him and the boy both watching her. White towel, black suit, white skin, black hair.

So many lengths. He always lost count. She was still swimming every morning when he left himself.

Two apartment blocks overlooked the pool. In a way he knew well from home he came to recognise the strangers who lived in them. The workers who trudged home at first light from the cannery or the vulcanisation plant; the man who hung cagebirds on his balcony; the old women who dried octopus on her washing line; the working women who put out clothes at dawn to have them done by lunchtime. Emine, he knew, would have liked them.

Further off stood a heavy low-rise, scores of windows in acres of concrete. It did not look like a building in which people would live, but neither did it look like a regular workplace. Its ordinary mystery became a fixture of his mornings. For the first few days he was too exhausted to do much more than eat when he came home from the dig, alone or with Missy, and he would forget about the low-rise until he woke and saw it there again. The lights would go out in one window and come on in another, silent and inexplicably purposeful, like warnings on a strange machine.

On his fourth morning he saw a figure moving in one of the building's lit windows. He followed it with his gaze as it came and went and came again. Only when it stopped moving did he recognise the uniform of a nurse. For a moment she stood profiled, tranquil at that distance. He couldn't see what ordeal or task she was attending to. Her head was bent. Merciful, like that of an icon.

He would wait on the hotel steps. At half-six Chrystos would come for him, every day as he had promised, always on time, always with his brother Giorgios, never with more than a nod to Ben's thanks, never with any of the others. The van could have held them all, but that wasn't the way things worked. The foreigners and the other locals made their own journeys, together or alone, according to a chemistry that Ben could not understand.

Missy was there first each day, setting up camp in her Gore-tex hoodie, her SUV parked messily in the shelter of the cypresses. Max came in Eberhard's silver Volvo 144 Delux, Jason and Eleschen later in Natsuko's hatchback, and Elias and Themeus last and by foot or perched double on a scooter. Sometimes Chrystos would pick up other people, an uncle and a teenage in-law who would get down at the village of Afisou, an older Maxis cousin with an antiquated shotgun and false teeth of the same vintage, and once with the uncle an old, old creature whose accent was almost incomprehensible to Ben, a tiny woman with oiled hair who nagged at Giorgios all the way, her cracked voice jabbing at him over some undefined and antediluvian grievance, implacable despite Giorgios's silence and the uncle's soothing remonstrances, staring at them all with relentless bird-black eyes.

He grew fond of Chrystos and wary of Giorgios. In Chrystos there was a dignity which in his brother became forbidding. Outdoor lives and reticence made both seem old, not that either was young. Chrystos had some English from his stints on other excavations and his years as a merchant seaman, and photos in his wallet of Newcastle England and Newcastle Australia, wrinkled shots of old sunsets and friends. But he was a quiet man and Giorgios quieter, his talk to the point and his points sharp.

If they talked at all on the way up it was sparingly, their three voices hushed, as if it were a sin to speak in the dark.

– You slept well?

– Thanks. And for the lift, again.

A nod. Chrystos's eyes still measuring the road.

– You never take the others?

The bridge out of town, the turning up to Afisou, and then – They make their own ways.

A sound from Giorgios in the back. – They don't mix with the likes of us.

– Us?

No answer at all to that. He tried again. – What about Elias and Themeus?

Chrystos harrumphed. – They are different again.

– Oh?

Afisou behind them. The roadside shrine under the pines. Claymore and Kleenex. The turning ahead.

– They live outside town. In their own place. It's not so far for them to walk. They prefer to take care of themselves.

– By the river, Giorgios said. Always they live by the rivers. Those people.

– What people?

– They don't trust the pipes. They don't like to drink from the pipes.

– *Athigani.*

– *Athigani?*

– *Yifti*, Giorgios said, and he understood, a first small equation coming clear. *Yifti*. Gypsies.

~

That first week he worked with the brothers every day. The others were never far off – the Skull Room, Max's prize domain, was just over the shoulder of the hill – but the pits kept them apart as they worked, or at least abetted their apartness. At lunch Missy would bring them together to discuss their finds and plan ahead, but they would dissemble after that, Eberhard drifting off to eat alone or sometimes going with Max and Jason to North Hill, Natsuko and Eleschen with them or some days cloistered together under the striped awnings, Elias and Themeus side by side by the shrine with their radio playing softly and homemade pastries on newspapers on their knees. Only Missy seemed to go where she liked, hunkering down to eat with Ben and the others at Long Hearth, or shoving up beside Elias and Themeus, or drawing up a director's chair beside the girls, her voice carrying as she butted in.

He watched Eberhard. Since he had arrived Sauer hadn't spoken to him. He wondered about that and what it might mean in the scheme of things. He wondered how it was that he had been with Eberhard at Oxford, had been in the same room as him for so many hours, and yet knew so little of him.

He recalled only two things about Sauer, two things in particular, each memorable because curious. Once, in his first year, he had been at the Institute, late for a lecture, and had ended up on the wrong floor. He had taken the stairs and had heard people talking below him. The stairwell had distorted the conversation, and he had seen Professor Foyt and Professor Lorne from above before he had recognised their voices.

Sauer? Lorne had asked. *Is he all they say?*

To which Foyt had coughed up a rare dry laugh. *For better and worse, I'm afraid. Still, that one is peerless.*

Another time, cycling home on Emine's bicycle, he had heard someone singing in the dark where the Oxford Canal ran between newbuilds, the voice very drunk but striking and sad, the song something old-worldly and German; and coming up beside the figure had seen it was Eberhard, alone, a tie loose on him, dress collar undone, singing as he walked. Afraid of being recognised he hadn't slowed down, but as he'd passed he'd been unavoidably aware that the other boy was crying.

He watched him. There was a distance between them, but there was a distance between Eberhard and everyone. Then he began to overhear things, a word or a look here and there, and to notice how the others tried to speak to him and were cut short, and he understood that this particular distance was new. That it was his doing.

They were not so different, he thought. Eberhard was not like Emine, who forgave and forgot. His anger lingered, like Ben's own. They were alike in that.

All that first week he waited for Sauer to say something. Every day he braced himself. He imagined the words and the method of delivery, the question or statement, spoken softly enough to hide malice, or loudly enough for them all to hear.

So you decided to follow me.

I'm sorry you thought you were invited.

Why is it that you followed me?

What are you doing here?

By the end of the week he understood that that wasn't the way it would happen. Eberhard had chosen to say nothing. He would go on avoiding him, and his avoidance would speak volumes. He would leave Ben unacknowledged, would go on not quite meeting his eyes, would go on looking through him as if he were the fog going out to the rivers.

He knew, of course, that he was not befriended by the others. That too did not need to be said. He had understood it instinctively the day he had arrived. He was not one of them. It was nothing new to him. It was how things had often stood with his older siblings, and after his childhood illness in many places, at school and in the odd jobs he had done before college. It was how some of Emine's wealthy friends had looked or not looked at him. He had stood at the peripheries of many circles, not quite accepted, half-admitted, the friend-of-a-friend, the last-minute dinner guest. He had never liked it, but he had never been surprised by it. It was the way things worked, the way things were. He had never had the wit or the poise, the sureness or the knowingness, the right words or the right manner. He had never had enough to be one of *Us*.

He saw that Missy was not one of them either, and that unlike him she didn't understand. *Us* were Eberhard and Eleschen, Max and Natsuko and Jason. Missy was different; too eager, too ingenuous. She struggled against their closeness with her relentless enthusiasm and was bewildered when she was rebuffed. Where Eberhard was the most donnish of workers, his director would have done anything to be a student again, one of the crowd. He wondered if he could explain it to her, the otherness of the others, unsure he had the courage to spell out something so brutal. What he recognised implicitly was, to her, an invisible force. He watched as she ate lunch with the girls, leaning towards them with awkward need, as baffled as a moth batting against glass.

The first week made no difference for him. He was no closer to them after six days than he had been after one. *Welcome*, Jason had said, but he had said it with a wink, Ben recalled, and he saw in the recalling that it had been meant not only as a joke, but as a joke on him.

Even so, despite Eberhard, despite *Us*, he was happy. He had not come to Sparta with any expectation that Sauer would be pleased to see him. He had come to Sparta for its own sake, and Sparta was a joy to him. All those weeks in Athens he had still been in transit. He had been the speed of light, relative to nothing. Not that Sparta promised him anything more. Not that it was a homecoming. It was not like coming home. It was like finding he had never had a home. It was as if he had found his place in the world.

He still carried his wedding ring. He would try and leave it behind only to find that he had picked it up on his way out, involuntarily slipping it into his coat pocket. Sometimes he would discover himself running it through his fingers in the pocketed dark, like a magic trick he'd bought and never worked out how to use. Or he would realise he was worrying at it, as the old men in the town square did with their strings of beads. And once he looked up from his work with a jolt to find it back on his wedding finger, as if it had uncoiled and crept there of its own accord.

The recollection of Emine began to seem muted by distance. Like a child scratching at a scab he made himself remember her.

The first time he had ever seen her: it was his first month at Oxford, Michaelmas term, and he was late for a lecture. Emine was coming down Beaumont Street with friends. It was bright weather and she was laughing. The group came on towards him together, all of them merry, leaving no room for him on the pavement. He stepped aside into the gutter, and as he did so Emine looked at him.

The gloss of her: that was what hooked him first. The lustre of her, like fresh split coal. The way her eyes lit up when they found him. Her collar was lined with a black fur which, he understood later, was meant to show up her hair. And as she looked at him standing there in the gutter her laughter faded. Not to nothing, but to a smile. Not a warm smile, but a pretty one, the delight in it veiled. As if he were a bargain, but the deal was not yet to be counted on.

Have you found someone else? he had asked, the night everything finally came apart. She had told him that she had made confession and that, her condition being intolerable, it was right for them to separate. She had said that she could no longer love him, and done so patiently, as if she were explaining some commonsensical thing to Nessie: as if it were the most natural thing in the world.

Have you found someone else?

She had shaken her head. Not as if she meant to deny it, but as if it were simply the wrong question. *It's not me*, she had said, *It's you.*

And he had understood. The worst thing was that she had not needed to explain. He had wanted so passionately to hate Foyt, to blame Foyt for the ruin of his marriage, but he had always known that the other man was no more than a symptom. The cause had been himself. After that night he had never asked her for a reason again. Much better to be kept in the dark, where there were still alternatives.

*

Ten hours a day, he made holes. He washed shards and hauled gear and sieved earth too, but most of the time it was the holes: it all came down to the holes. He made holes with trench shovels and augurs and corers and spades. He made holes with mattocks and trowels and fine brushes, slowly uncovering bones and urns, removing the earth grain by grain, like a child in a story given the first of three impossible tasks.

He began to dream of Therapne. The sun creeping into the pits. The air hung with dust, the walls trickling down. Chrystos and Giorgios digging beside him.

In the dream they dug until the light had gone, then dug until their shovels broke, the walls no longer trickling dust but something wet and warmish. One by one – Ben always last, seeing it first in their faces – they would understand that the wetness was blood, great tracts of it squeezing out of the stones. And even then they always still dug, even with that understanding, not terrified but triumphant, working at the fractured earth with their broken hafts, their hands even, with their fingers and their teeth.

*

He called Emine three times that first week, trying their apartment, unwilling to catch Foyt at the house. Twice the answerphone kicked in quickly, as it did when other calls were waiting to be retrieved – Emine had never liked checking them, had treated the backlog as a chore to be left to him. The message had not been changed, either, so that he left his monologues for both Emine and his old self.

It was Saturday when she answered. He was late back from the site and too tired for the restaurants. Instead he bought something from the all-hours shop on the corner (the old lady who ran the place a chain smoker with kohl-black eyes, who always looked – or looked at him – as if she had just then recalled an excellently dirty joke), eating in his room, the TV on, the War against Terror flickering far away. A woman in an orange jumpsuit, three figures standing over her, her expression not frightened but dismayed, as if she had just woken up to find, not that she was about to die, but that she had only slept too long and missed the visit of a favourite friend; and a leaner woman, a politician or general in civilian clothes, reading a statement to a room full of flashbulbs, her voice steady as she goes.

. . . *All individuals in all territories should be aware of the risk of indiscriminate terrorist attacks in public places anywhere in the world. Be vigilant, take sensible precautions. Do not assume* . . .

He showered, half-asleep on his feet in the water. He was in bed, the lights out and the TV killed, when he thought to try Oxford again.

He dialled in the dark. Emine picked up on the first ring.

– Hello?

Her voice was throaty, melodious, as if she had just been laughing. He was jealous instantly.

– Hello . . . who is it?

– Me. Is Foyt with you?

– *Ben?* My God, where are you? Why didn't you ring?

– I am.

– Hold on.

The line deadened. Muffled voices, male and female. He closed his eyes, already weary of her, hanging on.

– Are you still there, Ben?

– Is that him?

– No.

– Someone else, then.

– Don't be stupid, it's just a friend. Where have you been? You didn't call!

– You forgot to check the phone. I wrote to you too, when I got yours. I thought you'd have them by now . . . Are you alright? How's Ness?

A sigh, both angry and relieved, distorted by the line.

– She's better.

– Better than what?

– It wasn't anything. Just the cold. I told you that. She asks about you all the time–

Good, he thought, or felt. His gratitude was more feeling than thinking.

– And I didn't know what to say. I was worried about you. Where are you?

– Sparta.

– *Sparta?*

Now he was smiling. Weary but grinning in the dark. Triumphant.

– Sparta, you know. Council-house of trickery. Helen and Menelaus–

– I know what Sparta is, Ben! What are you doing *there*?

– Digging holes. I've got some work. There's an excavation here. It was all in my letter. It's going well, I think. There's eleven of us. It's just spadework but it's beautiful. Did you know Sparta was beautiful? I don't know why I never came here before. They've put me up in this big old hotel, I think you'd like it . . .

He waited for her to say something. The line had gone quiet. He closed his eyes and found he could still hear her there, just breathing, listening. There were other sounds beyond her, too. The hiss of heavy traffic, outside in damp Oxford streets.

He shivered, the place he had left behind seeming abruptly much too close. The low grey skies. The cold clear air.

– Ben?

– What?

– Are you alright?

– I'm fine, why?

– You sound strange.

– No I don't.

– You do. When you talk like that it makes you sound strange. I mean different.

For a second he didn't answer. He found himself becoming angry with her, as if she were questioning his sense, or faith.

– Ben . . .

– I'm fine, I told you. I'm different because I'm happy here.

– Oh. Well, then, I'm glad for you.

– You don't sound it.

– No, I am.

But she wasn't, he thought. Instead she sounded disappointed. Envious. As if she had been hoping for something other than happiness for him. Or from him.

Only after he hung up, on the cusp of sleep, did he realise he had never mentioned Eberhard.

Sunday surprised him.

– Someone is here for you, Sudoku said, as if the someone were distasteful and the fault were to be laid at Ben's door. It was after eight and he was still in bed, still half-dreaming of the pit.

– Who is it?

– I wouldn't know, I'm sure, Sudoku drawled. Will I say you are coming down?

He pulled on clothes, boiled the kettle, burnt his mouth, discovered that his shoes were lost, his thoughts all muddled up with hopes.

He discovered himself by the window, his morning ritual asserting itself. Sparta taking precedence, as if that should be all that he looked for. Full morning on the mountains. Buntings of clothes on balconies. The swimming pool unwavering, its lanes as straight as rules on paper. He remembered Natsuko, stopping for breath in the deep water, and remembering her, eel-dark, realised he was hoping most of all for her.

The lift was out and he took the stairs. An odd noise carried up the well, an insistent, ugly, snagging sound, like the grinding of teeth or untoothed gears, and as Ben reached the entrance hall he saw Chrystos in shirtsleeves, out of place in the hotel's marble and brass, a big man in a too-small seat, impervious to the twin glares of Sudoku and the cockatoo, his cap folded on the sofa beside him.

He held a trowel and a bastard file between his knees. He was sharpening the trowel with long strokes of the file, like a boy whittling a scrimshaw. He held up both as Ben reached him.

– A perfect point.

– Chrystos? It's Sunday.

– Eh. No holes today.

– So, you . . . we're not working somewhere else, are we?

– No. Here, he said, his English as halting as Ben's Greek, and he stood up and put down both hafted blades on an occasional table, gesturing. – For you. Take please. Souvenirs.

– Gifts, he said, and picked them up, their weights sinking unexpectedly in his hands. – Souvenirs are when you leave. Thank you. It's very kind of you.

– The trowel is good. Marshalltown steel. From Iowa in America. Not like the old things they lend you. With this the digging is not so hard. Keep it sharp, like how you saw. So now we go now?

– Go where?

– To sightsee. You don't want, you can say no.

– No, no, I mean it's fine. I just wasn't expecting–

– Then we will go now, okay?

The van was there as always, at first only the absence of Giorgios and the presence of sunlight distinguishing the morning from that of a working day. Only little by little, as they drove, did Ben notice other differences. Chrystos was more at ease, and by degrees more talkative, though whether through release from work or from his brother, he couldn't say. There were takeaway coffees for them on the dashboard, and the Sunday papers by Ben's seat. It was finally election day. The front pages were full of it.

– So where's Giorgios?

– At church.

– You don't go?

– It's not for me, he said. Then nodding at the tools, A joke.

– Are they? I thought–

– Gifts for you. A joke for her.

– For who? Sudoku? he said, and Chrystos frowned and laughed.

– Marina. My sister's friend. Very proud.

– Do you know Crossword too?

That made him laugh again, an oddly boyish giggling. – Crossword is a good name for her. Marina's cousin. Even worse. Lucky for me it was only one.

– You know everyone.

– Of course. Everyone knows everyone, here.

They were heading west, the plaza, its bars and colonnades already behind them. The cathedral loomed up, a crowd in the square in its Sunday best. Beside him Chrystos turned the radio on, surprising him again, burrowing through blocks of talk to veins of music, pop, Greek folk, humming tunelessly along.

– Today is an important day.

– Are you going to vote? he asked, and Chrystos glanced at him, a quick keen sideways question which he shrugged easily away.

– You don't?

– Sometimes.

– Sometimes you do not vote?

– Not everyone does, where I come from. It doesn't make much difference there. It doesn't change much, he added, unaccountably embarrassed, though it was a conviction he had held for as long as he could recall. – I don't believe in them.

– In who?

– Politicians. Like you don't believe in God.

– It is not the same.

– It seems the same to me. One kind of disbelief is like another.

– It is not the same. And I did not say I do not believe. I do not have faith. And that is also not the same.

He was relieved when Chrystos turned his full gaze back to the road.

The edge of town. The van jogging over potholes. Cars up on bricks in bare front yards. Concrete and red geraniums. A dead tractor under mulberry trees. Carillons of dogs passing them along from one dog-realm to the next.

– Here, Chrystos said finally, It makes a difference.

– Maybe you have better politicians here.

– I do not vote for politicians. I vote for politics, Chrystos said, tight-lipped. And then, relenting, Look. Up there.

He looked up through the smudged windscreen. The land ahead was rising, orchards of oranges giving way to less pastoral olive groves, the groves to rocks and Aleppo pines, and rocks and pines to the Taygetos. The western mountains were much closer now, and darker, too, shoulders and ridges blocking out the clear blue sky.

He blinked. A city lay concealed in the mountains. Wherever he could see through the trees were vertiginous cobbled streets, fortresses and palaces, lichened domes and buttresses. Gardens, towers, gates, and halls, all of them barely clinging on, their rooftops falling into ruin, their walls held up by vines, each tier capped by another tier, as fabulous as cloud castles.

It dizzied him. He muttered some empty sacrilege, *Christ* or *God*, and heard Chrystos's smile in his voice.

– Only a few find him here now.

– Is this Mystras?

– Mystras, the city of the Byzantines. You like it?

– It's beautiful! Beautiful . . .

They parked under the walls. A buzzard in the pines below went loping away through the air. Chrystos was rooting in the van, passing him out shopping bags full of food and bottled water.

Already they were high above the valley. He could see the river and the city below, and beyond them, miles away, the rise of the Parnon foothills. He traced the road to Therapne, found the ridge that marked the dig, then closed his eyes, breathing in the air of the strange end-of-the-world he had come to. Olives, woodsmoke, oranges.

– Laconia, Chrystos said. He had come up to stand at the car park's edge. In one hand he held a wide-brimmed, much-worn hat, in the other a HellaSpar shopping bag. He pointed with the hat, the gesture proprietorial. – Over the Taygetos, Messenia. Over the Parnon, Arcadia. Once there was a time when all this was ours.

– Ours? he said, and Chrystos tutted, as if it were of no consequence. He brushed off the hat.

– Here, for you. Ready?

The entrance looked unmanned, but as they reached it Ben could hear the squabble of a radio. An old man in the gate-booth waved them by, his head cocked to a sports phone-in. They went up through the shadowed gate and out into the sun-bleached streets.

He leaned into the ascent, soon finding himself out of breath.

Chrystos climbed with a farmer's stroll, lumbering against the gradient but always somehow still ahead, his voice hollow, booming back from doorways and vaulted passages, putting names to ruined buildings – the Mansion of Laskaris, the Palace of the Despots, the Convent of Pantanassa – his face bright-eyed with something that Ben belatedly recognised as pride. As if the palaces were his, and Ben an honoured visitor.

They met no one. At one turning Ben glimpsed something in black, a huddled, hurrying figure, but when he looked back it was gone, and rooks were rising over the rooftops, cawing and threshing at the wind.

Above the town a fortress stood guard, acropolis on acropolis. They struggled up the last few stairs and came out on the fortress-top, the wind blowing up from the south, whistling at the mountainside, nabbing at wrappings as they unpacked the food.

They ate in the shelter of the wall. The bread was Saturday's, and tough, but warm from the sun and their own exertions, and bread and water aside Chrystos had brought more than enough. A Volvic bottle one-third full with homemade pink wine, the smell of it as rough as meths. Big donkey olives and the smaller local kind, fresh from the harvest. Almonds and pistachios and slabs of cheese dusted with thyme. Snails in oil and herbs, wrapped up in dark-stained newspapers. The boiled bulbs of hyacinths.

– Once many people lived up here, Chrystos said, breaking the bread into fists and heels. – Hiding behind their walls.

– From what?

– Enemies. Whenever people here were weak they would live up in the mountains. Sometimes it is easier.

– To be weak?

– You don't agree. You think it is easy to fight.

– I wouldn't know.

– No? You don't fight for what you believe in?

He laughed. – I would, if I knew what that was.

Tsk! Chrystos was shaking his head. He took out a penknife, halved one slab of cheese.

– Try.

– It's good.

– From Trípi. Not far from here. Some say Trípi is where the Spartans took children born sick. There is a high rock where they were left. You know what I'm talking about?

– I wouldn't say the Spartans were heroes because they left children to die.

– Not heroes, I did not say that. I said it is hard to be strong. It is not easy to kill a child.

– Not easy for the child, either.

– Harder for mother than for child. To live down there, without walls, to be *Sparta*, not *Mystras*, the people had to be hard. So that is what the Spartans were.

– And now?

– Now is different. Now we are just people. There are no Spartans now.

They ate for a while in silence, sharing the bulbs. The rooks were back, Ben saw, watching from ridges and fissures, their voices echoing between outcrops of juniper and opuntia.

– In winter we come up here, Chrystos said, unscrewing the wine.

– What for?

– For this. To look and drink. The wine keeps us warm.

– Warmer indoors.

– Nothing to see, indoors. Also my brother brings things, for the people here.

– People still live up here?

– Some. Not many. Not young. In the convent there are holy women.

– Nuns?

– Giorgios saves something for them. Calor for cooking. Oil. Meat. Chocolates from Switzerland. They like the chocolates best.

– It must be hard up here in winter.

– The ice is bad but the view is good. We have a nice time. Five, six of us. First we go see to the . . . nuns . . . then we come to sit up here. We look down where our fields are. Some years it is all under snow, Chrystos said, and sketched out a line miles across the valley's gulf.

He took the wine, swigged it, leaned back, closing his eyes. After-images flickered in his private darkness. The sky's light and the snow on the heights. It would change a people, a landscape like this. A place of small horizons. The mountains reproaching departure. The valley a haven of green, cut off from the world. Something worth defending.

The stone was warm against his head. It came to him that there was really nowhere else he would rather be – Not Athens, Oxford or London – and he closed his eyes tighter, as if that reflex could trap the reflection. Beside him Chrystos was still talking, lapsing into his own language, the wine loosening his tongue.

– Like kings with kingdoms. That's how we feel up here. Really we are like boys. We come here to forget what we are becoming. None of us has the land our grandfathers had. Even the Chatzakos have less. There are more outsiders now. And the children go to Athens and the farming is always hard. Some of us build property. The Maxis have only two good fields. My cousins harvest the olives now. Giorgios and I find other work. Every few years you people come looking for Sparta. You hire us because others have hired us. We go again to the acropolis or Amyclai. We never find enough. You always leave disappointed. And all the time Mystras is here, where anyone can see it. Much more beautiful than anything you dig out of the ground. Much less work to find.

– Maybe that's why we don't come here.

– . . . You want it to be hard?

– No, no. We want to find something no one else has seen before.

– The things you find are not unseen.

– Forgotten, then, whatever. Secret. There were secrets up here too, though. I read something, about a man who went on worshipping the old gods here. Zeus. Poseidon–

– *Plethon.* Chrystos waved the name away. – In Rome they believed he was clever. Here not so much. Gemistus Plethon was not secretive. He did not keep his secrets well. Now you look surprised. You think all I do is dig? That I would never read a book?

– Of course not, he said, looking away, feeling himself blush at the crude lie. When he looked back again Chrystos was watching him, another of his sideways looks, this one amused and tolerant. – I'm sorry.

– *Pff.* No need. You give me the pleasure of surprising you.

They finished the last of the wine. The sun was climbing higher, the fissures of the mountainside filling one by one with light.

– You are not like the others, Chrystos said, as if it were a compliment.

– Others? he said; and realising, What are they like, then?

Chrystos took out a pipe and began to fill it, fretting over spilled threads, so occupied with it that Ben tried again.

– Missy said things were weirding out.

Chrystos shrugged, lit the pipe. – *Weirding out?* I don't know. They play strange games.

– Games?

– They talk about them, down there.

– What do they say?

– They don't behave like foreigners.

– Is that bad?

– Some say they are rude. They don't make friends. They keep too close.

– That doesn't sound so strange.

– They eat together, drink together. They do not stay at the hotels. They look for rooms in the old town, places not meant for visitors. They hunt together.

– They *hunt*?

– Eberhard and the quiet boy, Max, they know what they are doing. They buy from the hunting shops. They go for rabbits in the hills. Not just the boys. Also the girls. It is the wrong time for rabbits but that is not a problem. What they do is their own business. A friend of my brother has seen them. People think it isn't right. Not for women. Not for foreigners. It isn't what people expect. More to eat?

They cleared away the last remnants, stones and shells, the pages of old newspapers, headlines from *Estia* and *Stohos*, Chrystos leaning against the weathered wall as he stood, grunting at his stiff joints.

– So. What do you believe in, Ben?

– Believe in? Oh, well, not much.

– Not God? Not God, not politics. You should believe in something.

– Why?

– Otherwise it is too hard. Maybe you believe in yourself. You have faith in yourself.

– To do what? he said, and laughed, the echoes ushering his voice back oddly.

– To do well in your work. Archaeology. To find what is left of the past. Or to live a good life.

– I haven't lived a life which anyone would have faith in.

– That is a shame. If you think it. What is it you believe in, then?

It was a moment before he realised they were both still waiting for an answer. A wretched panic began to unfurl in him, a subtle coil of it at first, like the first loose threads of smoke. He nodded down at Mystras. – I believe in this.

– In this? This is just stones, Chrystos said, taking the pipe out of his mouth. – Old stones.

– No. It's history.

– You only believe in history?

– At least that's something, he said, What's wrong with that? But Chrystos only shrugged again, his face surprised, then bleak. He dry-spat and turned away.

– We should get back.

– Already?

– I have to vote, and you must want time to yourself.

They finished clearing and went down carefully through the ruined streets. There was no more talk on the way home. Chrystos dropped him by the hotel.

– Thanks for the sightseeing.

– You liked it?

– Very much.

– Do something for me.

– What?

– Stay away from the others.

– Well, that shouldn't be too hard, they haven't exactly–

– Even so.

– Alright. But I don't understand–

– No. But I see that you are easily surprised.

He stood there as the van pulled out, awkward with the sense of something unfinished. For the first time all week he felt alone. Only as he went up the hotel steps did he remember that he had forgotten his gifts. He turned back, raising a hand, and found Chrystos already gone.

∞

The afternoon was his own to kill. At first it seemed a luxury. He took his notes and went back out. For a while he walked, seeing the town as he had not all week, the shops shut but the streets crowded. He went by the museum, hoping he might find books there – something in the way of a library – but expecting to find it closed and not disappointed in that.

At three o'clock he ended up at a kafeneion in the square, a grimy place full of grim old men in saggy suits, like second-string mourners at a funeral, acquaintances of the dead, no one talking to anyone, the waiter setting out umbrellas and vinyl armchairs to catch the best of the cold March sun.

He ordered coffee, medium sweet, and made it last an hour, avoiding the waiter's eye. The light moved up and over him. It lit up the page in front of him and left him in sharp blue shadows.

Children were playing in the plaza, their mothers watching over them from tea houses and coffee bars. An old woman sat by the fountain, counting hyacinth bulbs from a green bag to a red bag. There were no young men, he realised. It was as if they had all gone off to war.

The waiter came to take his cup. He ordered more, not wanting it. The lights around the square came on.

Still he sat, writing at first, then not writing, only looking. Then only looking, not seeing. The pen lying lax in his hand, his hands and face as motionless as those of the old men sitting inside, each of them unutterably alone.

VIII

Notes Towards a Thesis

What else is there but the past? What else is there to have faith in? It is not in us to believe in the future. We distrust it. We cannot be convinced. We believe only in what our eyes tell us. Seeing is believing, but the future can never be seen, and so it remains unbelievable. We are too short-sighted. Even in our darkest moments we never believe, in our hot hearts, that we will ever change. We go blindly on. We have faith only in Then and Now.

At least we have something, then. At least then we have faith in history.

The Spartans set great store by faith. Their multitudes of dire gods were like the old deities of Gilgamesh – which three thousand years before had *Swarmed like flies over the sacrifice* – but their way of life, too, required fidelity. The Spartans believed in Sparta as fervently as they believed in any god. Their state was an America, a dream of perfection. They lived out their lives in the shadows of their beliefs, and saw the fruits of doing so through generation after generation. Their city's power was the proof that their faith was well placed. For half a millennium and more the Hollow Realm remained safe from the world, stronger than the world, the wall-less city inviolate, the red cloaked phalanxes unmatched.

And then, inevitably, their time passed. The greatest soldiers in the world were beaten. The enemy trod them underfoot into the mire of their own meat. Lacedaemonia was lost. The meadows of the Eurotas burned. The strong women of Sparta ran screaming into the streets. It must have almost seemed to them as if the Taygetos had been torn down. The gods they loved had failed them.

The Spartan dream had been destroyed. And what did they put their faith in, then?

✥

The Hellenes called two places Thebes. One was a city of the Egyptians, who called it No-Amon, *City of Amon*, the god whose name means *The Hidden*, and whom the Greeks worshipped as Zeus. The other Thebes lay in the heart of Greece, north of Athens, with Mount Cithaeron at its back.

The Thebes of Egypt still exists. Karnak and Luxor are its names. Half a million people live among its endless monuments. But of the other Thebes almost nothing has survived. Like the Sparta it destroyed it has become a place of absence. It cannot be forgotten, but nor can it be known except through legend, myth and history. Like Sparta it was a city whose strengths lay in the practice of war, and it was through war that its fortunes rose and fell.

It was not much loved elsewhere in Greece. The Thebans were seen as a brutal, cloutish folk. After Xerxes breached Thermopylae, the Thebans were among the few to offer him subservience, and having done so they then fought relentlessly against the Greeks at the final battle of Plataea. After the Persian Wars, when Sparta and Athens battled between themselves, Thebes sided with the Lacedaemonians, yet it remained a thorn in the side of both powers, too eminent to be ignored, too close to Athens for comfort, too far from Sparta's realm and reach to ever be wholly trusted.

Eight decades after Plataea Athens was conquered, its walls torn down. Sparta had won in war, again. Thebes saw its enemy beaten, but was not itself victorious. Its rivalry with Athens had dwindled as Athenian power had ebbed, to be replaced by other jealousies.

For generations, Theban men had fought under the Spartan kings. In doing so they had been changed. They had absorbed the Spartan ways. Years before Athens's loss, Thebes had begun gathering its strength. Sparta was its new enemy, and the enmity was mutual. In the same summer that Athens fell, the Spartan phalanxes marched north, taking the Thebans unaware, conquering their old allies just as they had their enemies.

But Thebes would not accept defeat, and Sparta lacked the wherewithal to rule the world that it had won. After a century of war it was no longer the great force that it had been. Nor was it ever geared for peace. The meshed components of its state – hoplites, helots, fearful gods – these were streamlined for war. Victory did Sparta no good, though it still had faith in itself. Its ways had brought it victory. The elders saw no need for change.

Thebes changed. Having learned from Sparta, it surpassed its masters. It raised a standing army of its own, a force known as the Sacred Band. Like the royal guard of the Spartans, the Band comprised three hundred men. Its uniquity arose from love. The Sacred Band was anticipated by Plato, who in his *Symposium* has this:

And if there was only some way of contriving that a state or army should be made up of lovers and their loves . . . then they would overcome the world . . . for who would desert their lover, or fail him in his hour of danger?

Three decades after the fall of Athens, and for the first time in living memory, a Spartan hoplite army was defeated in the field, a phalanx of a thousand broken by the Sacred Band – a force composed of one hundred and fifty homosexual couples. Four years later Thebes drove out its puppet rulers, and Sparta readied for war again.

For all that the Thebans had learned, their army was still outmatched. Their great leader – Epaminondas, of the House of Aigeidai – possessed only six thousand men. King Cleombrotus of Sparta marched with ten thousand. In Thebes there were signs and portents, the temples of the city all opening of their own accord, as if the gods offered their strength; but the signs in Sparta's favour were brutal in their simplicity. The triumph of the Sacred Band had been a minor oddity. Not for over four hundred years had anyone claimed victory against the full force of Sparta.

All began well for Sparta. Their army marched northwards unchecked, moving through the hills and capturing a Theban sea-fortress. With the taste of victory still fresh, Cleombrotus made for Thebes. By the road that led to Plataea – the place where they had once driven back an empire – the Spartans sighted their enemy. They camped near the village of Leuctra, and in the morning drew up their lines, the Thebans on the higher ground, the Spartans no fewer than eight shields deep, their cavalry edging ahead, their silent, red-cloaked phalanxes stretching for more than half a mile.

Not everything was as it seemed. Not every man in a red cloak – not even one man in a hundred – would have dared call himself Spartan. By the time battle was met at Leuctra, there were no more than fifteen hundred adult Spartans left alive. A hundred years of war, disease, earthquakes and Sparta's rigid laws had left the city with almost no men left to call citizens. So precious had those last become that only seven hundred had been sent to fight at their king's side. Those who swelled their ranks were the Edge-People of Lacedaemonia – the merchants, sailors and blacksmiths who were neither helots nor Spartans – with soldiers from Sparta's allies, and mercenaries from beyond, and even helots offered freedom if they would fight for their lives. And the riders edging out ahead, their mounts stamping at the dust of the plains – those men were hardly men at all, Sparta having little respect for anything but the phalanx, so that the Spartan cavalry was manned by the last of its boys, *By the least able-bodied of men.*

Nor were the Thebans as they seemed. Epaminondas began the day by sending away any man who did not have the will to fight. Those left to him were the veterans, men who had fought alongside and against the Spartans. His cavalry were skilled horsemen, raised to ride on the plains. And while the Spartans queued to kill in the manner of their ancestors – eight shields deep along the line, twelve where the king stood on the right – the Thebans had altered their ways. Epaminondas did not place his strongest men on his own right, as hoplite generals had always done, but set them facing Sparta's king, and ranked them not eight shields deep, or twelve, but fifty, with the Sacred Band at their cutting edge – the whole mis-shapen line withering along its length, all but the bulkhead holding back, as if most could not bear to fight, so that the Spartans did not face a phalanx like their own, but an army drifting away, its force all massed against one point, Cleombrotus, the Spartan king, *Like a trireme, with its spur on its prow.*

The Spartan horsemen rode out first, herding back onto the plains those men Epaminondas had sent away. It was then that the Theban riders attacked. The scattered Spartan cavalry was lost before their hoplites had begun to move, the orders from their king passing slowly along the thin red line. Their horsemen were thrown back into the spears of the Spartan phalanx just as the Theban bulkhead charged.

Around the king stood Sparta's greatest soldiers, its royal guard, its polemarchs and councillors; old men, trained all their lives for war. Against a force twelve shields deep they would have had no fears. Against fifty they had no chance. The Theban line broke them. Cleombrotus was dead before the army he had led had ever met its enemy. A thousand of his men were killed, and out of them, four hundred of the last living Spartan Equals.

Leuctra changed everything. To the traveller Pausanias it was *The most decisive battle ever fought by Greeks against Greeks*. But it was not Leuctra that destroyed Sparta for good. Epaminondas was not finished with Sparta yet. In the years after Leuctra he led his forces over the Parnon mountains, into the heart of Lacedaemonia. His armies had not come to fight. It was the helots they came for.

Epaminondas built them cities. In Arcadia his armies raised a capital where nothing had been. So massive were its features that the Greeks called it Megalopolis. The scattered peoples of Arcadia flocked to their new citadel. Epaminondas left them there, their love for him equalled only by their hatred for the Spartans who had ruled them for so long.

Westwards, beyond the Taygetos, lay the lost land of the Messenians, a people who had lived as captives for almost four hundred years. The Messene Epaminondas built them had walls thirty feet high and five miles in circuit, with towers all along its length, and an acropolis built into the fastness of the mountains. Nor did the invading army work alone. One by one, family by family, the captives of the Spartans came to rebuild for themselves a city that had not stood for thirteen generations. The face of Hellas was changed. The helots became Messenians again.

Sparta fought on for a few more years. Epaminondas fell on the battlefield, but Sparta was already dead. Perhaps it did not know it yet. The last of its Equals fought and fell. The enemy trod them underfoot into the mire of their own meat. The meadows of the Eurotas burned. The strong women of Sparta ran screaming into the streets. It must have almost seemed to them as if the Taygetos had been torn down. The gods they loved had failed them. The Spartan dream had been destroyed. And what did they put their faith in, then?

❧

What was Sparta, without its helots? It was a weapon rendered obsolete. It was a creature perfectly designed for worlds forever lost to it. It was a thing evolved to hunt and feed on one species of bird or fruit that had itself become extinct.

And what did Thebes gain in victory? What happened to the Sacred Band, which defeated the greatest army in the world?

Thebes became no more than a footnote between the rise and fall of powers greater than it would ever be. The old cities of Hellas had fought themselves to a standstill, grinding themselves into the dust of the plains. The brilliance of the Thebans was emulated and surpassed. Thirty-three years after Leuctra, Thebes was routed by Macedonians from the north. Only the Sacred Band held firm. Most of them died where they stood. After the battle, coming to the place where they lay, the king of the Macedonians wept, saying to those who stood with him:

Perish any man who suspects that these men ever did or suffered anything that was base.

The lovers of the Sacred Band never overcame the world. The Macedonians buried them where they had fallen, raising a monument to them in the form of a lion. But the monument was soon forgotten. The history of the Band became doubtful, uncertain, mythical.

In 1818 the monument was discovered. In 1879 the grave was unearthed. Two hundred and fifty-four skeletons were found there, laid together, in seven perfect rows.

IX

Burials

Have you found someone else?

It's not me. It's you.

He still dreamed of her. More mornings than not there was a trace of her. Nothing exact, just the warm sense of her and, under the warmth, the cold intimation of what he had done. Guilt, always guilt, ethereal and malignant as a shadow on an X-ray. He would find himself thinking of her as they dug, the past silencing him, cutting him off from the others.

He recalled what he had loved about her: loved about her still. Nessie. Nessie as herself but also as the sum of their parts, as the best and worst of them both.

Other, lesser things. The way Emine loved washing lines. Once, on the train to London, he had asked her what it was she saw in them, and she had laughed and told him he wouldn't understand. And then, as in other times and places with her, it was true that he had not understood, though he had tried. Maybe – he thought as he worked the earth – there had been something festive about them for her. The bright flags of skirts and festoons of underwear hung out in the sun. He could almost see that, though for him those domestic spectacles were embarrassing, exposed. *Common*, his mother would have said, peering down the neighbours' yards, her own washing safely away on racks and radiators.

The way she liked the smell of petrol, rolling the window down at service stations surreptitiously, as if it were a guilty pleasure. The way she flirted with old men as if it were good manners. The way she liked standing under trees in the rain. The way she hated talk of sex or money, so that at first he had thought her shy, had worried that she would be wary of sex itself.

Her body. The hollows of her neck. The hollows of the backs of her knees. The skin there, each cavity as taut and hot as a fontanelle. Almost feverish, the heat of her there. He had kissed her there in his sleep once. Not her breasts or her sex, but the backs of her knees. A ridiculous thing to do, awake or asleep. He had known nothing about it until the next morning, when she had told him, her eyes shining, as if he were suddenly glamorous.

He remembered the week they had spent in Ireland, in County Antrim, before the child, before even the marriage. It had been the summer holidays and Oxford had become oppressive with heat and tourists. They had got the hotel for next to nothing online. The first morning there had been a hammering at the door, the kind of heavy-handed knocking a policeman might make, and when he went to open it – alarmed, cold with sweat, pink coverlet wrapped around his skinny flanks, abruptly conscious of the Catholic girl in the bed behind him – there was nothing there but a trolley loaded with breakfast: smoked salmon and eggs Benedict under the tureens, potato farls in nicked steel racks, kiss-curls of butter. Ironed newspapers and a spray of wild roses; and nobody in sight, the whole thing seeming like an elaborate trick played by children or benign goblins.

Propped between the teapot and the cafetière was a card from the hotel, almost lost amongst the other freight: *Happy Honeymoon from all at The Hurdles!* They had debated sending the trolley back for as long as it took to look under the tureens, then had devoured it all.

Afterwards, sated and idle, they had been flicking through the papers when a bunch of flyers had fallen into Emine's lap. All were for local events – an outdoor evensong, a farmer's market – but it was the summer fair they fell for, the picture showing old carousels, a helter-skelter, traction engines. It was to be held all that weekend in a small market town on the far side of a nearby lake, only a few miles away as the crow flew. There were maps at the hotel reception, and they went down and planned the walk. Plotting with their heads together. It was eight miles by foot, though, and by the time they reached the place they were tired, soaked through by quick showers of summer rain.

And the fair had been gone. That was the thing he remembered. They had come round the corner to the village green – the Linen

Square, it had been called – and seen all the rides packed up to go. The carousels folded like gigantic umbrellas, the traction engines being loaded onto lorries backwards, like great four-square horses. Candyfloss trodden to mire on the worn-out grass.

They must have read the flyer wrong, they agreed, though their room had been cleaned by the time they got back, and they were never sure. Emine had cried on the way home, berating herself for doing so, insisting it hadn't mattered at all. But it had, somehow. The way their hopes had risen and then been defeated. It had felt terrible and ominous, as if they had been too late for their own wedding.

He remembered being in the house of his wife's lover. People were still arriving – familiar faces, faculty and college, delayed by the rain – but the rooms were already crowded with unseasonable flowers. There were girls in uniform leaning by the kitchen door, hired for the afternoon and already tired with boredom, waiting to wait on uncaring guests.

– You like them? Foyt asked, and for a disconcerting moment Ben imagined he meant the waitresses.

What was it he said in reply? The proliferation of flowers reminded him of funerals, the way cut flowers always did, but he wouldn't have told Foyt that. He was wishing he had come later or not at all. He was thinking that it had been a mistake, that seeing his wife and daughter wasn't worth this.

Why had he come? He must have been mad. He had thought of killing this man, had stood under the trees outside this house, one night, cold-faced and hot-hearted, and imagined the ways he would do it. He was thinking that it was her place already, even if she was keeping the apartment. Already she had begun to put her mark on her lover's home. She was there in her absence, in the disordered still lifes of the flowers, the kitsch elegance of the new/old twentieth-century furniture.

He was thinking all this, and in reply would have said nothing worth remembering.

– Emine bought them. Not much from the garden, this time of year.

Foyt reached across him to a vase of peonies, lifting the already-dying blooms on the tips of his fingers. They were standing together by the French windows. It was warm in the long room, the radiators turned up high. The professor was so close that he caught the smell of him, like sweet vinegar.

– Emine arranges them herself. Not quite to my taste, but there we are. She has this striking dislike of formality, doesn't she? Unusual in one of the Roman persuasion–

– Is she here? he asked, and Foyt looked up at him in apparent surprise.

– Of course. She'll be down later.

He looked towards the hall. Through the doorway he could see the first turn of the stairs. – Vanessa?

– Resting in the arms of Morpheus.

– I'd like to see them.

– Yes. This must be difficult for you. You look hot.

– I'm fine.

– Would you like to see the garden? The winter aconites–

– No.

– No, you don't like flowers, do you? Emine said. Stupid of me. A drink, then.

He took two glasses of wine from a passing tray, spilling one a little as he handed it to Ben. – I'm sorry. There, well. What shall we drink to?

– I don't really care. You choose.

He was a handsome man but small, so that he had to look up to meet Ben's eye. His voice was shy and his neck thin. A grey vein pulsed there.

– Alright. To Emine. I think I would like us to drink to Emine.

It's not me. It's you.

As if they were a comfort, he thought sometimes of all the other things she might have meant.

There had been the money. For some people that might have been fault enough. Emine liked money, was used to it, was adapted to its environment, and he had none. Even before she had entered the law her allowance had sustained them both. Her family owned a shipping company with fleets in Marseilles, Algiers and Istanbul, an old, declining business which had accumulated fortunes over the course of five lifetimes. Emine's father had taken well to Ben but friends of hers, he knew, had talked about him behind his back, had said that he lived off her. They had never been equal partners in those terms, but then there had never been much prospect of him attaining such an equality. And they had been complicit in it: if he had used her then she had allowed him to do so. She might even have liked it, he had suspected. The power it gave her and the hunger of his lack. The additive of that desire.

There had been her faith, or his lack of it. He had not been raised with the Church and had never had any cause to distrust religion, though he had never believed in anything much either. Her faith had been far stronger than his lack of it, and he had acceded to Catholicism as best he could; had been baptised, since it meant nothing to him and everything to her. That had been a mistake, of course. It had been harder to see the same done to Ness and to keep his mouth shut. He had not anticipated how it would rankle with him, that she should be claimed in that way before she knew her own mind. Marked; booked; brought to book. They had argued about it, and Emine had been angry, had stormed and wept.

And in other ways, too, he had not been faithful. It had happened three times in their years together. He would meet a woman whose need was a reflection of his own, whose desire was like a mirror. Each time he had been careful, and Emine had never given any sign of knowing. He could have done without any of them, if it had meant risking Emine or Ness, but they had talked about infidelity often, it had been one of the many What-Ifs, the things spoken of in the small hours, each looking not into the other's face but off into the confessional darkness.

He had been surprised to discover how much less than him she claimed to care about faithfulness. It meant less to her than their marriage and her own happiness. She was practical about it. If he slept with someone else she didn't want to know about it. What good would knowing do her? She loved him and wanted to be happy with him, even if it meant he had to lie to her. And he had respected that at least. He thought he had lied well.

Those were all reasons, but they were not reasons enough for Emine. She had divorced him against the grain of her faith. She would never marry again within the Church. She had said that he was a danger to her, body and soul. He had always known that it was Ness that she meant. First the What-If children and the One-Day children, then the child born after them.

When they had first met Emine had wanted four children. He had laughed at her then and had regretted it later. She was an only child of estranged parents, a Catholic father and a mother who had been a moderate Turkish Muslim by birth and Catholic by marriage and finally and passionately Muslim again. Her cousins were all on her mother's side and separated from Emine by the Mediterranean and her parents' mutual hostility. All through her childhood she had wanted siblings.

He had missed the moment when their roles had reversed. He had always liked the idea of family without having any ambition to be a father. He had agreed as he had agreed to much else; because it had made him happy to see her happy. If there had always been an anxiety when she had brought the subject up then he had only noticed it in retrospect. In retrospect, too, he had wondered if she had already begun to fall out of love with him then. She had stopped mentioning children, and when she began again it was to speak of the sense there might be in childlessness.

The first time he had discovered himself arguing for a family he had burst into laughter. They had been driving somewhere or other. He had tried to explain it to Emine, the way they had twisted round, but she hadn't found it funny, had told him to watch the road. And it hadn't been funny, of course, simply strange. He had been laughing at his own bewilderment.

It was later that day, when he was alone again, that the bewilderment had begun to crystallise into fear.

The night Nessie was conceived – certainly the night they both believed her to have been conceived – they had been to dinner with a colleague in London. It was May and hot, the Oxfordshire landscape acid-yellow with rape. The evening was one of duty rather than pleasure. They had both been working long hours that week and Emine drank too much in recompense.

Did he know what he was doing? He had to think so. He knew the chance and the mischance. He knew, when she prayed at nights, when the wishbone split her way, not what she wished for but what not. He knew what a vain and selfish hope it was, to wish for both conception and acceptance. That he would be forcing her, that he would be taking something she had denied to him: he had understood that.

He watched her all night, half a table away. Wanting nothing there but her, wanting her for good. He drove back through the sweltering London gloom while she talked in an effort to keep him awake, dissecting the evening, retelling bad jokes, laughing at embarrassments and petty misdemeanours. They were both tired on the way but the sight of home refreshed them.

They had made love before sleep, without protection – Emine had never been at ease with that – and easily inciting one another to desire, knowing one another as they did. But already something new had crept into it for him. A novel hunger.

Dimly, through the drink, he had thought it through again. Then he had begun to fuck her. He had raised her legs up over his shoulders, moving gently at first as her body adjusted. He remembered looking down into her dark eyes and seeing all the gentleness gone, the pupils huge and avid for him. Her own orgasm had been little and slow to break, muted by alcohol, but when he came himself he had almost fainted from the force of it. Old voices had come back to him in that state, London men boasting to one another.

I reamed her mate, I'm telling you. I slipped it up her sweet as that. I banged her up I swear, and oh my God you should have heard her singing . . .

He had come deep inside her, pushing desperately hard. He had put everything of himself into it. And as she had realised what he was doing she had tried to pull away, agile as a cat but not strong enough, and screaming all the while, *Ben Ben Ben!* as if he had scalded her.

In the aftermath he had been dazed by what he had done. They had talked half the night, in the dark, Emine exhausted and restless, pointlessly washing herself, kneeling above him in disarray, a silhouette against the window asking him what he had meant to do and why – why? – trying to understand him as he had tried to understand himself, raging one moment and weeping or laughing the next, but falling asleep finally in his arms.

It was not the last time they slept together, but certainly it was the last night they made love. In the morning she had been cold, and the coldness had never thawed. He had revealed an avarice in himself which could not be taken back or explained away. Besides, she had refused to speak about it again until the day she had left him. Sometimes it was almost as if it had never happened at all.

Several times, over the years, he had seen the vehemence with which she argued against abortion. He had never liked that in her, had hated the convictions which her beliefs instilled in her, but he had put his trust in them. It had shaken him when he came across the torn-up remains of an advice pamphlet, and much later a scribbled note of a doctor's appointment which she had never spoken of. It was a shock, to know not only that she was pregnant, but that she would ever have considered a termination. He had not known her decision until he woke another morning to hear her vomiting in the pre-dawn light. By then he couldn't quite believe that she would keep the child.

She had not let him be with her at the birth. She had named Nessie herself. Vanessa Catherine Alia Mercer. Emine had grown to love her as clearly as she had grown out of love with him. She had moved away from him perceptibly, inexorably, despite his best efforts to bring her back. It was as if what he had done were unpardonable, a crime, and he had known himself that it was, in a way, even if there was no name for it.

Loving lies, he remembered his mother saying of a girl in the street, four months gone the day she married. But that was different. That was not the same at all. *Rape* was a better name for it. From the Latin, *rapere*. To seize. To take by force. That was what he had done.

He had done it out of love for her. Out of the need to have her love him. And then – he had never known when or where – she had come across Foyt again, waiting for her. In the right place, at the right time. A famous man, faded but handsome. Secure. And old enough – as everyone said – to be her father, with his own children all grown and gone.

Monday he woke to the sound of rain. When he went to the window he could barely make out the streets and lots below. The swimming pool was a field of smashed safety glass. The reflections and multiplications of streetlights and brakelights were festive in the dark. A pink umbrella bobbed like a Chinese lantern from one awning to the next.

He got downstairs to find the lobby awash, the cockatoo screaming with girlish laughter, its left eye peering at the flood, dilating like a camera lens. Crossword and Sudoku were sweeping water from the courtyard into the street. They rested on their brooms to let him pass.

– What did I tell you?

Sudoku-Marina, grim and triumphant.

– What did I say, heh? *It rains!*

He waved a capitulation at her, hauling himself down the cascade of the steps. The van was outside, Chrystos leaning across to open the door. Again there was no Giorgios.

– My lazy brother gives you thanks.

– Why me?

– He thinks it's because you got sick he can sleep all morning.

– I wasn't *sick*.

– Sick or crazy, to walk in the rain. Either way, you make the director worry.

He sat back to hide his irritation. His mouth still tasted of last night's meal; cheap meat, cheap wine. As they pulled out he raised his voice against the thud of the wipers and the drumming of the rain. – So we're going up there? What for, if there's no work?

– Not up there. No work for us. For the sick boy the director has other ideas.

They turned right into Lycurgus Street. Ahead of them, towards Mystras, the foothills were all inkwash and watercolour. Just after the cathedral plaza they turned right again and stopped in a street of small shops. Chrystos pointed towards one. *Mavrakis Bakery & Imported Products*.

– Here.

– The director wants me to bake?

– Funny boy. Upstairs. Go to the side door, they'll be waiting for you.

– I'll see you tomorrow, then?

– Of course. Here, you forgot your souvenirs.

The HellaSpar bag. The martial clink of the tools inside. He shook hands and got out, ducking under the bakery's green awning as Chrystos drove away, his salute indistinct through the mottled glass.

The side door lay beyond the awning's submarine shelter. He ducked through a frill of rain and leaned on the buzzer, shouting his name twice into the unintelligible crackle of the intercom. By the time the door opened he was already drenched. He edged forward into an unlit hallspace, narrow stairs leading upwards into darkness, his feet squeaking on bare boards. The door at the top was ajar, a gamma of light showing. He pushed it open and went through.

A Formica table twice the length of a body. A stereo playing Radiohead to the audience of a human skull. Tupperwares, gigantic outsized tubs and kindergarten lunchboxes, their contents as indistinct as Chrystos's hand through the wet glass. A map of the ancient Laconian heartland, from Sparta down to Gythion. An aerial shot of Therapne on one wall, a Harris matrix facing it, the strata of the excavation reformed as diagrams. Electrics – a fridge, two laptops – murmuring to themselves in the shadows. The room's natural occupants – giant TV, davenport sofa, hatstand, smoked-glass coffee table – huddled around the far door, like refugees seeking asylum. An ouzo carafe full of spring squills. Two trays lined with silica gel, the spearhead in one encrusted with rust, the matter in the other riddled with verdigris. A laser scale, its twin red dots glittering on the fanned length of a shoulder bone. Natsuko bent over a microscope, her head raised, watching him.

A funny old bird, Missy had called her. She did not look funny to Ben. Frightened, maybe, frightened but brave. Righteous, too, like a cat discovered with a kill. Her eyes were like those of a deer, very dark and shaped like teardrops. He tried to think why she would ever be frightened of him, and then recalled the undelivered message, the day he had walked to Therapne. She must have imagined he would be angry, he realised, and then wondered if he was, and then why he was not.

– Hi, he said, too eagerly, making them both jump. Natsuko's voice lapped his own as faintly as an echo.

– Hi.

– Missy sent me. Doctor's orders.

– Oh!

He closed the door. It was ill-fitting: he could still hear rain blowing. – So, what do I do?

– Oh . . .

He wondered if her English had failed her, though he had heard her talking to the others in both English and Greek, laughing at Jason's jokes and jibes. If it wasn't that she had misunderstood him, it might be that she didn't know what to say to him.

– Is it just you here? he asked, and wished the words back as her shoulders drew together. She looked towards the far door and shook her head.

– Right. Well, I'll just. I'll put these down . . .

The hatstand was behind her. He dumped his stuff in the wiry corner by the computers instead. Another image of Therapne was tacked up in the shadows, a magnetometrical survey – the composition of the earth revealed in peacock-eyes of burnt orange and indigo – and he stood looking up at it as he shrugged off his wet jacket, trying to ignore the uncomfortable prickling of hairs on the back of his neck.

If he turned round she would already be at work again, he was sure, peeking into the otherworld of the microscope. But it felt as if she was watching him.

You're wet.

It was the first time she had said more than a word to him. As he turned he imagined that she was smiling; then he saw her and wondered why he had believed so. Her expression hadn't altered at all.

– A bit.

– No. Very.

– Well, it's pouring out there, you know. Cats and dogs, he added, angling for the smile, disappointed when she only blinked in incomprehension. – Doesn't matter. English saying. Anyway, here I am. You don't know what I'm supposed to be doing, then?

She shook her head, then reached up to tuck her hair back. She had gloves on, thin white ones, like a surgeon. For a long time – four seconds, five – she went on looking at him. She didn't seem especially frightened any more, only curious. Cautiously speculative.

Radiohead interposed themselves between them.

You're so very special
I wish I was special
But I'm a creep
I'm a weirdo
What the hell am I doing here
When I don't belong here?

– Eleschen will know, she said finally. What to do with you.

– Is she–?

– She is washing her hair.

– Oh, right.

– She has lice.

– . . . She has what?

– Lice. They like clean hair.

– I remember that.

– She is embarrassed about it.

– I won't mention it, then.

– No, don't.

Her face was guileless. If she was teasing him he couldn't be sure of it. If the three of them had been friends she might have been laughing at Eleschen. Except they were not that. Natsuko had avoided him since his arrival, after all, had barely spoken to him in a week. She wouldn't have shared anything with him at Eleschen's expense.

Lice. Nessie had had them, that last year, had cried inconsolably when he had used his mother's old nit comb on her. It was a children's affliction, to him. It wasn't something Eleschen would have, surely, nor something that Natsuko would share with him. Not with him, not so simply, after so many days of distance.

There were stools at the table, a scarred chrome-and-faux-leather set that looked like it might have been bought second hand from a twentieth-century cocktail bar. He perched.

– What are you up to, then?

She looked down at the microscope, as if surprised to find it there. – I am examining faecal deposits for intestinal parasites.

– Interesting.

– No. It is very *boring*, she said, and the smile broke through at last, her eyes diminishing to crescents.

Her front teeth were slightly crooked. She had a pock-mark on one temple, quite close to her ear. He only noticed it because her skin was otherwise perfect. He found himself remembering her morning swims. The slicked-back boy, loitering in the shadows. The gasp of breath that had echoed up to him, sometimes, as she turned between metronomic lengths. Her endless, effortless strength.

He leaned forward. – Is that true, about the lice?

– Yes.

– Are you laughing at me?

She shook her head again. The smile had gone. Her eyes were still on him, unafraid, but gauging him.

– No?

– No. Or.

– Or?

– Maybe a little.

The door behind her opened. He sat back, too quickly for it to seem incidental, not quickly enough for Eleschen to have missed it. She was dressed in a halter top and a bronze-brown hippy skirt, her face and shoulders still flushed from bathing, her hair turbanned in a ragged orange Disney towel. Wile E. Coyote chasing Road Runner upside-down around her scalp. One ear was free, pushed wide, elfin. She looked so different from the Eleschen of the dig – the Terminator shades and mountain boots – that he did a double-take, even though he had expected her.

She was smiling, mouth and eyes, the expression fading as she saw him. Deflating, as though she had hoped for someone else.

– What are *you* doing here?

– I don't know yet, he said, and, in a half-hearted effort to legitimise his presence, Chrystos brought me.

– Natsuko.

Her name was a reprimand, low with disappointment. Natsuko ducked her head.

– You were busy.

– Busy, right. Did you know it was Ben?

– The intercom is broken.

– So then it could have been anyone!

– But I'm not anyone. So that's alright.

Her eyes glided back to him, bluer than blue. The clothes made her look less American, somehow, more European, her eyes Austrian postcard skies.

– I suppose Missy thought I might help out . . .

– She didn't tell us.

– She didn't tell me. Look, I don't mind. I'll just take myself back to bed, I could do with the sleep, actually–

– No. She was rubbing her forehead, as if he were bringing on a headache. – No, don't be silly. You ought to stay, now you're here. Anyhow, it's raining.

– Thanks.

– Don't be cross. I didn't expect you, is all. Anyhow Stanton's right, you'll be useful. There's always too much for us. The guys don't like it. No mud or glory. Do you know your way around a lab?

– I should be able to get by.

Eleschen was talking over him, closing the door with a roll of her hip, tucking away that elfin ear, coming around the table to show him the cabinets, the computers, laying a proprietorial hand on the *memento mori* of the shoulder bone.

– Ask before you touch anything. We keep a lot in context, and we have the Findhut, but it's only got a padlock and we have to be careful. We keep the real treasure here, what there is of it, plus the database and paper trail. Too, we can do the basic measurements and chemical analyses. We send out for the hard-core tech, electron microscopy, X-ray microprobes. Stanton has us using Harris matrices, and she also has some new ideas on ceramic seriation and palynology . . . is any of this making sense to you?

It all made sense. She was talking fast, pressing him to fail, he thought, but it was elementary, a busman's holiday after the back-breaking week of excavation. He sat beside her, measuring and bagging finds, labelling them according to Missy's quirky system of annotation, adding tallies and entries to a ream of pre-existing notes, the two of them taking turns to weigh relics on a jeweller's electric scales.

All three of them wore the surgical gloves, as if they sat around an operating table. The Tupperwares lay open between them, their contents exposed to the anglepoise lamps. The parturient curves of amphorae. The butchered remains of animal bones. The lips of vessels.

Minute by minute the atmosphere eased. There was no talk beyond the necessary. The stereo was still playing, though the music had switched from Radiohead to something he didn't recognise, a wordless synthetic soundtrack, shallow and soothing.

The skylight brightened. He noticed it only when he sat back, needing to piss, and looking round saw the way it caught Eleschen's hair. Here and there a strand had escaped her turban. She sat utterly motionless, absorbed in the bones in her hands, but the breeze from the staircase caught the strands. It moved them as the sunlight illuminated them, burning them white as filaments.

She was beautiful. She was so beautiful that it made her almost asexual. Immaculate. There was no fecundity to her. It was hard to look at her, even to sit beside her, without dwelling on it. She was classically beautiful: Classically beautiful, like a statue carved from Pentelic marble. She had that paleness and those proportions.

He remembered learning – years ago – that the Hellenes had painted their statues. The lurid pigments had faded over the course of centuries. It was a discovery that had deeply disappointed him. It had seemed almost outrageous to him. As a boy he had believed that the ancient statues were perfect without adornment. Their austerity had been, for him, an inextricable element of their beauty. The features of gods and monsters, the dying and the victorious, all as unimpeachable as ice.

A shiver went through him. The lab was chilly, though he could hear the bakery workers moving around downstairs. He could smell the bread and feel the heat of the ovens through the floor. He wanted his coat, but it embarrassed him that the girls seemed so oblivious. It was cold enough that he could sense Eleschen's warmth, her arm an arm's width from his own.

There was a smell that rose from her, too, not of anything he would have expected – soap or skin or perfume – but a faintly unpleasant odour, a chemical rankness, and remembering the lice he glanced up straight into Natsuko's chiding eyes.

– Do you think I sound French? Eleschen said abruptly, and Natsuko broke off the gaze.

– French?

– When I speak Greek. My accent. Themeus says I sound like the French. Do you think so?

– I didn't notice. What did he think–

– He was just trying to flatter her. He is one of Eleschen's *admirers*, Natsuko said, eyes brimming with amusement, and Eleschen *tsk*ed.

– I don't see why you're so jealous. I'm sure you have admirers too. Don't you think she has admirers, Ben?

He floundered under their attention. Their laughter, when it came, was almost a relief.

– Ben, you're squirming!

– I'm just a bit cold.

– Sure you are. We're just teasing. Just having fun. So, anyway. Eberhard says you're at Oxford?

– More or less.

– Do you like it there?

– Not really.

– No? I always thought it sounded nice. Ivory towers. Tea and crumpets. Romantic evenings round the bar heater.

He cleared his throat, still uncomfortable with the conversation, though he had wanted it, had been hoping for the past hour that one of them would talk to him again.

– It has its ups.

– Oh, she said, as if an intermittence of *ups* were a disappointment. Then, – Do you like doing this?

– What?

– When we have all the pieces washed and laid out and we're getting to understand them, putting them back together, don't you love it? It's the most incredible thing. It's a jigsaw puzzle, except puzzles don't mean anything and this does.

– I do think of it like that, he said, Sometimes, but she pursed her lips and laughed, as if he left her unconvinced.

– Well I do, all the time. I remember the first time I did something like this. Like archaeology. We were playing near the highway, where we weren't supposed to be. I found this doll. She was one of those wind-up models. She had a pretty dress and a string in her chest and when you pulled the string she cried like a baby. I guess some little girl had dropped her out of a car. I was little enough to still have dolls too, but I knew my parents wouldn't let me keep this one. She was . . . well, old and dirty, but I wanted her. I hid her out by the water tower. Whenever I wanted to play with her I went out there. I thought a lot about the other little girl. I wanted to know who she was, how come she lost her doll. There was no label I could see. I decided to take her apart. I thought maybe there's something inside that would say where she was from. I stole a knife from home and some dressmaker's scissors and I cut her open. And inside there was this thing.

She stopped. She was frowning but still smiling, as if she had begun the story for her own amusement, and now discovered it to be less than satisfactory in that regard.

– What thing? Natsuko said, and Eleschen roused herself and shook her head at them.

– A record player. It was in her chest. It was right behind where the string went in. You don't believe me but it's true. There was this tiny turntable and a record and a needle. The record was about the size of a nickel and it was real rusty. We didn't have a record player but I knew what they were. When you pulled the string the record played the sound of the baby crying. It was strange seeing it there. It felt like I had cut her open and there was a heart inside. And on the record there were numbers and a name. It said *Anna*. And you know, for the longest time I really believed that that was the name of the little girl. But of course it wasn't. It was the doll's name. It was just the name the makers gave the doll.

She stopped. In the silence that followed Natsuko stood up, knelt down, and from somewhere under the table brought out a thermos.

– I have some tea.

– Is it Japanese? Eleschen said, and Natsuko nodded. – Not for me.

– It's good for you.

– I said I don't want any.

A look passed between the two girls, their mutual regard cool and intimate and beyond those things incomprehensible to him.

– Ben?

He drank the tea. He could feel them both half-watching, could half-see them doing so, in the uncertain periphery of his vision.

– So, Eleschen said, Ben, are you from there? Oxford?

– London.

– You're lucky. That must be exciting.

– El is from Athens, Natsuko said, and Eleschen laughed.

– Not the real one! Athens, Hicksville. America's full of them, and Spartas too. I wasn't from there anyhow, I was just studying there. Politics and anthropology, plus some music on the side. A regular Da Vinci, that's me. I don't know what I was thinking. I wanted to learn everything I could find back then, I was just grabbing everything I could. That was before I knew what I really wanted to do with my life. So how come you're here? I mean if you're at Oxford?

– I'm taking time out. A deferment.

– How long for?

– It depends.

– On what?

– On things, he said, clumsily evasive. He soldiered on, wanting to deflect the conversation rather than out of any real interest. – What about Eberhard?

– Eberhard?

– Did he defer too?

– How would I know? she asked pettishly, and not waiting for an answer – disinterested, bringing the subject to an end – picked up the bone in front of her. – Laco is bugging me. I don't get her.

– Who's Laco?

She pointed the bone at the skull.

– Ben, Laco, Laco, Ben. It's a stupid name, it's meant for a dog but Jason chose it and it stuck. This is the skeleton Max found.

He took the armbone from her. He weighed it lightly on both palms, a slender human relic. It was unexpectedly heavy.

– You don't notice anything?

– I don't know. It's quite large, compared to the skull–

Eleschen smiled coolly, as if she had told a riddle which he had solved too easily.

– You're warm. Try again.

He looked at the skull. Now that he did so properly he could see that its balance was subtly off. The teeth, the mandible and the skunt bones of the face were all normal, full-grown. It was only the cranium that was wrong. The vault that had once held a brain was too narrow, too low. He must have been aware of it, he realised, to have thought that the ulna was too large in comparison.

– She's deformed, isn't she?

– Right. Her brain case is too small, poor dear. Her brain will have been too, of course. She's near enough to average that she probably got by. She must have looked normal at birth or she wouldn't have been allowed to live. Guess why.

The blue of her eyes had turned fierce, not angry but challenging again.

– Something genetic, I suppose–

– Hah! Nope! Last chance, wise guy.

He shrugged, happy to concede, happier when Eleschen smiled, the ferocity vanishing instantly.

– It's mercury. She's full of it. The deformity means she was exposed in the womb, but the traces are so strong when she died that she must have been poisoned again in childhood or adult life. Mercury's horrible. It's indestructible, the body's really bad at getting rid of it, and it's more toxic than arsenic. Not that Laco knew that. That's what I don't like. Laco shouldn't know about mercury. She's over three thousand years old. The Chinese and the Egyptians were using mercury back then, in medicines and burials, but not the Greeks. If there was natural mercury up at the site, like cinnabar, then maybe she might have gotten it that way, but no one's ever found that. So Laco doesn't fit. She's going to make us all look really stupid. That's what's bugging me.

– Maybe she's important. I mean, if they were using mercury in Egypt, it's not so far–

– I just don't understand her. She's a surprise. I hate surprises.

She put the armbone down. Her eyes lingered on it. She was rubbing the fingers and thumb of one gloved hand together, absently, as if recalling the poison in the bone.

– Understanding is a funny word, isn't it?

– In what way?

– I mean funny strange. It's what we look for and what we do. We go down into the past in order to look up at the present. We only understand it when we stand under it.

She smiled at him sideways. Her teeth were even, stainless, perfect. – Don't you think so?

– I never thought about it, he said, and realising it, You sound like Eberhard.

She made a face. – Like I'm that smart.

– But you do, he said, I mean you are; but she had gone back to her work, and he returned unwillingly to his own tasks before pushing his stool back to stand.

– Washroom's through there, if that's what you want. Watch out for the roaches. We think it must be the bakery. Anyhow we can't get rid of them.

He saw no roaches, though he heard their faint skitter as he opened the door. He peeled off his gloves, relieved himself, splashed water on his hands and face, and didn't register that he was hearing more than two voices until he was already opening the laboratory door.

Jason craned round to look at him from the sofa. Eberhard was still standing by the stairwell. All four of them were talking at the same time, and all stopped as he came in.

– Hello, he said into the silence, and for a moment it seemed that no one would answer before Eberhard nodded and began unbuttoning his coat.

– How are you, Benjamin?

He closed the door behind him. The things he had imagined Eberhard saying came back to him in a rush that he pushed away, out of memory.

Why is it that you followed me?

– I'm alright. It's just Ben, by the way.

– Ben it is. You're finding things–?

– Fine.

– Good, good. I'm glad you're settling in.

He smiled as if he believed it. Eleschen was avoiding his eyes. Natsuko was hunched over her papers, as if trying to make herself as inconspicuous as possible: an animal flattening its ears. Jason was still smiling up at him, the expression hungry.

He edged between them to his place. There were two more tubs of pottery to be sorted, eight fragments of a wine-mixing bowl and a dozen pieces of white clay with a scribble burnish, significant in their age and foreign origins. Each potsherd bore a dot of nail polish on its inner surface, a provisional marking: blue glitter on the mixing bowl, coral pink on the white clay. He wondered abstractedly which make-up belonged to whom as he picked up one of the latter and let it settle on the scales, digits flickering on the display.

– You've been making friends, I hear, Eberhard said, his voice disembodied, still somewhere behind him.

– Have I?

No one seemed surprised that he sounded surprised.

– Dr Stanton seems to think so.

– Yes, she's good company. You don't seem to like her much.

– We like her well enough, Eberhard said, coming round, leaning by the computers, watching him work. Freed from the excavation he was dressed as he had always been at Oxford, his ironed casualware putting years on him. – And the Maxis brothers, you seem friendly with them also.

– Chrystos, anyway.

– Not Giorgios?

– Not so much, he said, and Jason made a sound, *tcheh*, halfway between a snigger and a sneer. – What?

– Nothing.

– It doesn't sound like nothing, he said, and looked up, knowing what Jason's expression would be – secretive, satisfied – before he faced it.

– You should be careful about the friends you choose.

– Why, what's wrong with them?

– Depends who you ask.

– He did not ask you, Natsuko said, but Jason's voice overrode hers, rising into an ostentatious, rhythmical oration.

– *You are old, Father Giorgios, the young man said, and your beard is incredibly white. But you fought in the war and we don't know who for. Tell me, sir, do you sleep well at night?*

– What does that mean?

– Nothing, Eleschen said tersely. Jason's just being idiotic as usual. He'll go away if you ignore him.

A lull. Jason lounging back on the davenport, infuriatingly pleased with himself; Eberhard opening the mail, a pile of parcels from the Fifth Ephorate of Prehistoric and Classical Antiquities. Some small talk about the possibilities for lunch, the chat passing around him as if he were no longer there. The stereo was still playing, though the music had changed again to a track with heavier bass and a more insistent beat. Eleschen leaned over and switched it off.

– Anyway, he said doggedly into the silence, He's not that old.

– No?

– No, not nearly. Come on, he can't be more than fifty. He wouldn't even have been born then.

– When?

– In the war.

– Which one?

– Which one did you mean?

– Not the one you reckoned, obviously. You know, I reckon you could be smart if you listened a bit harder.

– Jason.

– There have been a few, and they don't all end happily ever after, not here. Here, some of them don't end at all.

– *Jason.*

– What?

Eleschen picked up a sheaf of notes, walked over to the sofa and dropped the papers in Jason's lap. – Leave him alone. If you're that bored you can do some work.

Delicately, as if they were corrupt, Jason put the papers aside and stood, stretching.

– I'll pass. Looks like I'm out of a job anyway, now you've got Ben. It's all so cosy with Ben here, isn't it? Like a thriving cottage industry. Come on, let's go. Eb? he said, and Eberhard nodded again, his bespectacled gaze moving from Ben to Natsuko and on to Eleschen.

– You're not coming for lunch?

– Not today.

– But you'll come tonight.

– Not too early.

– Alright.

– Phone me before. We'll have to change.

– Of course. Goodbye, Ben. Until tomorrow.

The street door slammed behind them. He went back to work, methodically placing fragments on the scales. He cleaned the provisional marking from each shard as he catalogued it, dabbing it with polish remover and cotton wool. Hot pink, blue glitter.

In the hush he could feel his heart going, still overclocked with adrenaline. Pointless to be angry. He had known that Jason disliked him. He had suspected it all week, ever since the afternoon in the car. It should have come as no surprise.

It wasn't Jason he should be angry with. It should be all of them, even Eleschen. Even Natsuko.

The computers had gone quiet, the trickling of their processes as soft as those of egg-timers. There was almost no sound at all from Eleschen and Natsuko. It felt to him as if they were embarrassed, by him or by themselves. He kept his gaze on the scales and the inventory beside them, the core list of the lost and found.

CATALOGUE SECTION 5: SMALL FINDS (ARTEFACTUAL, FAUNAL, PALAEOENVIRONMENTAL)

AREA G

Context 0212:

#019-028: MH butchery debris.

#029: MH partial prismatic blade.

Context 0211:

#105: LH2 drilled lentoid seal-stone. On one face an intaglio of a Gorgon.

They worked on through the afternoon. There was little more talk, and what passed for conversation was desultory and nondescript, as if the morning had been a mistake or had never happened at all. At two Natsuko went downstairs and came back up with three pastries, greasy parcels of spinach and cheese still hot from the oven, bringing Ben his in silence, without meeting his eyes, with no more than a nod to his thanks.

They finished after five. Natsuko went first, putting on her hat and coat and leaving quickly, as if afraid that Ben would try and go with her. Eleschen stayed behind to turn off and lock up, so that he ended up going down into the street alone.

There was still an hour of daylight left. The sky was full of cloud again, but there was no more rain. The wind had picked up in its wake. It was blowing old leaves up into the trees, as if time were running backwards.

Long Hearth. He was squatting by the open hole, Indian style, keeping more or less dry, the brothers below him lost in their work, when he glanced up and saw Max looking as strange as he ever had.

The brow of the knoll half-obscured him. His habitual slouch was absent. He was very still, his face downturned. The land fell away so sharply beyond him that he seemed to be balancing, as if nothing but his concentration kept him from falling away towards the river.

Giorgios's voice came up to him, a muffled muttering command, and for a while there was work to do, buckets to be hauled, a mattock to fetch. Then he was unemployed again, and when he looked back Max was still there, still standing motionless over his excavation. He had moved around the Skull Room, though the adjustment was almost imperceptible. He seemed to be looking at the same spot as before.

He got up, his calves protesting. Max made no acknowledgement if he heard him come up at all. He was staring between his feet. His head was cocked slightly to one side. The hole in which he stood was an inverted ziggurat, the broad floor of the

Mycenaean room cut out in the middle to reveal its foundations; the largest of the foundation stones – two solid slabs of schist – laid carefully to one side, revealing a shaft grave beneath. Laco's bones lay exposed. Her skeleton was almost complete. They had removed nothing except the ulna and the skull. Her hands were clenched into fists.

As Ben reached him Max knelt, sniffed at the dirt, stood again.

– What's wrong?

Max shrugged. He was still frowning at the pit floor. – Something is buried here.

– That's good, isn't it?

That earned him a look, quick and disparaging. He recalled the way Missy talked about Max, her admiration edged with envy. He was a natural archaeologist, his talents as uncanny as those of a water diviner. He could see colours and patterns in the earth – the telltale signs of subterranean metals and structures – as if the topsoil obscured nothing. He had discovered the Skull Room where none of the technologies had done so. None of the others had believed him, at first, but he had insisted. He had simply seen the room's outline one morning in the lie of the dew.

– Is it important? he said, and Max scratched his shaven head.

– Maybe.

– Something buried with Laco–

– No. This is something new.

– Newer than what? he asked, but Max was no longer listening, seemed to have exhausted his limited capacity for polite conversation. Already he was down on his hands and knees, his face inches from the damp clay, like a man praying towards Mecca. Only when he rolled back on his heels did Ben hear that he was still muttering, to Ben or to himself.

– . . . Not yesterday. Before the rain. But it is hard to tell.

– Can I help? he said, wanting to, curious and eager, anyway, to prove himself not as foolish as he must already seem; and Max glanced up at him and away, uphill towards the others. No one was in sight except Themeus. His accent was stronger when he grimaced.

– Why not?

– What do you need?

– A trowel. A sharp one.

He went and fetched his Iowan gift. When he got back Max was already digging with a trench shovel, and Themeus was leaning over him inquisitively. Max took the fresh blade and went back to work.

He craned in closer. Firmly, delicately, Max was combing back the dirt. Silt clung to the blade. It reminded him of something, and after a moment he realised it was the nit comb. His own hands making that same motion, running the teeth through his daughter's hair. The dust of the eggs holding to the steel.

The dirt came away easily. Too willingly, as if it had already been turned. He wondered if that was what Max had noticed, and then what could have been buried there. The site had been untouched for three days. Something illicit, maybe; something stolen. But it was a long way from anywhere, Therapne, and any local would know that foreigners were working there.

It came to him abruptly that it could be something more dangerous, guns or bombs, and thinking that he took a half-step back, just as Themeus gave out a smiling exhalation – *Ah!* – and there under his own Marshalltown blade was fur – lush, wet fur – and in it, a single unblinking eye.

– What is that?

Max shook his head. He paused, staring back at the eye, then went on with his excavation. The body of the thing in the pit was long but curved around itself, elegantly self-contained, like a cat by a fireside. At first it seemed perfect to Ben, unhurt, and for a moment he wondered if they had dug up some hibernating animal: then he saw that the eye was not dark at all, but wholly absent, the socket full of rusty blood.

Beside them Themeus giggled. – *Laghos.*

– What's that?

– He says it's a hare.

– What's it doing here?

If anyone knew they didn't stop to tell him. Themeus was turning away, his teeth white in his wide dark face as he called his cousin's name, *Elias, Éla, Éla!* Whistling him over.

Elias was a head shorter than Themeus but older, less prone to excitement or susceptible to laughter. He stepped down into the Skull Room, hunkered down beside Max, nudged the bigger man aside.

– *Laghos.*

– *Eh.*

He pushed at the carcass with the heel of one hand, muttering to his cousin. Their Greek was strange, the language striated with alien grammars and intonations. Then, – Please give me this, Elias was saying to Max, his English unexpectedly clearer than his native tongue, his gesture indicating the trowel, and receiving the blade he hunched forward, turning the hare's long cheek with the point, his own head cocked critically, like that of a builder or a sculptor.

He touched the creature's neck with the blade – as if checking one last time for death, though Ben could smell it now, the potent reek of its rot – then pressed the trowel into the clay. For a minute he sawed and chopped, working at the wet packed soil. Finally he turned his head and took a breath, then lifted the body out.

It uncurled as it came away. Its underside lay torn apart. The raw blue meat lay bare. Bones jutted through the braids of guts.

– *Hah!* Elias said, and sat back, wiped his hands, propped Ben's trowel upright in the sod, and grinned at all and sundry, like a detective who has found the murderer's identity.

– *Tsakal?* Themeus said, and Elias shrugged, pushed out his lips, and echoed him.

– *Tsakal.*

– What's he saying? Jason said, and looking back, Ben saw them all gathered around. Jason and Eberhard, Natsuko and Eleschen, Chrystos and Giorgios, with Missy peering anxiously between them. Eleschen shook her head.

– I'm not sure. I think he said–

– They say it is an animal. Chrystos, under his breath. – Maybe a wild dog. Maybe something that is more trouble. There is an animal like a little wolf. Sometimes they do this with their meat. It is a long time since they came round here. Themeus says that two nights ago their people heard them. They believed it was maybe just dogs, but these things do not sound like dogs. Nothing sounds like this animal. In Greek we call it *tsakal*. You know it?

– No, Jason was saying, but Eleschen was nodding wordlessly. And suddenly it came to Ben too, a rare thrill of understanding going through him, electrical, as he crouched beside the coil of the hare, privy to its secrets.

– Jackal, he said. He means jackal.

ᘓᘐ

– *Canis aureus*.

– Golden dog.

– Golden jackal. El looked it all up back at hers. She might be along.

– Not the others?

– They're busy. Giorgios says they used to be like rats, but the farmers pretty much wiped them out. They go for the lambs and kids. Real kids, too. There were two children killed. It was a long time ago but you know how it is. People still talk.

– How come they bury things?

– Dunno, I don't think El got that far. Dogs do it with bones, don't they? Or is that just in the comics?

Late night. Jason and Ben, drinking Metaxa in the Hard Rock Café. For an hour they had been working their way down through the grades. Seven star, five star, three.

– What happened to four and six?

– Stanton, probably.

– Does she drink?

– Doesn't she just. The mantle lies heavy. Max wants to look for them.

– We could try HellaSpar, if they're still open.

– Not the brandies, you muppet, the jackals, Jason said, leaning through the background music. – Max doesn't think they'll be far. Up in the hills, maybe. Max knows that kind of thing. There are caves up there like you wouldn't believe.

He had been at the hotel, watching a satellite film, shoes off, shirt off, lights out, when Jason had come for him. There had been a banging at his door and when he had opened it Jason had almost fallen through.

So. How's Shovelmonkey Number Ten this evening?

Tired. Knackered. What do you want?

Lazy monkey. Knackered is for nags. Tired is for wimps. Come on.

Where?

Out. You need a drink and I need another.

They had found a snug at the back of the bar, a dim pool of light between claggy Naugahyde banquettes, cut off from the evening crowd by music and shadow, Jason shouting to be heard over the endless medley of U2 and AC/DC, resplendent in a scarab-green shirt and Eurotrash shades, his eyes straying to the girls on the dance floor, the diminutive body-built barman eyeing him with extreme prejudice each time he went up for more drinks.

– Another?

– Not for me.

– Come on, it's your round, and Oddjob likes you. He pours mine short, cheeky fucker.

– Why's that, then?

– Don't look at me. There was a ruck last time we were in here, some biker boys from Kalamata. It's not like I had anything to do with it. I was just a bystander.

He got the drinks, avoiding the gyrating crowds and the barman's gimlet eye – he poured short for Ben too when it came to it – and lined them up beside the empties. Jason raised his tumbler.

– To *Canis aureus*.

– The golden jackal. So why does Max want to look for it?

– Oh come on. Rabbits we could poach in Essex. This is different. This is real hunting.

– You didn't say he wanted to hunt it.

– What did you think I meant?

– Is that legal? he said, and Jason laughed.

– You need to get out more. Rabbits aren't exactly legal either. Eb and Max are the only ones with licences. The thing is, one, this isn't England. People don't go soft about animals round here. And two, the farmers hate rabbits the same way they hate taxes; and three, everyone hates the jackals, and last but not least – no one cares if you break the law anyway. They only care if you get caught. That's the way it's always been here. The Spartans were the same.

– And if you're caught?

– Caught at what? Everyone knows we go hunting already. If we don't get the jackal somebody else will. Come on, don't tell me you're not curious?

He sat back with his drink. Was he? He felt something. A double-edged excitement. An uneasy urging. Not curiosity in the hunt half so much as in hunting with them. And not curiosity so much as . . . what?

Gratitude. That was it. He was grateful to be asked. He recoiled from it out of pride, but had no doubt of it.

– Anyway, it doesn't matter. I'd be useless.

– Why?

– I've never fired a gun in my life.

– Yeah? Well that's the thing about guns, it's easy. All you have to do is point. So?

– I'll think about it.

– Suit yourself, Jason said, and then he was looking away, the invitation to join them already forgotten; perhaps revoked, if it had been an invitation at all; his attention drawn back to the dance floor, two girls there leaning close to converse as they moved to a slow syncopation.

A sense of regret filled Ben, a disappointment in himself, as if he should have given a different answer; as if he had missed a chance he wouldn't have again, and feeling that he thought of Emine and Ness, five weeks and half a continent away, their lives still going on without him, otherworldly, transmarine.

One of the girls was smiling at them, whispering to her friend, shaking her head. *Don't look. Don't look!* When Jason finally sat back he was grinning, the expression altering as his eyes ran over Ben.

– What's that, then?

He looked down. Somehow he had his wedding ring on. It had been in his coat pocket again. He must have been worrying at it, as he so often did when Oxford or his family were at the back of his mind. The gold was blood-heat, though he had no memory of manipulation.

– When's the big day?

– Funny.

– Yeah, it is. I was just thinking we might do some hunting here, offhand, and then you would've had to have said something. Except you did, didn't you? You let your fingers do the talking. What's her name?

– Emine. We're divorced.

– Since when?

– Since I left.

– Right. I'm sorry, he said, and Ben was about to say thanks, the word jogged loose in surprise at Jason's sympathy, when he ploughed on. – So, what are you, cock or cunt?

– *What?*

– Did she make a cock out of you? Or was it the other way round?

– It's not heads or tails.

– No? My old man's been divorced three times. My mum was number two. He's got a picture of Henry VIII in the garage next to the calendars and the road maps and he looks more like that fat knobhead every time I see him. Funny thing is though, no one ever kicks him out. My mum still carries a candle for him. It's the same every time. He's the one who leaves.

– It's not like that. It's not that simple.

– Suit yourself, Jason said, and then, almost imperceptibly over the bar noise, *Cunt*, so that for a moment the dislike came flooding back, as if they hated one another, though they didn't, when it came down to it. He had been wrong about that.

– What about you, then?

– Me? What do I look like to you?

– A shovelmonkey, he said, and Jason's eyes glittered in the mean red tint of the lights.

– Takes one to know one. But you're right. I've been living off digs for years. Somewhere hot every winter and then back to Europe with the swallows for the summer. I haven't been home in a long time. Never liked it anyway. Nasty little country. I've seen the world. Plenty of women in this line of work too. I get fucked off with the hotels and the factor thirty greasepaint and the spadework, but I never get tired of the women. Just look at us. I mean us lot. I don't know which way to look half the time. What about you?

– What about me?

– Which way do you look? I mean, you're divorced, so who would you go for? Given half a chance. Which you don't have, by the way, any more than I do.

It was unnerving, the degree to which the others took him back to the past. Jason reminded him of the London markets, the raucous, rookish closeness of the men and boys there: but they all reminded him of the politics of childhood. The strange alliances, the unlikely allegiances. The playground laws and interrogations. Questions with no right answers. What football team, which TV show, which neighbourhood. *Friend or foe?*

That was the trouble with Jason. It was as if they had been friends all the time and had only forgotten it for a while. As if friendship could slip the mind. That was what he still distrusted: the hand offered a second time.

– I haven't thought about it, he said, and Jason leaned across the table, creaking obscenely on the red banquette.

– Oh come on, don't be shy. Don't be silly. You're not queer so it's one or the other. Natsuko or El. Or Stanton. I wouldn't put anything past you.

He took off the ring, put it away. He should have got rid of it. He should sell it. But Sparta was too small. Someone would hear of it before too long. He remembered the gypsy woman in the ruined doorway, the day he had walked to Therapne in the rain, and then thought of Elias and Themeus. For all he knew they were family. What was it Chrystos had said?

– *You know everyone.*

– *Of course. Everyone knows everyone, here.*

– It's none of your business, he said to Jason.

– You are shy, aren't you? Listen, I'll tell you something for free. Natsuko creeps up on you. Face like a shitsu, arse like an angel. She's up for it too.

– How do you reckon that?

– Those T-shirts. *All This And My Daddy's Rich*. Loaded too. They all are, aren't they?

– Who?

– The Nips.

– She doesn't look like a shitsu.

– Oh doesn't she? Jason said, softly, and then Eleschen was beside them, standing over them like a Valkyrie, her hair in wet ribbons, her face gleaming triumphantly.

– Gods, I forged rivers to get here!

– It's raining *again*?

– Like Genesis. Who wants what?

– I think they're already closing up.

– Bollocks! Where's Oddjob? There he is. He's paid for it, see, he'll be here all night. You can rely on Oddjob, I'll say that for him. I'll have a seven star.

– Ben? she said, and he had the same.

Missy was calling for them. It was a fine day, the wind light and silent, and her voice carried her alarm clear over the hills.

When they found her she was kneeling by a row of Calabrian pines, east of Elijah's chapel, where the ridge fell to a shepherds' path. It was an out-of-the-way place, beyond and below the Therapnean heights. She had gone there to look for new findspots, but instead of the superterranean dips or knolls or lines of vegetable growth that might have marked underground ruins, she had come on freshly dug earth. A small disturbance by the wood's edge, the resinous turf of the pines turned and bared.

They were less careful digging this time, knowing what it was they would find – not gold or bronze, but meat and bone – or knowing at least the essence of what it would be: it was still a shock to see it uncovered, the first wing unfolding as it came free.

– Magpie, Ben said, and behind him someone echoed its name in Greek; and someone else exclaimed wordlessly, as if it was not a carcass they had found but buried treasure. Helen herself.

– One for sorrow, Eberhard said, his voice surprised as Missy turned her blade. The bird's feathers were untarnished, the wings green-black and white, lustrous as ivory and obsidian.

The light was good that evening, and they worked later than they had done before. Afterwards he walked up to the North Hill, looking towards the Parnon mountains. The sunset was creeping over them, but here and there were dark pockets ahead of it. From where he stood they all looked like caves, though most would be open rifts or ravines. There seemed to be thousands of them.

There are caves up there like you wouldn't believe.

He almost expected to hear them. The golden jackals. Their howling would be like that of wolves, he thought, though he had never heard wolves howl, not in the flesh. It would be like that but higher, less rooted. More ethereal.

Nothing. Only the voicings and belling of the goats, and the sound of someone toiling up towards him. He looked back as Missy reached him, hands in pockets, a thermos tucked under her arm.

– Hey! How are you doing? Want some coffee? she said, and passing him the thermos, I haven't seen so much of you lately.

– All work, no play, he said, and she laughed, though he didn't think he had earned it.

– Seems like you're fitting in great.

– Am I?

– Sure. You're good at this. And I mean the others like you. You're working out well. So what do you think? Are they up there?

He shrugged and shivered. It was colder as the sun went down, and the wind was picking up.

– It's just so weird, the way they bury those things–

They both turned at the scratch of the lighter. Jason was trudging up beside them. His face was wicked in the cupped glow of a cigarette.

– Jason, do you have to smoke all the time?

– It's just a fag.

– It's so bad for you.

– I'm doing it for charity. Cancer Research. Sponsored smoke.

– That's so not funny. And those are *so* rank.

An edge of plaintiveness had crept into her voice. It made her seem less like the woman he had got to know, more like the voice he had heard on the phone before his arrival. *I tell them all to call me Missy, but no one ever does.*

He saw Jason shift sideways, closer to her, like a cat that has found someone with an allergy. – Made in America, look. You're a Carolina girl, aren't you? Tobacco country, yeah? It's your neighbourhood duty to sponsor me.

He felt Missy bristle beside him.

– I thought you were on the Skull Room?

– So?

– So if you were, you didn't get a tarp down on Laco. Didn't I tell you about that before? You're the senior guy down there, Jason. Max might be a genius but he doesn't have your experience. If it rains tonight–

– It isn't going to rain, any idiot can see that. We did the tarp anyway.

– That's funny, because it wasn't there two minutes ago–

– Alright, alright. Jason stuck his cigarette in his mouth, his habitual grin transmogrified into a grimace.

– Tamp it down, Mister! Missy yelled after him, but he was already gone, walking away westwards, a gangly silhouette with the wind tugging at his faded shirt-tails, a Shaggy stepped out of *Scooby Doo* and befouled by the real world. Missy slumped, the air going out of her with a hiss: *Yess.*

For a while they stood without talking. It wasn't a comfortable silence to Ben, though Missy didn't seem to notice it. When he looked back he could still see Jason in the distance, below the stark ruins of the Menelaion, waving one arm in angry gesticulation.

He unscrewed the flask, poured a cup of Greek coffee – he could smell its sweetness in the cold air – and held it out to Missy.

Did you want some?

She took the cup.

– You don't like him.

He said it only to make small talk, but when Missy turned to stare at him it was as if she had forgotten his presence and was affronted to find him there.

– What?

– Jason. Sorry. It seems like you don't like him much.

– Quit apologising, will you? God.

– I meant, he began, and stopped himself with an effort. Missy made a sound in the back of her throat, somewhere between a laugh and a groan. After a while she passed him back the coffee cup. He had drained it, was running his thumb round the rim, fitting it back in place, when she spoke again.

– You're way off. Way off. I can look after myself.

– I didn't mean that.

– I mean it's not like we're here to *like* each other. This isn't some beach vacation. Cyriac wants results. I don't care what anyone thinks of me, as long as they dig.

Her voice was vehement, but the plaintiveness was still there. He wondered at that, the odd jar of assurance and doubt.

– Why wouldn't they like you? he said, carefully, not wanting to say the wrong thing again, trying not to mean anything by it beyond the question itself, so that he was surprised when she turned to look at him, her face softened in the dusk.

– Thank you, Ben.

– For what?

– For the nicest thing anyone's said to me in weeks.

She leaned in, hugged him. As she did so he smelled her. He had forgotten that perfume of hers, a summer scent of lotion and salt. He began to put an arm around her, meaning only to reciprocate, to comfort her, just as she pulled away. Her look had been open. Now it was indecipherable.

– What?

– I meant it. What I said when you got here. About it being good to have you here. It's not just about the dig. I'm not making a move on you, but–

– No, of course not. I didn't think–

– It's really good to have a new face. That's all. I hope you don't mind me saying all this.

– It's fine. Really.

She put her hand out for the thermos, busied herself with it, checking the lid, rolling her lips tight together. Only when she smiled did he realise how close she had been to crying. She had composed herself before looking up at him again.

– Well! I'll see you tomorrow. Sleep well.

– You too.

He looked back at the mountains before following her down. The sun had set. The caves had disappeared, their mouths lost in shadows.

ᘓᘐ

For ten days he lunched with the brothers. After Missy's daily meeting they would take their shares of the food laid out and go back to their pit. They would eat with their legs dangling underground – their feet four thousand years in the past – side by side and close for warmth, sharing olives from the Maxis orchards, talking of anything but work: of basketball and the Gulf Wars; of mobile phones and killing lambs; of the secrets of growing the perfect lemon.

He had liked that. They had all liked it, so much so that Missy had scolded them for it. *Look at you guys! Sitting on your butts like the three wise monkeys. See no spadework, hear no spadework, speak no spadework. Siesta's over, amigos!*

It had changed after Mystras. They had been less at ease in the wake of that. He had wondered what Chrystos had said; what he had done wrong that day.

It was not that they abandoned him. The brothers would head back to the pit, and when Ben went to join them Chrystos would try too hard with him, translating for his benefit, though he understood them well enough now. Even Giorgios would be less taciturn. Their friendliness had become forced. Then too there was less work for him, Long Hearth having been mined out, the great circumference of the hearth the deepest context, nothing but cold earth below it. On Friday Missy moved him to East Midden, to work with Natsuko and Jason.

He ate his lunch alone. Jason had disappeared somewhere with Max and Eberhard. Natsuko was with Eleschen, under the Gearhut's deckchair-striped awning. Now and then when the wind turned he caught a scrap of talk or laughter. There had been a mist that morning, the air in the pits wet and cloying – his fingertips had been like pegs as he worked – and though the sun had burnt it away by noon the cold had lingered in his bones. He swapped hands as he ate, pocketing one fist after the other, his nails coiled into his palms.

A pair of fighter planes went over, their black chevrons thundering east. He was huddled into his coat, and didn't notice Natsuko until she was standing over him.

– Hello, he said, and she smiled with her crooked teeth.

– You look cold.

– A bit.

– No. Very.

– Actually I'm freezing.

She sat down on the ridge beside him, their backs to the old excavations of the North Hill Mansion. Her coat was lined with some kind of fur, a deep black pelt. The wind moved it against her skin. He could see the pockmark by her ear.

She was holding out a sachet, a shiny plastic thing emblazoned with Japanese in cartoonish red and black.

– What's that?

– Guess.

– Heroin. Dynamite. Chicken soup.

– No!

– Shame.

– It's a hand warmer. Put it in your pocket, it makes heat for you. It's like magic. It's for you.

He took the sachet. She had begun to explain its use to him, her voice patient and musical, and he nodded as if he were listening. At the far end of the ridge Chrystos and Giorgios were playing backgammon on the steps of the Menelaion. He could hear the clack of the men, the *trictrac* of the dice. Beyond them the air was full of light.

– You like it?

– Sure, he said, and smiled to reassure her. She hesitated as she stood.

– Jason says you will be coming.

– Coming?

– With us. She cocked her head. To hunt.

– Oh.

– Are you? she said, and he found himself held there, locked into her eyes, which were not black, he saw now, but the deep ochre of old dried blood.

– I'm glad, she said, and it was only then that he realised he might have nodded. Then Missy was calling for her, calling for them all, and Natsuko was walking, three steps backwards like a dancer before turning away towards the huts and awnings.

Siesta's over, amigos!

❦

Saturday they worked till half-six. The days were getting longer. Even so they raced the sun to pack the last of the gear away. Torches dancing over the green for a lost spirit level, a map gone missing.

Jason was posing for Natsuko, a tripod slung across his shoulders, an Indiana Jones-James Dean-Beach Boy captured on picturephone. Eberhard was crosslegged and barefoot, relacing his boots. It had been a poor day's work, both of the new pits striking an impassable honeycomb of limestone three feet down, but only Missy seemed dispirited. The mood among the others was restless and excitable.

He was standing at their edge, looking towards the Transit van where the brothers stood waiting for him, when Eberhard glanced up at him.

– Are you busy tomorrow?

– Why?

– I want to take you out. I hear you've never fired a gun. You should do so before Tuesday week. What time shall I call for you? Would six be too early?

– Six is fine. Tuesday week?

– Unless it rains. The moon is full then.

– We'll go at night?

– They hunt at night, Jason said, and turning, he saw that both Jason and Natsuko had stopped their play to listen.

– Six it is, then, Eberhard said, and pulled on a boot as Jason started for the cars, his hand clapping Ben's shoulder as he passed, gripping him there.

– Coming?

– What for? I've got my lift.

– Now you've got a better offer. We're going back to the girls'. You haven't even met Sylvia yet.

– Who's Sylvia?

– Ah, who is Sylvia, what is she? You'll never know if you don't come.

– Look, can I meet you there? Chrystos–

– Forget him, Jason said. His grip tightened.

He shrugged him off, walked down the slope to the van by the northern track. The brothers were already inside. Chrystos leaned from the driver's window, mobile in his shoulder-crook, smiling ruefully in the reflected highbeams.

– Bad news. Our sister visits friends. Giorgios is cooking. He still makes food like a soldier, always enough for ten. We need another mouth to feed. Ready?

– You go on.

– We can wait.

– I'm busy, he said, and heard Giorgios hurrumph in the interior dark, Chrystos frowning as he folded the phone away.

– Busy. Busy with your foreign friends?

– Only tonight.

– You know what I told you.

– I haven't forgotten.

– No? We will see, Chrystos said quietly, changing gears, the van already pulling away, its white bulk rocking down the track into the concealing dark.

> ***Canis Aureus*: Golden jackal, common jackal.**
> **Carnivora of the family Canidae.**
> **Regions: Palearctic, Oriental, Ethiopian.**
> **Biomes: desert, grassland, forest, scrub.**
> **Conservation Status: unthreatened.**
> **Body length: 3'. Body weight: 24lbs. Standing height . . .**

A carillon of laughter. The din of a glass-pack muffler. There were lights in the orange trees outside. Walking back from the girls' place he had wondered what they were meant for. It was two weeks to Independence Day but Lent still had a month to run. Thin crowds converged outside the shops or at the bars around the town square, yet there were few out on the streets even on a Saturday night. Only the young bloods were in good spirits. The older people huddled over their drinks and chat, as if they were living through hard times and the worst might not be over yet; who could tell? Who could tell.

Natsuko and Eleschen lived on the cathedral square, a stone's throw from the laboratory. They rented one floor of a crumbling villa, a building with a tired grace the postwar blocks around it lacked. The rooms were dirt-cheap, high-ceilinged, ornate and icy: there was no heating, and the landlords – old folks from New Mystras – had nailed up the fireplaces. A month before Eleschen had prised off the boards and used them for kindling, but the chimneys had vomited back smoke and they'd had to flirt assiduously with the widower upstairs to avoid calls to the fire brigade and complaints to the owners. The rooms still reeked sweetly of burnt olive wood, the smell almost masking the scents of perfume, candles and dog.

Sylvia had taken to him. At first she had rushed up to the girls, weeping for their affection, claws skidding on the boards; but later, after Natsuko had taken her for a night-time walk, it was Ben that she had watched, finally trotting over and collapsing into his arms. She was a Laconian breed, white with liver spots, a round muzzle and long, soft ears; a beagle kind of dog, descended from old hunting stock.

– Where did you get her? he had asked, stroking the sow-purse ears, and Max had laughed, the sound of his humour rusty, like a big cat's cough.

– Corinth, Eleschen had said. I bought her there. But Natsuko had leaned towards him, her eyes obsidian.

– She *stole* her.

– I did not!

– She told Max to stop the car. She said she felt sick from the road. She went into a restaurant to ask for a glass of water. Then she came out with Sylvia. Jason said *What is that?* Eleschen said *This is Sylvia.* Eberhard said *I didn't see dog on the menu.* Eleschen said *I feel better now. Let's go home.*

– It's *Sylvia*, Eleschen had said, prim and tart and simmering. Not *Sirubiya*. Two syllables. Can't you learn to talk properly? But Natsuko had been giggling, and Jason had roared with laughter.

– Why would you do that? he had said to Eleschen, and Why would she do that? To no one in particular: but Eleschen had still been cross, going to fetch glasses and loitering overlong in the kitchenette, and no one else gave him an answer.

They had drunk brandy to keep warm. Natsuko had cooked fish and rice, wrapping sardines in vine leaves. No one had taken off their coats to eat. It had reminded Ben of old war films: greatcoated soldiers eating by candlelight in derelict Norman mansions. Eleschen had fetched bedclothes for anyone still chilled, and he had taken a blanket even though he hadn't needed it. He had felt anything but cold. It was enough to be with them.

Jason had talked too much and Eberhard hardly at all. Eleschen had asked about England again and for want of anything better he had tried to amuse her with the markets, making the best he could of his family's business, making her laugh even as he edged away from all real talk of family (and Jason watching him, a cat-got-the-cream, but saying nothing of Emine). Later Eleschen had played for them, folk songs on a Greek violin, but she hadn't gone on for long, the instrument being hard to tune and her fingers numb. Natsuko had asked for his middle names and had written them out in Japanese, and Max – grumbling and sighing and confessing to be flattered at the girls' coaxing nonetheless – had done the same in his native Georgian, the script like something out of Tolkien, all fishhooks and tongues of flame: and later still and less sober he had stood to recite Georgian poetry, a sherry glass gripped at the stem in one big hand, his smile gap-toothed in his pockmarked face and the verses full of harsh wishes. *If our lives are bitter, let our deaths be sweet.*

It had been small talk – little of it mattering in itself – but he had loved it all. The ease of their friendship. The way their conversation could die away only to flare up again, out of nothing.

– I love it here, Eleschen had said, just as he was thinking the same thing himself. They had been talking about the dig but had fallen quiet, and the words had carried, though Eleschen was muffled in an eiderdown and besides had spoken matter-of-factly, as if what she meant by *love* needed no emphasis beyond the fact of its own mention.

And Eberhard had shifted in his ladder-backed chair, his shadow mantling across the high walls, his own voice soft but distinct as always.

– All Europe loves Greece. It is dear to us as a grandfather. It is lovely as a granddaughter.

He had left after two. The others had already gone. He had lingered for as long as he reasonably could. Natsuko had been dozing, a pyramid of bedclothes surmounted by shining hair. Eleschen had seen him down. He had got a drowsy goodnight kiss at the door.

He had still not been sleepy himself and so had walked back by the town square, hoping to find a club or bar to keep him for another hour. The last few long days' work had left him too tired to sleep, his thoughts weary and energised, and the burials had unsettled him. And he did not want to be alone.

Beyond the town hall, between the offices of the Guild of Ice Cream Manufacturers and a lurid hybridised kebab shop/cocktail bar/nightclub, he had found an internet café open. The dozen machines were all occupied by teenagers playing shoot-'em-ups, their Nazis and GIs hunting one another through massive multi-player online bombstruck ruins, the attendant watching over them with dispassionate tolerance.

– How long will they be? he'd asked, in Greek, and the boy-herd had shrugged and run a thumb down one razored Nike-swoop footballer sideburn and answered in dour Australian English.

– Long as it takes them to die.

He had put his money down and gone to wait in the kebab club. The inner rooms were barely lit, their crazy-mirrored walls obfuscated by a mingled haze of souvlaki and cigarettes. Two goth girls with long green drinks had watched him with panda eyes. An insomniac DJ stood alone at the back, nodding over rap metal.

He had bought a beer and a side order of meat, picked his way through his charred pork, then had drunk up and gone back to the café. The pack of boys had left and their overseer had been alone, polishing a pair of twelve-hole boots. The concussive thud of bass still shuddered through the walls.

The golden jackal's enemies are leopards, wolves, and men. It subsists on small mammals, insects, fruit and carrion. It is also a fast and efficient hunter. *Canis aureus* rises after dusk and ranges over a territory of one square mile. Though it pounces on smaller prey, larger quarries will be run to exhaustion before being disembowelled. Near human habitations the jackal may attack livestock and scavenge in waste. It is a recognised rabies carrier . . .

His emails had awaited him. He had paged through them unwillingly. Here and there amidst the junk were messages he might have read: should have read, if he were a better man. One from Ted, two from his mother, a dozen forwarded from work. He had opened none of them. He had resented them, the way they pulled him back to the margins of another life, the one he had left in tatters. He had not left home to find them.

From Emine there had been nothing.

A dog had barked outside and the boy-herd had thrown down his boots and sauntered out to cadge a kiss from its bleach-blonde owner. The dog had looked like Sylvia – he had recognised the breed – but had lacked her temperament, baring locked teeth at the boy-herd despite its owner's chidings. He had thought of the jackal then, the wild dog up in the hills, and turning back to the console had entered its Latin name.

***Canis aureus* lives and hunts in families rather than packs. The animals pair for life. Hunting in tandem they may kill in two attempts out of three. This kill rate drops to one in five for jackals that hunt alone.**

The jackal has a large and distinctive repertoire of howls. The most distinctive, the pheal, is a rising and falling wail that carries for many miles. The jackal howls at the moon, at the kill and in concert with its mate. Choral howling can be considered a form of betrothal . . .

At first he had found nothing but the bare bones of weight and height. He had searched on idly, trying to piece together an understanding of the thing. After an hour he had sat back, thinking that he had given up: but his hands had gone back to the keyboard again, his fingers doing their own talking.

Jackal: an eastern word deriving from the Persian. The animal is significant in many Eastern mythologies. The Egyptian Anubis – god of the dying – was portrayed as a man with the head of a golden jackal. The association may have arisen from the jackal's recorded habit of burying kills, as well as from its unconfirmed practice of scavenging in cemeteries.

To reach the guiding hand of Anubis, the dead first had to proceed through a crowd of terrifying monsters. These beings – Flint-Eyes, Gut-Eater, Shining-Tooth and Bone-Crusher – waited for the newly deceased at the mouth of the underworld. To reach Anubis in safety, the dead were directed to chant, _I am pure, I am pure, I am pure, I am pure._

Anubis led the souls to Osiris, deity of death. There the jackal-headed god would take the hearts of the deceased and preside over their weighing. Checking the tongue of Osiris's scales, Anubis would balance each heart in its canopic jar against the counterweight of a feather. Those hearts borne down by deceit were eaten. Only the lightest of hearts were permitted to enter the endless reed fields of Aaru . . .

The boy-herd had fallen asleep, his head propped on his boots. Outside the square was empty. The kebab bar had closed. The sky was awash with stars. The Snake's Head and the Hunting Dogs. The Northern Crown. The Kneeling Man.

He did up his coat and hurried home. The hotel lights had been left on. He stole in through the empty lobby and up to his single room.

∾

Along the empty river road, past the Therapne turn. Upwards into the eastern hills, the Delux jouncing over holes. The sun creeping over a bluff where Eberhard turned off and slowed across the wild sage and thyme. The Volvo coming to a halt amongst a maze of wildflowers.

– Where are we?

– Nowhere. Those trees are white mulberries. I'd hazard a guess this was a plantation once. The Venetians and Ottomans both being fond of silk. The Spartans themselves would have hunted here, of course. Hunting was meaningful to them. Almost as sacrosanct as war. Now it's used for grazing, if at all.

– Never seen no one up here, Jason said, and swung his feet off the back seats.

– It's Maxis land as I understand it, though it's up for sale.

– Do they know we're here? he asked, and Sauer smiled with nothing but his eyes.

– I would have thought you could answer that rather better than I. Help him choose a gun, Jason, would you?

He leaned on the warm silver hood while Eberhard stalked off with a box of clay pigeons under one arm, stooping here and there for stones. Along the ridge, by two windbent trees, were a series of miniature cairns, none of them larger than a molehill. Behind him Jason rummaged in the car until the boot popped open. Five boxes lay inside.

– First time, you said?

He nodded as Jason joined him. The boxes were not mundane. They were entirely too well-made to be innocuous. They were finished in oak and brass, as if they were meant for miniature burials.

– Join the club. I mean it was mine too, when Eb and Max brought me up here.

– I thought you were the big expert?

– Not a lot of guns in Luton, to be honest. I'm just a fast learner. Scared?

– Not yet.

– Don't worry, you'll get used to them, he said, and reaching in he unlatched a case and tenderly brought out the first gun.

He had never held a firearm. He had never had the chance to do so, had never wanted to.

It was unexpectedly beautiful. He had seen weapons that possessed the quality before. A collection of Japanese swords with hilt-guards of oxidised steel, inlaid with electrum praying mantids and plum blossoms in pink gold. A Damask blade with a scabbard of shagreen and lacustrine velvet. Celtic pommel-works. Hoplite panoplies.

The gun in Jason's hands was like those things. It had a magnetism. It drew him. Its beauty arose from its function. It was as finely tooled as the classic car beside them. From a distance guns had always seemed frightening to him, ugly mechanisms, brutal means of inflicting harm. Eberhard's gun was all those things, but it was alluring despite them. Alluring because of them. It lured him.

It had two barrels laid side by side, the pair as long as an outstretched arm. Nothing was affixed to them, no scopes or straps. A metal tooth made do as sights in their cleft extremity. Their black tubes flared like the conclusions of bones where they joined the weapon's thorax. The handle was carved of a dark veined wood, its grain full of whorls and cloudscapes. Above the trigger, on the cheeks, two birds were incised in gold. A pair of fowl roused into flight.

– Take it, go on. And, There! Jason said, pleased as Punch, as if admiring a new suit. You're a natural. To the manner born.

He lifted the gun, settled its weight. Sighted along the bores. It could only be a trick of the light that made the mulberries at the ridge seem closer. A breeze moved in their bare white antlers. Eberhard was propping up clay pigeons in their shadows. He stood back from the last of the cairns, dusting off his hands, gazing up towards the sunrise.

Jason pulled the barrels down. – Easy, tiger.

– Is it loaded?

– Might have been, for all you knew.

– How did Eberhard bring these over?

– Didn't. Got them in Athens. You should've seen the salesman's face. Sweat pouring down his smile. Definitely working on commission. He's got a hunting licence too. Used to come here with his family. You can drive down here from Germany. They make their money from guns, you know, Eb's lot. El says they're all rolling in it.

– These must have cost a bit.

– Five grand a pop.

– All set? Eberhard said, and as he reached them, How does that feel, Ben?

– Like I'm going to shoot myself in the foot.

– It wouldn't be the first time, I'm sure. Try not to be nervous. Look. This is the trigger, this the safety. This selects the firing barrel. There's no more to it than that. It's not a complicated piece. Shall we give it a try?

Eberhard broke the gun for him. Jason fetched a box of shells. He slid a pair in, thumbed them home, closed the breech, levelled the gun.

The little cairns with the sun behind them. Pillars of rain in the far distance. He breathed in deeply and stopped breathing.

For a moment there was no sound at all. It was as if the world had retreated from him or from the thing in his hands. Or it was as if the inverse were true, as if he had drawn back into his skull, like a snail into its shell:

and then there were sounds everywhere. He leaned his cheek to the gun's cold cheek and heard the water down below. The fissured limestone of the river. A black bee droning through the thyme, as heavy as a shotgun shell. Birds crooning in the mulberries.

– In your own time, Eberhard said, and he swung the gun and fired and fired.

Only once, when he was small, had he seen his father in a fight. It was a hot summer and the crowds in Church Street simmered and boiled between the market stalls. They were all there, his uncle Maurice, his dad, the kids and their mum helping out. Uncle Maurice had come up trumps. He'd bought a job lot of hand-held fans off a fellow in the Commercial Road, and from a friend who owed him favours a load of fizzy drinks. He'd driven down to Smithfield that morning for a block of ice and they'd smashed it up in an old tin bath and laid a hundred bottles down. They sold the fans at forty pence, three and a free drink for a pound, and as long as the sun was shining people couldn't get enough. Lolly and Coll and Ted and he stood round the bath's glittering hoard, opening bottles, drinking as much as they could stomach, all buzzing with sugar in the sun, their tongues peppered with bubbles. Fanta and Lilt in thick cold glass with paper straws.

They were flicking drink with the soggy straws when Lolly saw Mr Marinescu. Mr Marinescu owned the ice cream van, *Marinescu Refreshments (Ices, Ice Drinks, Mind the Children)*. He parked every weekend outside Granada TV Rentals. He didn't speak good English but he was nice, had given Lolly a Mivvi for nothing once on account of her name being funny. Now he was pushing his way in through the crowd. He held people back with his big round shoulders. He had his scoop in one fat hand, like a hollowed silver egg. He talked with Uncle Maurice and their dad, their heads nodding together, and just like that the fight began.

The first thing was Uncle Maurice sitting down. He put his hand up in the air the way that children did in school (*Sir! Sir!*) and with his hand still raised sat down, missing his fishing stool and vanishing behind the bath. That made them laugh, all four of them, and then their mum was gathering them, ushering them, their heels tripping on the kerb, and looking back he saw the scoop in Mr Marinescu's hand, the silver smeared raspberry red.

It seemed unlikely, looking back, that he had never seen his father fight. He knew it happened, knew he fought with Ted, their mother, other men. Once at tea the phone had gone and it had been Sol Ullmann, who somehow made a living from nothing but stale knockdown chocolates, ringing from the box outside his lock-up, and someone – two men! Three! – crashing around inside; and Ben's father ran out of the house; and when Ben saw him at breakfast he seemed quiet, kind, almost peaceful for once, the kitchen smelling of Dettol and fry-ups, and as he cut his eggs his knuckles like knobs of raw mince.

His mother had got them away and they were not the only ones. The fight seemed to have blown a hole in the packed mass of the Church Street crowd. Everyone was shouting except Ben's father. Mr Marinescu was yelling about the iced drinks. He shook his scoop as if it were a knife or evidence. His face had gone white as his shirt. Then Ben's father nodded, as if he agreed with all of them. He stepped towards Mr Marinescu, one hand out to conciliate until it brushed aside the scoop, the other coming out of nowhere, like a coin kept up his sleeve, and jabbing Mr Marinescu fast in the neck and face, once, twice, three times – *four* times – and the ice cream man already down, the hot tarmac blacking his knees, and as Ben's father stepped away the crowd cheering, and someone *ahh*ing, as if he were a brilliant act. A juggler, a conjurer, a human cannonball.

He had never been so proud of his father as he had been then. He had carried the feeling with him for days, cherishing it.

Now he felt it again. The gun in the boot and the two birds with it, collared doves, Eberhard said, beautiful things, as beautiful dead as alive, their tea-greys and tea-pinks and pale gore wrapped up in newspapers and plastic bags; and Jason and Eberhard smiling as they drove down, arguing over how to cook the birds, talking about him, over him, and both proud of him, it seemed, happy with him and happy for him. And the thrill and the surge and the rush of it still fresh as the blood and the smell of the gun.

He went to turn on the lights.

– Don't.

– So you can see what you're doing.

– I can see what I am doing.

– . . . What *are* you doing?

She was picking up things here and there, moving from bathroom to bedroom, from wardrobe to bed. Her hair fell to one side like a shadow as she sorted through his clothes, his books, stared at the laptop on the desk, gazed at the razor on the black glass shelf. It was evening and the daylight was long gone.

– Natsuko? he said, and she paused in her circling and looked down at him as if surprised to find him there, seated on his own unmade bed. – What are you looking for?

She raised her shoulders and let them fall. – You shouldn't shave yourself.

– Why not?

– You cut yourself.

– Do I?

– Here, she said, and stepped in, reaching to touch his neck, down at one side by his ear, and feeling the blood-spot crusted there he raised his fingers and caught her own.

– The ring's in my coat. If that's what you want.

– No, she said, and moving away, You don't keep pictures of her.

Of them, he thought, and said instead, I've never seen the point.

– Why?

– I remember them. I don't need reminders.

– Do you miss them?

– Every day.

– It must be nice, to have a child.

– Yes.

– Boy or girl?

– Girl. How did you end up here, Natsuko?

– Max.

– He was a friend of yours?

She didn't bother to answer him. She was at the desk again, leafing through his thesis notes (or whatever kind of notes they were now), seemingly absorbed in them until she let the book fall shut and drifted towards the window. He watched her opening the blinds, looking out, thinking how different she could be. Sometimes the mischievous telltale, sometimes this calm, mirror-eyed creature. Unreachable.

– Natsuko?

– Max does not have friends. Maybe Eberhard is his friend. Eberhard is a very admirable person.

– Listen, can I ask you something? When I arrived, and there wasn't a message for me did you do that on purpose?

– Yes.

– Why?

– We didn't want you here.

– But, I mean–

– We didn't know you then.

– Oh. He stood up, rubbing his palms on his jeans. – Would you like some tea?

– Not yet. What does your name mean?

– Nothing.

– All names mean something.

– Ben is just Ben. Or anyway I don't know what it means. Mercer means merchant, if you really want to know. It's a good name for us, actually. We've always been selling something. Off the back of a lorry half the time.

– What are you selling, Ben Mercer?

– What do you want me to sell?

– My name means Sweet Little Summer. You can see the pool from here.

– Every morning.

She turned as he came up behind her. For a moment he thought she would step into his arms, but instead she smiled and put out one hand again, this time against his chest. Not pushing him away, but spreading her fingers across his breast, as if to tell him to wait a little, or as if she were measuring him.

X

Notes Towards a Thesis

Monday 15th: no Maxis brothers today. The cousin is delayed in Athens and the olives must be harvested. To harvest the olives (the Greeks say) is more important than to fight the war.

Crossword came up in person with my wake-up call and Chrystos's apologies. Bad news calls for room service. Her eyes go everywhere, two grey mice scurrying after the smallest scraps of unhappiness.

Eberhard drove me up. We met at his with time to spare. We talked about nothing much. Elections and politics. Almost like friends.

He has good books. I found this:

All executioners are of the same family.

And thought of this:

Happy families are all alike; every unhappy family is unhappy in its own way.

All extremisms are also alike. Does that mean all extremists are happy?

Sparta, with its secrecy, its perfect, prehistoric strength, its arrogant brutality, its panoply of gods, its young bloods coming down at night to kill *the sturdiest and the best*, its mothers turning from newborns swaddled and cloaked, bawling and gone; its sly reptilian deadliness–

What is the type of Sparta's extremism? What is the Spartan pattern? In the terms of our age it is Left, Right, East and West. It is a meeting of all degrees and compass points. It does not resonate because it is strange but because it remains strangely familiar. The good extremist thinks he walks backwards, against the ways of the world. He thinks himself happy because others are unhappy and because he is unlike others it must be so. But his logic is false, and in any case he is not unlike others. He is akin to all those who have pushed themselves beyond the limits where the dial clocks back to nought. All extremisms are alike and in Sparta all are prefigured.

I go on calling these my notes. I don't know what kind of thesis I could rake up out of them now. I've botched the job: why go on with it? I've lost sight of my end. I have no argument. I have misinterpreted the most basic facts. How can I keep writing at all when I don't understand what I have written?

The Spartans had little time for outsiders. They were sparing with their respect. Even when their hands were extended in friendship they were tight-fisted with their trust. They were cautious even of those of their own whose stations took them abroad. Too often their emissaries would both learn and forget too much. The further that Sparta's power reached, the more often its kings and admirals returned to find themselves no longer at home with the old severities. Degenerate habits would be noted in them. They would desire rich foods and prefer fine clothes. They would hold themselves apart from and above the company of their equals. They were found out in the possession of Athenian silver or Persian gold. In dutifully going out into the unhappy world they had been contaminated by unhappiness. In the end they would be cast out again, or killed, immured in the sanctuaries where they hid, their bodies brought out on the brink of death, that the gods be spared their corruption.

Did the Spartans fear the world outside? Did they guard against its jackals and wolves? Their wall-less city claimed fearlessness. The Spartans had faith in themselves until the day they were destroyed. And yet their faiths themselves – their gods – are full of flashes of terror. If it was not the world without they feared then what was it, unless themselves?

Their longest and most brutal war was reserved for their enemies within. The Romans and Athenians wrote of the Crypteia. Little is extant and nothing certain. As so often where Sparta is concerned, nothing has been unearthed which sheds any light on the rumours of others. The secrets are still buried deep, if they were ever buried at all.

Crypteia means *The Secret Matter* or *The Time of Hiding*, *The Hidden Ones* or *The Hidden*. It was an enclave and a service. It was the young men who undertook to serve and the acts undertaken.

The magistrates from time to time sent out into the countryside the most discreet of the young men, equipped only with daggers and the necessary supplies. During the day they scattered into obscure and out-of-the-way places, where they hid themselves and lay quiet. But in the night they came down to the roads and killed every helot they caught . . . the sturdiest and the best of them.

The most discreet:

The Hidden were selected not according to martial prowess but by merit of cunning and circumspection. By mental capability. This reflecting the nature of the Hidden, which was not a military force except in the last extremity; was firstly, rather, an instrument of subterfuge and terror.

The Spartans were not unique among the Greeks in admiring subterfuge. Odysseus, the slipperiest of kings, is loathed by Homer's Achilles – *I hate the man who says one thing and hides another in his heart* – but both are heroes even so. It is only that the valorous hero dies while the discreet one survives.

The young men:

Paidiscos; *boy-like*; nineteen years of age; between boyhood and manhood.

The necessary supplies:

What did the Hidden eat? Hunting was of ritual importance to the Spartans, but the Hidden could not have hunted freely. Nor could they have built open fires. By definition they were to remain concealed. Their period of service is unknown, but it may have been as much as a year. The valley here is lush but the highlands would offer little foraging. Onions and chestnuts, walnuts and snails. Hyacinths and pomegranates.

The helot farmlands would offer better pickings. Theft – if accomplished – was admired in Sparta. There is a story of a Spartan boy who stole a fox, hid it under his cloak, and died from the wounds it dealt him rather than face the shame of failure (and this has come to seem a strange parable, a muddled, inscrutable Chinese whisper, though Apollodorus gives the fox as a symbol of Messene, the long-lost city of the helots, whose lives were Sparta's greatest theft and whose masses were an army at its back).

Theft was admired, and so too were the qualities of scavengers and carnivores. Aristotle condemned the Spartans for raising men to be like wolves. Xenophon records a Spartan threat – the promise to devour an enemy raw – that equates the consumption of unrefined flesh with martial ferocity. Ferocity, tempered with control, was a quality the Spartans admired: Ares Thereitas was not the god of a people who fought in cold blood. I think the boy-men of the Hidden stole what they required, and ate as animals eat.

Obscure and out-of-the-way places:

Where did the Hidden rest? The winters are dreadful here and all seasons are unpredictable. Jason says there are caves in the mountains. People lived in them once, tens of thousands of years ago. In the mountain caves, a Hidden would have found both concealment and shelter.

But in the night they came down:

The Spartan territories possessed three notable areas of higher ground: the Aigaleon, Taygetos and Parnon mountain ranges. Since the Hidden inhabited the highlands during daylight, it can be assumed that these ranges were at times occupied by them. In such positions they were ideally placed not only as sentinels against foreign incursion, but as watchers of those within the kingdom.

Nightwork served several purposes. To control their vast majority a permanent nocturnal curfew was imposed on the helots. Spartan numbers would have made such a measure impossible to enforce were it not for the Hidden. Without the fear inspired by the Hidden such subjection would not have remained a reality.

The curfew was not inconsequential. Spartan armies bound abroad left their territories under cover of darkness. The defence of the state relied on the helot population never knowing what force remained to guard against their slumbering giant.

How did the helots see the Hidden? They must have known of them. It was vital that they knew of them, but important too that they never knew too much. Nothing is as frightening as the unknown.

They were not a learned people. They would live for thirteen generations without formal education. The Hidden must have seemed supernatural. Monsters in the shadows. Warnings against those who thought to wander too far or wonder too much. What killed the lamb that strayed last night? What is that moving in the trees? Don't say that name. Don't speak of that. Come back, my love, into the house.

The sturdiest and the best of them:

The killings themselves served three functions. Firstly, they inculcated fear: but Sparta also made use of eugenics among its own people, and its Hidden will have brought to their homicides a eugenic understanding of what it was they undertook. Secondly, then, the culling of a strong or clever helot would be seen as the elimination of troublesome stock, of singular sources of potential rebellion; and lastly, as the means to weaken the helot race as a whole.

The Hidden would also have been well suited to performing the exposure of Spartan infants. While exposure of deformed newborns was common in Greece, in Sparta alone the practice was state-controlled and scrupulously applied. The monster (*teras*) would be adjudged as such not by the father but by the Council of Elders. The process of exposure was also known as *The Hiding*. The Hidden were under the age of marriage: they had no true experience of paternal feeling, or how it feels to gain or lose a child. The secrecy of the undertaking, its state administration, and its execution in the higher regions of the Taygetos or Parnon mountains, all suggest that exposure would be naturally delegated to the Hidden.

. . . What did it mean, that the helots were human? It is Aristotle who describes how Sparta would declare war on its captives at the beginning of each new year. The declaration was needed precisely because the humanity of the helots was recognised. To kill in wartime was no crime; but that is not to say, of course, that such killing was without consequences. That the soldier commits no crime does not mean he is innocent. That the law pardons him does not mean he goes unpunished.

The Hidden did not work alone. Terrorisation took many forms. Part of a Spartan child's education was to watch a helot humiliated by being forced to drink unmixed wine. In Sparta's declining years the helots were ordered to wear insignia in the form of caps made of animal skins. At other times suppression became extermination. Thucydides writes of the culling of two thousand helots who answered a Spartan call to arms. The same is retold by Plutarch:

The helots who had been found brave had wreaths put on their heads to show their liberation, and they went in a procession to the temples. But not long afterwards they vanished – more than two thousand of them – in such a way that no man could say, then or afterwards, how they had come to their deaths . . .

XI

Shoot-'Em-Up

Little by little the nights were getting warmer. For a week he slept poorly, windows thrown open to allay the Soviet blast of the hotel heating. He would lie awake for hours, listening to the town outside – an insomniac bird shrieking in its fourth-floor cage; a coming and going of music; a wolf-pack of revellers – and then would fall asleep with archaeological slowness, not passing between two distinct states but descending through intricate strata of consciousness, subconsciousness, unconsciousness.

Emine began to fade, first from thoughts, then from his dreams. A whole day would pass, and as lay awake he would realise with a stab of guilt to the heart that he had not thought of her. He wondered if it was what he had set out to do in leaving everything behind, this salving reduction of memory. And then sometimes it did not feel a salving, but like a tearing away.

He wondered if even Nessie would come to mean less to him.

Monday night he slept at Jason's. That morning as they worked he had told the others about the kebab club, hamming it up to make them laugh, but Eleschen had been enthused, had begged them to go back with her for supper and cocktails, and even Eberhard had succumbed in the end. They had gone home to change and then had met up at the bar, sitting in the confusion of smoke and mirrors with Faith No More ringing in their bones, Natsuko drinking Grasshoppers that stained her tongue lizard-green, Eberhard arguing with the cocktail waiter about which sugar to use in an Absinthe Drip, Max dancing with himself – laughing at his own gracelessness – and then with the panda-eyed neo-goths Ben had seen in the place before. When Eleschen had been invited on to a name-day party by two military students (*Galinis*, they had called her, meaning blue-eyed and unlucky, though neither had looked as if they could believe their luck when she agreed), the five of them had followed in her wake to a flat at the west end of Thermopylae Street. He had soon been drunk enough to hope Natsuko might come back with him, but the girls had left together, hand in hand on the stroke of three, and Jason's place had been round the corner; and besides, he had had cigarettes.

He slept for an hour and woke as darkness faded. He was hung-over but no longer drunk. His thoughts ran clear as if he were well rested. He picked his way across the bombsite of the bedsit to the galley kitchen, ran the tap and dipped his head and drank until his head sang with the cold. Weariness hit him as he stood, and he retreated to the sofa and lay down again, on one side, watching the light fill the windowpanes. He could see Jason still asleep. There was so much crockery around and in his bed he seemed to be laid out in a kitchen sink.

He was woken again by a cacophony of machines. The computer was on in the corner, the bellows-drone of its overclocked fans accompanied by the death throes of a war game left to its own devices. The clock-radio and TV were playing and Jason was shaving at the kitchen counter, humming, dancing, baring his neck, working blind, edging his goatee with a battery razor, gulping last night's coffee from an unwashed wineglass. Beyond him a weatherman was conjuring the sun while, on the radio, a singer grieved for long-lost Byzantium.

> *City of God, City of Light,*
> *Constantinople, like the Phoenix,*
> *Will rise again, will rise again!*

He belched and tasted the night's champagne, sour as bile against his teeth. There was something wrong with the weatherman. He was still trying to work it out when Jason danced round to face him.

– Oh, it's you.

– Of course it's me.

– I mean you're up. I didn't think you'd make it. Want coffee?

– No.

– Sure? It's best served cold. Like revenge and pizza. Sweet dreams?

– I don't remember . . . What time is it?

– Too early to think about. Me, I was hoping for Eleschen, but all I got was the time I got narked. I did underwater archaeology for a bit but I lost my nerve after that. Narked is when the nitrox gets you. A decent operation you use helium mix on deep dives but this one wasn't quite decent. They called themselves archaeologists but they were selling the stuff on to collectors in Tunis. Don't tell Stanton I told you, right? So you start to get narked at fifty feet and at a hundred you feel like you've had a good few solid vodka shots. I was twice that deep and it was dark down there. I was a state. I didn't know if I was coming or going. I thought I was going to throw up in the tubes. I could have got my weight belt off but I was scared of going up too fast. I saw someone do that once and the blood was running out of his ears. I was lucky they found me when they did. Anyway I had enough of that, that was my last dive . . . what's up with you?

– What do you think?

– Oh, the new spiky hungover Ben. I like you better this way.

Late, he thought: that was what was wrong with the weatherman. He should have been washed and dressed by now.

– Where's my watch?

– How would I know? Stop worrying, we've got . . . ten minutes. Shit. Natsuko's always on the dot too. The bathroom's all yours anyway. *Mea culpa* in advance. Come on, cheer up, have a coffee. Look, there's a clean mug here. Get dressed, I'll warm it up for you.

He found his watch in his boots and strapped it on. It was Natsuko he had dreamed of, he remembered, though he could recall nothing more than her face. The pock-mark at her temple. Her deer-dark eyes, sometimes cautious, sometimes fierce.

– Do you think people grow into their looks?

The radio was still blaring music. For a moment he thought Jason hadn't heard. Then, – Not in the way you're thinking.

– What am I thinking of?

– You're thinking of Eleschen, you dirty boy. Aren't you?

– If I was it wouldn't be in that way.

– Liar. You're as bad as me. With Eleschen it's always that way. What did your wife grow into, then?

– We just grew apart.

– My heart bleeds for you. Got a picture?

– No.

– Eb said you'd say that.

– What? What else did he say?

– That you play your cards close to your chest. Which is a compliment coming from him, trust me, he likes quiet types. And that you wear your learning lightly but your troubles like chains. Whatever that means. I can see where you might get in trouble, mind you.

– Why's that?

– You're gullible. You know you are. And you're a classic nympholept.

– What's that?

– From nympholepsy. A passionate longing for the unattainable.

– Sounds like you.

– Me? No, I'm realistic in my passions. Oy!

– What? What?

– Don't go back to sleep. Talk to me.

– Only if it'll make you stop.

– No chance. So where are you from, then? Hampstead, I bet. Primrose Hill.

– Cricklewood, he said, and Jason clicked off the razor and laughed like a drain. – What's funny about that?

– Nothing. I had you pegged wrong, though. You knowing Eberhard at Oxford, I thought you'd be . . .

– No, not really. He pulled himself up again and began winnowing the blankets for his shirt. – I told you about my family.

– Doesn't mean anything. Nothing hard-up about the markets these days. You could be some nob selling yoghurt. Doesn't even mean it's true. People say all kinds of things when they're in strange places. With strangers they can be whatever they want. Not that we're strangers any more. Still, Eberhard mixing with the hoi polloi, well well. And there was I thinking you were one of those public schoolboys with the perennially fashionable Cockney accents.

He walked boots-in-hand to the window and unlatched it, filling his lungs with pine and woodsmoke. On the windowsill was a flowerpot, four marijuana seedlings praying to the sun. The sky over the mountains was clear, the last stars still undiminished. The day was starting fine.

On Thermopylae Street a police car had pulled over onto the pavement. The driver was leaning out towards an old gypsy woman in a sheepskin coat. She huddled away from him, trying to edge round the car. Her face was thrawn with fear or anger.

– Gorgeous out there, isn't it? I love this country. Don't you?

– I do.

– Best place on earth. Cradle of civilisation.

– Come and look at this.

– I am. Who would you shoot first?

He craned round. Jason had one eye shut, his hand curled into a gun, the two fingers of the barrel resting lightly on Ben's shoulder.

– Get off me.

– No, really. If you had the chance? The gypsy or the policeman?

He looked back at the scene. – Or you.

Jason patted him. His voice moved away. – I like your lateral thinking. Won't solve any problems though.

– It might, if it stops you talking. What problems?

– The troubles of Greece. It's a shambles out there.

– I don't see anyone asking for your help.

– That's because they're proud, that's all. The whole place is going to the dogs. Someone needs to sort it out.

– By shooting gypsies.

– Nah, they're alright, I'm just having a lark. They wouldn't be top of my list, anyway.

– Lucky them.

– I'd sort it all out if I had the time and the brains, though. You should think about it too. Takes work to keep things working. It's a dirty job but someone's got to do it. You should talk to Max about it, he's the ideas man. I'm coming back here when I'm old, you know. I'll get a little place, a house and a few olive trees. Maybe some goats. Goats can't be hard.

– That wasn't what you used to say. You called Sparta a shithole.

– I can lie, can't I? That was ages ago. I didn't know if I liked you then. Sparta's not for everyone. You and me: not her and him. Come on, get your boots on.

– I am.

– Good boy. Here, Jason said, and there was the coffee, hot and black and impossibly good. – Drink up, you look like you could do with it. Hope you're going to be up for tonight.

– What's tonight? he asked, and the weatherman smiled and vanished into an ether of advertisements as Jason leaned at the window beside him.

– Tonight, he said, We hunt.

❧

The goats came down to the dig that morning. They were pretty creatures, mild-mannered as sheep, inquisitive as tourists, their familiar bells ringing as they strayed here and there among the pits, their voices rising in complaint when Chrystos shooed them away from the huts and shepherded them back towards the hills.

He remembered the one time he had seen wild goats. It had been on Ithaca when he was a child. They had been driving through the mountains when the trees above them had burst open. Two Minotaurs had come crashing down the steep embankment into the road. His dad had sworn and thrown on the brakes, but the goats had been oblivious. The car and its pale occupants were like so many ghosts to them. Nothing had mattered to the animals except themselves.

The way Ben remembered them they were massive, big as horses or bulls. Their coats fell down in thick foul skirts of piss-stained white, tramp-black, and rust. One had shouldered back up the slope while the other struggled to its feet; and then the pair of them had charged, their horns clashing with a sound like trees splitting. Ten or a dozen times they had come together, locking and wrestling, and as the Mercers had sat watching, the windows all rolled up in fear, the smell of the creatures had filled the car like gas, their musk inescapable, the power of it unmistakable, and its double-meaning, too, clear as a voice raised in anger. The rank ripe stink of their sex. The unassailable eminence of their violence.

Four of them worked at East Midden, where Eberhard had hit

upon a hoard of oyster shells and the smithereened, blackened remains of a multitude of storage jars. When lunchtime came they ate in silence, looking up now and then to the higher hills and the mountains beyond, then cat-napped together in the shelter of the cars – Eleschen's head on his shoulder, Max's breathing thunderous in his ear – and woke to Missy's voice, their hands tender, their shoulders aching.

At sunset they drove down. The evening was still clear and cold, the day's warmth fading with the light. They had agreed to meet at ten and he went back to the hotel for clothes and showered while he had the chance, scrubbing soap through his beard and hair. He rang down for a wake-up call at nine, set his travelling clock for the same, then found himself too wired to sleep and – luxury! – ordered supper up, eating cutlet and rice and spring greens at his desk, his books and papers sprawled around him.

He left late despite all his precautions. The moon was clearing the mountains as he went half-running under the orange trees and through the long shadows of the colonnades. The others were at the girls' before him.

– You're late, Eleschen said at the door, more tersely than he felt he deserved. He felt the tension as she led him upstairs even as he realised how rare it was, to see them ill at ease together, their nerves rubbing raw on one another. Only Eberhard was calm, sharing out on the floor six miscellanies of tools – torches and binoculars, reflector-bands and whistles, hunting knives and shotgun shells – while Max paced up and down between the fireplace and the long windows and Natsuko cradled Sylvia, the dog's face woeful and alert, a masticated Converse just out of reach.

– She wants to come.

– She always does.

– She can smell. She could help hunt.

– She is not trained.

– People hunt here. Maybe she was raised–

– She is too small. She could get hurt. Jackals are fierce, like wolves. A wolf would break her up like chicken bones–

– But you don't know. Please? Eleschen?

– Hmm?

– Is Sylvia a hunting dog?

– You know she is, but that doesn't mean–

– She is not coming.

– Max, it is not fair that you always decide everything! she said, abruptly fierce herself, rebellious with anger, and Jason laughed where he sat barefoot, cutting his toenails on the ratty sofa, cupping the small-change in one hand.

– Who said we had to be fair? It's always Max or Eb who decides, in the end.

– Nevertheless, Eberhard said, We should be in agreement.

– How about acclamation, then? That's how the Spartans did it. Cheers for and boos against?

– No need to encourage the hound, Eberhard said, still without looking up from his division. – Normal discussion ought to suffice. Eleschen?

– Oh, I don't care. Let her come. Jason, *God*, you are so foul, will you please not do that here?

– Jason?

– I got to, they hurt when I run–

– *Jason.*

– Not on your life. She can't even catch her tail, let alone–

– Yes, alright. I also feel as Max does, which brings us to two for and three against–

– What about Ben? Natsuko said sulkily, and Jason sniggered.

– Oh yes. What about *Ben*?

He felt his stomach lurch. It felt as if he had walked in to hear them laughing over him. Eberhard looked up from his work, his expression not surprised, only a shade too courteous.

– Yes, of course, I'm sorry. Ben. Do you have an opinion on Sylvia that you would like to share with us?

– Bring her, he said, and Max groaned and strode away while Eberhard took off his spectacles and began polishing them, as if to delay or avoid the need to take the conversation further.

– Why? Max said, turning back. Why do you say bring her? I tell you why. Because it is Natsuko wants it. Because it is you who wants Natsuko. Excuse me, no. You think because you shoot two little birds you know suddenly all about hunting?

– No, no, I know I don't, he began to say hurriedly, but Natsuko was answering for him, Jason was butting in again, Max was yelling, and his own voice was feeble with awkwardness, as if he found himself caught up in a domestic argument between friends.

– He does not need to say why! No one else has to–

– Ben and Nat? Fat chance. Ben and Sylvia, if he sits up and begs–

– Like little dogs, both of you!

– Look, sorry, I know I don't know anything, I just think there's nothing to lose. I mean why not bring her along? Just to see what she can do? If she's at home with the guns, try her. You know how to hunt, Max, you decide when we get there. Maybe she can follow a scent. If she's no good, leave her in the car. Bring some water and a blanket. She's used to being by herself. She won't be any trouble there. I don't see that it's such a problem.

Max scowled, his scarred face vicious. – *You* are the problem! There were no disagreements until you came–

– No, Eberhard said abruptly, and looking back at him Ben saw that, for the first time since Metamorphosis, Sauer was smiling at him, without irony or rancour. – He's being quite sensible. When he puts it so well it doesn't seem a problem at all. Don't you think so, Max?

They were all watching the Georgian, he realised. There was a difficult silence before he unfolded his arms, threw them up and let them fall with a slap against his thighs.

– Alright. Too much talk. We're wasting time. Bring her, then. If she gets in the way I will shoot her myself.

– She is a good dog, Natsuko said, and stood with Sylvia grinning in the cradle of her arms. – You'll see.

– Well, there we are. Now, if there's nothing else, Max is right, it's getting late. We can't afford to miss the moon. Are we all ready for the off?

~

Their nerves took them in different ways. At first Jason was all chat, egging on Sylvia in the back (*Who's the big hunter? Who's the big hound?*), nagging them to put the radio on; but he fell into a sulk when Natsuko shook her head no, and after that there was no sound except the panting of the dog until they reached the excavation, following in the dim red wake of the Volvo's tail-lights.

They parked just as they always did, side by side under the cypresses, as if it were a working day. They all three jumped, and the dog gave a half-bark, when Max came tapping at the window to tell them to switch off the headlights. Jason got out, still muttering, Sylvia scrambling after him, investigating the car tyres, sniffing after shadows. Ben watched the pair of them go, hardly aware of them, attuned to the intensity of the girl beside him.

Therapne came clear as their eyes adjusted. The full moon riding high. The trees a noctilucent silver. The huts and hills and stepped ruins rendered in silent monochrome.

– Ben? she said, as if he might not be there, might have faded away into shadows, and he reached for her hand in the dark and found it.

– Here.

– It looks strange. Like an old film.

– It's just the moon.

– Are you sure?

– What else could it be? he said, and seeing her smile he understood for the first time that she was not nervous with fear at all, but with excitement.

– Maybe we have gone back in time.

– You'd like that, wouldn't you?

– Yes.

– Why?

– Because the world is bad.

– The world was always bad.

– No. It was better at first. Then it got old and it went rotten.

– Natsuko?

He leaned in as she turned her head, felt her meet his kiss. Felt her begin to melt. Her lips opening, softening. She touched her mouth as she pulled away, as if he had crushed her there.

– Not yet.

– When?

She shrugged. – Not yet.

– When I'm one of you?

– One of me?

– Not *you*. You know. You do.

– No, she said, Shh. Silly.

– Why? Why am I silly?

– Because you'll never be one of us.

She kissed him again before opening the door. They stepped out into the night. The others had moved on from the cars. He couldn't see where they had gone and was about to call for them when Natsuko started away, walking up towards the North Hill, and following her, looking past her, he saw them waiting there. The four of them as colourless and motionless as standing stones.

He caught the whiff of cigarettes before they reached the ridge. The wind was blowing from the east and he wondered if that was a good thing. Both Max and Jason had lit up, toting shotguns and smokes. The other guns lay by Eleschen's feet with Sylvia stretched out beside them. Max and Jason were staring north, Eleschen and Eberhard east. No one was saying anything.

A minute passed. Eberhard sat down. The dog glanced at him and yawned carnivorously.

– What are we looking for? Ben said finally, and Max rounded on him, his face a lunar grey, light flashing off his reflectors as if he had put on armour. Eleschen answered him, her voice faint and strained.

– We're not looking, Ben. We're listening. The jackals howl at the moon. That's why we came tonight. And it'll help us hunt. Us and them. If they make a kill they'll howl again. Better for us. It helps us both, the moon. Max came up at the weekend. He says they won't be far away. All we have to do is wait.

– And listen, Max said, under his breath.

Silence. The glow of an ember. Jason dropped a cigarette, mashed it underfoot.

– Nice clear night, he whispered, and when no one answered, Quiet though.

– Not with you here, no, not at all.

– It's a Tuesday. Eberhard, murmuring. – Some have considered it an unlucky day ever since Byzantium fell to the Ottomans. Most are not so superstitious, but hunters do not like to take chances. No one wants–

– Quiet! Please!

Midnight approached. The moon was still ascending, sailing through mottlings and spumes of cloud. He squatted down and stood by turns, the cold creeping into his joints.

– How long do we wait?

– Tired so soon, Jason?

– I'm just asking.

– You talk too much.

– Because he's nervous.

– No, I'm just bored. I think I'm coming down with something.

Eleschen's laughter, off in the gloom. – You're such a hypochondriac.

– Better hypo than klepto!

Eberhard turned his owlish face. – At least you know you'll be proved right. Hypochondriacs always are, in the end.

– Funny. And you could've brought some tea instead of all this poxy kit. I'm going for a slash.

His eyes were still acclimatising. He could see the excavations now, ranged around them like pitfalls, as if the hill had been fortified against some nocturnal attack. His hearing, too, was heightened. He could make out the traffic in town, a truck changing gears by the northern bridge, dogs barking towards Afisou; and then, with uncanny clarity, the patter of urination, the small, pathetic sound of Jason breaking wind, and Natsuko's glove-muffled mirth.

Max had wandered off eastwards, disgruntled with the lot of them. Eberhard was entirely still, arms on knees, chin perched on hands. The wind came up, catching at the last frail filaments of his hair.

He looked at Natsuko. Her dark hair was patinated white. He edged crabwise towards her. She ignored him as he came but buried her face in his coat as he reached her, stole her arm through his, guided his hand into her pocket.

– How can you be hot?

– Not me. Hand warmers. Here: magic.

He closed his eyes as she led his fingers to the alchemical heat. He was so cold that he could feel the warmth creeping up his knuckle joints, into the dense heel of his hand, up the bones of his arm. Like the poison that killed Socrates, he thought, the hemlock that began at his toes and ended at his heart.

– Ben?

Eleschen was holding out a gun to him. The bores were wavering too close to his face, the mouths a dark figure-of-eight. Two hollow black infinities.

– There aren't enough to go round, now. We didn't plan for you. Eberhard thought you should have one.

He nodded, took the gun. – Is it loaded?

– Not until we hear them. There's no hurry.

He shut his mouth tight again to stop his teeth from chattering. Eleschen was still talking, dreamily envious.

– Eberhard says you can really shoot. I've never been much good at it.

– What'll you do, then?

– Mind Sylvia. That's okay. The Spartans hunted with dogs. Dogs and nets and spears.

– Is that what we're doing? Being Spartans?

– Well, there are worse things to be.

Silence again. Eberhard still quiet. Then Natsuko's soft voice at his shoulder. – Don't you think so, Ben?

– I don't know.

– Do you love Greece?

– Of course I do, he said, and Eleschen laughed almost soundlessly.

– Then it's easy! There wouldn't be a Greece at all if there hadn't been Spartans. Greece needs its heroes, do you see?

– I know that, he began to say, not knowing if he meant to agree, only halfway persuaded; and then the howling began.

It was an alien cry, neither canine nor lupine. It was unlike any sound he had ever heard an animal make. His skin crawled. The pheal rose and fell like a siren, eerie and silver and unearthly. It seemed to come from everywhere, from all around and overhead, as if the moon itself was screaming.

Time leapt. He struggled to his feet, the others exclaiming and scrambling around him. Jason was running back towards them, a fresh cigarette rolling away into cinders. Max was turning this way and that, his face raised urgently to the light. And then,

– The dog! The dog!

He looked down at Sylvia. Her hackles were up, her lips rolled back, her teeth bared to the black-flecked gums. She looked like a different animal, larger and wilder, lycanthropic, the moon transforming her. She was making no sound at all, not only no answering cry but nothing, as if she meant to give no warning to the thing howling off in the dark. The whole of her – eyes and ears and trunk – was magnetised, fixed on the North Pole of the eastern hills.

Someone put his gun in his hands. He found himself loading it. Beside him Max was doing the same, breaching weapon after weapon, dropping a shell, fumbling for more. Then they were running, all of them, in a straggling line.

When had they planned how to hunt? They had not decided anything. In arguing about the dog they had forgotten that most essential thing. And yet he saw that as they ran – down the hill, over the scree, across the dusty, musky thyme – they left their first panic behind.

They shambled the first hundred yards, falling over themselves, out of breath, out of sheer luck missing the pits; but then, gaining a second wind, they found their pace and their places. Eberhard and Max were leading them, drawing them into a shallow crescent of guns, though it was Eleschen who was furthest ahead, her stolen dog leading them on across dry stones, wet sighing ground, towards the inner dark of the trees.

Moonlight strobed them through the branches. He lost sight of Eberhard, then Max. He could still see Jason to his left and Natsuko off to the right, her gun much too long for her and held out straight in front, the way that riflemen bore arms in old paintings of old wars.

The howling came again, much closer. He stopped and realised all at once that all of them had done the same, that he had been the last to catch whatever it was that had passed between them. He scrabbled for the torch at his belt and saw, not far ahead, the flash of moonlight from an armband. The others were still going on, but slowly now, and quietly, though he could hear them here and there. The snap of twigs underfoot. The dice-click of stones. The stealthy hiss of someone pressing through the brush.

Afterwards he could never tell how it was that he lost them. One minute he could still hear them, the next there was no sound at all beyond that of his own progress. He stopped, groped for the torch again, listened for a painstaking stretch, then caught his breath and snapped it on, pointing the beam down at his feet.

The forest leaped up around him, the trees and rocks larger, uplit. The undergrowth was impenetrable, the sky entirely out of sight. A sense of loss washed over him. He had been one of them, whatever Natsuko had said. He had felt part of them for – what? A minute? It felt more; was less – and already he had failed them.

For some time he stood unmoving, straining to make them out. He heard nothing but the trees, the susurration of the wind, the gallows creak of limbs and roots. It was as if they had vanished. As if they gone on into some place barred to him, like children in an old story, and he the lame boy left behind.

His face was cold. He reached up, wiping his cheeks, and realised that he had been crying, the act seeming so shameful that he cringed, as if he had wet himself.

He thought of going back. A part of him still wanted that. To not be lost, searching for them, but to accept what he was not. To get it over with and have his failure complete. But then he thought that they had run ahead again, that there had been a simple sign he had missed, and that they might still want him there. That as much as he needed them, they might still have need of him.

He raised the torch, scoured the trees, then put it out and went on. His hands were shaking. With the left he gripped the slick stock of the gun, the other arm raised like a shield against the clumps and beards of gorse that grew wherever the trees had failed. Twice he fell, the second time catching the gun against his knee, the barrels rammed into his guts. Then the woods began to thin, the moonlight stronger than before, and stepping out of the last pines he found himself in a burnt-earth clearing, and the jackal standing, watching him.

The night had become so bright that he could see it all in colour. The clearing was a blackened field, the trees at its edges part-burned, as if lightning had struck and fire crept only so far from the epicentre. The jackal was pale in contrast. Something lay dead at its feet, a slick mess of pelt and viscera. The jackal had been nuzzling it: its muzzle was still dark and wet. It seemed like a wolf to him, but smaller, long and muscular: a lithe creature, built for speed. Its coat was old-gold and black with, on its chest, a bib of white, like a flaw of milk in dark honey. Its ears were long, pricked up. Its eyes gleamed yellow-white. Its face was weird and devilish. Its mouth was fixed in a crude smile.

His scalp ached. His hair was trying to stand on end.

Only as the creature began to move did he realise it had not seen him after all, had only sensed him through some less precise means. It went off at a neat, fast trot, leaving the kill behind, pausing once to sniff the air. It headed not towards him or away, but south, along the hills. At the wood's edge, by a blackened spur of rock, it stopped and cocked a leg to piss, and yawned, as Eleschen's dog had done. And remembering the dog, he remembered the gun.

He swung and pulled in one act. The trigger hardly made a sound, only a smothered click, but even as it came to him that he'd left the safety-catch on the jackal stopped, one foot still raised, posed in the moon's limelight, and looked his way again, its face both sly and innocent.

The trees to the east crashed open. Someone – Eleschen, white-haired – burst out, the hunting dog with her, no longer silent but baying, an anarchic howling ululation. And all around the two of them came other figures, wild things staggering into the light.

The jackal froze. For half a beat he thought that it would double back through the mob of hunters. Then a shot went off and it had turned. Its mouth grinned as it came on. It loped towards him, swift and low. As it closed he heard it growl. Its eyes did not seem scared but fierce, as if it meant to run him down. As if it thought that he would flee, the hunter turned into prey, a quarry like any other, to be chased until it fell.

The gun lay slack in his hands. He shouldered it again. Sighted along the double-bore. Readied the catch. Readied himself.

Just as he fired – it seemed to him – the creature leapt out of his way. The motion was so languid, so uncaringly graceful and unthinkingly beautiful, that he cried out, his voice caught between despair and admiration. And then the thing was flinching back, its length writhing and tumbling, its own voice rising above his own, purer and more articulate. Its scream going up and up, and the hills full of his own thunder.

൭൬

Morning found them sprawled on chairs outside Afisou's one taverna. They had been drinking for five hours, the owner grumbling at first, closing up as they arrived, begrudging even the first drink, then warming to Eberhard's orders, the cash advanced for brandies by the glass and by the bottle, for bread, olives, cold meats and wine – the best wine that he could find, Asirtiko from the Cyclades, Black Laurel dark and sweet as chocolate, and four bottles of old Chablis, still sound, bought in better days and gathering dust ever since on the shelf above the beer-stained bar where the owner napped with the TV on while they saw out the night.

The candles had guttered out. The sunrise crept across their remains. The owner shuffled out again with coffee, spoon sweets and tall glasses of Spartina. Natsuko was collecting wax, kneading figures out of it; a bow-legged family of dogs, women and men. Eleschen was basking, legs stretched out on the taverna steps. Eberhard and Max were playing chess as if each meant to prove the other drunk and himself sober. And Jason was still talking, had not stopped talking for a second since they had come down from the clearing in the woods, their heads full of moonlight and gunpowder.

– The dog was good. *Good dog*, yes you were! She was, though, wasn't she? I mean we couldn't have done it without her. The way she went after it. Like she was inside its head. Like one of those Yank missiles. Garage door at fifty K. You were wrong on that one, Max, weren't you?

Max nursing coffee, tapping at the choice of knight or pawn.
– The dog was good.

– Dead wrong on that you were. And Ben! How good was Ben? We were all wrong there.

– Jason, Eleschen said, slow-lipped. She had her sunglasses on and had rolled up her trousers and knotted her shirt, the sun on her belly and calves. – You're embarrassing him.

– Embarrassing us, more like.

– Embarrassing yourself, at least . . .

He came up behind Ben's chair, leaning over him like a London drunk, hugging him, his beard rough and his breath smelling of half-digested wine. – Kept his head, didn't he, while all about were losing theirs? We almost didn't ask you, you know. We thought you'd be the weakest link. It was my vote that tipped it. And now it turns out you're our point man, our hotshot . . . it was a bloody hot shot. The way you took your time. Waited. What a killer you are. Didn't you think so, Eb?

No answer. Sauer was sat back from the chess game, still awaiting his move, an empty glass in one hand, his chair turned to the cars and the road.

– Eb? Jason said again, and Eberhard started and wiped his face. The dawn was still no more than lukewarm. Even so he was sweating.

– It was well done.

– Is that how it always is, Ben said, Hunting?

– No. The intensity is in proportion to the ferocity of the game.

– Do you think the Spartans ever felt like this?

– Yes, I should think they did, Eberhard said, and Jason leaned over him again, off balance, voice barely coherent against his ear.

– We're the real Spartans now.

– What if there are more jackals? Natsuko said. She was arranging her dogs and men in a circle, man dog, man dog, as carefully as if they were votive offerings.

– Then we hunt again, Max said, and Eleschen groaned.

– Oh come on! Once was enough, wasn't it?

– What's wrong with you? You loved it up there!

– Sure, but now I'm scratched all over. Except I suppose we'd have to go back, wouldn't we? I'll sure sleep better when they're all gone.

A moment's peace, the first in hours. He extricated himself from Jason, propped him up in the next chair, watched him fall asleep with his mouth wide open on his hands. The TV muttered and boomed inside. A cockerel crowed up at the top of the town.

– Why would we have to? he said, and Max glanced up and cocked his head, as if the question made no sense. – I'm not saying it wasn't . . . it's not that I didn't like it. I just mean why hunt them all?

Nothing from Max in reply but a Cold War thousand-mile stare. He tried again. – You said we'd have to kill them all–

– I said that, actually, and I didn't mean *have* to, Eleschen said. She sat up, pulling down her clothes, untangling her hair. – Oh look, I don't know what I meant. I'm so tired I'm not thinking right. What time is it?

– Seven, Eberhard said. Time to go.

– Go where? he said, and Natsuko laughed.

– To work. Did you forget? Stanton will be missing you. She likes you.

– Good. I like her too, he said, and Natsuko leaned across to him, smiling, stretching like a cat.

– Not like me.

– No, not like you.

Eberhard went to settle up. Eleschen shook Jason awake. Max came over with the Volvo's keys.

– You drive. We pick up the other car tonight.

Is Eberhard

– He's fine. Just drunk. Like all of us, except you.

– I'm not sober–

– You'll do, Max said, and met his eyes. His own, Ben saw, were small and grudging. – Jason was right.

He went and waited by the car. The others were still gathering themselves. The sun was creeping on up the hill between the last houses and olive groves. The cockerel crowed again. It sounded triumphant to him. He threw the keys up and they sang in the air in the seconds before he caught them.

ↂ

Only later did he wonder what happened to the jackal. His memories of the night's end were haphazard, everything after the kill confused by exhaustion and adrenaline. It was Natsuko who told him that Max had driven out of town that night and thrown the body in the river.

He didn't like that. It seemed wrong to him, disrespectful. The animal dragged under, the plush dark fur plastered thin. The buckshot weighing it down, the rot bearing it up, the spring floods filling its lungs, the rocks breaking its teeth and bones. But it wasn't an animal by then, of course, and he could think of nothing better for it; and Natsuko was in his arms, and he had other things to think about.

Thursday he ate at Eberhard's. His apartment was on the main plaza, next to a lurid Mister Donut – a place like a Hopper painting gone wrong – on the top floor of the long-defunct Hotel Panhellenica. The elegant ruined facade – the peeling yellow plaster and the tall grey-weathered wooden shutters – reminded him of the girls' lodgings but, inside the old hotel was grander, the rooms still with a few fittings, oak and mahogany and green brass, great spinnakers of net curtain, and an ironwork balcony with a marble table like a butcher's slab and perilous rattan chairs.

– You brought more books.

– They came last week. That's all of them now. I had nowhere else for them.

He worked his way along the shelves while Sauer changed out of work clothes and carried off the food they'd bought.

– Nowhere at college?

– Not any more. I don't plan to go back. Do you?

– I'm not sure yet. I thought you liked it there. You seemed made for it.

– I found it stifling. Too many old minds. How hungry are you, Ben?

Latin, the Golden and the Silver. Three shelves of German, two of Italian. A section of musical scores, then Russian and a phalanx of Greek, Ancient and Koine and modern, eight rows high, that turned the corner of one wall and went on, spine to spine, almost to the door. Thucydides in blood-red calfskin.

– Starving.

– Good! My mother used to say that hunger is the best cook. With luck it will make up for me.

He wandered down the corridor, past an array of luggage (stacked cargo boxes, a doctor's bag, three ancient age-cracked leather suitcases) into a windowless kitchen. An extractor fan had been fitted at some point, its aperture a rough hole bashed dead-centre in the exterior wall, its blades long since congealed solid with grime. The kitchen units were more recent additions, their flawless whites as out of place in the old room as Eberhard was at the stove. He was making an omelette of sorts, cracking eggs one-handed straight into the pan, his face frowning with absorption, the apron bound over his shirt patterned with roses and robins.

– You look a right mess. So does that.

– Thank you. You get the smallest egg.

– How did you end up here?

– In Sparta? Oh, we used to come. Often, for holidays. The English always want islands. The Germans lack that obsession. I will let you into a little secret: we get the best end of the bargain.

– I meant the dig.

– That was Max. He recommended us. He gave our names to Dr Stanton, and so . . . here we all are.

– You knew the others?

– In a way. All of them, in a way, Eberhard said, and nodded at the new bread. – Can we make use of that, do you think?

He found a knife, cut up the loaf, filled a green-glazed jug with water. The room was clouded with the smell and haze of eggs and hot oil.

– In a way?

– We corresponded. I mean over the internet. We met, the five of us, on a site suited to our mutual interests. I'm sure you know the kind of thing.

– Did you ever meet them?

– Max, once, years ago. The others never, until now.

– Why does Eleschen steal things?

Eberhard glanced up at him, still frowning, half a mind on the eggs. – What kind of things?

– Sylvia. Clothes too, I think.

He wiped a forearm across his glasses, raised the pan, slid the omelette onto a plate, turned off the hob and began to cut. Without the hiss and spit of the oil the kitchen was abruptly quiet.

– How did you know about the clothes?

– The lice, he said, and Sauer laughed.

– The lice, of course. That's perceptive of you. She was out with Natsuko one night. This wasn't long after you arrived. She jumped over a garden wall and took some things off a washing line. Natsuko claims to have been very shocked and not an accomplice at all. It was blankets, not clothes, I think. Their rooms being so cold, you see. But otherwise you're quite right.

– And is Jason right too?

– Is she kleptomanic? No! At least, not so far as I know.

– Then why steal– he started, and Eberhard turned, his face easing, a plate in each hand.

– I think you know why. I'll take these. There's wine in the fridge. Bring that and the water, if you could.

They ate on the balcony, silent until the plates were cleared, the lights coming on bit by bit below, illumination spreading from the cafés to the streets.

– I do know what you are, Ben said, and the rattan creaked precariously, Eberhard leaning to pour the wine.

– Do you? What am I, then?

– You're playing a game. It's just a game. Isn't it?

He felt a tremor of relief when Sauer shook his head.

– It's not a game. On the contrary. What we do here is in earnest. You should understand that too.

– I'm trying to.

– I know you are. You're doing very well. Much better than I had expected. Even Max has been impressed.

– Was it some kind of test? The hunt? he asked, but Eberhard shook his head, shrugging the question off.

– I saw you once, you know. By the Oxford canal. You were on a bicycle.

– I didn't know you'd noticed, he said, and then, because it seemed impossible not to go on, You were crying.

– Yes, I was.

A bat flicked through the dark. He thought of Metamorphosis. The eggs tinctured with blood, monstrous, red as a warning. He reached for the glass Eberhard was offering and drank off half of it straight, glad of the wine's astringency, his stomach gripped by nausea.

– Are you alright?

– I'm fine. Did you . . . had you lost someone, then?

– Lost? No, no. My family are alive and well. Well fed, well heeled, well set. Counting their hoards like Nibelungen in Berlin, London and New York. No, there are no losses there. Not fatal ones, at least.

– Why were you crying, then?

– For Sparta.

– But, he began, and didn't know what else to say; and said, But you were in Oxford.

– But Oxford is alive and well. Or at least it thinks it is. No one need shed tears for Oxford. That place is happy with its lot. Are you happy, Ben? he asked, and Ben answered without thinking.

– Happier than I've ever been.

– I'm so glad, he said, and raised his glass. – To happiness?

– To happiness.

Dig Sermons was their name for them. Missy called them other things – *Halftime Talks*; *Team Dialogue* – but more and more, that last fortnight, the lunchtime meetings had become less dialogue and more soliloquy. The ten of them would sit listening, or appearing to listen, or not even stretching to that, like children at the back of class texting gossip between their knees. Natsuko would be eating already, Jason eyeing up Eleschen, Themeus picking his teeth, Elias nudging him, Max and Giorgios brooding, and Missy's eyes would seek out Ben's, appealing always for his help, entreating and impeaching him, angry and sad, her voice speaking only to itself.

– Okay! The sun is up, the sky is blue, it's beautiful and I love you all, but my feet are wet and I hear my spare socks calling to me like

Ligea and Leucosia. Gather round, citizens. What's in the news this morning?

Friday. A cobalt sky. The pits like so many open graves. Bees crashing through the cyclamen.

– Hello? Calling Planet Spartacus, is anyone receiving me? What's happening underground? What do we got? Pigsties, potsherds, palaces? Come on guys, talk to me.

Jason beside him on the Menelaion steps, cigarette in lax fingers, kneecaps poking through his jeans, skinny as a glam rockstar, whispering down Natsuko's neck. – What's that?

– Stop tickling.

– If you tell me what that is.

– Fermented soybeans.

– Like beer?

– Beer is bad. This is good. Power breakfast. Want to try?

– You couldn't pay me. I've seen spew looked better than that. That's frightening, you eating that–

– Jason! How's the fishing today?

– What?

– No bites? No catches? No buried treasure? Where are you on, my man?

– Bronze Trench.

– So when I came by earlier it looked like you were doing something. Is your work on a need-to-know basis only, or can you share with us?

Chrystos grimacing, raising his hand before Jason found a counterpunch. Missy turning on him like a rat on veal.

– Chrystos!

– We found more infill to the west. Jason was working with me.

– Great. That's the Late Helladic fill?

– It goes down through three levels now. The pebble paving and two clay floors.

– Thanks, Chrystos. Now that might not seem like much, but a pit context is always worth following up. You all know digging's hard work. You know no one ever dug for nothing. Still . . . the consensus today seems to be that things are slow. Anyone disagree?

Nothing. The gyre of a skylark. Max opening a newspaper.

– It's slow. I take the heat for that. The new pits didn't pan out so good. What I want to say today is this: it's been worth all the work so far. Already we've found some fantastic stuff. A new shaft grave. A burial. Six thousand small finds and counting. That's more than we were hoping for, and I don't think we're done here yet. Another month, maybe three weeks, we'll up sticks and move down the hill and see what Orthia has in store for us. But until then I need you all–

– What *is* that? Eleschen said, and before Missy could bridle (her face was flushed, Ben saw, and sweating) Max was getting to his feet, head bent, one hand raised in admonition. Only then did he hear the whining.

It came and went, in just the way that a child would cry and falter and cry again as it began to forget the origins of its unhappiness. Its source was still some way off, but getting closer, or at least louder.

His first thought was that it was Sylvia. The notion came to him that a door had been left unlocked and that somehow she had followed them, the way that dogs in stories did. There was a strain of fear in her voice, a wheedling apology, as if she knew she had done wrong and whined by way of confession.

– Sylvia? he called, and took a step up the ruins. The whining began to rise again in the trees beyond the chapel and the shepherds' path, the place where, eight days before, Missy had found her burial. Eleschen was clambering up to him, pulling roughly at his sleeve.

– Someone's been teaching her new tricks, he began to say, but looked down at her halfway through and saw that something was wrong.

The whining stopped. As it cut out there was a last ejection of sound, a noise lying somewhere between a dog's bark and a big cat's growl. And then the voice returned again, ascending, up and up, like smoke, and hanging there, like smoke, reaching some perfect awful pitch, not animal and not human but sad and mad and heartbreaking.

He turned his face away from it. Max was already running, helterskelter up the slope past the chapel and on down, falling once on the infirm ground before he reached and crossed the shepherds' path. Natsuko was crouching, her hands over her ears, Chrystos bending over her. Jason and Eberhard were by the sheds – Jason looked to have dragged them there – inaudibly arguing. Eleschen was gazing at the trees, her hand still on his arm, her cheeks and lips white as her hair; the skin around her eyes blue-white, as if she had been drained of blood.

– What was *that*? Missy was saying at his back, What was it? Excuse me, will someone please tell me what that was?

– *Tsakal*, one of the Greeks answered, and then cried out excitedly. He looked round and saw Themeus, arm raised past him at the woods, and turning back he saw it there, beyond the trees, watching them.

It was not his jackal: not *his* jackal. It shook him that that surprised him. This animal was like the first – the same famished, infernal grin – but smaller and less beautiful, its coat patchy and rabbit-grey. It was misshapen, too, its head too small, its legs too thin to hold up its distended form.

A crash echoed back from the woods. The jackal ran up the rise beyond and stopped to look back again. It stepped over the top and was gone before Max came out of the pines. They watched him scramble after it, making hard work of the higher ground, going no further than the ridge, standing there for a long while before he came trudging back, waving their questions away, snatching up his trowel like a sword, hunkering down by the Skull Room.

He didn't see the others that night. Eberhard drove him down to town with Max still as a carving in the front and Eleschen in the back beside him with her arms folded tight across her chest and her face pinched, as if she felt a draught, though she leaned towards her door and kept her face to her window. The only talk on the way was an interminable argument in which Max asked Eberhard not to hum and Eberhard said he had not been humming, and Max insisted that he had and hummed the tune to prove it, and Eberhard calmly stated that, be that as it may, he never hummed, that he found humming distasteful, though he would sometimes whistle or sing . . . and so on past Afisou and down as far as the HellaSpar by the track to the Ortheion, where the gypsies offered their girls and loitered for coins they saved for cigarettes and country wine. It was odd too, he knew, for Natsuko and Eleschen not to go home together, and he wondered if they had argued themselves, but couldn't screw up the courage to ask.

Eberhard dropped him by the hotel and drove off as Ben turned to ask what they would be doing later. As he reversed the Delux he was already talking to those still in the car, his mouth twisted into a snarl. The look on his face was one of angry alarm, and Ben looked down the street to see what had startled him; but there was no traffic at all, the road empty except for trees, the orange trees and corpulent palms, and the kiosk vendor selling phonecards to a black man on a mobile phone, his rarity as striking as that of a Nubian in Imperial Rome.

He lasted two hours alone in his room – pacing and reading newspapers (*Protests against NATO Troops*, *Kidnap Family in Plea*, and *More Bombings Expected in Madrid*, as if bombs were now forecast, like rain) – then rang Natsuko's mobile, and getting only her recorded message (the voice too high and kittenish, a parody of her own) he put on his muddy boots again and went out, first to Eberhard's, then on to the cathedral square and up to Thermopylae Street. He found no one in, or no one who would answer him, and when he walked back by Eberhard's he saw no sign of Sauer's car.

He stood in the town plaza, by the lit plate glass of Mister Donut, looking up at the sky through the trees. Somewhere a band was practising, the sound of brass warming the air. It was almost Independence Day. The weather had turned colder again. The stars were overcast, the moon a lowbeam through fog, and part of him was sorry while another part was glad.

ꕥ

Chrystos found him the next afternoon. He was working back to back with Jason in the cramped shaft of East Midden, both of them with trench shovels, not talking much and not at all about what had happened last night, Jason's curses and jabbing elbows being answers enough.

He had hit raw rubble for a third time, was yanking out rocks like bad teeth, twisting the shovel blade, when he felt a shadow fall across him, and looking up at the pit mouth, blinking into the sun, he saw Chrystos peering in.

– You missed an easy bit. Just there.

– I'm saving it for later, he said, and stopping to catch his breath heard Chrystos chuckle down at him, the pit walls hollowing out the sound.

– Like the best meat. I wanted to talk.

– What about?

– The jackal you killed.

He heard the scramble of dirt behind him, as if Jason were not getting up but falling. East Midden was deep but not long. They would be stood close together.

– It didn't look dead last time I saw it, he said, and Chrystos smiled again. The light was odd on his face. It threw him into silhouette but lit up the lines around his eyes. It made him look kindly and old.

– Not the bitch. I mean the dog.

– The bitch? Jason said in his ear, but he could hear that he already understood just as well as he did himself.

– The bitch is carrying. She should not be out of her home. She must be very hungry. Very hungry to have come here, where people are, to find her mate. But she will not find her mate. Because her mate is dead.

– How do you know?

– Because she came.

– We didn't kill it, Jason said, and Ben jumped at the harshness of his voice. The undertow of fear and anger. – We take rabbits, birds, that's it.

– Sparta is a small place. Everyone talks to everyone. If someone else–

– Then no one did. Maybe a car hit it. They must just die sometimes.

– Sometimes.

– It wasn't us. And what the fuck's it got to do with you?

– Nothing. Your business is your own.

– What happens to her now? Ben said, If the other one is dead?

Chrystos put his hands on his knees, readying himself to rise. His eyes were still on Ben's. Later it occurred to him that he hadn't looked at Jason at all.

– You saw her. She cannot hunt and eats for many.

– Will she die, then?

– Yes, of course. If one is killed, then all are killed, he said, and drew back, and was gone.

ঌ৩

He didn't see the bitch again for five days, except in his sleep.

Sunday morning he dreamed of the den. It was a fissure in the rocks, half-filled with rubble and loose earth. Narthex and opuntia bracketed out the light, but he could hear the jackal, its breathing on his neck in the dark, its panting in his ear like Jason's in the pit. Now and then there were other sounds, too, a whining and a dull, irregular, rasping grind, like a file drawn across a trowel, and after an unbearable time it came to him that he was hearing the creature eating itself.

He woke to the smell of chlorine. The shower was on, and Natsuko's sneakers, T-shirt and jeans were heaped pink-white-blue on the floor. He hadn't given her a key, but somehow she had found a way to let herself in that last week. He suspected the slicked-back boy, had wondered if he should be glad for himself or jealous of him.

She was naked when she came in, and he lay, pretending sleep, watching her moving around, making tea, drying herself, stealing his dressing gown, until finally she looked up and caught him.

– Bad man.

– Good man. Come here, I'll show you.

– No. You're too bad. Too lazy.

– Why, what time is it?

– You slept all morning. Like a cat.

He checked the clock and swore, although he'd had no reason not to sleep in; and then the dream came back to him, and he threw off the blankets, not wanting to return to the fissure and the grinding.

The kettle was reaching a boil. The noon light came in the window, slanting downwards through the vapour. Natsuko was gone again, back into the bathroom, singing.

– You sound happy. Where have you been?

– Swimming.

– Always swimming. You must have been a fish in a past life.

The hair dryer started up next door, on and off, bursts of noise drowning out fragments of her. – . . . dolphin. That's why I like eating . . . not all morning. Also church.

He went and got the kettle. – Church?

– . . . sometimes. We go with Max. He believes very strongly. And the Greek ways are very precious.

– I didn't know, he said, pouring. – I thought Japan was something else.

– Where I come from there are Christians.

– So you believe in God? he said, and felt her arms around him, still moist from the shower, luxuriating in him.

– It is important to believe in something.

– I dreamed of the jackal, he said, and held her hands where they were twining into his hair.

– To dream of killing is good luck.

Not that jackal, he thought, and said, Is that what your God tells you?

– No. But I have many gods.

– Lucky you. What's bad luck, then?

– To dream of being killed, she said, and drew him round to face her.

⁂

The next night it came to him again, one nightmare bleeding into the next.

He saw the first creature, drowning, its eyes flayed out by river grime. As if Natsuko had cursed him he dreamed of the killing itself, the hills, the woods and the clearing rendered in silence and slow motion. And finally he dreamed that he woke alone to find Stanton by his bed, her head that of a jackal, her eyes those of an old god, and her hands held out to him, to guide him through the underworld.

He woke to barking in the yards outside. He got up as quietly as he could, not wanting to wake Natsuko.

He was about to shut the window when he heard a sound further off, beyond that of the dogs and higher, pitched in falsetto. At first he half-convinced himself it was a siren, an emergency crew somewhere far off, going to or from some crime or accident.

Already, though, against his will, he recognised the jackal's voice. That distant loneliness and wrath. The raw thread of it strung through the duller bayings and chitterings of the town animals.

– Is that her? Natsuko said, drowsy in the dark behind him, and he nodded, listening. – How close is she?

– Not very close, he said, and locked the window as he shut it.

෴

Sometimes, when he kissed her, she would go utterly still. Motionless, like an animal. It was as if she was waiting for something. He didn't think it was him.

Their sex, too, bewildered him. He would look into her face – her head back, her collarbones like wings – and see the pleasure that he gave her, and still he did not feel he had her. He possessed her and possessed nothing. Afterwards, sometimes, alone, he would remember that and know that one day it would enrage him.

She sat beside him in the bed, hair falling straight across her breasts, eating yoghurt and honey from the jar.

– What are you thinking? he asked, and she stopped to think, then to look down at him, her eyes dilated in the dark.

– I am thinking of nothing.

෴

By Thursday all was well with the others, if not with himself.

Jason was back on form, telling anyone who would listen of the summer he'd worked in Astrakhan and dug up seven skeletons, all dressed in rotted sable furs, one with a golden fob watch as round and thick as a halved apple. At the dig sermon Eleschen spoke excitedly about the Skull Room: Max had uncovered a pair of urns two feet below Laco herself: inside them Eleschen had found votives to Apollo and Artemis in their role as the twin gods of disease; and with the lead figurines the residues of what seemed indisputably to be medicines. Honey, opium, ground root of cyclamen, and quantities of powdered cinnabar, the red sulphide of mercury.

Even Max was sanguine, breaking off his relentless work to sit with Themeus and Elias under the eaves of Elijah's chapel, chatting with them about small things, the sun bathing his pockmarked face and rare stone-Buddha smile.

They broke early despite the good weather, Missy announcing a few hours' leave for Independence Day, revelling in their temporary approbation. They cruised down with the windows open, Eberhard conceding to put some of Jason's music on – the best driving compilation (Jason said) that side of Berlin – with Eleschen singing along in snatches, her voice throaty and fine, her arm hugging the car's warm flank, her fingers opening for the breeze.

They were passing the first outhouses and allotments of Afisou when she stopped singing and sat up.

– Oh, she said, her voice falling, Look. And as they did Eberhard slowed to a crawl, the wind of transit dying around them.

A pickup truck with smoked-glass windows lay parked on the bend of the village road. Someone had hosed down the tyres. Mud still clung to the flatbed's sides. The driver's door stood open, a toolbox on the grated step. The front wheel on that side was off, the wet chrome hub a polished shield, the chassis jacked up on concrete slabs.

Hung from the back of the cab was a long thin grey rag. It looked heavy, so that at first he thought it must have been soaked by a clumsy pass of the hose. Only as their car closed with it did Ben see it for what it was.

The jackal had been strung up by the tail. Its hindlegs and forelegs hung down; only one ear jutted up, as if still listening. Its guts had been roughly cleaned out. One long wound ran up to its chin, another down each limb to the claw. The belly flapped empty and wide.

Its head swung clear of the truck's bed. As they passed it by he saw its eyes, narrowed to slits, and finally the white snarl of the teeth trapped in its perpetual grin.

Silence in the car, stretching like held breath. Traffic was backed up before the main road and it was slow going until they were over the bridge. Then Eleschen leaned forward by Eberhard, her white hands gripping the seat back.

– Should we be worried?

– Not at all.

– But where do you think–

Jason, muttering. – They must have got it last night.

– Jason's right, Eberhard said. If something were going to happen we ought to have seen the signs by now. We were well placed for that. Besides, the body wouldn't be displayed, not like that, if anyone had found anything.

– Found? Ben said, They found her, didn't they? What else is there to find?

No one answered him. They drove up past the hotel, not slowing at Eberhard's but going on towards the cathedral square. The bunting lights were not yet on, nor were the streets crowded, but people were out in numbers, children and best clothes on display, and everywhere there was an air of festival vitality.

– Time for a drink, Jason said. – Who's up for it? First round's on me.

– What would they find? he asked again, but still nobody replied.

– This is an appalling song, Eberhard said phlegmatically, and Jason kissed his teeth.

– I've heard the shite you listen to. You wouldn't know good music even if it blew your bloody eardrums out.

They came out by the square. Two priests passed down the broad cathedral steps, old women clambering up around them, all of them – women, priests – in black, busy and sure as ants. Doves scattered around the car, their wings flashing in the sun.

– My definition of a bad song, Sauer began, and Eleschen cut him off.

– I wish it was summer.

– Why? he asked, still bewildered, but caught up in their relief, infected by their happiness, wanting to understand – wanting that more than anything – and Jason laughed, not unkindly, as Eleschen leaned into him, turning her face to kiss his own.

– Because summer is so beautiful here, Ben. Because we'll be finished with everything by then. And because I want to hear the cicadas singing.

XII

Notes Towards a Thesis

Last night I heard sirens again. This morning the streets reeked of smoke. Some still clung along the river.

Crossword told me about the fire. She collared me out on the steps where she was watering the road trees. Her face came alive with the pleasure of telling it.

It was the *yifti* (Crossword said), all of them drunk as Russians to celebrate the festival. The women drink just like the men and none of them have the heads for it. The children are insolent and the women (Crossword said, taking my arm) are worse than the men. They keep knives in their skirts. The fires happen all the time because they love to see things burn, they make so many fires just for the prettiness of it. It was an old building went up, out on the road to Gythion. Not that there would be much to burn, those buildings being so tumbledown, half of them already gutted in one way or another.

Later I talked to Elias. Elias tells it differently. He says it was local men, seven or eight of them, who came down looking for some fun. One girl was hurt. No one was burned. The police and the firemen came. And that is all he says.

Siren. From *seiren*: binder. The Sirens in the old stories are monsters of the seas and rivers. Ligea and Leucosia are their most ancient names. They are birds with women's faces, or women with the tails of fish. Their voices are beautiful, so beautiful that they can hurt. Their songs are full of hooks and lures, and with them they fish for men. They are men's fear of women made flesh. A man who hears the Sirens sing forgets his life; forgets himself. His ship is wrecked and down he goes, or he stands listening, transfixed, and dies of the hunger he has forgotten.

First you will come to the place where the Sirens live, the creatures that seduce men. Those fools who get too close will never leave again. The Sirens who lie in the meadows will charm them with their sweet singing, although the dead lie deep around them.

How did Sirens become sirens? The monster draws us in. The device warns us back. They seem like polar opposites. As if the word that once meant *north* has twisted round to point at *south*.

What were the jackals to us? Did they draw us or warn us? They didn't mean either, of course. They didn't howl for us.

The voices are what stay with me. The sirens woke me last night and I thought I was hearing ghosts, the jackals sounded so like them. I sat down to write this note when I realised I was listening for them again. Their voices are lodged in my head like hooks. I am enmeshed in memories.

What kind of sirens were the jackals? I think they were both Sirens and sirens. A warning and an allurement.

Easter is coming soon.

Themeus has begun bringing Eleschen gifts. At first he was too shy to offer her things to her face. His own face blushes Indian-dark when he does. Elias laughs and Max looks angry and is, I think, embarrassed for him. Themeus creeps up on her at lunch, as if she is an animal he doesn't mean to startle (one that might run, or might bite?) and leaves her eggs wrapped in fig leaves and celebrity magazines and last season's wild honeycomb, its ruined gold-black labyrinths suspended in old olive jars.

Her hair is paler, now there's sun. My Spartan blonde, Eberhard calls her. Jason says Themeus isn't her only suitor. Half the town men are half in love with her. The cadets worship her. The older ones loiter in the cathedral square in ones and twos every evening. Come Easter, Jason says, she'll be buried in offerings.

Jason told me something about her. He says her family are Amish. She told Jason she can't go back. Her family won't eat with her. She left because she loved music. Music is evidence of pride. Pride is a deadly sin. She was nineteen when she went to live alone in a town called Athens.

So Eleschen tells Jason, but Jason doesn't believe it; he thinks music can't be it, that it must be *something juicier*. And so Jason tells me, and who can I believe? Jason is full of stories. Like a historian, he believes only in ulterior motives. But we were drinking when he brought it up, and he is more honest when he's drunk. It's the only time he tells me things. And he is the only one of us who ever tells me things at all.

They play strange games, Chrystos said. He was right, but the game isn't the heart of it. They play at being Spartans with their secrets and their ridiculous thefts and hunts. They are like cats practising kills. They are like children, whose games are cruel and facile or meaningless to anyone except themselves. But the game is . . . something like a joke told to avoid telling the truth. It is a comedy mask. There is more to it than play. Eberhard had no need to lie. It isn't just a game.

They hide things. They work at it. They're not much alike except in that. If fear is the theme of the Spartan gods then theirs is secrecy. What am I saying, then? That they have something to hide. That I think they are testing me. That I think they have something up there, something in the caves.

XIII

The Cave

– An outing!

Friday: Eberhard's. He was in the kitchen for ice. The others were all out on the balcony, pacing their drinking as the moon came up. He could hear them out there, their voices faint through the dead blades of the extractor fan.

Warm gin, Natsuko had said, making a moue of distaste, and before he could offer himself Eleschen had spoken for him. *There's ice. Ben will get it for you, won't you, Ben?*

Eleschen was talking again now, her excitement punctuated by the crack of nutshells. She was chain-eating almonds, the only edible supplies they had found in Eberhard's kitchen. Before she finished one she was on to the next, cracking them on the butcher's slab table, her empty shot glass like a gunshot. He knelt to open the freezer and heard pigeons scattering from the eaves overhead.

Eavesdrop: Natsuko's favourite English word. It made her think of rain, she said. She said she had always loved rain.

In Japan it rains very much.

A lot, you mean. England too. Cats and dogs.

Why cats and dogs?

You could come. I'll show you.

Maybe, she had said, *One day*, and she had sounded so nostalgic and melancholy, had made it sound so impossible, as if England were cut off from them by centuries or outer space, that he had burst out laughing.

Crack!

– Will you stop that, El? I can't hear myself think.

– That's no great loss. What outing, Eleschen?

– I don't know yet, I just thought of it, but isn't it a sweet idea? I think we should go.

– Go where?

– Who cares! Somewhere nice.

– Have we earned it?

– Sure we have. Come on, guys, don't be so stuffy.

– We haven't achieved anything yet.

– All the more reason, then. It'll inspire us. We'll go somewhere *inspiring*.

– How could we be anywhere more inspiring than here?

He closed the freezer and went to the sink, the ice fracturing when he ran the water, the voices briefly incoherent, though he knew them well enough to tell them apart without discerning a word, knew them like old friends, would have known them anywhere.

Eleschen was laughing when he shut off the tap.

– We could go tonight even!

– It's too late, and we're all too drunk.

– I'm not. I'll drive. Who's coming?

Crack!

– *Will you bloody stop doing that?*

– Only if you find me something else to eat. Which you won't, because you're not gentleman enough to help a girl out, and anyway you can't because Eberhard lives on books and dust. Like a spider. Like a bug.

– I don't suppose I can be both, since spiders live on bugs–

– You can eat me, darling.

– No, you're too vulgar. Anyway, these are much nicer.

– I'm nice. You won't know till you've tried.

– Where?

Max's voice. Ben had almost forgotten he was out there. It was a talent of his, that unobtrusiveness. Notice slipped away from the Georgian like oil from water. It was an odd trait in a big man. His face – Ben imagined it – would be as grudging as his voice.

– Olympia. Or the sea! We haven't been since Gythion, and it was so cold then. Come on, we've got a whole weekend. It isn't far.

The whole weekend was Missy's doing. The mood up at the dig had changed for the better that morning, the coolness thawing to a new cordiality. Missy had seemed bemused, and then inordinately pleased, her pride unfathomable until she buttonholed Ben, asking him if the afternoon off she'd declared yesterday had really been so special to them.

She had saved her trump card until the afternoon, announcing just as they struck camp that tomorrow she would have to go to Athens to give her progress report to the Cyriac Foundation. While she was gone they deserved a full day's holiday. *Because you've all been such great sports*, she had said, and Ben had blushed at the bribery as she blushed at it herself.

He shucked ice into the green-glazed jug. The last cube clung to his fingers, and he hissed and peeled it away, no longer eavesdropping, already tired of it, wanting to be back with them.

– Better not Gythion again.

– Why not? It's not a bad idea, a dirty weekend by the sea.

– You've no one to be dirty with.

– Except himself.

– There'll be tourists down there now, they're always game for a laugh.

Now Jason's eyes would be roaming the square. He had shaved his goatee that last week. The stubble had already grown back in, hollowing his cheeks. It made him look less comical. He seemed more voracious, perhaps more threatening: a rejuvenated Tom Waits or Jack Nicholson, a sexual predator, a crackhead driller killer.

– We have responsibilities here.

– Nothing that won't keep.

– Someone will have to see to it.

– Yes, of course. That could be done tonight.

– We could go paddling.

– Skinny-dipping.

Natsuko, sighing and shifting into the last of the sun. – We could go *swimming*.

– It's this waiting. I'm so tired of it.

– It's almost over now.

– Is it?

– It must be soon, one way or the other. Easter is just around the corner.

Silence. In its lacuna he realised he had lost the thread of the conversation. He had missed something, had heard them wrong, he thought; and then Eberhard was talking again, his voice as guarded as Eleschen's was irrepressible, and hearing the far-off sound of his name he stopped, stock-still in the kitchen door.

– And Ben?

– Enough of Ben.

– He'll be upset.

– He is an impediment.

– Oh come on. He doesn't mean to be.

– He doesn't know anything.

– And who would he tell, if he did?

– You don't like him much, do you, Max?

– I don't trust him.

– You don't trust anyone.

– He likes us.

– He loves you. Lucky girl.

– And so he would say nothing against us.

– Eb's right. Let him come.

– I don't care either way, I just want to see the sea. And sand. Let's go somewhere with sand, can we? I've had enough of mud and stones and waiting.

– Pylos, then.

– Gythion is closer.

– We can't go back to Gythion.

– It is not sensible to leave at all . . . but Eberhard is right. If we have to do this, then Pylos is safer.

– *Sandy Pylos!* Like in the stories, Eleschen said, so ingenuously delighted that by the time he rejoined them it was all decided.

∾

They left by the Langádha Pass, up through the gorge with the first light behind them, over the boulders and scree of the tops, peak after peak rising above them, then down into a second night, darkness dug in under the pines, dawn unbroken in Artemisía, the sun not catching up with them again until the hairpinned descent to the dusty green orchards of the Messenian plain.

By eight they were at Kalamata, the traffic slowing along the city's clogged arteries, first Natsuko and then both cars stuck behind belching gridlocks of long-haulage, bikers swerving between coaches, flatbeds stacked with watermelons, chickens in teetering highrise coops, bread and fibreglass and ice. Then they were through, and already the sky ahead was lucid and nacreous, as if it met the sea just beyond the horizon.

They changed drivers by the airfield, Ben taking over from Natsuko while Jason saw to Sylvia, the dog bug-eyed and ecstatic with thirst, gorging herself on bottled water before frolicking wickedly out of reach in the giant calamus grasses beside the road. By the time they had cajoled her back they were far behind the others, but there was only the one road ahead and he drove fast, overtaking tractors and weekend drivers until the Volvo came in sight, a pocket silver racer between green banks.

The road turned south-west after Messene. Jason was channel-surfing the radio, fishing for police frequencies. Natsuko was gazing out, shadows filming her face. The dog was asleep and agape.

Let her come, Eleschen had said, the night they had argued over Sylvia. And Jason had said the same about him, that last night on the balcony. They had talked about him as they had the dog, as if he too were no more than that. They had not done it to his face. That aside there had been no difference.

He shivered, and a moment later felt Natsuko's hand, warm on his neck.

– What?

– Nothing. It's fine, he said, and smiled back, as if it were true.

And wasn't it? He had never felt better. The conversation on the balcony seemed insubstantial, unsubstantiated. There was only the faintest unease in him, the old feeling of having gone wrong somewhere; of having lost the thread of his life as he had lost the train of the others' talk. Odysseus, lost at sea. He had almost grown used to that. Other feelings were fresher in him now. His passion for the country around him. The happiness of finding friends, of being among those he loved. The freedom that rose in him as they drove seawards together. They had let him come with them. That was enough. He was content.

He wondered where it came from, that new sense of freedom. He felt released from something. He wondered if it was his old life, or the gridlocked city falling behind, and then realised it was neither of those so much as it was Laconia. He had spent a month inside its mountains. He had become inured to its oppressiveness.

– Are we there yet? Jason said, and Sylvia woke up whining, as if she understood his grievance, and just then a roadsign came up to assure them that yes, they almost were.

ꙮ

He caught up with Eberhard just as Pylos came into sight. The Volvo fell in beside him – a glimpse of Max and Eleschen spitting like cats in the back – and then overtook again, speeding to beat oncoming traffic, one lazy hand extending from the driver's window, regally waving Ben to follow. The town was an amphitheatre of terracotta roofs and whitewashed walls clinging to the hills below them, but they turned away from it, following the coast road north.

– Where am I going now? Natsuko?

– I'm asking, wait.

He heard her speed-dial, then stilted talk.

– He says there is a secret beach.

– Shouldn't we get rooms first? he said, and Jason yawned and stretched, seat rolled back to the max, feet stacked one-two on the dashboard.

– Relax, will you? Why waste the day? This time of year they'll be crying out for us.

Now the sea was beside them, black as anthracite in the harbour, bright as stained glass in the shallows. An island sheltered the bay, a long Here-be-Dragons procession of vertebral humps.

– Eberhard says the island is Sphacteria. He wants to know if anyone would like to hire a boat tomorrow.

– Not tomorrow, not in this lifetime. What's wrong with him? Tell him there's nothing there I want to see. Anyway, I came to prop up the beach, not bone up on more history . . .

The island still ran parallel with them. He watched it as Jason grumbled on. Named, it had become familiar, its rugged face resolving like that of an old friend in a crowd. It was the first place where the Spartans had ever surrendered, their hoplites starved and besieged by sea, their enemies burning the island bare. Athenian hirelings creeping along the tops with slings strimming through the smoke, like Davids going to meet their Goliaths.

– Here be dragons, he said, talking to no one so much as himself, but Jason nodded, his own gaze still lingering on the island, as if he felt the same thing too, the sense of a history so old it had almost crossed into myth.

Pylos was like Sparta in that, its modern insignificance overshadowed by a legendary past. *Sandy Pylos*, and *Sacred Pylos*, Homer had called it. And there had been something else, too, some other momentous event besides the surrender of the Spartans . . . what was it? Something almost modern – *Not your period*, Fischer at the British School would have said – though more than that he couldn't grasp, the memory of a word cleaving to the tip of his tongue, the definition of it just out of reach.

But that was Greece. The endless cycle of vicissitudes: all of them, for better and worse, remembered, retold and recorded, not dispassionately but ardently, so that the daughters might learn from the mistakes of the mothers, and the sons avenge the fathers. Revenge after revenge, on and on, since before the invention of history itself.

A sign came up for the town beach. Eberhard kept on past it. They drove in convoy now, close enough for Eleschen to turn, gesturing like a drama queen, pointing at Max, mouthing for help in comical desperation.

A village had grown up around the turning, a ramshackle strip of convenience stores, foreigners here and there even this early in the season, women with bleached-blonde bangs and balding men in Bermudas trying on hats and sunglasses, admiring themselves in hanging mirrors, cocking their heads like parrots in cages. On the sea-side of the road Europop played on hotel verandahs. A handful of younger tourists waited at a bus stop, the men red-necked, a toddler crying or crying with laughter; it was hard to tell which before they were gone.

Natsuko had gone to sleep, her cheek propped on the back of one hand, as elegant and desirable as a girl in a Pre-Raphaelite painting.

Eberhard was gathering speed. The village thinned to outskirts and was gone.

A river. Fallow fields. One lonely house, a row of cacti standing guard in rusted feta cans. A chapel and a wrecker's yard, a man walking from one to the other, shouldering a jack as long as his arm. Then they were turning onto an unmarked road, the surface reduced to dirt and dust, twisting between old acreages, the view of what lay ahead always screened by eucalyptus or calamus, laurels, olives, blossom trees, the smell through the open windows of salt and iodine: and then a cliff rising above them, dark and grim with the sun behind it, the sea strobe-lit at its feet, the beach suddenly opening out in a stupendous crescent of coral white, and Eleschen already out of the car, kicking off her shoes, running, screaming, shrieking, running.

Later, sated with sun and sea, they climbed the southern headland, Natsuko, Sylvia, Eberhard and Ben, ploughing uphill through the dunes, their ankles pricked by gorse, ponderous black carpenter bees droning around them and away through thickets of sea-thistle and thyme.

There was a cave below the heights, and they stopped in the shelter of its mouth and looked back at the beach below. The others were Lilliputian, Jason smoking in the shade, Eleschen an indolent sun goddess, Max reading the newspaper, bolt upright like a yoga master.

– Look at them, Eberhard said, Basking in their own glory. The lizard, the cat and the shark.

He was wearing a Panama, an old one, the fine weave coming apart at the brim. It made him look surprisingly different. Locking the car, then stood in the surf, trousers rolled up to his bony calves, he had seemed out of place, a hesitant young bank clerk dipping his toes at the beach. The Panama changed that. He looked less upright in it, more debonair, less trustworthy. Altogether riskier.

He was leaning on Ben's shoulder, emptying sand out of his shoes, dusting off his hands with a flourish.

– Which is the shark? Natsuko asked, and Eberhard grinned, sharklike himself.

– I'd say they all have their moments. Shall we go on?

– Where to? Ben said, but the others were already off, all of them quicker than him, none of them much out of breath, Natsuko nimble, Eberhard wiry and loping, Sylvia cavorting through the scrub.

They skirted downwards to the south, the headland rising between them and the open sea. Inland, a freshwater lagoon cut them off from the world beyond, the sand blackened around its shores, the water baking in the sun, foetid and eerily silent, what sounds there were magnified out of all proportion, so that when a snake jackknifed out of their way Natsuko's scream and Sylvia's howls were deafening concatenations, thrown back at them by the cliff above, more frightening to all of them than the snake had ever been.

They emerged by the town beach. Natsuko had brought water and they sat in the shade of a tamarisk and shared a half-bottle four ways. Two old men in black swimming trunks walked up, down, up the strand, nursing prize bellies and cigars. Beyond them a pack of girls were playing beach tennis, kicking up spray alongside rows of grass-skirt parasols. Sphacteria faced them all, its northern tip looming across a narrow strait.

– We could swim that, he said, thinking they'd both jump at the idea, his high spirits sinking just a shade when neither of them did.

– My watch . . .

– We hide it, under a rock.

– It's too far for Sylvia.

– Besides, Eberhard said, There's plenty to see here, and no need to swim for it.

– I thought you wanted to get a boat?

– I did. And then I wondered if Jason wasn't right after all. Why follow in the footsteps of those who surrendered?

His voice had cooled.

– But that wasn't what he said–

– But perhaps it was what he meant. Jason is often less plain-spoken than people realise, or give him credit for. He knows his own mind, and knows how to keep it to himself. Ready? The old castle is just up here.

They started off again. The path ran seawards and upwards, curving away and doubling back around the green bulk of the headland. The sun was higher and hotter now and for a second time he found himself lagging. At first both Eberhard and Natsuko kept his pace, but Sylvia was soon out of sight.

Already they were high above the sea. The hillside below was steep, shapeless wild olives and cypress giving way to a boulder beach, monstrous eggs and domes worn smooth by the Ionian; and high above them, to the north, the broken outline of a fortress, crenellations white in the noon sun.

– Is that where we're going?

– That's it.

– It's not exactly round the corner.

– You sound like Jason when you whinge.

– I'm not whingeing, I'm just saying . . .

They climbed a set of ruined stairs, the last of the flight more handholds than footsteps, stone pegs wedged in sheer dry earth, Natsuko offering a hand he ignored first and then refused rudely, tetchy with sun and failure. Overhead, between cypresses, spiders had laid web after web, great dusty grey labyrinths.

– What was it happened here? he said, and she glanced back at him, her expression anxious, as if he had asked what year it was. – Not the Spartans, I mean something else.

– Navarino, Eberhard said. He was well ahead of them now, his voice coming and going between the trees. – Nineteenth century. The last great battle between ships of the line. It happened just by Sphacteria. For all intents and purposes it marked the end of Ottoman sea power. The armada of Ibrahim Pasha was annihilated. Three thousand died by fire and water. A good day for Greece. A fine day for Europe, you might say. English, Russians and French watching Musselman ships burn through the night. The admirals understood what so many have since forgotten; that this is the last frontier of Christendom. There are some paintings of it, none of them terribly good, although the ships make a pretty show. The *Kastor* and the *Konstandin*, the *Sirène* and the *Scipion*, the *Asia* and the *Albion* . . .

He was out of sight before his voice faded. The two of them

climbed on together. Two lizards flickered out of their way, slim as blades of grass. Sylvia barked a question somewhere downhill; uphill Eberhard whistled back.

– It is nice to think of, Natsuko said, and he gritted his teeth, more annoyed than ever by her sure-footedness, and more than that by her strangeness, by all of their strangenesses.

– What is?

– Navarino.

– Is it?

She smiled at him over her shoulder. – Of course! You don't think so?

– I think water is nice to think of. And lunch. I don't think Navarino–

– It is the beginning of the new Greek freedom. The end of tyranny.

– Tyranny's a strong word for it. I doubt the Ottomans saw it that way.

– There is no Europe without Greece.

– Yes, but–

He took another step towards her, blinking sweat out of his eyes, shaping up for an argument, and felt scree shift under his feet. The breath went out of him before he realised he had fallen, the pain hard on the heels of the impact, his ribs creaking under pressure; and then he really was falling, not all at once but sliding backwards and downwards in ludicrous slow motion.

His hands were clawing for purchase. The heat of limestone was against his cheek. He was spread-eagled on a sunlit rockface. The whole thing was almost funny until he felt one foot swing loose, and looking down he saw the way the rock to which he clung ran out, morning glory trailing from the overhang in breathtaking blue festoons, and cypresses far too far below, one terrifying funnel web spun between them, as if waiting to catch him.

– Don't look down.

He looked up. Natsuko was an arm's length away, cheeks flushed, voice hushed, as if she might blow him away. He swore between his teeth.

– Shh. Can you climb?

– Of course not! If I could–

– I can reach you. I think so. Wait . . .

– Don't be stupid. Get Eberhard–

– He's too far. I won't leave you. Take my hand.

He reached for it, slipped, felt her catch his wrist. Her fingers thin as wishbones.

– Will you help? I can't do it by myself, she said, out of breath at last, and he put his head back and roared another oath. Eberhard's voice came back, somewhere far-off and questioning; and then Natsuko was laughing, lovely audible bubbles of pleasure that made him want to shake her or kiss her.

– Ben!

– What?

– Do you want to fall?

– What bloody kind of question–

– Don't you trust me?

He met her eyes. Not black, he saw again; blood-red. The sun entered deeply into them, the darkness of the irises suffused with faint ochre crypts.

– Alright.

– You believe in me?

– Yes! Yes, I believe in you.

Some great weight lifted away from him. He pushed and kicked at the face of the rock as Natsuko began to pull. She was much stronger than he would have guessed, even knowing her so well. It was as if he hardly knew her at all. Her face was relentless, contorted, and still grinning as she reeled him in, into the circle of her arms.

For a few hours afterwards – lovely hours, to him, though he would not have confessed it to anyone – he was the sole centre of their world, a cherished child. Eleschen and Natsuko made him an invalid's bed in the dunes above the beach, a smooth nest of sand and towels, while Jason recounted accident disaster stories, even Max squatting beside him with a first aid kit from Eberhard's car, curing his grazes with Savlon, probing his ribs for breakages: but there was no real damage done, and at some point he fell asleep, and when he woke no one was there but Natsuko, warm beside him.

– *Yashashii, ne.*

Her voice made her sound as if she was smiling.

– What does that mean?

– You should be sleeping.

– You woke me up.

– I thought you were going to fall.

– I didn't. You caught me. What does it mean?

– It means you have a soft heart.

– Don't you?

Her head was on his chest. He felt her face move against him, eyelashes tickling him, the sand still warm under him.

– No.

– No? What kind of heart do you have, then?

But he was almost asleep again, and if there was an answer he never heard it.

ꙮ

Evening found them in the square in Pylos, drinking Camparis and orange under cyclopean oriental planes. Eleschen and Max were bickering over backgammon, the Georgian watching every move, staring out the dice, Eleschen on a winning streak, all insincere innocence. Sylvia was hunting cockroaches between the maze of legs and tables, trees and vending booths and fountains. Eberhard and Natsuko were picking through the Saturday newspapers, reading them cover to cover, as if starved of real life. Jason was watching the sun go down, the island half-eclipsing its incendium.

– Look at that.

– It's pretty.

– Pretty! It's beautiful. Like the end of the bloody world.

– Or the beginning. It looks so ancient.

– *Take from the altars of the ancients not the ashes but the fire.*

Eberhard stirred, mantis-thin, propped on his elbows over a broadsheet. – Blake, isn't it?

Jason nodded, sucking on ice, eking out the dregs of his drink.

– Never liked him that much.

– I didn't know you were on close terms.

– Hardly ever says what he means.

– But he always means what he says.

– That's what I *mean*, Eb; what does that mean? Blake's so New Age. These days he'd be right into all that crystal dolphin tribal bonding bollocks.

They ran out of conversation again for a while. Jason was thoughtful, for once, cracking the last of his ice in his teeth. – Funny, all this being Spartan once. All that way we came.

– All this and more. Not that most Messenians realise how lucky they were.

– Lucky? Ben said, and Eberhard closed the newspaper.

– I'd say so. Fortunate to serve greatness.

– Unfortunate kind of servitude.

– Oh, no doubt some would disagree, but service can be its own reward.

– Is there news? Max said, and Eberhard shook his head as Jason pushed his chair back and stood, Eleschen crooking a grin at him.

– Where are you sneaking off to?

– Wherever the fancy takes me. Goodnight, sweet ladies. Don't wait up.

– There he goes, out on the prowl, Eleschen said. Max frowned.

– Go too. No one's stopping you.

– No, I'll just cramp his moves. Anyway, it's not my style.

Her gaze was still on Jason, ducking away between tables and trees, and she shrugged and began to pack away her books and sunglasses and lotion.

– Off to bed?

– Yup, I'm beat. Max, walk me back?

He brushed himself down as he stood. There was an ineptitude to it that was so unlike him that Natsuko turned away, towards Ben, smothering a smile.

– What just happened? he said, once they were gone, and she giggled while Eberhard sighed impatiently.

– Nothing new. I find it all unnecessarily intense. I know opposites are meant to attract, but they seem to find each other so very repellent, when they're sober.

Natsuko was gathering herself, taking Sylvia's lead, leaning down to kiss him goodnight. He watched her follow in the others' wake. Just as Jason had promised, they'd had no trouble finding rooms, four rundown rear-window doubles that Eleschen had wrangled for less than half the summer rate, even with the dog in tow.

A breeze came in off the sea, bringing with it the smell of the harbour, leafing through the headlines. Eberhard straightened them but no longer looked at them. He sat as if alone, making no move to talk.

New Algerian Terror Threat. 9/11 Blow to Bush. Violence Mars Athens Football Game.

– The hat suits you, Ben said, when the silence began to weigh on him, and Eberhard jerked back to life, his hand going to the Panama.

– Yes? It was my father's. I always liked it myself. He presented it to me to celebrate my Oxford Fellowship. That pleased him very much.

– He must be proud of you.

– Must he? Eberhard said, and took off the hat. I'll tell you something, Ben. People often assume my parents are dead. It's a gross assumption, don't you think? I find it offensive, but I know I must encourage it. For example, I know that I tend to speak of them in the past tense. I think I do it because we're no longer close. My father and I, especially, are similar in many ways, but we have grown apart. We hold such different beliefs. He had his plans for me, but they are no longer the plans I have for myself.

– I'm sorry, he said, awkwardly, out of his depth, wishing only for the shallows, for lightness, as he so often did with Eberhard. – Sorry about the walk, too.

– Don't be, please. I'm just glad nothing seems to be broken.

– I'd have liked to have seen the old castle.

– There's not really much to see. It's only the view that's impressive.

The sun had gone down. A tanker was moored out in the harbour, its lights plumb-lines across the water. A few small yachts were coming in soundlessly towards the marina. Eberhard was looking out at the dim shape of Sphacteria.

– I heard you talking, he said, surprising himself at least as much as Eberhard, whose head turned only lazily, eyes still focussed on the distance.

– Talking?

– Last night, on the balcony.

– I see. I can't recall that anything scandalous was said . . .?

– Why can't you go back to Gythion?

– We had some trouble there. Jason got into an argument. I wasn't there to see it. I believe he was thrown out of a shop.

– When?

– A couple of months ago, I suppose. Some time before you joined us. We hired a boat down there. Plenty of wind and too much rain. I did the same thing as a boy.

The wind caught at Eberhard's hair. He pushed the last thin strands out of his eyes and smiled again.

– You sound unhappy, Ben.

– No, I'm not. Not at all.

– Good. I didn't think you were. You must tell me, if you are.

– Sometimes you leave me out.

– Out of what?

– If I knew that I wouldn't be left out, would I?

– Don't be angry. We are trying.

– But you keep things from me. Like the jackals.

– How did we keep them from you?

– You lied to me. You said it was just a hunt–

– I'm not sure I ever said that–

– We killed it so the locals wouldn't. You didn't want anyone up by the caves. That was all it was. That was why it died.

No reply. Eberhard, chin on hand, one knuckle pressed to his lips, as if stopping an answer. Ben leaned closer to him.

– That's why we killed it, isn't it?

– There's no use pitying it. It would have been killed anyway.

– But there's something up there.

– There are lots of things up there, I'm sure. There are so many caves–

– Are you playing games with me?

A man at an adjacent table broke into sudden raucous laughter, and Eberhard looked sharply round at his English bulk and noise before replying. – I told you. I don't play games.

– Chrystos thinks that's all it is. A game. Missy too.

Eberhard sat back. He spread his hands on the table as if they were winning cards. – Let them think.

– But you do, don't you? That's what you do. You let them think it's just a game. You play at playing Spartans because no one cares about a game.

– In a way. Yes, in a way. Do you trust me, Ben?

– You all keep asking me that. I would. I want to. I would if you trusted me.

– Quite right. That is the question. Do we trust you? Natsuko does. Jason does. Eleschen is open to it. And Max does not, but then Max is religious in his distrust of everyone . . .

– Is there something in the caves?

– Yes.

– There's something there.

– I just said so. Yes.

For a moment it was as if he had fallen again, the air going out of him. He took a deep breath and sat back. He experienced a moment of clean clear triumph. Honoured: that was how he felt. As if he had just received some quiet, long-sought word of praise.

Eberhard was nodding at him, unruffled and amused. – So now we trust one another. I always knew we would. You always had that quality. You're one of those who seems to be searching for a place in which to put your trust. A destination. Some people find that search painful. It becomes a burden to them, to not believe in anything. You had your marriage once, at least–

– What is it?

– It's not easy to describe.

– What period? Is it Classical?

Eberhard laughed and shook his head. He had turned to watch the ebullient Englishman again: when he looked back at Ben his eyes were bright with agitation. He leaned forward, whispering, more eager than Ben had ever seen him, ironing down the paper tablecloth under his winning hands.

– It's priceless.

– Tell me what it is.

– No. Much better for you to see it yourself.

– You'll show me?

– Yes.

– When we get back?

– When we get back. You've earned that chance, Ben. I'm sure the others will agree.

– Promise?

– I promise to put it to them, though we've discussed it often enough. I know their feelings. Now, in the meantime, I'd like another drink. A Scotch, if you can find one, two if you'll join me. Would you mind?

Somehow they lacked the time to make it back to the secret beach. In the morning Natsuko persuaded him to go with her to matins and the liturgy, all of them except Jason making the breathtaking climb up to the white domed church, the lustrous, candled gloom inside almost as mysterious to him as it had been in childhood, pungent with beeswax and myrrh, the priest a young man smiling shyly through his paternal beard, giving out blessings for travellers and the dying, for new cars and rain. Jason was still in bed when they returned, and they pottered around till past noon, abandoning their church clothes, Eleschen luxuriant and louche in her too-short hotel dressing gown, Ben yawning and bone-idle and magnificently bruised, all of them except Eberhard playing Texas Hold 'Em under Jason's drowsy tutelage before migrating down to the square for an afternoon measured out in beers, frappés, taverna wine, and platters of sweet hot fried squid at a breezy end-of-jetty table.

It was eight before they left, and long past midnight when Ben woke and saw mountains against the stars, the Parnon and Taygetos familiar and inimitable as any Westminster skyline. Their black ring closed in on him, no longer threatening or confining. The streets outside, the small-time shops, the colonnades, the hotel steps, all of it known and intimate, sheltering and welcoming.

ꙮ

The bruises blossomed. By morning he was marked from hip bone to sternum, the blood seeping under the skin, the contusions ripening into shades of toadstool green and Wedgwood blue. Two tiger-stripes still shadowed his ribs like X-ray images. For five days he worked with Natsuko at the Findhut, Missy refusing to allow him down into the pits.

Those first days after Pylos he thought of the cave all the time. The need to see it ate at him. But Eberhard did not come for him, did nothing, would barely speak of it, frowning the only time that Ben reminded him of it, muttering a sharp *Not yet*, his face closing like a helmed mask, as if it were unpardonable to mention the cave at all.

He would be doing something else – inventorying mussel shells, cleaning Dark Age bones – when it would come back to him, vivid as the sight of blood, shocking not just in itself, in something being concealed, but in the way it brought to light the substance of his deeper thoughts. The longing to see the cave was always in his system, subliminal, subcutaneous, intracerebral. It waited in the back of his mind for some memory to trigger it – mountains, shadows, sunlight, pain – like an addiction, or an infection.

Priceless, Eberhard had said, under the oriental planes. There had been no time, that night, for Ben to think about what that meant. But even that one word was shocking in its way, that single detail, so unexpected in the harsh light it cast on all of them.

It was a fine line, the one that lay between the passion of the archaeologist and that of the collector. Intellectual passion: passionate avarice. The best archaeologists would skirt the line, flirt with it, but would never cross it. Now and then, in archives, at sites, Ben had seen the avidity in the eyes of those who risked falling for beauty. The inscription on a Moghul ruby; the gold ropes of a Celtic torc; the miracle of Seahenge. It was always seen as a fall, that step, in the world of discourse on ancient things. It was the greatest offence, that descent from thought into desire.

It's priceless.

ꙮ

He took Natsuko out. There was a place in New Mystras which Eleschen said would be perfect.

It was a mild evening, a foreshadowing of summer. They drank outside while the meal was made, the wine flavoured with saffron, the slopes around them dissonant with unseen mountain streams.

She wanted to talk and he let her. She told him about Japan. Her parents owned a vending machine firm, a franchise with operators across the Kyushu region. There were machines for videos and magazines, food and drink and cigarettes: they had grown rich on cold beer, hot noodles and soft porn. Natsuko had been close to them until the age of twelve; then she had begun to be ashamed of them. Their wealth was selfish and tasteless. They had abandoned their own parents' religion and traditions. The shame had grown as she had herself, not coming and going as the familial embarrassments of her friends did, the school-gate ignominies of overweening mothers and fathers in low-grade company cars. Her parents cherished her, and she hated herself for hating them. She had moved out as soon as she could, going to college in Nagoya.

Her first passionate love affair had been with a professor there. He had inspired in her a zeal for all things European, the arts especially, the list of icons seeming to Ben unpredictably nostalgic – Pheidias and the Beatles, Aesop and Aristotle, Beethoven and Housman – the fervour for them and their worlds drawing her first to Berlin and Rome and finally to Athens.

– And Sparta.

– I am very lucky. It is a special place.

– I know. I feel that too.

– Do you?

– I talked to Eberhard in Pylos. Did he tell you?

She went quiet in that way she had, like an animal stilling itself to avoid attention.

– You don't want to talk about it.

– I don't think I should. They did not say I could.

– Do you always do what they say?

– Always. Almost.

– I won't mention it, then. Not if you don't want me to.

Her face was indefinite in the dusk. So pale as to be luminous, so faint as to be ambiguous.

– Are you smiling?

– Maybe.

– It's hard to tell out here. I don't know what I'm missing. Let's go inside.

– Not yet. Please, I like it here.

– Alright.

The smell of grilled meat came to him on the breeze. He felt a craving, simple and instinctual.

I love you, he began to say, but she reached across to him just then, putting her hand against his lips.

– You don't know what I was going to say, he said, but he thought she did.

– I don't need you to say it.

– What if I want to?

– No. It's like a wish. You'll ruin it.

– Tell me then.

– No! That's the same.

– Tell me, if you think it's true, he said, and she shook her head and bent closer, smiling: he could see it now. – Alright. Are you happy, then?

– Yes.

– Happy to be with me?

– Yes. I am so proud of you.

◎◎

April had begun.

In the mornings when he left, and at night when he returned, the town was listless, the hoteliers and shopkeepers impatient and distracted, the crowds in the squares on hold, the avenues holding their breath. Easter was almost upon them. Everything waited.

Overnight – so it seemed to him at first – the impatience reached the excavation. From Pylos they had carried back a residue of high spirits, of languorous euphoria, that lasted all of three days. By Thursday morning it was gone. A new mood took its place.

He noticed it first in his friends. The general expectancy seemed to have intensified in them. Missy showed no symptoms, was desultory and drawn, but Eleschen was excitable, energised by unlikely things – a new outlying pit beyond the shepherds' path; the first find there of a pig's skull. Even Natsuko was quiet that morning when they woke and vague all day at the hut. Max was not to be disturbed, burying himself in work, and when not working in newspapers, snapping pages flat in the wind. And the tempers of the others frayed, suddenly and without warning, Jason talking a mile a minute one moment and snarling the next, Eberhard cold and aloof if anyone dared speak to him.

It frustrated him at first, the way that Sauer made him wait. Then it became bewildering, his impatience cooling into unease. A new distance had grown between them, between him and all of them, even between him and Natsuko, not the old unfriendliness so much as a fresh watchfulness. It frightened him that he might lose them and never understand why. He wondered if they had argued over Eberhard's promise to him, or if their thoughts were simply elsewhere and left no time for him. But then sometimes it seemed to him that the mood wasn't new at all, that their tensions had been building for longer than he knew, and all that had happened overnight was the moment of his own apprehension.

❧

On Friday he was still slow rising, and so cantankerous with pain, bickering over pointless things, that it was no surprise to him when Natsuko took herself off to pick up Jason and Eleschen, threatening to come back for him only if he stopped nagging.

He had only just got down to the lobby, could see the car waiting, was on his sheepish way out to the street, when Marina called him back to the desk, tapping a note in her palm.

– For you.

– Are you sure?

– *Po-po-po!* said the cockatoo, its pink crest flaring up like something venomous, and Marina clicked her nails at its cage.

– Of course I'm sure. Now finally you get messages you don't want them any more?

It was a postcard of the Parthenon with the Elgin Marbles frieze biroed in. The message was writ large, the handwriting cursive and soft-edged, as Emine's was, though it was not hers.

Dear Ben,
Athens's rocks!

Want to come for dinner? I know you're busy these days but I want to pick your brains. Are you free tonight? Otherwise anytime is fine. Just you, hope that's OK, because my place is real small.

You probably don't know where I am. I'm here ~

9 Cosmos Apartments, 42 Oreas Elenis ~

which is down by the bus station. Leave room for moussaka,

love Missy XX

The car horn sounded twice. He folded the card away before he opened the street door and waved down to Natsuko, kissing her hard as he got in, losing himself in the rush and noise of the morning and the four of them.

Only as they came up to Therapne, pulling in by Missy's car, did he think of her again. She was right, after all. He had never been to her place, hadn't known where it was, had never thought to ask. Really, he had never thought of Missy living anywhere.

☙

– Ben! You found me! Come on in, don't mind the mess, I don't know where I get this junk, it just follows me everywhere, like a goddamn junky albatross . . . listen, the food's not ready yet, so can you be an angel and start getting drunk for me? There's wine out on the table there. It's red, is that alright for you? My family's all allergic, so red's always a treat for me. I won't be too long, okay?

It was a small flat, four floors up in a prefabricated block, the stairs and walkways outside windblown and rusted, and the room he entered low-ceilinged, a television droning indistinctly through the partition walls. The table had been laid for two. A gaudy waxed tablecloth, a halfhearted poinsettia and a faded equipage of posters all failed in their efforts to brighten the cramped charmlessness of the place. He had expected something else – if not the space of Eleschen's then the scholarly grace of Eberhard's – and he kept quiet as he managed the wine, embarrassed into silence.

– Did I put the corkscrew out?

– I found it.

– Sweet! Pour me too. So was Pylos good? It sounded swell. Wish I could have gone with you all.

The living room and kitchen were connected by a serving counter. Through it he could see Missy peering into a mini-oven, her face lit up raw and anxious by its elements.

– What about Athens?

– Oh, you know. I'm not really a city girl. Anyhow I got our funding. Laco went down real well, she got them all excited. The Gods of the Deep Pockets smiled on us. Mercury's worth its weight in gold when it turns up in the Late Helladic. You come back next season, I'll have a hole with your name on it.

– That's great, he said, mechanically polite, Congratulations.

– Thanks! Are you hungry, Ben?

He drifted over to the posters, glass in hand. They were student staples, mostly, their corners stained and pin-pocked from years of migration. Audrey Hepburn in opera gloves. Kurt Cobain with wings. Muhammad Ali in the ring, towering over his enemies.

– Ben?

– Starving.

The Lion Gate of Mycenae. A child's guide to hieroglyphs. Einstein, with the electrocuted hair and the kindly eyes, seated at a writing desk above a line of florid text.

The world is not dangerous because of those that do evil, but because of those who stand aside and let them do so.

– Do you like what you see?

She had come up behind him, quietly smiling and quiet in her house slippers, her arms folded tight around herself as if she felt a draught. Her hands were mittened in oven gloves shaped like the mouths of animals: one crocodile, one frayed bear. Her cheeks were pink with the heat of the kitchen.

– I always loved that one myself. Some days it's my favourite. Einstein was so wise, don't you think? You want to look around some more? I can give you the tour. I mean it's nothing much. It's just here and the bedroom.

She was standing by his shoulder, close enough that when she looked at him he could smell drink on her breath.

– Maybe later, he said, and she smiled, swift and bitter.

– Sure, I understand.

– Missy, he said, not letting himself think through where her name might take them next, but then a bell rang and she turned away, her voice rising.

– It's chow time, folks! Sit down, I'll serve. I guess you want everything?

They ate without much talk, at first, the quiet punctuated by the brittle clink of cutlery, the high points of the TV show next door, Missy's subdued offers of more carrots, more beans, and his own acceptances and refusals. Almost immediately he knocked over his glass and Missy ran for kitchen paper, dabbing the spilled wine with a soothing *There, there*, as if he had cut himself. The table was so crowded with stuff it made all movement hazardous, a weird full regalia of archaic implements, coasters and napkin rings and trivets, a cruet of oil and vinegar, place mats and serving mats showing four chipped Scenes of the Great Lakes at Sunset.

She began speaking again abruptly, and brightly, as if the dejected silence had never fallen between them.

– Did you ever notice the thing with Giorgios?

– The what?

– How the others treat him. I mean they *really* don't like him. I mean they're not overflowing with love for any of us, except you, but with Giorgios it's different. Didn't you ever notice that?

– I don't know, he said, and for a minute went on working at his second collop of moussaka. – Jason said something, once.

– Oh, he did?

– About the war. It didn't really make much sense. Giorgios can't be that old.

He looked up in time to catch her face. – That was what I was worried about. That kind of makes it my fault. God! I don't see why they care, it's really none of their business.

– What isn't?

– Okay. When we started here it was just four of us. Max, Themeus, Elias, me. We're short-handed though, so Max calls some friends and I look for locals with experience. Stella – she's at the Department of Antiquities – she comes up with the Maxis brothers. Only at first it's just Chrystos. Then we get the files out and there's Giorgios. Experience to die for. I ask if he's retired, and Stella says no, he's hanging around, but there's bad blood there. How if we hire him it'll be tough if we want anyone else.

– Because of the war?

– Not that war. I guess Jason meant the Cold War. That was close to the bone here. Greece would have gone Communist, you know, in 'forty-four, except America and the Brits would never let it happen here. So Greece got thirty years of awful puppet governments. Giorgios was an army man, but only in the seventies, when the Colonels were running things. He was just a young buck, but he was stationed in Athens, and the story that goes round and won't go away is that he was in the tank that broke down the Polytechnic gates on November seventeen.

She stopped, awaiting some sign of recognition from him, scandalised when he shook his head.

– Oh come on, Ben! Where have you been all your life? November seventeen, 'seventy-three? There was a big student protest against the Colonels, and being the army they . . . sent the army in. I mean like snipers and tanks. A lot of students were killed. It's still a big deal here. No one forgets *anything* here, and this wasn't just anything. This was like the Greek Tiananmen Square. There was even a terrorist group named after it. November 17. Communist-anarchist-nationalists, can you imagine that? So *Greek*. They hated anyone who poked their oars in here, NATO, the UN, Turkey, and the Americans, of course, and the Brits too, you know, because the Colonels had all of us behind them. They killed a lot of people too. I mean the terrorists. They only caught them just last year. They were a really strange bunch, wow. Quiet. I remember they kept talking to the press in Latin. And one of them was a beekeeper, and there was a painter, too, he did religious icons

. . . so anyway, Giorgios. Since then, people round here, a lot of them don't like him. He brings back bad memories. But I kind of feel sorry for him, you know? That was all thirty years ago. He was just a kid following orders. So I hire him, and Max asks me about them, the Maxis brothers. And I tell him.

She stopped again, turning her glass, not playfully but unhappily, frowning into the dregs.

– What did he say?

– Squat. Not a word. He was real angry though. You know how he gets. He's pretty scary sometimes. He's real political too, did you know that? He asked me to send them away. And when I didn't . . . well, he didn't leave or anything, and then we were super-busy with all the others rolling up. So I thought it all went back to normal. We never got on that well, it wasn't like anything changed there. I thought it all blew over, but I guess he told the others. Made some big deal out of it. And then Jason told you. But I don't see why they care! What does it matter to them? Anyhow, maybe I shouldn't say it, but sometimes the past should just stay buried, don't you think?

The last of the moussaka had gone cold. They cleared away the remains, then sat on a tiny balcony that opened from Missy's box of a bedroom, nursing coffees and Greek brandies in novelty shot glasses.

The sky was moonless, overcast, its darkness almost inseparable from that of the mountains below.

– You know, people are so superstitious here. When I moved into this place the landlady came round to give me this thing of salt. Like a little thing of it. I thought it was roach poison, but it was just *salt*. I was supposed to throw it around. To scare off the Evil Eye.

– And did you?

– Nope!

He heard her laugh, low and warm, off in the darkness to his right.

– Trouble is, you only get to be a cynic until the bad voodoo kicks in. After that, not believing feels like a false economy.

– What was the bad voodoo, then?

– I don't know yet.

He looked at her. His eyes were adjusting to the dark. She was leant on the railing, chin cradled on arms, a distant traffic signal just changing to green behind her. As he watched she turned her head towards him. Her neck was bare, broad and sleek, muscled and beautiful. He could feel her eyes on him.

– Do you?

– Is that what you asked me here for? he said, and she laughed again, the sound cutting out in a sob.

– No. I asked you to get you into bed. At least I managed the bedroom. Don't worry, Ben, I know you're spoken for. I'm not utterly blind.

– I'm sorry.

– Don't ever say that. Do you, though?

He shook his head, not turning away. He saw more than heard her sigh. Her voice was a whisper when she spoke again.

– Something's happening.

– What is?

– I don't know. Something bad. Bad voodoo. It's my dig. *My dig.* I don't want to be innocent. I don't want to be the one to stand aside. Do you see?

– Yeah.

– Would you tell me, if you knew? Ben? You'd tell me, wouldn't you?

Her eyes were those of a mournful drunk. They shone in the green signal light. He leaned in and kissed her face. Her forehead, her wet cheeks.

– Of course I would. Of course I would.

The hotel wasn't far, a half-dozen blocks north-west. He walked on north instead, up towards the edge of town.

A truck had broken down outside the HellaSpar, the hazard lights beating, three men crouching by the exhaust, conferring in grave voices like doctors around a bed. He walked clear of them and on.

The lie was still fresh on his lips. He could almost taste it. It was distinct, discrete from the food Missy had made him or the wine she had given him. It lay in his mouth, the lie, the acrid after-sense of it. It was vital and poisonous as salt.

The last streetlights gave out. Beyond them the gypsy ruins lay in gloom, only here and there an oil-drum lit up, and the highway lights in the far distance, high up on their poles like UFOs. As he passed one doorway he caught the sound of singing, a woman's voice, but this time no one called out to him.

He heard the river before he reached it. On the bridge he stopped. The nearest highway light was down, leaving the crossing in darkness.

He leaned out, looking east. At first he could see little more than the road to Afisou, the village a dull nebula. Then the foothills came clear to him, and finally, higher still, a faultline across the sky: heavens and mountains, black on black. And somewhere in all that was the cave, still denied to him.

He rested his head on his arms, the way Missy had done. His own warmth was comforting. Below him the river was still high with spring snow-melt and rain. Where the water churned the foam was bright as if with phosphorescence.

His hands were playing tricks on him again: he was holding his wedding ring. The gold was warm but cooling. He tried to recall the last time he had worn it. Not for a while now, not since before the hunt. Why did he still carry it? Only because he didn't know what else on earth to do with it.

He put it on. Held out his hand, like a newly-wed. He circled his ring-finger and thumb. There was a shadow-animal Ness had loved which began like that: what had it been? A donkey, or a goat.

He loosened the ring, running it from thumbnail to fingertip. He felt it hang at the meeting point. He let it swing, his hands together over the water.

He found himself thinking, not of Emine or Ness, nor even of Natsuko, but of Missy. Her eyes in the dark with the green behind them.

Necessary, too, the lie. Necessary, as salt was.

He let the ring go. He lost sight of it before it hit the water. Any splash it might have made was swallowed up in the larger noise of turbulence below. The rush and roar of it. The many tiers of sound.

The grinding of a stone somewhere, shifting in the river's bed.

൭൦൭

Missy called in sick. The message was sent to Chrystos with a texted list of instructions so exhaustive that, of the foreigners, only Ben listened through to the end. The others wandered off where they liked, Eleschen and Jason idling, Eberhard stalking away with Max to the Skull Room, leaving Chrystos grim as his brother and Themeus giggling fretfully, watching them all with wide white eyes.

He worked at the Findhut at first, as Missy had asked, but by noon there was nothing left to do and he ended up at the new pit with Natsuko and Jason. Eleschen had christened it the Pigsty, and the name had stuck, just as Laco's had, even as it grew obvious that it wasn't that, Jason finding one by one the familiar evidence of another junkyard-midden: the smashed bole of an amphora, two burnished shards of tableware, a goat's narrow shoulder blade scarred with laniary grooves. The magnetometry had raised Missy's hopes of something more, the outlying area a deep stain of old-blood brown fading to blue, but they had found no iron or stone to justify her optimism. It was good to work there even so, the going being easy, the topsoil a tender piney loam so close to the woods, the trees themselves not so near that they had to fight their way through heavy roots.

Natsuko sat crosslegged on the grass beside them, sieving earth into a bucket between her thighs. Jason dug with his shirt knotted around his waist. It was a hot day, and dry: they all wore handkerchiefs bandit-style against the dust. There had been no rain in a week. The local newspapers were full of warnings of forest fires and global warming.

Neither he nor Natsuko said anything much as they worked. Jason did all the talking for them. That last week his monologues and diatribes had taken on a new nervous force, his background noise stifling all efforts at conversation.

– I did this cave in Morocco once. Seven Spanish women and me. No money to write home about but I owed myself some fun. I'd just come off a job with these American ethnologists. That's when you live in context. This project's up in the highlands in Papua New Guinea. Neolithic context, but the pay's good so it's alright with me. The first two months we get no protein. We're supposed to hunt wild pigs with Neolithic weaponry. First day we go out hunting and we find the pigs, no problem, but they all come charging at us. Tusks, screaming, everything. They don't look like what you'd expect. They look like something off *Doctor Who*. After that two of the lads get some kind of pig-phobia, so then there's six of us to hunt. We go out every day, but now all we see is eyes. All they do is watch us. Soon we're all getting the willies, and we're hungry too, but no one knows how to hunt and the pigs are like ninja pigs, Vietcong pigs, those evil manky little bastards . . . so then it's been a month and we all look terrible, like shrunken heads, and there's this bloke called Boff with a big thing about McDonald's, it's all he talks about, all the Happy Meals he's going to eat the day he gets out of there – we call him McBoff and he likes it. He does us Neolithic cave paintings. Mega Macs, Chicken Biscuits, Shamrock Shakes. One morning we come down and he's built a shrine to McNuggets. He's praying at the shrine. We're going nugget-mad up there. We hear about these missionaries who sell tinned fish out of their church but the boss won't let us go, he says we have to *stay in context*. Anyway, that's where we are when this nice old lady comes up from the village with her three boys and two big crates of corned beef. They tell us we're very funny but now we have to stop because we're upsetting the pigs. That night we eat six cans each. That was the best meal I ever had. Corned beef, I'm telling you. Corned beef . . .

– Ben.

There was a moment when he didn't recognise the voice: hesitancy made it unfamiliar. He looked up into the light, wiping dust out of his eyes, and saw Eberhard's silhouette.

– What is it? he said, but he already knew before Eberhard nodded, the Pigsty abruptly as suffocating as a locked room. The others had stopped work, Jason leaning on his spade, breathing hard, head cocked, one eye on him. Natsuko smiled down at him, her eyes shining.

– When? he asked, and Eberhard squatted down by the pit,

staring a question into his face, and finally nodded again and said, Tonight.

ꩰ

It was just the two of them. They went to Eberhard's first. It was still light outside. Later was safer, Eberhard said, and besides, they should eat.

They dined in circumspect silence. He felt no appetite, at first, but there was food for once, cold quail from a meat grill on the square, so delicate and delectable they ate even the bones.

Eberhard dealt with his brace with efficient brevity, then crumpled his napkin, tossed it down and watched Ben gnawing his remains, not standing until he was finished.

– All set?

– How do we get there?

– Nothing fancy. Car and foot. There are a few things I should pack, actually, do you mind? I won't be long. You could make coffee, if you like.

He rooted in the kitchen, finding a packet of Papagalo and an ancient verdigrised briki, and boiled up the dusty grounds. The froth spilled over as he poured, scalding his fingers, and he swore at himself as he ran cold water. He was no longer excited, but ill at ease, with a nagging sense of already being late for an appointment.

He could hear the shower going, and he took the coffee next door, left Eberhard's on the writing desk, then carried his own cup with him along the shelves, foraging for distractions, finding nothing fulfilling, discovering himself back at the desk before he knew it, his circumnavigation complete.

It was a new arrival, the desk, its worn green leather inlay already buried under layers of paper. He leafed through them with his scalded hand. A month's supply of newspapers. A sheaf of notes in Eberhard's decisive, indecipherable script. A diary of game seasons from the Hellenic Hunters' Federation. A yellowed, white-bound pamphlet.

He picked up the pamphlet. It was familiar, though the cover was blank and, because of that, it took him a moment to recognise it as the one that Eberhard had been reading, the night they had met again in Metamorphosis.

He put his cup down on the newspapers, next to Eberhard's, opened the pamphlet and turned past the flyleaf. On the title page were three abbreviated lines of Italian: he translated as he read.

The Birds

*

Ten Ways to Sing of Freedom

*

Milan, June 1973

He spread the pamphlet wider. The pages flickered open. His Italian was not good. He read only where his eyes fell.

The Sixth Way is to relinquish the platform. Sing as loud as you will, the message reaches only so far. The time will come when the song is not enough. There are ears the message must reach and will not reach from the platform.

Then the platform must be relinquished. Then is the time, not for song, but for action–

*

Do not be ashamed to feel afraid. Instead make a weapon of your fear. Fear secretes acid. Let it burn.

Nor should you shy away from terror. Do not disregard it. The careful application of terror is also a form of communication.

– Keep that, if you like.

He dropped the pamphlet and looked up wildly. Somehow without his noticing the light had almost gone. A faucet dripped in an adjoining room. Eberhard stood behind him, drying his hair with a towel. His hair was darker on his chest, bestial and luxuriant. His eyes slid from Ben to the pamphlet and on to the cups.

– That smells good. Which is mine? This one?

He found himself nodding. Eberhard picked up the cup.

– You learned how to make this in Athens, did you? At least something good came out of that. That seems a long time ago. I hardly knew you then.

– What's that?

– This? Eberhard said, and picking up the pamphlet, This is as it says, a manifesto. Or a manual. I suppose it's more a methodology than a statement of belief. I found it in a shop in Oxford some years ago. It cost . . . let's see. Two pounds fifty. But I think I got it for less.

– What are The Birds?

– Were. They were an Italian group of anarchists. Their enemies called them anarcho-communists, not entirely inaccurately. The members have all retired now. I met one of them once. She lives quietly. Not peacefully, I think. The group began in Lombardy. They were marginal but vigorous. They still have some interesting things to say. You're welcome to borrow this. Ben?

He had stepped back, he realised, was still moving away from the desk, the yellowed pamphlet and Eberhard himself. The twilight seemed to fall between them.

– Don't be afraid.

– I'm not, he said, and in saying it knew he was.

– You don't need to be. You're safe with us.

He had reached the balcony doors. The worst thing was Eberhard's calmness. Through the dusk came the pacific sound of bells, calling worshippers to vespers.

– I don't know you.

– Of course you do. And I know you. You've changed.

– Have I?

– A great deal, and for the better. Separation has done you good. Don't stare like that, it makes you look ridiculous. We're not monsters, Ben. We're your friends.

– I thought you were.

– You know we are.

– How can I? I don't know any of you. I don't even know what you're doing here.

– But you do. We're here to dig, like you. You might have had other reasons for following me, of course, given the state you were in when I found you. It shouldn't be such a surprise that we have other reasons, too. We would love, all of us, to find something of Sparta, to see that greatness rediscovered. But we have other interests here, and for those the dig is useful. It helps us keep up appearances.

– Why would you need to do that?

Eberhard put down the pamphlet, arranging it squarely atop the chaos of the desk, as if putting off an answer. The lights of the square gleamed vaguely off his wet scalp. – Well, I think you know. Essentially, yes, I think you do.

– I don't.

– You're lying. Lying to yourself. You've known enough to guess at it for a long time now. You've been wilfully blind to it. You've let it dawn on you until it has become so blindingly obvious that it is impossible for you to ignore. You can't imagine how glad I was when you finally faced up to it, when you faced up to *me*, in Pylos. You've certainly tried my patience, Ben.

– That's all shit, all of it. I thought you were mucking around–

– Playing games? No you didn't. You knew it was more than that. You asked me as much, once, and I told you so. Not that you ever asked too much. Better not to have all the answers. Easier to be uncertain. You preferred to remain in the dark. You wanted to be with us, and so, for as long as you could, you chose to see in us only that which you wanted most in us.

– That's not true, he said, but it was only a flat refusal: it lacked the force of contradiction. The shock he felt, he realised, was almost uncoloured by surprise.

The acceptance of it came to him as something unnaturally held back. It was gradual at first, a trickle of stale recollection; then it became a landslide, a flood, an inundation.

He saw that they had been very kind to him. They had let him into their circle. They were strange children, elder children, who had let him play a game he had never quite understood. There had been rules which no one had explained to him, which he had never really grasped. He had not been grasping, after all. He had never asked much of them. He had asked them questions, but somehow never the right questions. He had put up with Jason's bigotry and Max's stubborn hostility, but most of all with what seemed to be his necessary ignorance. He had needed them, needed to be with them, more than he had wished to know what they kept from him. Even in Pylos, when he had finally demanded answers, he had been content with half-answers. He had cherished his contentment. It had been enough to be with them, even if he wasn't one of them, not really, not one of *Us*.

He had known all manner of things. He had known that there was something in the cave. He had understood that the game of the hunt was more than a game. For as long as he had known them he had known that they were hiding something. He thought he might even have had an inkling – but how could he have understood anything, then? – the first night he saw Eberhard again, reading alone in the meat grill in Metamorphosis.

Understanding is a funny thing, isn't it?

– It's time, Ben. It's time that you believed in something, Eberhard was saying, but there had been more than that, something he had missed again. He shook himself clear of himself. – You look pale. Are you sick?

– Of course not. Stop worrying, I'm fine.

– Sit down, here. Better?

– Yes, thank you.

His voice sounded strange to him. Too shabby and vulnerable. The room felt colder. He put his face in his hands. When he looked up Eberhard was going away, through the dim room and out of sight, down the hall towards the kitchen.

– Eb, he said, then more audibly, Eberhard?

There was no answer. After a minute he got up and followed down the hall. Eberhard had the cupboard open, was unpacking water bottles from a satchel onto the empty shelves.

– What are you doing?

– I'll take you home.

– I thought we were going to the cave.

Eberhard's voice had been gentle. Now there was a new terseness to it.

– You seem to think I've made a mistake with you. I can't say I'm not disappointed, but I'm willing to take your word for it.

He closed the cupboard as Ben came up. His hand remained on the door, as if he were protecting it.

– I didn't say that.

– Didn't you? You've made it very clear. For which I should be grateful, since we have no room for mistakes.

– That's not fair and you know it.

– Do I?

– You promised.

– And in good faith, but you say that I misunderstood you.

They were head to head now, their voices low, like a couple in a public place locked in some unspeakable argument.

– You trusted me, you said.

– So I did. I still do.

– So tell me.

– Are you certain you want me to?

– I still want to go with you.

– That's not the same thing. I don't doubt that you want to be with us. I don't doubt you at all, in fact, or you wouldn't be here tonight. My only concern is that you may doubt yourself. You seem to be in two minds, Ben. I'm asking you to choose. It's time to choose. There is no going back.

A silence fell between them. Through the clotted extraction fan he could hear pigeons hobbling along the eaves. Then even the birds stopped moving, and it was so quiet that he became aware of the sound of his blood, faint and deep, beating behind his ears.

– How can I make up my mind, when I don't know what I'm making it up about?

– You'll have to trust me, I suppose.

Out of nothing he thought of Emine. The memory of her was very sharp, sensual, and so meaningless, so little to do with anything in this new life, that he pushed her away as if she were nothing.

– Alright.

– What do you want?

– To be one of you.

– Then you will.

– What are you? he asked again, and Eberhard hugged him before turning and opening the fridge, the weird light of the machine falling askance across his face.

– Come and see.

ঞ

It was a quiet night, the trucks on the highway intermittent, and after Afisou nothing, only the engine and the road, and the stars of insects pinwheeling towards them, headlit and colliding and gone.

He had not been to the site after dark since the night of the hunt. He had been excited, then, thrilled by their togetherness. This time he felt, not excitement, but a wearing anxiety that soon deepened into weariness. The stuffy warmth and the darkness instilled a lethargy in him. They spoke little, and when they did he found his tongue and thoughts sluggish.

– I never asked why you were in Athens.

– I didn't want you to. I'm afraid I steered you away from it.

– Were you buying the guns?

– That was another trip. No, I was there to watch. We had begun what we have set out to do, oh, a few weeks earlier. Max wanted one of us to observe the . . . reaction to our first action. I went to Athens for two days. I needed to be discreet. I wanted a quiet place to stay, somewhere not too far out of town, but off the beaten track.

– Metamorphosis.

– I chose it for the name. It seemed appropriate. I did think it was a dismal place, I don't know how you put up with it. The hotel was atrocious. But then we would never have met again if it wasn't for that. I am glad that we found you, Ben. You were made for us.

They had turned off the river road, up the hill towards the site. The track was louder under the wheels. The trees had put on a wild new growth which swooped and slapped against the windows.

They came out onto the tops. Eberhard coasted in under the moonshadows of the cypresses.

– We walk from here. Can you manage a bag?

– I'll try. I don't know why I'm so tired.

– I think it may be mild shock. We must take care you don't get cold. I don't suppose a bit of fresh air will do you any harm.

His head began to clear, in fact, as soon as they set off. It was a cloudless night, and the cool air was invigorating. They climbed North Hill between the pits, then descended diagonally across a field of scree and a hollow of boggy ground. Only as he saw the trees ahead did he realise how nearly they were following in the footsteps of the hunt.

They entered the woods together. Eberhard took his arm. They went on more slowly as the trees thickened. The satchels were heavy, packed full. There was a torch strapped to one of them, but Eberhard shook his head at it. There was no path that Ben could see, but now and then Eberhard would stop, casting about in the dark.

A cluster of boulders loomed up to their left, a natural dolmen, familiar to him as a thing once seen in a dream and since forgotten. Then they were at the clearing, its blackened waste dreary without the luminous presence of the creature they had killed. Weeds had sprung up since the hunt, tall things with heavy heads, their buddings ashen in the dark.

Eberhard's voice came back to him, hushed, as they shouldered through.

– I believe these are asphodel. Homer's harbourers of the dead.

– They look like weeds. I thought they were meant to be flowers.

– I don't suppose they mind what you call them. And no doubt they'll come into flower soon enough. They seem to grow just as well here as in any Underworld.

The land began to rise, gently at first and then more fiercely, until the pines gave way to clinging growths, and they were more climbing than walking.

They came out onto bedrock. Eberhard was ahead of him, hands on hips, catching his breath: his own was long gone, and he squatted down, gulping lungfuls.

After a while he became conscious of the silence. He could hear the wind, faint in the trees and rocks. A goat cried somewhere far away. There was no human sound beyond that of their own breathing.

He looked back west. Sparta was miles off, a rigid network of brightness crisscrossing the lowlands. He felt a quickening of the pulse, a gathering euphoric sense of both accomplishment and anticipation. The night itself was no longer dark. The moon had a dirty cast – as if the high air were full of dust – and the sky a vestigial lucidity, a corona of light pollution circling the horizons.

A stone clicked on the rocks behind him. He looked up and saw Eberhard, his head obscuring the stars.

– Come on.

– How much further?

– Not far.

– You always say that.

– Do you want to go back?

– Too late for that, isn't it?

He stood up. They went on. The going was quicker on the rocks, but here and there he caught glimpses of crevices and sudden drops. He stayed close to Eberhard, walking with his arms spread, ready to fall again. A song began to go round in his head, distracting and maddening, nagging at him for half a mile before he recognised it as an absurd snatch of an old Christmas carol.

The night grows darker now, and the wind grows stronger.
Fails my heart, I know not how: I can go no longer . . .

The land began to rise again. They came to a sheer face of rock. A lone cricket stilled as they approached.

– Are we lost?

– This is the way.

– I can't do that.

– Of course you can.

– Does Natsuko? he said, and Eberhard chuckled.

– Two of us come, twice a week. Natsuko is fearless, she puts even Max to shame. I suspect she would be more ferocious than any of us, if push ever came to shove. Does that make you feel better?

– No.

– Follow where I go.

They began to climb. He smelled woodsmoke, a faint warm trace of human habitation from somewhere far below. The rock bit into his hands. He was glad of its solidity. Then Eberhard was reaching down, helping him the last feet, and as he crested the top he saw the mountains, their snowcaps blue in the moonlight, and below them the caves.

The slope that led up to them was steep and studded with scrub. He began to lag. By the time he reached standable ground Eberhard was sitting on an outcrop, a thermos lid cupped in both hands.

He slumped down beside him, shrugged off his satchel. His shirt was steeped in sweat. Eberhard held out the lid.

– Here.

– What is it?

– *Sidherítis*. Mountain tea. Try it, I find it helps.

They sat side by side. The air was growing colder. He could feel the warmth of the outcrop beneath him.

– Up there, Eberhard said, and Ben followed his gesture. The mountains began in earnest less than fifty feet above them, breaking loose from the foothills, a mass of limestone heaving skywards. All along the face were the outlines of caves, concentrations of darkness. Lips and mouths and clefts.

– There are so many.

– People lived in them once. Twenty thousand years ago this was an acropolis of troglodytes. Greece begins with her caves. The earthquakes and the road builders demolish many over time, but what remain are still countless. Ours is the nearest from here. It's tall and narrow and there's a fig tree growing in it. You'll smell the fig when you're close. I found it a long time ago. I used to come here as a boy, to get away from things. My family, primarily. I found it a peaceful place. There are more impressive caves, but this one has advantages. It's one of the reasons we're here at all. I mentioned it when Max first told me he was coming here. Our plans were all theoretical until he saw it for himself. The cave inspired him. And Max inspired us.

– Is it safe?

– Safe enough. Go carefully. It's tight at first but you can stand inside. Walk nine steps – count them – before you use the light. You'll see that you have to crawl again. Look in the satchels before you do and you'll find something to put on–

– You're not coming?

Eberhard shook his head.

– I wish you would.

Eberhard reached for the lid, shook it out. – Better you go alone.

You may want some time to yourself. Take the satchels. Remember what I said. You'll know what else to do.

His ribs ached as he stood, the bruises a week old. He took a satchel on each arm and trudged up the last stretch. The scrub gave way to maquis and he shouldered through. At the cave mouth he looked back. He could still see Eberhard, motionless against the distant lights of the Laconian plain.

The mouth was narrow, tapering up out of sight from a mass of growth. He got down on his hands and knees, the satchels swinging under him. The earth was dry and soft, like the sand at Pylos, on the secret beach. He could smell fennel, figs, opuntia.

He began to crawl under the thicket. Brush scraped along his back, not painfully but alarmingly loud, as if his clothes were being torn open. As he tucked his head into his chest something – an insect or a bird – fluttered and flew out past him. A branch whipped across his face and was gone.

The air changed first. He felt it cool. He went another foot and stopped. Under his hands the ground was unyielding. He could hear the echo of his own breathing. The undergrowth was behind him: he must be inside the cave.

He began to rise, putting out a hand, and cried out as he pitched forward onto his knees. Where the walls should have been there was nothing but darkness and sepulchral cold.

He fumbled for the satchels. For an interminable moment he thought the torch was gone before his fingers closed on it. He yanked it loose. Switched it on.

The cave came to life around him. The walls were just beyond his reach: he must have barely missed them. The thicket crammed the mouth behind him. The alien cast of a cicada clung to a low branch by his face. A pigeon huddled against one wall, an emaciated thing with one wing hanging awkwardly and both claws clenched into fists. High above the two of them the space dwindled to a fissure, a chink, a hairline crack, the torchlight jittering into shadows.

As he stood he brought the torch down, sending the light inwards. The space was small, an air pocket, thirty feet deep at most. It was the wrong cave, he thought, and for a moment he imagined the shame of going back to Eberhard to ask him for redirections. Then he saw the way the light struck one creased fold of rock and flashed out of sight into it, from the walls into deeper space, a convoluted vanishing point.

Eberhard's voice came back to him: he had used the torch too soon. He shuttered its face with his hand. It was going to be hard to turn it off again. The cave was dim around him, but a residue of light still seeped between his fingers, blood-red, warm and comforting. There was a movement at his feet, and looking down he saw it was the pigeon, hobbling crabwise away from him or his illumination. He took a deep breath and then another, as if he were about to plunge into water, and switched off the torch.

The floor of the cave was smooth, rising towards the furthest recess: he knew there were no crevices, but with the light gone he began to doubt it. He lurched forward into the dark. A dry branch snapped under his foot. He took a second step.

On the fourth step he paused. He could hear something ahead. A scrabbling or a gnawing. It stopped and started, stopped and began again, surreptitious, like a mouse inside a wall. It was the bird, he told himself, the echoes confusing its location. But he knew it was not the bird.

He took the last five steps in a rush and snapped on the light. There was limestone a foot from his face, yellowish, blueish, black. He had almost run headlong into it. The only way onwards, to his right, was a ridged orifice of stone.

It was smooth, its edges calcified, as if it had been burrowed out by water. It tapered as the cave mouth did: only by the floor was there room for him to go on. He shone the light inside. The crawlspace opened out. More than that he couldn't tell.

He sat down beside the hole with his back against the stone. He hauled the satchels around, unbuckled them, and unpacked them carefully onto the ground between his feet.

Bread. Six round loaves of it. Water, which he had known was there, feeling its counterweight as they climbed: eight litres in four segmented bottles. A ball of blue nylon string. A bar of Nestlé chocolate. A mask.

He took out the mask. It was a latex head, skin-tone, the scalp hairless. The face dimpled and sagged in his hands. For a moment it was familiar to him: a horrible old man with half-moon eyes and an obscenely puckered mouth. It was one of the ritual masks from the Sanctuary of Artemis-Orthia. Then he had it flat, and the mouth and eyes relaxed and became mournfully anonymous.

He couldn't put it on. It was the mask which brought it home to him, all at once, crashing down. The cave around him, and the night outside. There was a Hallowe'en mask in his hands. He tried to remember the point at which it had become definite, his presence in this time and place. The point of no return.

There is no going back.

He pulled on the face. The rubber yanked at his hair. The hood came all the way down to his neck, hanging stiffly below his chin. Instantly he began to sweat. There were no nostril holes and he took one suffocating breath before he understood. His breathing echoed unevenly as he packed the satchels and knelt by the orifice.

He inched his way in. The crawlspace was as smooth as its mouth had been, as if it were the product of an organism, or organic itself. The air was warmer inside, and there was a new smell, too, not that of the stone or the rubber mask but something animal. A faint, foetid, faecal scent that made him retch with fear.

He kept going. At one point he felt the walls against his shoulders. Then he was through the worst of it, and as the passage broadened out he discerned the beginnings of a second cave.

It was much larger than the first. The roof above was jagged, hung with dry, broken stalactites. The far walls were out of sight. The floor was deep, shelving down sharply from his ledge towards the outer limits of his light.

There was something down there.

It was near the blind end of the pit, perhaps fifty feet away. It was moving, though his first thought was that it might be only incidentally animate, a heap of leaves or ash or driftwood directed by some subterranean current of air or water. Then he saw it was working at something, scrabbling at a stone overhang, erratically but doggedly, as if hunting for sustenance, and the fact of its life became unavoidable.

It was squat, dark, and quadrupedal. He remembered the jackals, but this thing was bigger and cumbersome, with no alertness or grace. For a moment it seemed to him that it was a pig, a massive farm-bred animal, the wrongness of that in the darkness worse than anything. Then as his eyes adjusted he understood that it was not that either, was not four-footed at all, the main mass of it a heap of blankets or pelts, and the limbs scratching at the overhang each concluding in a hand.

His light furred the stone around it and it stopped its foraging with a jerk and turned in a circle. It raised an arm against the glare and then began to shamble towards him. As it came the blankets and sheepskins fell back from the head, and he saw that it was certainly a man.

He dropped the torch. The light flared and went haywire. He caught the pommel as it skittled towards the edge. When he had it steady again the man was closer. He was no longer young but was big in bone. His hair was almost gone, though he had a moustache and a newer, paler growth of beard. His mouth was open as he stared upwards and his eyes were screwed up against the light, the expression faintly imbecilic.

No sound except for the conjoined echoes of their breathing. Finally the man licked his teeth.

– Good evening.

– Hello.

His voice was not his own. It was lipless, distorted by the mask.

– Do you know how I know?

– What?

– *Good evening*. How do I know to say good evening?

– I don't know, he said, and the man smiled, pleasantly, as if they were discussing fine weather.

– There is a bat. Only one. I thought they lived together, like the birds, but here there is just one. It's not here now. It's gone to hunt. So then I know it must be evening. I hate it. It shits everywhere.

He said nothing. After a moment the man raised a hand, as if he meant to wave.

– Can you see this?

His accent was provincial, Ben thought, though his voice was distorted too. It was hoarse from disuse and his teeth clenched oddly around certain words or syllables. There was something clotted in his beard, a dirty pussy crust around the wet shine of his teeth. – Can you see this? he said again, and Ben shuddered.

– I don't know what you mean.

– My hand. The man smiled terribly and spread his fingers into a star. – Look. It's cut.

– I can't–

– I try to climb. I keep trying. Of course I try. Come up to the edge, he said, and when Ben shook his head he took another two steps himself. Now the hand was raised above his head. The nails were black and broken. The palm was stained a vivid ochre.

– See it now?

– Alright.

– It's bad. Rotting. I'm rotting to death. So you see, I need a doctor.

– I'll tell them, Ben said, and the man stopped smiling. He moved his hand to his forehead and blinked into the light.

– I heard you yelling. Which one are you?

– No one, he said, and the man laughed.

– You all say that. You're all the same. Are you the Englishman? Yes, that's you. It's not like you, Englishman, to be yelling like that. Someone might hear you. They might find this, this . . . I don't remember. I forget words now, you know. Atrocity. This *atrocity*. But listen, Englishman, you don't sound like yourself today. Maybe you need a doctor too. Maybe you're rotting, like me. Come down, we can rot in hell together. What is today?

– Saturday.

– That's right. I lose count sometimes, now. I lose track of my bat. I lose track because I hate it. The little fucker shits everywhere . . . Saturday. What month is it?

– I can't tell you that.

The man laughed. – You all say that! But I don't see why. I don't see why, eh? Come to the edge, boy. I can't hurt you.

– I'm sorry, Ben said, and the man lunged forward, suddenly frenzied and strong, scrabbling at the pit wall, his black nails scraping on the rock.

– You're not him, are you? Jesus Christ, which one are you? Who are you? Help me. For God's sake, boy, help me, help me if you're not him!

– I'm sorry, he whispered again, and the man began to shriek, his mouth puckering in rage, his face crumpling like the mask.

– Fucker! Arsefucker! Whoreson! Bastard, I'll kill you, I'll eat you alive, I'll . . . oh, for the love of Christ, please! Please? Please! Please!

The shrieking followed him. He had no conception of what he was doing until he found himself back at the entrance, flailing at the undergrowth with the torch-head and his empty hand. He stopped only as the shrieking faded.

He sat down. He noticed time passing only when the dry cold of the stone began to permeate his clothes. He thought of that. The old man sleeping in the cave, the cold creeping up into him.

The pigeon was crouched across from him. Its eyes were bleak, empty of all interest in him. He found it in himself to be surprised that it had not fled. He wondered if it was dying.

The mask was wet with sweat and saliva. He wiped at it uselessly, then peeled it off and shook it out. After a while he realised he could still hear the man in the pit. He was no longer shrieking, but his voice rose and fell distantly, an ululating sound, not wordless but made indecipherable by echoes.

You'll know what else to do.

One of the satchels was still round his shoulder. He got up and rescued the other. It was halfway across the first cave. Once he had gone that far it was not so hard to keep going. He put the mask back on. At the wormhole he got down on all fours. To keep the torch ahead he had to crawl on his elbows.

He crept to the edge of the pit. The old man was huddled below, rocking on his haunches. Along the wall beside him were faint, dry streaks that might have been blood or faeces.

He opened the satchels again. He tied the string around the neck of the first bottle and began to lower it. Half the ball was unspooled when the bottle began to swing, bumping along the wall of the pit, and the man stopped rocking, his eyes rising to the bottle first and then on upwards. The expression was that of a figure in a religious painting, a martyr gazing heavenwards, patient, expectant, fanatic.

– I'm thirsty.

– Untie the string.

– What else is there?

– Bread.
– Just bread?
– Some chocolate.
– Ah. That's good.
– Did you really cut your hand?
– Bastard, the man said, and untied the string, cradling the bottle in his arms.

It was slow work. They were both clumsy in the torchlight, labouring together without much helpful talk. Without any prompting from Ben the man collected up a litter of empty bottles and tied them on to be reeled up. Once he asked again if Ben was the Englishman, his voice doubtful and querulous. When they were finished the man lay back, wrapping the sheepskins around him. He looked older, lying there: later Ben would understand that it was because he looked so like a corpse. His gaze drifted up, but his eyes were empty, like those of the bird. There was nothing in his face. It was like meeting the eyes of a baby, a newborn whose sight was so weak it perceived nothing but the vaguest outlines of anything beyond the immediate. He hoisted the satchels and left, ripping off the mask, crawling back through the caves and the curtain of undergrowth.

The night had become beautiful. The moon was paler, sailing clear. An aeroplane was heading west, its altitude so extreme that it seemed to make no sound at all. Elsewhere the landscape was timeless. The hills were mythical. Silvered.

Eberhard sat where he had left him, a sentinel looking out across the hollows of the valley. Ben trudged down the slope. His legs were numb, and the scrub snatched and tugged at his feet. When he reached the outcrop he dropped the satchels and the mask and sat down, not facing Sauer or Sparta but looking back up towards the caves.

It was a long time before Eberhard spoke, and when he did his voice was soft and meditative in the moonlight.

– His name is Kiron Makronides. He is sixty-nine years old. He was born in Epirus to a military family. During the war his father was one of many who served the Germans. He fought against the communist resistance and died an undistinguished death in the

Epirot mountains. After the war the family lived with an uncle stationed in Lárissa. Kiron became an officer in the armoured cavalry. He married young and well and received a post at the Armour Training Centre in Athens. In 1967 he was promoted to a captaincy. One night that spring his superiors overthrew the lawful government. I expect you know that story.

An owl cried somewhere below. He shivered, hearing the man's voice in it. In the moonlight the cave was clear, a splinter of darkness in the lunar face of the mountain.

– It would be bad enough to say the powers of the world did nothing. The truth is they did everything. The coup would never have occurred if not for America. Socialism was strong here. The West feared its sympathies. For twenty years America groomed the Greeks, seduced them with wealth, interfered with them, subtly or brutally as the times required or allowed. The relationship was that of abuser and child. You think this is hyperbolic. The metaphor is too violent. What other form of metaphor should one use to describe violence? That spring the American ambassador called the coup a rape of democracy. In reply the CIA chief of station in Athens asked how one could rape a whore. One has to admire his honesty.

He turned to watch Eberhard. His voice was still meticulously calm. His arm lay along his thigh, the hand and thermos cup outstretched. The posture was like those of the figures in the museum, alongside the masks. *Chthonic Deities.*

– That spring there were soldiers who found it hard to obey their orders. Kiron was not one of them. He was one of those young officers who feared and loathed the communists as if they were mythical monsters. He believed those who called the coup a revolution to save the nation. It was all beautifully organised. Athens was seized in the small hours. Ten thousand were arrested by dawn. Many of them were old people whose names had been on file since the war. They were held at the racecourse on Phaleron Bay until arrangements were made for their imprisonment or exile to the mountains or the islands.

– Kiron was at Phaleron. His posting there frustrated him. He wanted to be on the streets, where the nation was being saved.

Instead his revolutionary duty was to maintain the hygiene of old men. Among his many charges was Panos Eliopoulos. In his youth Panos had been an officer of the resistance. At Phaleron he commanded the respect of the prisoners and the antipathy of his warders. Among the lower ranks there was some talk of what should be done with old soldiers like Eliopoulos.

– On the fifth day of the coup Kiron oversaw the hours of afternoon exercise. Five hundred prisoners at a time were led out onto the track. As six o'clock approached Kiron ordered the last back to their cells. Many were still queuing when Kiron took Panos aside. The men who were with Panos say they heard the captain and the old man speaking in a friendly way as they walked towards the track. When they reached the racing lanes Kiron drew his pistol and struck Panos across the face. He went on beating him after the old man fell. After he had stopped moving Kiron turned him over and shot him once in the chest.

– The camp commander knew the Makronides family. Fifteen years before the coup he had served with Kiron's uncle in Korea. The death of a prisoner was a tractable problem to him. The racecourse at Phaleron was sand rather than turf. The evening of the killing two junior officers from the Armour Training Centre were ordered to water the sand until it was soaked clean of blood. The commander's report concluded that Panos had been killed while attempting to escape on his way to the toilet. The cause of death was a single bullet to the heart. The bullet had been fired by a second lieutenant, Kopris Kotsarides, who bore no responsibility, since he had acted in accordance with his duty, but who nevertheless did not appear on any other army records that survived the military regime.

– It took only seven years for the junta to destroy itself. Its leaders and torturers were put on trial. Some were convicted. Most not. Many records had been burned and others falsified. Some of the leaders died in prison, but most are now growing old on handsome country estates: the torturers went free long ago.

– Many crimes were publicly forgotten. Kiron Makronides is only one of many who have gone unpunished. Most of them are still alive. There are murderers and torturers who betrayed everything that Greece is and has been and should be, and who live as happily ever after as children in fairytales. Kiron is exemplary. His life has been full of rewards. He has had an enviable career. At his retirement he held the rank of lieutenant-general. He is still employed as an advisor to two national companies. He is a Knight Commander of the Order of Honour and the Order of the Phoenix. This will make you smile: when we took him, two months ago on his yacht, he was polishing his medals.

– Why are you doing this?

His voice sounded querulous, like that of the man in the cave, and Sauer turned and looked at him strangely, as if he had spoken in some indecipherable ancient tongue.

– Because some things are worth fighting for.

– What things? What will this do? Eberhard, how is this a fight? You're as bad as he is, you're just punishing one old man, I can't see–

– The punishment is incidental. A week from now, on Easter Day, Kiron will be free to go, assuming our demands are met. But those are incidental too.

– You're mad.

– If I am then so are you. So is Kiron. Everyone has their own shameful little streak of madness. Most hide their neuroses and manias as best they can. They act out an ideal sanity which very few ever possess. And in the end the charade is ludicrous, because we all suspect that we aren't alone in what we feel. We come to realise that others must behave as falsely as we do ourselves. We never hide these things nearly as well as we hope to do. What point is there in pretending? Everyone is a little mad. The only relevant distinction is that some admit to it. Are you angry with me, Ben?

He answered automatically, lightheadedly, his voice far off and disembodied. – I used to be angry all the time.

– You should be now. There's no sanity in anaesthetising yourself. There are things to which anger is the only sane response. The life of Kiron Makronides. The forgetfulness which allows it. You should feel angry about such things. Have you ever admired Sparta, Ben?

All my life, he thought, but he didn't say it, not wanting to give

Eberhard that. – That's got nothing to do with this. I don't see what you hope to gain–

– We hope to focus minds. People forget too easily. They have no appetite for the past. They need to be reminded. No one remembers the murder of Panos Eliopoulos, but they will. No one wants to take account of the crimes of America. Except the Greeks, of course: the Greeks need less reminding than most. But Greece is where we choose to act, because Greece matters to us. This is where the West begins and ends. This is the birthplace and the easternmost frontier. The frontier is where we are needed most. Greece is weak and deserves our help. The Spartans understood. We fight the same fight as they did. We came here to remind ourselves that others fought as we do. Sparta gives us hope–

He had stood up while Eberhard was still talking. He was seized by a desperate urge to get out of the range of his voice. He would leave him sitting there. He could find his own way home. He could pack tonight and take the first bus out in the morning. It was no better or worse than he had done before. He would put them all behind him. Nothing was stopping him.

It wasn't true. It was too late. The cave stopped him. He had seen it now. Already he knew he would never excise the memory of it. The knowledge was inescapable. The man in the cave wouldn't let him go.

And was even that the whole truth? Didn't the others stop him too? They had been kind to him, in their ways. They had trusted him. He didn't want to leave them. There was even a part of him, a small and pitiful part, that wondered if their judgement might not be better than his own: he hoped that he would realise, soon, that what they had done was right, and that it was only he himself who was in the wrong.

A silence had fallen on them. Eberhard was waiting for him to speak, he knew, but for a long time he could find nothing in himself that he could have put into words.

– He cut his hand, he said finally, and Eberhard sighed.

– Badly?

– I don't know. I don't think so. He says he needs a doctor.

– We'll see to it. Did you talk much?

– A bit.

– Better not to, next time. Loose lips sink ships. Did he say anything else?

– He asked if I was the Englishman.

– Ah? I'll have a word with Jason. Natsuko told me that he and Kiron were getting on a little too well for comfort.

– Are you going to hurt him?

– We've no intention of doing so. Why would we want to do that?

– I won't say anything. I won't tell anyone.

– Of course not. I'd hardly have brought you here if I'd thought for a second that you would.

– Why did you?

– It became a possibility as soon as you came trailing along after me from Athens. You worried us. You are intelligent and quite perceptive. There was a chance that you would learn of us against our will. That would have been dangerous. You left us very little choice, unless we were willing to drown you in the Eurotas. Which we were not, I hasten to add. And as it turned out we liked you. We wondered if we might use you.

– How?

– We're hardly professionals, Ben, if what we are doing can even be spoken of in terms of being a profession . . . though perhaps it is one of the oldest? In any case, we need all the help we can get. Let's talk about it later, you've done enough for one night. You gave him the food and water?

– Of course.

– Shall we go, then, for now?

The way down was easier, the satchels light, the rocks and trees and asphodel seeming to offer no resistance. They didn't speak again until they were in the car and driving along the track towards the river road. He felt none of his earlier lethargy, only physical tiredness and a slow tide of panic. It came and went along with his sense of the cave, the madness of it unbearable one moment and the next no more pressing than the news of some distant war.

– Is it about money?

– We assume that money would be dangerous. To demand it we would have to receive it. The receiving of it would put us all in jeopardy. Jason was all for a financial arrangement, but Max was against it. He can be vociferous when it suits him, and he has some experience in this kind of thing. So, no, it isn't about money. We're asking for freedom. An exchange of prisoners.

– Who?

– People like us.

– You did it by sea, he said, and Eberhard nodded, eyes fixed on the road.

– It was plain sailing, most of the way. Max had details of the yacht. Kiron moored at Laurium, not far from his estate. Since his wife died he sails often. We followed him out to sea. He was helpfully drunk. The only trouble was of our own making. Jason got into a fight in Gythion on our way back. He was wound up very tight by then. It was already late and he insisted on buying champagne. Someone in the shop made an ignorant remark about Natsuko. What we were doing was new to all of us, except Max. It was difficult for us all, but Jason found it hardest. We drew more notice in Gythion than we would have liked . . . but it went smoothly, all things considered.

– Are you like The Birds?

– Not very. Times have changed.

– How?

At first Eberhard seemed not to have heard. His voice had been dismissive, and when his answer finally came it had become so divorced by the din of the road that it hardly seemed a reply at all.

– You mentioned hope. That is the change. You know what *utopia* means?

– It's a pun, from the Greek. *Outopia* and *Eutopia*. *No-place* and *Good-place*.

– A pun, exactly. The man who coined it intended both meanings: so, an impossible paradise. Strange, isn't it, that so many people remember only the latter? They fasten on the idea of paradise, not on the impossibility. Why is that?

– I don't know.

– Hope. I think that's what it is. I find that heartening, don't you? The times have changed, but there is still hope. Thirty years ago, in the days of The Birds, the world was full of those who still openly hoped for utopia. Some put their faith in Communism, some believed in God's will on earth. Now the Wall has fallen and the churches stand empty. The times have changed, but the capacity for hope has not. The question is, what to hope for? Where will people put their hope, when there is nothing left to believe in? That is the change and the chance and the challenge for us. Some say this is a cynical age, that people hope for nothing but personal gain. I think that is a mistake. There will always be those, like you, who are searching for more than selfishness, Ben, for something greater to believe in. You are not innocent. You understand the nature of utopia. But even if we accept that some things will never come about, we must do what we can. It is our duty to hope for great things. Do you understand?

– What do you care?

– I care very much. I'm sorry, Ben. You'll need some time.

– You sound like The Birds, you know. You talk like a bloody manifesto.

– This isn't the age of the manifesto. No one reads. No one listens. They only watch. They only want actions.

– Actions speak louder than words.

– Not any more. Now actions are the only language worth speaking. Words say nothing. Here we are.

They had drawn up by the girls' place, at the edge of the cathedral square.

– What are we doing here?

– Drinking our cares away, I expect. You have some leaves in your hair, incidentally. Shall we go in? The others will have begun by now. Natsuko is cooking for us. I hope we haven't kept her waiting.

❦

He woke angry. He was in her arms. He was so entwined that at first, when he tried to rise without waking her, he found that she wouldn't let him go. She frowned at him in her sleep and muttered a refusal, lovely and imperious and inextricable.

There was no milk – it was Palm Sunday, and besides the complimentaries had begun to reappear less often as March had given way to April, as if he had outstayed his welcome – but he boiled the kettle as always, made tea and drank it black, nursing the cup by the open window, looking out across Sparta. The hotel still felt deserted, but here and there were new signs of habitation. Three towels had been pegged up on the balcony of one of the better rooms, the wind bellying them like flags. It had become unseasonably warm: the local newspapers were full of reports of freak early tourists and cicadas.

The swimming pool was full of navettes of brightness, late morning light reflected down from the regimented windows of the apartment blocks beyond.

His head ached like a hangover, though he hadn't touched last night's wine. He had hardly drunk or eaten, had barely spoken. It had been as much as he could do to let the others' conversation wash over him, their small talk coming and going, their companionship working at him. He had been sure when he arrived that nothing they could do would change the way he felt, knowing what they had already done; and yet when it came to it, when it was time to go, he had been sorry to leave them. Just as he always was.

A dog barked out on the edge of town. For the first time in weeks he had dreamed of the jackals. He had been in the cave again, the torchlight filtering down, and when the prisoner had advanced into sight his head had no longer been human. He was a hybrid, a dog-man, a jackal-god. He had become Anubis.

The bed creaked behind him. He didn't look away from the window. He heard Natsuko getting up, her yawn, the pad of her feet on the tiles, the flush of the toilet muffled at first by the bathroom door. He leaned back for her kiss just as her arms came around him.

– You left me.

Her voice was chiding. Her breath was sweet from sleep. He couldn't help but return her smile.

– I'm still here, aren't I?

– You let me sleep alone. I want to sleep with *you*. You're mine, now. Don't leave me again.

– I'm not leaving you, he said, and drew her down.

He spent the afternoon alone. Natsuko hatched an eager plan for a hiking picnic, but he couldn't face the mountains any more than he could her. He wanted to work on his thesis notes, he said, but he saw in the fall of her face that she knew it was a lie, even if he didn't quite know it himself until he sat at the desk, his head in his hands, his eyes staring unblinkingly into the laptop's lunar light.

Don't leave me, she had whispered again as she left. How often he had longed for Emine to say just that.

He wondered if he would betray them. Eberhard trusted him, but even Eberhard could be wrong. Emine, too, had trusted him once.

There was a police station near the museum. He would sit in a windowless room, smoking the cigarettes offered him, while the duty officer took down the foreigner's mad story and finally, reluctantly, sent his least favoured juniors sweating up their hollow valleys, all the way to the caves.

No. Not like that. He would telephone. It could all be anonymous. There was no need for any name except that of Makronides. There was a phone on the highway, out on the stretch where the lights were gone. He could do it at night. No one would see him there. Makronides would tell them things –

Are you the Englishman?

– but by then he would have time to explain, to tell the others what he had done, and why. To make it alright: to get them gone.

What would they say? What would he see in their eyes? He couldn't do it. He couldn't face them. It was unbearable.

He would leave them, then. He was practised in that. At one point, that long afternoon, he stood up and began to pack. He lost his temper with himself even before he gave it up. He had been right before, on the outcrop below the mountains. The cave couldn't be left behind. He had seen it now. It was too late to close his eyes to it.

He sat unmoving in his chair until the light began to go. It was a warm day even then. His shirt was soaked with sweat. He thought of heroism and cowardice. Of Orpheus, who looked back, and Perseus and Heracles, who joyfully killed all who stood in their way. Half-men and monsters. Medusa, the mortal Gorgon, whose gaze was cavernous and cold; whose head was twined about with the scales of dragons.

Have you set foot in Libya?
Have you had the task of Perseus?
Have you seen the eye which turns all to stone?

XIV

Notes Towards a Thesis

Words say nothing.

How can it be true? Words *say*. It is all they are. If they say nothing then they are nothing.

It is true. Words are nothing if no one hears them. Why do I write at all? My hands move in front of me, but the letters which proceed from them are silent and invisible. The thesis I will never finish might as well have never been begun.

I won't write again.

Easter Week is here.

Easter: last of the Mysteries. Even its name is mysterious. Its roots are in the north, in ancient words for light and dawn. Its roots lie in the south, in the names of gods who long ago became the tarnished demons of younger, all-consuming faiths.

Ostara, in High German, from *Ostar*: sun-bound, sun-tending. From which *Ostar-manoth*, April, the month of openings and beginnings.

Eostre, goddess of the North. No image of her has been unearthed. No prayers to her survive. Only a Christian, writing thirteen hundred years ago in a monk's cell in Northumbria, ever calls her by name, or claims Easter as her observance.

Ishtar, goddess of Babylon. Queen of Heaven, Queen of the Bow, Light of the Earth, Opener of the Womb, who invaded the Underworld and was imprisoned, buying freedom only with a vow to send another in her place. Returning to the living, and finding her husband Tammuz not mourning her as was fitting, she let the demons take him; but his sister Belili followed him, and begged the ruler of the dead to let her bear half his suffering, so that for six months of each year Tammuz, the god of plenitude, still returns to the sunlit world.

From Babylon, like progeny, Aphrodite and Artemis, Orpheus and Persephone.

But then the Greeks have no Easter. It is *Pasoch* to them, after the *Pesach* of the Jews (whose worship came out of the East, from Ur and Babylon). *Pesach*: the passing from slavery to freedom, death to life, earth to heaven, and night to light.

There is no mystery to it. There is only a coincidence of names, a confluence of themes and sounds, millennia of whispers. There is no mystery because it is all the same in the end, just as it was in the beginning. There is darkness. Then there is light.

Nothing is ever really hidden.

XV

The Hidden

On Tuesday they found the jars.

That week the hills were full of guns. Lent was almost over: the lambs were going to the slaughter. There had been a truce of sorts, a delaying of collisions. Missy had come back to the dig. She stayed close to Chrystos and Giorgios, Themeus and Elias, working with them when there was anything to do, loitering when not. She shied away from the others. The excavation had divided into two camps, Missy and the Greeks by the huts and the old pits to the north, the other foreigners at the new trenches to the south. Missy looked drunk half the time and miserable when not. She was afraid of them, Ben saw: afraid even of him. She spoke only occasionally to him and to the others never in his hearing. There were no more dig sermons. The others didn't miss them.

On Monday night she was plainly too drunk to drive home, and from then on the brothers took her with them every morning and evening. Chrystos looked after her by day. He talked to her, kept her talking, whenever there was a chance to talk. Occasionally he would say something that would get a smile out of her. For a while her head would go up, and she would work with something of her old pride and vigour. Ben wondered if she was proud of herself for coming back. He understood that it must have been hard. Not that it was brave. Her silence wasn't bravery, any more than was his own.

Monday night, awake, alone – though Natsuko still slept beside him – he realised what he waited for. It was his own impotence. As long as the man was in the caves, he had power over them. He could set Kiron free, if that was his decision. And yet what he wished for was for the decision to be taken out of his hands. He waited for his power to pass. For an end to things.

The world is not dangerous because of those that do evil, but because of those who stand aside and let them do so.

ಌ

Tuesday broke like summer. The drive up was sweltering, and when they spilled out into the dappled shade of the cypress trees they found Therapne different, not to the eyes but to the ears, the hillsides full of the ecstatic chanting of the freak cicadas.

They parked by Eberhard's Volvo. Themeus and Elias had arrived before them, too, were already dutifully toiling at the dark blots of the old pits. They didn't look up from their work as Ben and Natsuko, Jason and Eleschen clambered past the chapel and down towards the Pigsty.

They had dug hard those last eight days. It was as if the source of their anxieties lay underground, could be discovered and eliminated. The new excavation had grown out of all recognition. One pit had become two, linked by an exploratory trench, a long wound in the loam spreading southwards into the trees. Max was convinced there was more there than the junkyard-midden they had found under Missy's direction, but so far it had all been fruitless. Nothing had come to light except the poorest of small finds and the labyrinthine roots of smoke trees, holm oaks and pines.

They worked in pairs that morning, Ben with Jason in the southernmost pit. The digging was hardest there, and he was glad of it. The more intense the work he found, the easier it was to lose himself, to reach the humming, mindless point where he became an animal, a cutting, digging thing that had no time or cause to think of more than the task ahead. Only sometimes, as the hours passed, was he dimly aware of Jason kneeling beside him, still talking breathlessly but incessantly as he had all that last week (and wasn't that just his own method of reaching for the thoughtlessness which Ben sought through other means himself?), his trench shovel wielded any which way, just like Ben's own, like a hammer or a spear, like a dagger or an oar.

He stopped only when he realised that Jason was gone. He backhanded sweat out of his eyes and, looking up, saw the others, the five of them eating together, in the shelter of the trees.

He threw the shovel out onto a heap of overburden and looked for the time. It was after one. His hands were bleeding. He folded his arms, pressing the hurt into his sides. His breathing slowed. He could hear the others talking indistinctly, and the cicadas. An arid, primeval laughter.

Ha. Ha-ha. Ha-ha. Haaaah–

He hauled himself out of the pit and made his way through the outlying pines. Jason raised a hand. He was dressed for the beach, Ben realised, and now lay in the shade, spreadeagled on a bed of needles, not indolently but bonelessly, more like a corpse than a sunbather.

– The soldier returns from war.

Ben lowered himself down next to him. – Don't call me that.

– It's what you are. You've got the guts. Not everyone does. I saw what you did to that jackal.

He lay back and closed his eyes. The smell of the pines was overpowering. He could feel the pulse of blood in his hands, could hear a song thrush overhead. Eleschen murmuring: Max muttering.

– Listen to the cicadas!

– I hear.

– They sound like they never get tired. Like the sea never gets tired. Remember Gythion, before we sailed? The sun came out and you said you always liked the seaside. You looked so handsome. Can we go back there one day?

– No.

– I liked it there. I liked things better then.

– Things are fine now.

– I know. I'm not saying . . . I just liked it. The cicadas reminded me, is all. They make it feel like summer.

– The gypsies don't like them. They say it is bad luck, when the cicadas come too soon.

– Don't say that. Why are you saying that?

Jason nudged him in the ribs. He was grinning sideways, eyes blacked out behind sunglasses. – Natural born killer, you are. We need people like you. You've even started to dig like one. You deserve a medal, mate. The Order of the Shovelmonkeys.

– Shut up, he said, softly, but Jason wasn't listening, was raising his hand again in a salute.

– To Greece we give our shining blades. Aren't you hungry? The cheese is alright. There's wine too, if you're up to it.

He looked up at the others. Eberhard was asleep, as far as he could tell, shirtsleeves rolled up, scalp sun-pinked. Natsuko was tearing heels off a cottage loaf, like those he had taken to the man in the pit. Her face was streaked with grime. Eleschen was wearily spilling wine into three mismatched glasses: she held out one as he watched and Eberhard opened an eye and reached out to accept it in ophidian slow motion.

From where they lay the pits were out of sight: the dig felt far away. And how would they have looked, from that remove? Like tourists who had found an idyllic picnic spot. Like London workers, drinking too much on the annual office outing. Festive, too, languidly foreshadowing the festivals that would soon begin in earnest all around them – the week would be a short one, with no work from Friday to Monday. A watcher might have envied them, might have thought them beautiful, or fortunate, or desirable, might have wished that he could sit down in their company. But only from a distance.

Max was reading the papers. His head was bent into shadow. Of his face Ben could see nothing but the jut of his brows and the pearlescent grey shine of his teeth. His grin, as he turned the pages, was a rictus, fixed and menacing as that of a gargoyle.

Natsuko had explained the newspapers. On the yacht at Laurium they had left instructions for the release of three men from a prison outside Athens. With their names had been the conditions for the sending of two messages. One was to appear in acknowledgement of their terms, one when the terms had been discharged. Each message would appear in the form of a personal advertisement, to be printed every day for a week in four national newspapers. The first message had appeared hastily, only a day after they had taken Kiron Makronides. After the second came, and Max heard from the men themselves, then Kiron would be freed. But the second message had never come. They had been waiting for two months. Easter was the deadline they had given, and Saturday the last day on which the newspapers would come before it was all over.

Who are they? he had asked, *The men?*

Just men, she'd said, *Good men*, and kissed him, stopping the questions up in him. Crawling up over him, her hair falling across his face.

Eberhard brought him food. He ate what there was in silence. He was surprised to find himself, not loathing them – though he did sometimes loathe them now – but thinking of how hard it must have been for them to work as they had those last months. The days at the dig with the nights still pending. The evenings of waiting, of planning and patience, and every three days the long dark climb to the cave.

Eleschen woke him. Somehow he had fallen asleep with his head in her lap. She looked very lovely, smiling down at him.

– Ben?

– Where am I?

– Right here, silly. You dropped off. You were talking in your sleep, and you looked so uncomfortable . . . Feeling better now?

He sat up. His mouth tasted of cheap wine. Bitter lees. – What time is it?

– Late. It doesn't matter really. No one cares about this now. Sleep some more–

He stood stiffly, Eleschen standing beside him, embarrassed, dusting off her clothes. They were walking back towards the Pigsty in awkward silence when they heard Jason's yell.

He ran the last yards to the pit. The others were already there, so packed together that at first he couldn't see what they clustered around. When he looked up again he saw Chrystos and someone else, up on the skyline by the chapel, and somehow the thought that they might have witnessed what his friends had found before Ben had himself was awful, grossly unfair. He jumped down, pushed his way between Eberhard and Max, and saw it.

For a moment he thought it was only a jar. It was cheap ware, wide-mouthed, made for the kitchen, not the table. The clay had been fired almost black along one flank. In hacking through the roots Jason had broken it open. Inside, in the shadows cast by the pit and the huddle of those around it, Ben could make out a human skull. It hung inverted from a coiled train of vertebra, the cranium white and delicate as an egg, and no larger than the circumference of his fist.

In the end there were fourteen of them.

Those were the last days of the dig, although they didn't know it yet. For that brief space they worked together again. There was room for only four at first, abreast and back to back, in the southernmost pit where the jars lay, but the going was hard and they worked turnabout, Missy with Max, Chrystos with Ben, Max with Chrystos, the others lingering to watch, or carrying the finds away.

He wondered how it would have been if they had found the jars before the dig had come apart. It would have seemed exciting, then, he thought; a cause for celebration. Instead they worked almost in silence. The sinewy roots and fragile clay made the labour tortuous, and the knowledge of what the jars held stilled them, instilled a dullness in them, a snappish intensity. Even with Chrystos beside him, it never seemed to Ben that anything had been forgotten or put right, or that their renewed collaboration could mend their differences, or make them friends again, as they had been, in the beginning.

Each evening they parked the cars by the Pigsty and worked with the motors running, the fumes and clamour of the engines drifting down into the pits through the crossed star of the headlights. Elias found the fourteenth jar on Wednesday, after dark, but after that there were no more, or no more that they ever came upon, and towards sunset on Thursday they began to drift away, their goodbyes and happy Easters half-hearted at best, Elias and Themeus going first, then Missy and the brothers, so that the six of them were the last to leave, Therapne stark and beautiful as it had ever been in the dusk behind them.

Eleschen and Natsuko had examined the first eight jars by then. Seven held a single form, the eighth a pair. Those last were the worst. Their skulls were enlarged, lantern-jawed. Their foreheads were humped and crenellated, more like those of horned animals than human infants. Four of the others were deformed in the same way as Laco had been, their heads pitifully small. Three were polydactylic, or syndactylic, or both, their digits mutiplied and fused. The last and least of those seemed perfect, as Eleschen laid it out, Max the first to find its only flaw, a pockmarked nub of bone. The vestige of a third thumb.

They stopped at the HellaSpar for wine. By the time they reached

Eberhard's there had already been an argument, into the aftermath of which they wandered like unwelcome strangers. Max sat out on the balcony in ferocious isolation. Eberhard's composure was brittle as he admitted them.

– What happened here, then? Jason said, too loudly, much too avidly, as Eberhard took the wine.

– Nothing this won't heal.

– Sure? I mean we can piss off, drive round the block, if we're interrupting–

– Do be quiet, Eberhard said, and for a long time Jason was.

– Well. Would anyone like to eat?

There were some eggs, four smoked trout, a dark bread, and a green leaf Eberhard had found in the market but which nobody recognised, and which remained bitter even after it was boiled. Max came in and sat with them, though he ate nothing and none of them could manage much when it came to it. Afterwards they brought in the ramshackle wicker chairs and drank in the sitting room. By then the wine had softened them.

– Why did they bury them like that? Natsuko said finally, quietly, as if the bodies in the jars were almost unmentionable. Max's chair groaned as he answered.

– No one buries them. The father chooses to expose his child. He puts it in something. A jar. He takes it out of his house. If the child is healthy he leaves it for others to find. Sometimes there is nothing wrong with it. The father has no food for it. He doesn't want another girl. Then maybe someone takes the baby. If no one wants it then it dies. But these babies are different. No one will ever want these ones. The father is ashamed of them. To him these ones are monsters. He puts them in the jars and takes them where no one will look for them. The old place down the hill where people throw their broken things. They go on throwing broken things. Soon no one knows the jars are there. But no one buries them.

– What do the bones say, Eberhard asked, too tired or grave to articulate it as a question, and Eleschen stirred, uncoiling in her armchair.

– It's mercury. Just like before. The damage is so bad the mothers must have ingested it.

– Why would they do that?

– Fear, I guess, of something they thought was worse. Plague, or anyway disease. Mercury kills off some infections. I mean it kills all kinds of things. It looks like Laco died of something like that: the votives and the medicines we found with her point to it. I guess they thought they were protecting themselves.

For a while none of them stirred. Jason lit a cigarette, shelving off ash into his empty glass. Out in the square a woman laughed delightedly, the sound jarring, too loud and out of place. The streets were quiet otherwise. In a few hours it would be Good Friday, the day of mourning.

– What are we going to do? Natsuko said, and only when Eberhard answered did Ben understand they had moved on; that they were no longer speaking of the children in the jars.

– We begin again.

– How? Jason asked, just as Eleschen said – Where?

– With ease, and anywhere. There are hundreds of Kirons. They can't hide them all from us. We see out the excavation and make things up with Dr Stanton–

– Bollocks to that.

– We may need her trust, and if not then her references. It won't be so hard, Jason. She's been crying out for our friendship.

– Let her cry, Max said. Why waste our time with her? We do not need another dig. Soon Greece will be full of tourists . . .

– I could be a tourist, Eleschen said.

– If that's what we choose to do, then alright. In any case, we need to find fresh hunting grounds. We've kept our hands clean here. No one knows what we've done–

– Ben knows, Max said, and he answered automatically, out of nothing more than the desire to defend himself.

– And Kiron.

Their heads turned towards him, all at once, in the dark, Eleschen hissing.

– *Max*, stop laying into Ben, can't you? He's one of us now.

– Is he?

– Well, anyway, just leave him alone. And what's this about Kiron?

– He knows our voices, Eberhard said, thoughtfully. – Ben also told me that he knows some of us are English. It's unfortunate, but it's not enough to distinguish us. We leave him well away from here, as planned, and no one will ever be the wiser–

Jason giggled abruptly. He held up his hands as they looked at him. – No, sorry.

– What's wrong with you?

– Nothing, I'm just thinking out loud. Don't mind me.

– I don't see that there's anything to laugh about.

– Depends on your sense of humour, Eb. Mine's black and you don't have one. No offence. It's all turning to shit, that's all.

– What is?

– All of it. Us. Those bastards up in Athens are going to call our bluff, and now we start digging up monsters.

– You're being premature. We could still hear from them. And irrespective of whether we do or not, the jars have nothing to do with what we've accomplished–

– No?

Jason was shaking his head, shuffling upright out of his chair, lighting a new cigarette, and waving out the match, the movements all confused in the dimness, chaotic and ungainly.

– What do we think of Sparta, then, now we've found their *accomplishments*? I bet Helen was proud of them. How many are there down there, do you reckon? You'd think they might have guessed they were doing something wrong after the first dozen–

– Don't be ridiculous. Medicines are poisonous, it's in their nature. To judge between the dose that heals and that which harms is incredibly hard. People still misjudge that now. Look at the Victorians–

– Who cares about the Victorians? I didn't come here because I look up to the *Victorians*. What I'm saying, all this time, here we were, worshipping at the feet of Sparta, following in the footsteps of Sparta – that *is* what we were doing – digging for the glorious accomplishments of Sparta. And here they are, and they're horrors. *Eh?* So much for fucking Sparta!

He left soon after Jason's outburst. Natsuko came with him. From the street they could still hear Max and Jason shouting, four floors up. As they crossed the empty square Natsuko took his arm and held on to it until they reached the hotel's light.

– Monsters, he heard her whisper, hours later in the dark. Her breathing was deep and even. She might have been speaking in her sleep. When he bent over her face he saw that she had been crying.

It came to him, as he watched her, that what Jason had said was no more than they had all felt. He had done what he always did, had said what others would not, could not bear to lay out in words. But they had thought it, all the same. The same anger and dismay had gripped them all as they had unearthed the jars, bearing them up out of the ground: finding, after all they had done, not the glories, but the horrors.

They woke at the same moment, or so it seemed to them, their eyes opening to one another, as if they had not only slept but dreamed together, though neither of them could remember anything they might have dreamed.

It was late, but outside the streets were full of shuttered shops and unlit windows. The hotel felt funereal. They had missed breakfast and walked up to the cathedral square to eat with Eleschen and Sylvia, but found them gone, and the rooms stale and hollow with absence.

Natsuko cooked and he helped her. Out of nothing, in the tiny kitchen, she made enough for both of them and more, enough for four, then six, or eight, her face determined at first, then sweating and panicky in the dull stove-light. Grilled aubergines and stuffed courgettes and peppers with preserved bracken fronds, sliced Laconian oranges with honey and cinnamon, rice balls with seams and cores of pickled plum and salmon skin and ginger simmered in wine.

– Isn't this enough? he asked, as she was pressing rice in her hands: when she glanced up at him, answerless, it looked as if she was praying.

Afterwards she dozed in her old narrow bed while he sat beside her on the pillow, leafing without much interest through Eleschen's dog-eared books – *Funerary Architecture of the Minoans*; *The Site of Giv'at ha-Oranim* – or looking out of the dusty window at the sunlit cathedral. Now and then women would enter, some with their arms full of flowers, their activity as mysterious to him as that of birds or insects. Natsuko woke again before noon, and they wrapped up the food and filled the fridge. The sight of the shelves stocked full and bright seemed to cheer her. She found her mobile, tried Eleschen's, and wasn't downcast when there was no answer.

– Let's go away.

– Go where?

– I don't mind. Just us. Can we?

He sat down beside her, lowering his voice in the empty apartment. He could not keep the excitement out of it. – Do you mean leave?

She thought about it; chewed her lip; shook her head.

– But would you? If I did?

– I don't want to be here. Maybe, if you want to, we can go on our picnic now?

They packed a lunch and set out west, through the outskirts towards Mystras. Natsuko had been there only once, as he had, and the walk was longer than either of them expected, but she didn't seem to mind, and he was glad, himself, simply to walk along beside her, the sun on their backs and Sparta falling behind them.

It was a beautiful day. The air was so clear that the mountains had stepped closer, leaning in, their highest peaks still white. He was smiling up at them, searching for the ruined city through the rising trees, as they reached the first of the Taygetos villages.

Three steps later he realised that Natsuko had stopped behind him. They were nearly at the village church. A group of boys were working at something in an empty lot beside the churchyard. Two were dragging branches down the road: a third was throwing the spokes of a broken chair onto a heap of wood that already rose above his head around the foot of a makeshift gibbet. A rag-man hung from the crossbeam.

– What's that?

– The Judas. They burn it.

– When?

– Tomorrow night. Midnight is when Christ comes back from the dead.

The rag-man was headless. The tallest boy was on a stepladder, unsmiling, trussing up its many-fingered hands.

– What do they burn him for?

– For his betrayal.

They went on past. A girl came down towards them, smaller than the boys, hauling a plank twice her height, her face fierce with determination. Natsuko took his hand.

Mystras was closed. They rested on a bench by the locked gate to the lower town, then walked down to the restaurant where, ten days before, he had not said that he loved her. The building was deserted but steps led up to the terraced garden. They spread themselves out on the grass and ate until their stomachs ached, then lay under the advancing shade of a strawberry tree.

– It's a sundial.

– A tree-dial. What time does it say?

– I don't know. I can't read tree-dials.

Around the lawn the spring flowers had wilted in the greenhouse weather. A gunshot sounded, up in the hills, echoing between peaks and ruins.

– It says it's too late.

– It's wrong, then.

– I've done bad things.

– Everyone does bad things.

– Not like this.

– Eb said he'll be alright.

– We were never going to hurt him.

We can leave, he meant to add. *We can do it together. I can't do it alone.* But when he rolled over he found she was asleep again, curled up on herself like a hibernating animal. Her face was pale: only her lips and the yellowish shadows under her eyes gave it any colour. Her mouth had fallen open, an upturned *U* in the crook of her arm, like that of a tragedy mask. He got up and cleared away their remains and then sat looking down at her. He wondered what was buried in that head and heart.

ᘓᘐ

A hour before sunset they began the long walk home. Natsuko stopped again before they reached the outskirts, by a shuttered house.

– Where are we?

– Guess.

He looked around. It was a desolate stretch of road, neither quite countryside nor town. Two auto-wrecks sat up on bricks. An old tractor leaned drunkenly under a row of mulberry trees. He had seen those before, he remembered, the first time he had been to Mystras.

– I give up.

– Max lives here.

He looked up at the house. He had never been to visit Max, had never been invited nor wanted such an invitation, had known nothing about his place except that it was somewhere beyond the edge of town.

– Why does he live out here?

– He is shy. Not that one. Down there.

He followed her gesture. A track led past the shuttered house to another, smaller and unkempt. A light was on in one window. The first colourings of sunset showed through the struts of an unfinished second floor. Smoke rose beyond it, a thick grey train against the southern sky.

– He's in. See?

– It smells like he's got his own Judas.

– They don't burn him tonight. I said.

He had upset her, bringing up the Judas. Too late to wish it back. He searched for something else to say, new talk to bury the old.

– Missy told me once that Max was just a nickname.

– His name is Lasha. It means Light.

– Why Max?

– It comes from his family name. It is more private for him.

Private? he almost asked, but he didn't really care, wanted only to be gone. – Come on, let's go home.

She started towards the track. He called her name after her, making a complaint of it, but she was already out of sight and all he could do then was follow.

Max was beyond the houses. The field in which he stood was littered with broken breeze blocks and petrified sacks of cement. His back was to them as they came round the corner. He was bent over a bonfire a dozen yards from the house. In one hand he held a stick, in the other a bottle. He was poking the fire with the stick. The bottle hung aslant, his fingers loose around the neck.

As they got closer their faint dusk-shadows loomed across the house and Max turned his head, staring them down before he raised the stick in greeting.

It was a warm evening, but the three of them still drew in around the fire. There was no talk at first. The pop and hiss of the flames seemed to dispel the need to speak, and the dim shifting of the light made the others indistinct to Ben, their expressions softening, as if the heat were melting them.

– What are you burning? he asked finally, and Max shrugged.

– Things I am finished with. It is good you came by. You are just in time.

– For what?

– To help.

– With that?

– With drinking. My friend Natsuko and my very special good friend, Ben. Three friends, one bottle. That is the best way. Come, drink with me.

He held out the bottle to Natsuko. He laughed – a cheerful, rolling-drunk belly-laugh – when she took a sip and held it trembling at arm's length, her face contorted. Ben took it out of her hands.

– So. My friends, Max said, then stopped. To Ben it seemed that he had been about to ask why they were there, but instead he poked distractedly at the fire again. The flames were dying down. It was mostly newspapers, he saw. Reams of them. Arcs of red edged slowly through them.

– We looked for Eleschen today.

– You didn't find her.

– You know where she was?

– Church. There is no rest for the wicked, Jason would say. She is coming here tonight.

– Where will you go? Natsuko asked, and when Max looked at her through the smoke there was a keenness to them both that was suddenly incomprehensible to Ben, an affinity in which he could not share.

– Why? What happens tonight?

– The funeral of Christ. Very sad, very beautiful. Come with us, Ben. You will see something.

– No thanks.

– You don't believe in Christ? Or you are tired of your friends?

He could think of nothing to say to that. He had been to church with them in Pylos, after all. Max nodded benignly, as if he had already answered. He turned back to Natsuko.

– Ben is tired of his friends. Eleschen is coming soon. Stay. We can go together.

He watched her hesitate. The smoke of the fire stung his eyes and he raised the bottle, narrowed them and drank, feeling the spirit burn. When he looked again Natsuko was shaking her head. Her face was full of apology. It was for Max, not for him. And Max was looking back at her, at both of them, in dumb surprise.

– So it's like that. Is that how it is?

Neither of them answered. A scintilla of charred paper floated up between them and winked out. Max laughed.

– I'm glad for you. You know why? Because then Jason is wrong. If everything else turns to shit Jason will still be wrong, if you have each other.

He sighed and scuffed his boot at the fire, still seeming not angry but wry and weary, as if all his anger had already been spent. He reached out an open palm towards Ben.

– Give me that.

He took the bottle. He drank the spirit like water. It ran across his face as he stopped and he wiped himself, his chin and shirt, laughing again in the thickening dusk. He tipped the bottle to them when he was done. Somehow he still sounded sober.

– To my good friends, Natsuko and Ben. I never liked you. You make me glad.

Ash blew up around them, a vortex with Max at its eye. Natsuko had moved closer to Ben. There was something in the other man's face, a fatal humour, which he found hard to look at himself. He gazed into the fire instead. Among the newspapers he could make out a smaller shape, he realised. The outline of a slender book. A booklet or a pamphlet, its cover white against black char. The flames were sinking low around it.

– We should go.

– So go, then. Go. Run away together.

– Your fire is dying, Natsuko said, but Max shook his head, nudging the papers again. He was no longer smiling.

– No, I don't think so. This will live all night.

Natsuko was on the phone. She was listening, her face pinched, her body hunched over the table. He could hear Eberhard's voice, very faint and calm, and although he couldn't make out the words he thought he understood everything.

They were sitting at a café under the town square's colonnades. On the table were four newspapers, two in front of each of them, the pages blotched with spillages and weighed down with coffee cups, coffee saucers, the water jug, their sunglasses.

There was no news for them, and no more time for it to reach them. It was Saturday. The streets were crowded with traffic, city workers making it home by the skin of their teeth for their family Easters. The square itself was quiet, the few pedestrians hurrying, as if the town were under siege and its open places dangerous. There was a euphoria to it all, still stifled, bated, but too great to be held in check for much longer. It was ten hours to midnight. Everything waited, except them.

– No, Natsuko said into the phone.

Then – I don't know. *I don't know.*
And then – Nothing!
And then nothing.

❧

That afternoon they walked. Natsuko wouldn't talk to him, had withdrawn into herself, and nothing he said seemed to help, so that they went on side by side but separated by their wretched thoughts, haphazardly wandering, one belatedly following the other. Going nowhere, losing themselves in the backstreets as best they could: as if they could have lost themselves.

In one street an old woman with grey whiskers gave them two eggs and told them to eat them tomorrow. In another the gutters were full of a bright flotsam of dead flowers. By the hospital children were letting off firecrackers, two old men frowning at them tolerantly from the doorway where they sat washing potatoes.

As it was getting dark they came out of an alleyway and found that they had been turned round. They were back in the town square. Natsuko's feet were sore and they sat by the fountain. She handed him the eggs and took off her shoes.

When he said her name she shook her head, as if he had asked a question. She sat with one foot cradled in her lap, looking away from him. The lights were coming on. A church in one of the streets was outlined with strings of blue neon.

– Leave with me, he said, but she shook her head again and began putting on her shoes.

– Will you keep mine for me?

– What?

– My egg.

He looked down at them. They were dyed unevenly. Rust-red and terracotta, ochre and cinnabar.

– You're going to leave without me.

– It would be better.

– Better how?

– Better for you.

– That's not true. I want to be with you.

– I want to be alone. Only tonight.

– Did I do something wrong?

– Everyone does. You said so. Will you take me home?

He walked with her to the cathedral square, waited while she unlocked the door, walked home with the feel of her kiss still fresh on his mouth. The streets were getting crowded by the time he reached the hotel. He fell asleep to the sound of fireworks and churchbells.

❧

In the morning he couldn't find her.

He went to the apartment first. When there was no answer there he tried her mobile from a payphone on the square, then walked down to Eberhard's.

Eleschen opened the door. She was in a dressing gown with his hotel insignia. He wondered when she had stolen it. She looked bewildered to see him. Her hair was wild. The morning sunlight caught it, turning it nebulous.

– Ben?

– I woke you–

– No, no. Don't be silly, I've been up all night. What do you want?

– Can I come in?

– Sure, why not?

He followed up the stairs. – Is Natsuko here?

– Did you expect her? Jason is. Eb was but he left just now. We've been trying to find something to eat. You know nothing's open *again*? Only the bakeries, and they're not even selling bread, they just rent the ovens out for lamb . . .

A radio was playing in the kitchen, pop music filtering through, the jollity of it out of place in Eberhard's sitting room. The windows had all been thrown open and the curtains billowed in.

– Jason! Ben's here.

– What's he got for us?

– Nothing.

– Tell him to fuck off then.

The room felt oddly hollowed out. It was a moment before he realised it was because the shelves were bare: Eberhard's books were gone. The other furniture, too, had been cleared of incidental possessions, everything but the writing desk swept clean. The old luggage from the kitchen hallway stood queued against one wall.

– You're leaving, then, he said, and Eleschen smiled, breezy, shrugging off any embarrassment.

– It's a shame. I'm going to miss Sparta. This was the perfect place for us.

– Where will you go?

– Somewhere sunwashed, I hope. I could really handle some sunwashing.

Can I come?

He only thought it: he didn't say it. It was a question she could have answered already, an offer she might already have made, if she had meant to make it. And it was only the weakness in him, the mouseish, hungry, bony boy, that made him want to ask at all. He wouldn't have gone with them if he could.

One of us, Eleschen had called him, the night the dig had ended: but he was not, had never been, would never be that. Eberhard had been wrong about him. There was some lack in him, or them. He had been sure of it that evening, in this room, in the dimness, when they had spoken of beginning again, of finding another Kiron.

That night, watching Natsuko sleep, he had known that he wouldn't go with them. It was only that he hadn't known, until now, that they knew it, too. That they had given up on him. That he had disappointed them.

He wondered if they still trusted him.

He lifted a curtain back. Down in the cathedral square five girls and a boy were chasing one another in endless circles, concentric, eccentric. Behind him he heard Eleschen sigh and sink down into a chair.

– We missed you last night.

– I didn't know where you went.

– We were all here.

– I was tired anyway.

– We could have been tired together. We're still friends, aren't we, Ben?

He turned round. She was sitting in the old armchair with her head leant back and turned slightly towards the kitchen. Her dressing gown had fallen open. Her thighs and throat and the gown itself, the folds and scrolls of it, were all flawless white.

– You look like marble, he said, softly, and her head rolled towards him, though her eyes were elsewhere.

– What?

– Nothing. Sorry. Of course we're friends.

– That's good.

– I can't find Natsuko.

– Poor thing. Come here, I'll make it better.

Something diaphanous enfolded his head. He stepped away from the curtains, fending them off with one hand. His knee glanced against an obstruction – the side of the writing desk – and glasses rattled and chimed, an empty bottle teetering before he reached out and caught it. Between the glasses was a bowl full of broken pottery. Eleschen was laughing.

– Oh *Ben*! Defeated by curtains. What are we going to do with you?

The pottery was old, the whorled red clay stained grey and black. Therapne potsherds, he thought, and a part of him was outraged that a sign had been scratched on each, a cross on some, a nought on others. Beside the bowl stood the green-glazed jug.

– What are these for?

– A game.

He picked up the jug. Something dry shifted in its depths. He looked up at Eleschen and found her eyes on him.

– It's a vote. What were you voting on?

– I told you, it was just a game.

– Hello, soldier! Where's breakfast, then?

He turned in time to parry the arm meant for his shoulders. Jason had come in from the kitchen, a cigarette in his mouth, sunglasses in his hair. He raised both hands, a tumbler in one.

– Fuck me, it's the Spiky Ben! Excellent, excellent news. I always liked you better this way. You should drink more. Hangovers suit you. Try this, go on, I don't know what it is but it does the job. There's nothing else left in the house. You can have some in that if you really want.

He let Jason take the jug. He shook it, muttered indistinctly, then upturned it over the bowl. Shards of pottery clattered across the desk and fell, taking a wineglass with them.

He got down on his knees and began picking up the nearest pieces. – Butterfingers, Eleschen was saying, but Jason was laughing.

– What are you doing down there, you prat? Leave it, it doesn't matter now.

He stood up, emptying fragments into the bowl. Among the glass he had retrieved were three potsherds. Each was marked with a cross. His hands were shaking. Jason was pouring from his tumbler into the jug, holding it out. He grinned when Ben took it.

– There! That's better. What are we going to drink to?

He pointed the jug at the bowl. – What's this?

Jason looked owlishly at Eleschen, then back at him.

– Were you deciding where to go?

– No need for that. We'll go where Max and Eb tell us. Bit Athenian, potsherds, anyway. Old School democracy. We tried to do it the Spartan way, but we just ended up shouting at each other.

– What was it, then? he asked again, but Jason shook his head. His eyes were still smiling as he tipped his glass. – It doesn't matter any more. Let's drink to something else. To Mrs Mercer. How's that? Her health. Such as it is.

– What?

– You know. Eb told us all about it, when Stanton said you were coming.

– What are you talking about?

Jason leered. – Oh come on. No need to be shy with us. No point being coy now. We're your friends, Ben, we know what you're like, remember? We've seen you *hunt*–

– There's nothing wrong with my wife–

– Not for your want of trying.

The room had gone quiet. He could hear Eleschen breathing. The radio in the kitchen, the tuning lost, gone to static. Laughter in the square.

– She told her bloke, of course, and he told Eb. What's his name? Professor something. You know him, anyway.

– I never hurt her.

– Very Greek, I thought. Rape in the Classical sense. Not that I'm criticising. What you do in the marital bed, that's your business. Anyway, I didn't mind. I thought you sounded promising. Nasty. Hungry. Spiky. That's what we wanted out of you, the Nasty Hungry Spiky Ben–

He swung the jug. It caught Jason across the crown and broke open with a hollow resonance. The handle was still in one piece, attached to a bellied curvature, and he brought it up, like a shield or a weapon, though Jason was already on his knees, his hands over his face, laughing merrily.

– Oh, now, that wasn't nice, was it? That wasn't nice at all. That hurt!

He knelt down in front of him. *Are you alright?* he began to say, but even as he did so he caught sight of Eleschen.

She was still sitting in the armchair. She was watching them patiently, as if they were children who needed to be watched: tolerantly, amused as the old men the day before, the potato men, watching early firecrackers.

– That really hurt, Jason whispered, and then he was on him, rolling Ben back on his heels. He was on top of him, still talking, though Ben couldn't make out anything except the motion of his teeth. One hand was in his hair, the other was coming down. It came at him again and again, quickly at first and then more slowly, each blow heavy and sure, workmanlike, like a shovel being dug into his neck and eyes, his face.

The sound of goat bells woke him. He was still lying on the floor in Eberhard's sitting room. He turned his head towards the sound. Under a stack of wicker chairs he could see Eleschen's hands and legs. The dressing gown swished against her calves. Her hands were holding a broom. The green shards of the water jug clinked across the floorboards as she swept them up against the wall by the packing cases. Like bells.

He let his head roll back. The ceiling of the sitting room had been painted an uneven pink. Terracotta. Cinnabar. His eyes were wet with tears. Their warm salt filled his sockets. He could feel them running back across his brow, into his hair. He reached up to wipe them away and when his hand came down again he saw that it was covered in blood.

He woke again. Something was nudging his ribs, insistently, like an animal, and he thought of the jackals and the hare and flinched away from it.

– He'll live, Jason said. His voice sounded funny and Ben tried to look up at him and found that he was blind.

The music was playing again. He could feel the breeze from the windows, could smell cooking on the air, meat roasting, Paschal lamb. His mouth filled with saliva. He began to choke and rolled over on his side, opening his mouth, letting it spill over his lips.

He could see Jason's bare feet. His eyes were sealed to slits with his own congealing blood. He brought a hand up to his face and tried to wipe it away. Twin pains lanced back into his skull, as if his hand were full of glass, and he groaned and lurched back and up.

They had dragged him into the middle of the room. Jason was sitting on the sofa, a dishcloth around his head, a second held to his cheek. He was crouched forward, trying to light a fresh cigarette. The stub was already stained pink. Finally he got it lit and, sitting back, saw Ben.

– Well, you're a sight for sore eyes. Your eyes look sore anyway. Don't know if that's quite the same thing, though. Here.

He threw the dishcloth in his hand. It slapped across Ben's neck, unfurling wetly. He picked at it until it fell away.

– Eleschen's making tea. Want some?

He shook his head. The sofa creaked. He drew back as Jason's shadow fell over him.

– That wasn't nice. What you did. Look what you did to me. I look like Lawrence of fucking Arabia. I should kill you, you know.

– Where's Eberhard?

– Out.

He tried to sit up. The writing desk was behind him and he slid himself back against it. There was something else he had to ask, something he had to know, but it took all his effort to lean back. The words eluded him, eelish, flickering into the dark.

– What is it? You think Eb's going to help you? You better think again. You've never been on the wrong side of him. If Eb had been here he would have taken you apart. He would have lamped you out. He'd rip your fucking head off, mate. Tell you what, though, I'll tell you something, I'm glad you took a swing at me. I am, if I'm honest with you. I've been wanting to do that for a long time, ever since you turned up like Johnny No-Mates on our doorstep–

The words came back to him. – Where is he?

– Ain't here, I told you.

– He's gone to the cave.

His eyes drifted shut. When he opened them again Jason was still gazing down at him, head propped on one hand. His smile was curious.

– He's gone there, hasn't he?

– What if he has?

– That was the vote.

– What if it was?

– He won't do it.

– He asked for it. Max was all geared up, but Eb said no. He was well up for it.

– Jason, you can't do this.

– We have to.

– You're not a bad man–

– We have to see it through. It's not like we want to. It's not what we had in mind. I liked him, as it happens. No one else did, but I thought he was alright, considering. We used to have a chat. It's all gone to shit, though, now. Max says we have to start thinking about next time. They need to know it's not a game with us. We need to get the message through, loud and clear. What do you think you're doing?

He was getting to his feet. One of his eyes was closing up and when he tried to lean against the desk he missed and almost fell. By the time he was straight Eleschen was there, setting down a tray with three tulip-glasses of tea.

– Guess what? I was just clearing out when I found this sugar in the freezer. Isn't that the weirdest? He doesn't live on dust, after all. Do you take sugar, Ben?

She was looking up at him as if nothing had happened. His voice as he answered seemed heard, not spoken, as if he were listening to an invisible, immaculately courteous stranger.

– No thanks. I don't think I'm staying. I might go home now.

– You could sleep here. The sheets aren't packed yet. The bed's made up.

He turned away. Behind him he could hear Jason laughing around his cigarette.

– Shh, Eleschen was murmuring. – You should stop him.

An exhalation. He smelled smoke. – He won't find any help today. Anyway, there's not much left to stop, Jason said. And by the time he gets there there won't be much left to find.

He started towards the door.

∞

He got as far as the hotel before he needed to sit down. The slicked-back boy was sullenly watering the road trees, but as he caught sight of Ben he dropped the hose and backed inside.

There were no taxis working. He saw one coming down the boulevard and got himself up off his bench to wave at it, but as it came closer he saw it was full of children and infants, old men and old women, all on one another's laps and knees, an entire dynasty on their way from one feast to another, and the driver scowled at him and picked up speed towards the square.

He was sitting down again when Crossword came out. She had a sponge and a bowl, but when she saw him she put them on the bench beside him and stood with her arms akimbo.

– I need help.

– I can't understand you. What are you saying?

He licked his lips and tried again. – I need to go to Therapne.

– To where? You need to go to hospital, is what you need.

– No, not now. Will you drive me?

– It's Easter. Bad enough I have to work at all.

He pulled out money, tearing a note. – Sorry. I've got some more inside. If it's not enough you can put it on my card–

– What happened to you?

He looked up at her. The light was high behind her, shining through her hennaed hair, lighting it up like Eleschen's. – Please help me.

She unfolded her arms. – Spiridon, she said, raising her voice without turning, and Ben saw the boy, loitering on the steps. Crossword was fishing in her purse, holding out keys, and the boy took them and sprinted away.

The car, when it came, was gigantic, plush and black, with turquoise upholstery. Crossword had Spiridon fetch two towels from the hotel laundry and lay them out inside. – Don't bleed, she said, even so, as Ben got in, and then, Tell me again, where it is you have to go so much?

– Therapne.

– The Menelaion?

– Yes, he said, but they were already going, his head pressed back against the towels by the acceleration. They were still warm. They smelled sweet as fresh bread. He thought of Metamorphosis.

– You work there, Crossword said after a while, With the American girl?

– Yes.

– Nice girl.

– Yes, she is.

– You left something, maybe?

He nodded, though of course she wasn't looking at him. – I did leave something up there.

He only realised he had slept as he came awake again. They were already climbing, the car rocking as Crossword turned up onto the Therapne road. He could see her almond eyes narrowed in the mirror.

– Some Easter this is.

– I'm sorry, he said, but his voice was a croak and he wondered if she understood.

– Oh, you're awake, are you?

– I'll pay for the car.

– Keep your money. Who are you running from?

– I'm not running.

– Of course you are. After this we're going to the hospital. And next thing to the police.

She peered round at him. Her face was sympathetic but intractable, like a publican asked for drinks after last orders.

– Fighting like that. At Easter. Who did this to you?

– My friends.

– Some friends. Well, here we are. What did you leave?

A silver car was parked under the cypresses.

– It's not here.

– You're joking, right?

– I'm sorry. I had to come.

– You had to come. God help us. What about me? Look at this, there's nothing here. Just ruins. Useless. Now we go.

He opened the door as they began to move. Crossword hissed as she craned back at him. – If you get out I won't wait.

– You don't need to. Thank you. You don't know what you've done. I don't even know your name.

He got out. The window descended beside him. Crossword glared out at him. – My name is Glykeria.

– Thank you so much, Glykeria.

– You're crazy. Get in the car. We're going to the hospital–

He began to walk. All the way round the North Hill he could hear her calling after him. Then there was the sound of the car, and finally the silence of the hills, which was not silence at all but a sea of white noise, the endless chirr of the cicadas everywhere around him.

He fell once as he crossed the scree. It became easier after he reached the trees. The pain was only in his head and it was dampened as he picked up pace. By the time he reached the field of asphodel he was going at a clumsy jog-trot. Then he was out, the rocks ahead, and the sun caught him in the face.

He began to climb. His mind kept circling back to Jason and Eleschen. He tried not to think about them. Twice he thought he saw a figure, a dark blot on the slopes a mile or a half-mile above, but each time, when he looked again, there was nothing there.

He came to the sheer face of rock. At the top he stopped to get his breath. When he checked his watch it was not yet one: he had not been at Eberhard's for long. When he began again there was a throbbing in his skull, and once a splitting pain, as if he had been sunstruck.

He could see the caves ahead. He was a hundred yards from the outcrop when he realised he would have to rest. There was a terebinth just ahead and he walked the last dozen steps and sat down suddenly under its low branches. He could see the cave itself, their cave, the fig tree a dusty green in the daylight, the mouth a black crack angling out of it; a negative lightning.

He could hardly breathe. The tree trunk was hot against his wet back. It smelled of turpentine. He lowered his head and felt his heart slowing from overdrive. He shut his eyes against the pain and when he opened them again he was lying on his side, curled up, the way that Natsuko had lain in the garden beside him, and he cried out, knowing that he had fallen asleep again.

He stumbled to his feet. As he reached the outcrop the fig tree began to move, as if a gust of wind had caught it. A figure was crawling out from under it. He shouted Eberhard's name, but even as he did so he could see that it didn't look like Eberhard.

It was an old man. He was tall, stooping as he stood. His face was somehow both strange and familiar, long and foul with white, white skin. He looked like a creature that had never seen the sun. Reeled over one shoulder he carried a thick coil of rope. He wore a full satchel and, sheathed at his belt, a hunting knife. He was smiling down at Ben, and as Eberhard's name echoed back from the mountainside above them he nodded, raised a hand in greeting, then held it to its lips.

The fig tree was still moving. Its lowest branches shuddered. He heard Kiron's voice, still carrying the cave's echo, muffled by the undergrowth, grumbling, raised in a doubtful question. Then the old man was squatting down, reaching up, peeling off its rubber face, lifting something from the ground, and when the figure stood again it was Eberhard after all, and he had a shotgun in his hands.

He turned and levelled it and aimed.

⁂

After the gunshot, the chorus returning. The stir and clash of the cicadas, shy at first, still listening, but louder on the heels of silence. And the sun somehow louder, too, or fiercer, its pounding a paean of light so great that it deafened him. The hot thunder of his own blood filled the smooth bore of his skull until his thinking quailed and burned.

The mountainside full of echoes. Eberhard breaking the gun. Leaning the breech over one arm, as if its side-by-sides weighed nothing. Peering into the undergrowth, and cocking his head as if he, too, were listening.

And smiling as he came away from the thing splayed five ways in the dark. And coming with him through the brush, following him, lingering, the smell of thyme and gunpowder.

– There, he said, his voice easy, and glanced back once towards the cave.

– What have you done? Oh, oh, Christ, what have you done?

– I've done what needed to be done. And now you're ours, Ben. Now you are. Now you're one of us.

XVI

The Careful Application of Terror

He turned and began to walk away. He had gone a dozen paces when Eberhard called his name, disappointed and pacific, and he broke into a shambolic run.

He expected to die then. All the way to the end of the standable ground he could hear Eberhard laughing. He laughed like a man watching a good comedy alone in a darkened room: not extravagantly, but in impulsive fits and starts, each bout of pleasure lapsing back into another avid silence. Each time the silence came he waited for the sound and feel of the gun.

As the start of the descent came into sight he was blundering through the scrub, his legs beginning to cartwheel with the downpull of the slope, and all that he could do to stop himself going over the edge was to fall before he reached it.

He toppled over sideways and rolled to a halt in a bed of sagebrush. Something echoed off the mountains, then, a dry retort, and he shut his eyes until the next one came, and he understood that Eberhard was clapping.

He looked back for the first time only as he began the climb down. He expected to see Eberhard still standing there, but instead Sauer was crouching, no longer watching Ben at all, but working at something on the ground. His shoulders and arms moving like those of a man washing his hands.

He went down steadily, at first, thinking of nothing but the rocks, losing himself in his attention. Then he remembered Eberhard, and the urge to look back again grew in him until he missed a hold and nearly fell. As he reached the trees he saw, at the edge of his vision but with compelling clarity, an old man with a long white head crawling down silently towards him, and he glanced back wildly; but it was only a bird of prey, a great black thing with a white neck, turning gyres through the air between him and the caves above.

By the time he came out by the dig his breathing was monstrous. The silver car was still there. The doors were locked. He found a dead branch under the cypresses and crawled into the car's shadow. The trunk end of the branch was sharp and he stabbed at a wheel with its point, but he didn't have the strength for it. He broke the windshield instead, smashing it in hopeless anger, leaving the branch sunk in the glass, looking around one more time as he started down the track.

He reached the river road and began the trudge northwards. He could still smell the mountains on his clothes. Terebinth and thyme. He only imagined the gunpowder.

The road ahead was so empty that at first, when he heard the engine, he thought that he was dreaming it. Almost too late he realised that it was coming from behind him, the sound echoing off the riverside eucalyptus, and he turned fearfully.

A tractor was coming up the road. He put out a hand. A squat man in a flat cap and shirtsleeves sat atop the tractor: a flatbed trailer was hitched to the back. He passed Ben very slowly, nodding without looking at him, dignified as a horseman, going inexorably on.

He dropped his hand and began to walk again. The verge was overgrown. His feet moved through the sere spring flowers. The tractor sounded far away when he heard its engine change, but when he raised his head it was pulling over only twenty feet ahead.

The man looked down as he reached him. Nothing in his face acknowledged the ruin of Ben's own.

– Good Easter to you.

– You too, he said, but his voice whistled and sang, as if his ribcage were full of birds.

– I go only as far as Afisou.

He climbed into the trailer in silence. The man gestured for him to hold on, then turned away as he lay back. The steel of the flatbed floor was baking. He heard the gears shifting position, the rising roar of the engine.

The sky was moving ever so slowly above him. He could see the back of the man's head. His hair was white as wool under the cap. As they passed the roadside shrine he took one hand off the wheel, took off the cap, crossed himself, and put the cap on again.

A vehicle was coming up on them. He closed his eyes as it overtook them. By the time he found it in himself to raise himself up, the car was already far ahead, so distant that he could not be sure if it was silver; though he thought it was, was almost sure. Sauer racing on towards Sparta.

He lay back down. He was shivering, though not with cold, and the engine was lulling him to sleep. When he opened his eyes again the sky was wheeling over him. They had reached the village, at last, were turning up the street. He lay still until the tractor stopped.

They had pulled up by the taverna where the six of them had celebrated, the morning after the hunt. The doors were locked and shuttered. His driver sat waiting, not looking back at him.

He got down and turned back. The tractor was still running, the sound of it loud in the street's enclosure. The man leaned down in his bucket seat and came up with a bottle of water.

– A hot day to walk, he said over the engine's noise, and Ben reached up and took the water. It spilled down his shirt as he drank. He wiped his face as he offered it back. The man shook his head.

– Thanks. I didn't mean to be walking.

– I see.

– I need help, he said, but his voice was soft and the man was no longer looking at him, was gazing up the street like a horse scenting home. The tractor shuddered and inched forward.

– Thanks, Ben said again, but he couldn't raise his voice over the engine's roar, and the man didn't look back.

His legs had stiffened; his knees felt spongy and tender. It took an age to make the walk down to the bridge. There was a telephone just beyond it, on the highway, where the lights were gone. There was money in his pockets but it fell through his fingers as he pulled it out, the notes blowing away towards the gypsy ruins. He put his bottle down and picked the coins out of the dust.

He stood up, fed the slot, dialled. Natsuko answered on the first ring.

– It's me.

– What's wrong?

– Where were you? I looked. I couldn't find you anywhere–

– I'm here now. Ben, what is it?

– Kiron's dead.

– You saw?

She whispered something in her own language and began to cry. He leaned into the hot shade of the hood and closed his eyes and waited for her.

– Ben, oh, I am so sorry. What are we going to do?

– Leave with me.

– Now?

– I need you.

– Where are you?

– By the bridge. On the phone.

A pause. Voices whispering on the line. The ghosts of dead conversations.

– Natsuko?

– I'm coming. It will take a little time. There are some things I must bring–

– Hurry.

He hung up and sat down. The road was very still. The bottle was next to him on the pavement. He had finished it, was starting to drop off again, when the hatchback pulled up in front of him. He raised his head as she came round, and of course she began to cry again, keening frantically as she kissed his eyes and cheeks, very gently, butterfly kisses, as she helped him into the car.

They were driving north. He watched Sparta in the mirror as the road began to climb. The streets were diminishing. The buildings were white as salt.

– What did they do to you?

– It doesn't matter.

– They *hurt* you. No one said–

– I deserved it. We all do.

Her eyes looked at him sideways, feral and dark. He put his hands over his face. – I don't mean that. I don't mean you. Listen to me–

– Shh.

He felt her reaching for him, tentatively, one hand still guiding them. Her hand was on his neck, in his hair, like Jason's, and he shuddered at the touch.

– It's alright now.

– Is it?

– Yes. Because, look. We are going now. We are going away together.

She took his hands in hers, holding on to them, drawing them both down. They were almost at the mountains. The road was still empty, eerie as an English motorway on Christmas Day. A single car crept up behind them and he watched it until it passed, white and anonymous. Natsuko's back seat was full of luggage, a suitcase and a sky-blue sports bag, a HellaSpar carrier stuffed to bursting with T-shirts, toothbrush, hairbrush, jeans.

He looked at Natsuko. She was no longer crying but her face was still fierce. Her eyes were edgy, dancing across the road ahead. She was so quiet she might have been holding her breath. When he whispered her name she flinched.

– What?

– Where are we going?

– Where do you want to go?

– I don't know, I haven't thought. Just . . . somewhere else than here.

– Athens.

– Alright.

– Then we can fly away together.

– Alright.

Their talk was rapid and so quiet that it felt to him as if they were a single mind which thought aloud.

– It's so far, though.

– Not today.

– No, it won't take so long today. No one's going anywhere, are they?

– Everyone is where they want to be.

– Except us, he said, and she nodded.

– But at least we are still going.

ᘓᘔ

The plain falling behind them. The mountains closing like great gates. The flickerbook shadows of trees. Goat bells. The smell of thyme. Snowtops floating in the clouds.

The highway like a ghost road. Tripolis shimmering in the sun. A cavalcade of children riding children throwing fireworks. Air pockets of music through which they passed like ghosts themselves.

The smell of meat in every town waking him from deep drifts of sleep. Afternoon light on Natsuko's face. Sunlight stippling her cheeks through the plane trees in village squares. The shadows of her eyelashes.

– You look like a dream come true.

– Are you awake?

– I think so.

– Then I can't be a dream.

Corinth, the canal opening under them like a hangman's trapdoor. Lamb roasting under awnings by a chapel in the olive groves. Judas burned to black lumps and clots on a black gibbet by the road.

– Eb took him outside. Why did he? He could have killed him in the cave.

– It would have made him hard to move.

– Why would they need to?

– I don't know.

– At least we can tell someone, in Athens. We can tell them everything.

– No.

– Why not?

– They are still our friends.

– They were never my friends. They'll think that we will. They'll want to stop us. What if they're following us?

– It's alright. They won't follow us.

Attica, the Greek heartland wasted with factories. The mountains and the sea. The blue battlefields of Salamis. And then Athens ahead of them, the Parthenon turning the colour of blood, the sunset behind them.

⁂

They drove through the streets in silence. The car stank of their fear and flight.

The city was unnaturally quiet, depopulated by Easter. Only as they came up to Constitution Square did they start to see people, the hotel cafés and the avenues under the trees still jammed with tourists and the young, the four-square facade of the National Parliament above them, the plaza loud and bright with jarring illuminations and music.

They stopped by the Hotel Grande Bretagne. Its windows rose in ranks, uplit and palatial. There were crowds outside, dining under green awnings, waiters moving between the tables.

– Why are we stopping?

She pushed her hair out of her face. Even after the hours of driving her expression seemed unchanged, her features still marked with that same nervous intensity.

– Ben . . .

– What?

– I didn't tell you.

– Tell me what?

– I didn't want you to be angry. Please don't be. There is a thing I have to do.

– Thing?

– For them. Something for them.

– No.

– It's an easy thing.

– I said no!

For a while she said nothing more. His panic and anger rose into the quiet until he felt they might choke him. She had leaned back from the wheel, her head turned – white skin; black, black hair – looking out at the crowds in unseeing distraction.

– We're done with them. Natsuko. Love. We've finished with them. It's just us now.

She shook her head, still not meeting his eyes, and all at once he understood.

– They know we're here. They knew where we were going. That's how you knew they wouldn't follow us. Is that it?

– Yes.

– Did they tell you to bring me here?

– Ben . . .

– Are you with me, or them?

– You!

– Look at me.

Her face was wretched. – I couldn't help it. They were there when you called.

– Where?

– Eberhard's.

– Why didn't you tell me? Was he there? Eberhard? He'll never let us go. You don't know what he's like, you didn't see him, at the cave . . . oh God, God. Why didn't you say?

He was shouting, pleading with her. He didn't know for what. For the past to be undone. Her eyes looked huge in the car-dark.

– I promised them.

– Promised *what*?

– It is just one more thing. Only one thing. We must say nothing to anyone, and we must leave something here. A message for the authorities. Then they will let us go! Ben?

His head had begun to ache, the pain returning beat by beat. The car was stifling. He rolled down the window and leant out into the night air.

– Let me do it. Then we can go away, Ben. We can go away together!

Two men went past, young and sleekly groomed, their cocky smiles fading as they looked at him and away. His face was clammy. The metropolitan evening felt much warmer than that of Sparta. He could still smell himself and something else, much better. Oranges, that was it. Orange trees, breathing in the dark.

– Please?

– They'll never let us go.

– They said they would.

– And you believed them?

– We'll go somewhere new, then. Somewhere they don't know.

– Where?

– Anywhere, she said, closer to him. – Anywhere. We can start again.

– You promise this is the end of it?

– I promise.

– And then we go away, he said, and when she echoed him, Tell me what to do.

He heard the smile in her sigh and turned back as her arms came around him.

– Thank you so much!

– You don't have to . . . I don't want to talk about it. Just tell me what it is.

She nodded once and let him go, unclipping her seatbelt, her motions urgent, her voice still soft. – You have your cellphone?

– I don't have anything.

– Then I will give you mine and I will find a callbox. I will go first. To see it is safe. When I call, you bring the message. The authorities will find it quickly, here. Then we can go. You look so worried.

– Because I am!

– Don't worry. Trust me.

She opened the door and swung herself out. He looked back as she did so. On the rear seat her bags sat huddled: the only light was that which came in from the lamp posts in the square. The HellaSpar carrier had fallen down, spilling into the footwell.

– Where is it? The message?

– I'll tell you when I call.

– Natsuko, wait, let me go first, he said, and she leaned down, smiling, reaching in to stroke his face.

– I will do better. You look too much like a bad man.

He put his hand up to catch her own. – I forgot about that.

– Silly. Don't forget me.

She kissed him and walked away. She moved smoothly through the crowd and the trees, heading deeper into the square. Just as he thought he had lost sight of her she came to a stop and looked back. His eyes had blurred where she had touched them. It made her face seem white with misery. She raised a hand and was gone.

He needed more air. He opened his door, took the car keys and got out. Natsuko's phone was in his hand, its mouldings already slippery.

He waited for her. There was the sound of fountains, a smooth background tranquillity under the discordancies of the music in the square. Under the trees the sleek young men had found a gathering of friends, or those they wished to be their friends for the evening. They were dancing by the light of a lamppost with four heads. In the twilight they became Bacchic grotesques.

He stood with his back against the car. Beside the road a line of black men were selling handbags laid out on white sheets. There was no expression on the vendors' faces. A police car cruised by, slow as a kerb-crawler. A man and woman in matching shirts were trying to talk together into a single public phone, the hood surrounded by small children perched wearily on suitcases. One of them was drowsing off, her hand curling into her hair.

Like Ness, he thought. Like my daughter; but the thought felt untrue, or undeserved. He could no longer picture his child's face. It was as if he had given up that world – the best as well as worst of it – for the place in which he found himself.

He checked the phone. No messages. He had begun to worry that he'd missed the call. He could see the time, but it meant nothing to him. He didn't know how long Natsuko had been gone, only that it had begun to feel too long.

She was what he had left, he realised. He had hoped for more, for the love of the others, but at least he still had her. That was something. Perhaps that would be enough. They could not go home – he would not lead Eberhard home – but they could start again, as she said. He could live with that. He could still be happy, if she would be happy with him . . .

Where was she? He looked at the time again. It jarred that she was still gone. He realised that his hands were shaking. Voices nagged at him, his own and hers and those of the others, all of them commingling in his memory, as if they issued from one mouth.

You're going to leave without me.

It would be better.

Better how?

Better for you. We need to get the message through.

Did I do something wrong?

Everyone does. You said so. What do you want?

To be one of you.

Then you will. You're ours, Ben. Now you are. Now you're one of us.

A sickness or a morphia began to spread through his limbs. It was an effort to turn and look down into the car. He could see nothing in there but the dim mass of the bags.

He got back into the car. A truck went past, full of laughter. He was being foolish now, imagining nightmares. She was not going to leave him. They were going to go away together; she had said so. She had said so. And a message was just a message.

To calm himself he pictured her. A list of Natsuko, the things he loved, like that he had once made of Emine. The way her front teeth were slightly crooked. The pock-mark on one temple, quite close to her ear: he had only noticed it because her skin was otherwise so perfect. Her morning swims. The gasp of breath that had echoed up to him, sometimes, as she turned between metronomic lengths. Her endless, effortless strength.

A woman called out by the hotel, and he looked round, but it was only a tourist, a Japanese woman gesturing to a stranger with a camera.

The police car was going past again when the phone went off in his hand.

– Hello?

– It's me.

Her voice was a whisper, its velvet brushed rough with excitement. He could hear the shushing of a fountain at her end of the line. Music, close by. A concatenation of wings. He looked up. Birds were wheeling above the trees.

– Are you alright?

– Yes. You can bring it now.

– Which is it?

– The blue one.

– The sports bag?

– Yes.

– Where are you?

– The middle of the square. There is a fountain near me. There is a man playing a guitar. He will find the bag. We will leave it behind him.

– What if he doesn't tell anyone?

– He will. It will frighten him. Ben?

– What?

– Don't look inside.

– Why?

– Promise me.

– Alright.

– I love you.

– I love you too, he said, but by then the line was already dead.

He leaned back in his seat. The back of his head throbbed, as if someone waited there in the dark. A figure sat staring at him.

Don't look inside.

Promise me.

He turned wearily and lifted the sports bag towards him. It was heavy and ungainly, dragging and snagging as he got it between the seats.

For a long time he only sat there, the bag resting on his lap, his hands resting on the bag. Five minutes passed, six, before he began to unzip it.

Inside there was nothing that looked like a message. There was no room for anything except a single Tupperware tub. It was oversized, one of the largest of those they had used in the laboratory. There was something inside it; he couldn't make out what. An indistinct round mass.

He thought of the laboratory. Natsuko's face as she faced him, frightened but brave. Righteous, like a cat discovered with a kill. And smiling, her eyes diminishing to crescents. And watching him, guileless.

Natsuko is fearless, she puts even Max to shame. I suspect she would be more ferocious than any of us, if push ever came to shove.

He peeled open the tub.

Something in dark wrappings. Bloodied sheets of newspaper. Out of the blue he thought of Foyt, the bastard, the thief in the night. But Foyt was no thief, and the thing in the wrappings had nothing to do with him. It was only that it reminded him of the cockerel, the special dish Emine had once made for him.

He is a dirty vain old cockerel.

Oh, he had not liked the look of those claws; but then the meat had been so good that he had been rendered speechless.

He groaned. He was going mad, wasn't he? The thing in his lap was nothing like the cockerel. His mind was trying to escape, to think of anything but this thing, which was so much bloodier than the cockerel, and heavier, heavy as a kantharos. There was less flesh to this, more bone.

A shudder ran through him. He shut his eyes. There was a delicacy to his sanity he remembered from another time, a frailty like that of water tension. He could hardly bring himself to look again, to be sure of the thing that lay in his hands.

Its swaddled face gazed up at him. He could see the hollows of Kiron's eyes.

– Natsuko, he said, Oh, Natsuko; but he had begun to cry, and his teeth to chatter, mangling the name, muddling it into a nothing.

He pushed the head away from him. The bag straps tangled with his feet. He was stumbling out into the road. He was tripping forward and vomiting into the gutter. He could hear the telephone ringing. His lover calling him.

And now? Now he was running away again. Running away, like the coward he was. He was still on all fours. How silly, he thought. How wretched I am!

He could hear applause – was Eberhard there with him? – and then the sound was lost in the crescendo of a car horn. Headlights swung into his face and past him. He went on, crabwise, like a dog wounded in traffic. He looked up at all the people who were looking back at him.

Get away from me, he tried to say, but the only word that would come was her name. And yet it seemed her name was enough, because the evening crowd was parting, its human elements stepping back from him.

He got to his feet. Strangers still moved around him, keeping their distance.

There was still something he could do for them. He found his breath and began to speak. He was telling them what was happening, he was telling them everything he had to tell, everything he understood, he had no more secrets from anyone.

No one was listening to him. He clenched his teeth in despair. He did not have time to convince them. Soon Natsuko would come for him. The thought filled him with terror.

There was the car, its doors still thrown wide, like arms. He began to walk away from it. People closed around him, but no one moved with him. He was among them but alone within them.

Where was he going? Where could he go?

He would go away from them all. He had already left Natsuko, hadn't he? And wasn't she the last? Nothing else would be so hard. It would be better to be alone. He would hurt no one then, it wouldn't matter what violence he brought with him, and, somewhere, one day, he would find somewhere to rest. There would still be somewhere for him, some dark and unexpected place.

The crowd began to thin. There were sirens in the distance, but he was approaching quieter streets. The loneliness of the crowd gave way to a deeper loneliness. He turned down a narrow way, lowering his head, watching the plod of his feet. His heart began to calm.

And as he walked it came to him that he was leaving even himself behind. He could no longer feel his extremities, nor the blood-beat of his heart.

It was as if he had run so far, and so fast, that he had escaped himself. He had thought that impossible, once. He was leaving his body in his wake. Or no, that wasn't quite right. It was as if he looked down on a body as it abandoned him.

That was it. And that was right.

He walked on, alone.

Acknowledgements

Victoria Hobbs, Julian Loose, Jean Vaché, Caroline Hill, Amelia Hill, Stephen Page, Rachel Alexander, Zoe Pagnamenta, Walter Donohue, ASB, Bomi Odufunade, Catherine Argand, Chris and Jen Hamilton-Emery, Denise Johnstone-Burt, Sam Edenborough, XB, Pip Pank, Anthony Thwaite, Professor Mary Beard, Cricklewood at large, and the Company of the Luckless.

Baronessa Beatrice Monti della Corte, for Bruce Chatwin's tower.

Drue Heinz, for a conversation on Lake Como.

Eton College, Newnham College, and the Royal Literary Fund.

Professor Richard Jenkyns, for good advice on harps and gods.

Terry Buckley. It's all your fault, you know.

Hannah, always.